TRACY M. JOYCE

ALTAICA

BOOK ONE IN THE CHRONICLES OF ALTAICA

Published by Cassilis & Co. in 2020

www.tracymjoyce.com

ISBN: 978-0-9924619-0-4 (paperback)
ISBN: 978-0-9924619-1-1 (ebook)

Cover design by Karri Klawiter (www.artbykarri.com)
Map of Altaica by Magic Owl Design (www.magicowldesign.com)
(Based on colour original by Marilyn Jurlina)

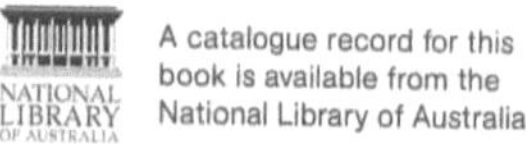

A catalogue record for this book is available from the National Library of Australia

DEDICATION

To the military historian in the family, my husband Robert, in thanks for his love, support, excellent library and scholarship!

To my dear friends and tireless 'beta-readers': Bronny and Marilyn. Wow! How can I ever thank you for your endless enthusiasm and hard work. You gave me faith in myself.

The final test—Thanks to Clive and Elleni.

To Michelle and Jess for getting it all in shape.

Books by Tracy M Joyce

The Chronicles of Altaica
Altaica
Asena Blessed

The Tales of Altaica
Rada
(coming in 2020)

www.tracymjoyce.com

THE CHARACTERS IN ALTAICA

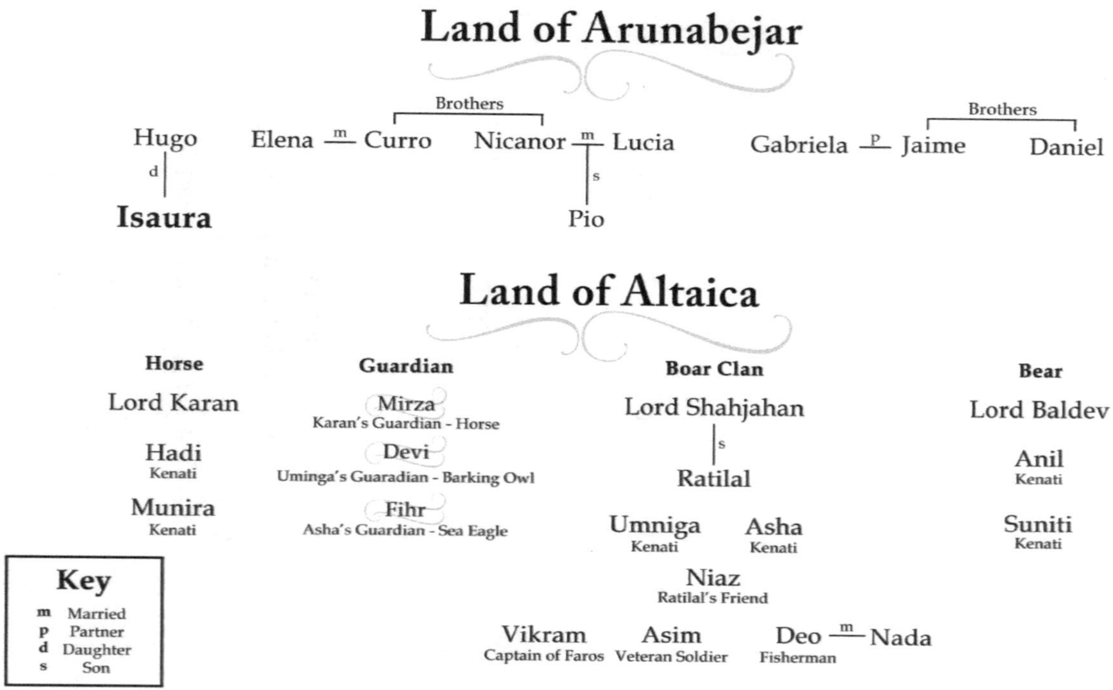

Land of Arunabejar

Brothers: Curro — Nicanor

Hugo | Elena —m— Curro | Nicanor —m— Lucia | Gabriela —p— Jaime | Daniel

Brothers: Jaime — Daniel

Hugo —d— Isaura

Nicanor & Lucia —s— Pio

Land of Altaica

Horse
Lord Karan
Hadi — Kenati
Munira — Kenati

Guardian
Mirza — Karan's Guardian - Horse
Devi — Uminga's Guaradian - Barking Owl
Fihr — Asha's Guardian - Sea Eagle

Boar Clan
Lord Shahjahan —s— Ratilal
Umniga — Kenati
Asha — Kenati
Niaz — Ratilal's Friend
Vikram — Captain of Faros
Asim — Veteran Soldier
Deo —m— Nada — Fisherman

Bear
Lord Baldev
Anil — Kenati
Suniti — Kenati

Key
m — Married
p — Partner
d — Daughter
s — Son

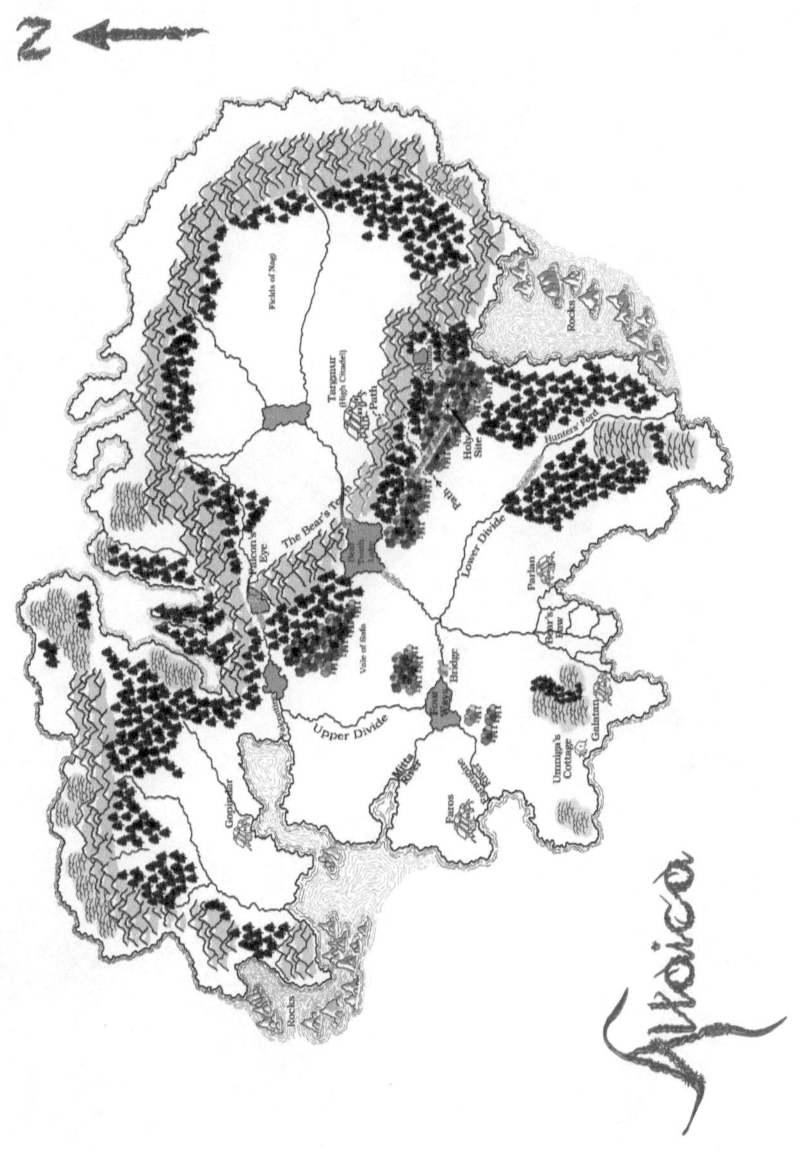

For more detailed maps please visit

www.tracymjoyce.com

CHAPTER ONE

ISAURA had taken a chance coming here. She desperately hoped that she had not made the wrong choice by giving in to her curiosity. Time was precious and although she started out early, she had yet to make it home. She kept up a brisk pace and negotiated the steep, increasingly rocky, goat path up Mt Majula. Isaura wove between tall pines, her lithe frame moving quietly and fluidly from their shadows into the patches of early morning sunlight that dotted the path. She paused when the track wended its way down an overgrown ridge. Drawing a deep breath, Isaura left the path and began scrambling nimbly up the ridge among the large rocks. The trees grew steadily more sparse and spindly as she climbed. The air was bracing, reddening even her tanned cheeks; her breath became laboured as the way grew more arduous.

Her pace had slowed, yet, driven by dread, she surged up the last section of her climb. At the base of an enormous flat boulder, she bent over with her hands on her knees to catch her breath. Straightening, she looked with determination at the lip of the rock just above her. Isaura jumped, latching onto the rock edge with her fingers. She scrabbled for purchase with her boots, levered herself up and dragged her body onto its flat top. She loved this spot; it was her refuge, but after today she would no longer have it. She knew there was no time to think like that; besides there was so much about life here she wouldn't miss.

Walking to the other side of the rock, she surveyed the wide plains below her. *They're already here!* Stretched out along the plains, a vast column of Zaragarian troops marched toward her with row upon row of cavalry, foot soldiers, siege weapons and wagons. Devastation lay in their wake. From her perch, Isaura could see the huge pillar of grimy, sooty clouds that billowed above the burning market town of Santentē. Smaller spires of smoke and blackened land pockmarked the rest of the plain, as if some malignancy had infected it.

Isaura was mesmerised by the orderly march of this enormous army and fancied she could hear the rhythmic pounding of boots as they flattened the land beneath them. Her eyes were drawn to the smoke and the pall that hung over the horizon. The contrast between the chaos they had inflicted and the regimented order and discipline of the army sickened, fascinated and terrified her—this was an immense, relentless, ruthless machine.

Zaragaria, a desert country, east of the Snake's Tail, with few fertile tracts of land, lay in the west. For generations the warlike tribes there had feuded amongst themselves, posing no threat to the rest of the land. They were looked upon as a rabble of inferior savages. However, Aitor I, the great grandfather of the current Zaragarian Emperor, had united them with promises of riches and freedom from the harsh life of their desert home. No longer a rabble, they conquered their neighbours. Word of their brutality spread. Their need for land was satisfied but Aitor's need for power was not. Steadily they increased their influence, conquering more countries through war, politically astute marriages or murder. Arunabējar stood in their way and, while lacking in mineral resources, it was fertile farming land—perfect for supplying an army. It was a food bowl and a gateway to those few remaining lands the Zaragaria had not yet conquered. With a relatively small army, it never stood a chance.

Isaura had never prayed. There were too many religions and so many gods now, each claiming theirs was the true way, that she thought them all ridiculous. To whom would she pray, even if any of them were real? Now, however, as a wave of dread and nausea settled in her stomach, she thought perhaps if ever there was a time for a prayer, then this was it.

'Majula, you and Araceli are the oldest gods; the father and mother of all. My friends keep to the old religion, they pray to you. Keep them safe.' She stared at the host arrayed in the distance below her. 'Please keep them safe. Give me the skills to help them.' A zephyr curled around her, brushing her face gently, then was gone.

Anxious to leave, she spun around to lower herself from the boulder. As she did she was distracted by a distant glint. The river snaked through Laguta, on their border, through the plains and forests of Arunabējar to the sea. She stared hard, squinting, wishing to see it again to be sure. 'No. Surely not? Damn it! They're on the river too.' Dismayed, her thoughts raced to the old river barge she was to sail to rendezvous with her friends in order to escape. Panicking, Isaura leapt from her lookout and scrambled down the slope at a frantic pace. Her feet slipped and she skidded on her backside onto the narrow goat trail, dislodging stones and sending them careening down the hillside. She leapt up and pounded along the trail, her earlier fatigue vanishing in the face of her fear.

As she descended, the trees allowed only speckled patches of early morning light to penetrate the canopy. Isaura paused, breathing deeply, one hand braced against a tree trunk, her lungs and throat afire. Something whizzed past her face. She spun around just as an arrow lodged in the tree next to her. *Oh shit! Scouts. Please, get me out of this. Think, girl.* Isaura surged forward, reserves of energy she was unaware she possessed renewing her flight.

As she fled, a voice called out. 'C'mon, I told you someone was up there. Those rocks didn't tumble down for no reason. Get her!'

Her blind panic subsided as she ran; Isaura was assessing, planning. She knew at least two were behind her. A branch snapped somewhere to her left. *There's another! Come on, Isa. You know this place, they don't—think!* Not following any obvious path, she ducked, weaved, and leapt through the vegetation hoping to lose them. Isaura heard them cursing as they tripped over fallen branches, which she had jumped, in the dim light. A smile crept across her face, but vanished quickly as she realised that those behind still dogged her. There were no further noises to her left, yet her instincts told her the scout was still there.

Veering to the right, she connected with a clear, well-travelled animal path. She heard the two behind her stumble onto the clearer path.

'We have her now!' More footfalls joined theirs in the pursuit. The narrow trail continued downhill amongst a multitude of tall tree ferns, whose fronds arched over the path, reducing the light even further. It angled around a steep slope littered with generations of fallen debris, forcing her pursuers to keep to the trail.

Finding another burst of speed, she put as much distance between herself and the enemy as she could, before she rounded a bend and the path widened. Isaura peered at the left side of the path. A mammoth tree trunk lay half buried on the outer limit of the path. Over the years more ferns had grown on and around it. Gingerly, struggling to stop her hands shaking, she parted the fronds of a large fern, revealing a dark hole between the trunk and the track, whose entrance was narrower than she remembered.

Shit! Please fit, please fit, please …

Heart pounding, Isaura carefully lowered herself into the hole, trying not to break any fronds as she passed. She cursed as she felt more dirt crumble away around her. She wedged herself under the tree trunk, concealed by the overhang it created. Precariously balanced and clinging tenaciously to a tree root, she struggled to maintain firm footing. Peering down, Isaura was grateful that the dirt she had dislodged had not cascaded far down the slope. Would they see it? The wait for her pursuers seemed interminable. *Where are they?* The forest was quiet—waiting. The temptation to look gnawed at her. Isaura heard the soft scuff of a boot—close. They were right above her. Barely breathing, she fervently hoped the now wider hole remained concealed. She began to sweat and her hands felt slippery on the tree root. Teeth gritted, she prayed, *Please. Gods, please …* A terrified squeal nearly slipped from her as guttural voices sounded overhead.

'We've lost her.'

'We can't have …'

'She was running like a rabbit, she's probably ahead of us somewhere.'

'This is a waste of time. It's just a girl …'

'She could be a scout.'

'Did she look like a bloody scout?'

'What was she doing out here then?'

There was a pause, as if they were waiting for instructions. The silence stretched. Isaura waited. Finally, a harsh voice said, 'Enough. We've orders. We'll head back to the others. Follow this path for a bit. If my instincts are right we're not far from the forest road anyway. If you see her, then you can have your fun.'

She did not hear them leave. Isaura's heart was pounding. Her instincts screamed, *Don't move. It's a trick.* She waited until the forest noises began to return; only then did she leave her cover and head for home, praying she was not too late.

Breathless, sweaty and dirty, Isaura slowed to a walk when she entered the forest clearing that sheltered her home. She did not want to appear panicked in her father, Hugo's, presence; it would only start another argument and she needed no delays. Isaura had not made up her mind what to do about him. She and her friends had agreed to flee downriver from the enemy rather than stay. Months ago, they had acquired an old river barge, and had kept it camouflaged in the overgrown backwaters of the river not far from her home while they repaired it.

However, Hugo wanted no part in their plan. He was adamant that they would be safe in their home. This little clearing was his refuge and he rarely left it. Isaura had no idea what her father was seeking refuge from and asking had always resulted in him withdrawing inside himself. Days of silence followed, which were tempered only by his surreptitious resentful looks. *Mama, I wish you were alive—you could always handle him.*

Hugo spotted her the moment she slipped into the clearing. 'What happened to you?' His abrupt voice travelled from the herb garden. He received no reply. His slight frame became rigid as he drew himself up to his full height; his bald pate shone in the sunlight. Isaura always thought he looked ridiculous when he adopted this imperious stance, yet today she couldn't laugh. His bushy grey eyebrows drew down as he scowled; his old hazel eyes bored into hers. 'You went up the mountain again, didn't you?'

Isaura nodded, still deep in thought.

'Well, what did you see?'

'The Zaragaria—they are coming. Father, I have never seen so many soldiers.' She paused. 'They are in the forest.'

Eyes wide with fear, he asked, 'Did they see you? Were you followed?' The questions shot out of his mouth like accusations.

'They chased me, but I led them away; I lost them.'

'I told you we will be fine. They will not find this place.'

'You didn't see the size of their army. You know their reputation. Those who don't get killed will wind up as slaves.'

Hugo narrowed his eyes. 'Don't tell me you are still in favour of this insane scheme to escape. It's madness. They've no idea what they are doing. I knew I shouldn't have believed you. I should have untied that damn boat and let it float down river. I trusted you!'

'I am concerned for my friends, that's all. I have to take the boat to them; now I can pass on the news.'

'I don't know why you'd bother. You know what they think of us.'

'Nic and Curro are not like that …'

'Hmf. Don't you believe it girl. Deep down they all think the same. You're a throwback to your mother's kind. You wait—push comes to shove and you'll see. You mark my words.'

Isaura held up her hands placatingly before heading into the cabin.

'Make me tea before you go,' Hugo ordered.

Inside the cabin, Isaura placed the kettle on the hob, barely restraining the urge to slam it down. *I haven't got time for this!* Her insides began to churn. *He's not right. I have friends here, good friends.* She paced, waiting for the water to boil. She had to decide what to do about him. Her instincts told her to leave him, but her conscience kept bringing her mother's face and words into the forefront of her mind. How often had her mother told her how much they owed to him? How their life would have been different if he had not found her mother. She knew her mother had been right, though it was a bitter pill to swallow. Finally, a chance to escape and her conscience was nagging her to save an old man, who was quite possibly insane.

Twenty years ago, her mother and Hugo had fled here. They had found this cottage abandoned and claimed it. They were foreigners in a backward country where all strangers were regarded with suspicion. To make matters worse her mother was from the Hill Clans of Matyran—a race about whom more was whispered than known. The Hill Clans had become more reclusive after the Great War when mages unleashed raw power and wreaked havoc throughout the land. Magic was despised and feared, particularly amongst the lowlands, like Arunabējar, which had been devastated during the fighting. The Hill Clans were rumoured to use magic. Isaura thought it was a myth concocted by the ignorant.

Luckily at the time the village had lacked a healer—something in which her mother was highly skilled. Her mother had worked hard at gaining acceptance here, for Isaura's sake; her knowledge and her gentle disposition eventually saw her succeed. Upon her death Isaura had inherited her role, though she knew she could never fill her mother's shoes.

The kettle was boiling. Absently, Isaura fetched the teapot, placing it on the bench. She stared at the teapot as if it might bite her. *Where's Hugo?* She looked through the kitchen window and frantically scanned the garden for him. Finally she spied him about to straighten up from his labours and venture inside. Hastily filling the waiting pot with hot water, she quickly grabbed two pottery mugs. Isaura ran to her medicine satchel, fished out a small container, unstopped it, and sprinkled some powder into one of the mugs. 'Shit!' she cursed when a liberal amount escaped the vial. 'Damn!'

Hearing Hugo stomping his boots clean outside the cabin door, she hastily stoppered the container, tossed it into her bag and raced back to the kettle and teapot. Taking a deep breath, she feigned nonchalance, poured tea into both mugs and then put two huge spoonfuls of honey into Hugo's tea, cringing as she did so.

'Why the face?'

Isaura hoped her fright was not evident. 'You have your tea so sweet, I don't know how you stand it.'

He shrugged and sat down at their small table as she passed him his mug. 'How much honey did you put in it?' he groused. 'Ugh.'

Isaura looked at him quizzically.

'It's too hot.'

She took the mug from him and added some cold water. 'Better?'

He nodded as he sipped his tea.

Come on old man, I haven't got all day.

'I'm sorry, Isaura, I should have known you would keep your word to your friends—and to me.'

She stared hard at him, but nodded.

'I know you have made the right choice. We will be safe here. We have always been safe here. Your mother and I chose this spot because it is hard to find.' He paused, savouring the tea, never noticing Isaura gazing at his cup like a hawk. 'Should we be discovered, we will still be safe. Every army needs healers, girl. All will be well, mark my words.'

Deluded old fool.

'This really is very good tea.' He stood up. 'I think I'll have some bread … Oh my … By the gods … I feel …' Hugo looked at the mug, then at Isaura with dawning horror. 'What did you do?' He took a step toward her, then collapsed.

Isaura nudged him with her foot. Satisfied with the lack of

response, she gathered her medical bag, bow and arrows, threw as much food into a sack as she could and raced to the old river barge. Reaching the barge, she ran nimbly up the gangplank and tossed her things inside the small cabin. She looked at the mooring line. *I could just go …*

'Damn it!' She dashed back to her home, grabbing the wooden wheelbarrow from the garden as she passed through. Trundling it into the kitchen, she looked with disgust and exasperation at Hugo's still form. Isaura hastily threw some bedding in the bottom of the wheelbarrow, then bent down to pick him up. Her heart skipped a beat as she wondered if he was still breathing. She placed her hand upon his chest, sensing its faint rise and fall. *Thank the gods!* She couldn't help but smile at this thought. *Calling on the gods again? Maybe you are reforming.*

CHAPTER TWO

'WE can't stay; you know that. You know what the soldiers will do to us,' Curro said.

'But … have we enough supplies … our things …?' Elena replied.

'It will be enough.' His grey eyes softened as he took her small hand in his large calloused one. 'We've been over this. We have water, tools, food, some weapons, all waiting there. With what the others have organised, we should have enough to follow the river downstream to the ocean. Then we can sail along the coast to Matryan and be safe.'

Elena's terrified eyes toughened with resolve. She picked up her pace; the others would be waiting. 'Let's hope Isaura will be there,' she muttered.

Curro stiffened. 'She will be. Ever since we were children, she has always done what she said she would.'

'So you and Nic keep telling me.'

Curro dropped her hand. 'I'm sure the others will tell you that as well. Ask Lucia, Dan, Jaime or Gabi—they all grew up with her. They know …'

'Of course. But you and your brother are …'

'We are like her brothers. She is only five years younger than me. You grew up with her too; you know what she's really like.'

Elena opened her mouth to argue. Curro raised his finger and placed it gently upon her lips, silencing her. He lowered his forehead to hers, then cupped her face in his hands. Her brown eyes softened, and the tension in her round, fair face eased and the soft smile he loved so well teased the corners of her lips. Curro traced the outline of her lips with his thumbs before kissing her. He straightened his tall frame with a sigh and ran his hand through his cropped dark hair. 'We've no time for this,' he said apologetically.

They headed off again. Curro looked back over his shoulder. 'I'm sure ours is not the only village to think of this. We're bound to see others on the river.' He readjusted the rolled leather bundles in his hands; one contained the basic tools of a smith, the other weapons. 'It's wide—if we stay in the middle we should be out of harm's way. I just wish we were sailors,' he finished with a grin.

With a wry grin, Elena shook her head. How he could joke at a time like this was beyond her.

Both became subdued as they walked through the deserted village. It had never been a bustling place, yet the absence of human activity was unnerving. A roaming dog raced around the corner of a building after a chicken. The couple jumped in fright: the sound was unnaturally loud in the dead village. The chicken's high squawk was abruptly cut off. All they could hear was birdsong and the whisper of the breeze through the leaves. It should have been soothing, but Elena shuddered.

'What's wrong?' Curro asked.

'This. It's wrong … It just feels so wrong.' She shuddered again.

Curro smiled gently. 'It's just empty, that's all.' He placed his arm around her shoulders, giving her a squeeze. 'Come on. Let's not linger here.' Looking around the village, he silently cursed his nagging doubts. Anyone not coming on the boat, unless too old, had already fled overland. *Is this really the right thing to do?* Curro thought. He caught Elena's worried glance. If his wife doubted him, then how easy would it be for others to doubt him as well? 'Are you with me, Leni?'

She nodded.

'Good. This *is* the best way.'

They hiked in silence, with Elena still nervously looking over her shoulder as they took the shortcut through the wood. She clutched Curro's hand. Her eyes darted furtively from shadow to shadow. A stick cracked to her left. She began to quake.

Curro kept her hand firmly in his, encouraging her along.

Nearing the edge of the wood, they could hear raised voices. Curro gently extricated his hand from Elena's grip and crept forward to observe from behind cover. Gathered in the clearing on the bank of the river were the villagers, standing amongst a vast array of household goods. A massive chest was balanced precariously in a wheelbarrow, and someone had even brought a feather mattress. He could see his friends, Jaime and Daniel, amidst the crowd, yet Curro remained concealed—waiting.

Jaime and Daniel were twins. Jaime was a miller, tall and broad shouldered. Daniel was a weaver, wiry and slight of frame. Both had a quick wit, a keen eye and a mischievous sense of humour. Right now their outraged faces blazed as red as their hair. Jaime was vibrating with anger. Daniel, although clearly annoyed, was trying to pacify him.

Jaime bellowed in disbelief. 'You can't bring *that.*'

'But it's been in my family for years,' exclaimed the pompous, rotund matron.

Elena giggled nervously beside Curro.

He looked at her sharply. 'Ssh!'

'Oh? Shall I tell your husband that we can't fit him in because you want to take your china instead?' Jaime was seething. 'Or shall I tell Bertran the baker that he will have to leave his two children behind?' He was met with shamed silence.

'Now, now, Jaime, don't be so disagreeable,' Daniel chirped. The matron's eyes lit with renewed hope. 'Come, Jaime, give me a hand.' Daniel grabbed the handles of the wheelbarrow, staggering a little under the weight.

Jaime frowned. He wasn't in the mood for this. 'What are you doing?' he hissed as he steadied the load.

Winking, Daniel upended the wheelbarrow in the river. The chest and its contents sank like a stone. There was a quiet chorus of giggling from the children present. 'Now,' he said gleefully, 'we're going to check what you're all planning to take. Unless we approve, it doesn't get on the boat.'

'Who are you to tell us what to do?'

'You've no authority over us!'

'No right!'

More angry voices added, 'Why should we listen to you?'

A deep baritone voice carried clearly across the crowd. 'Because I said so.'

Nicanor the carpenter, Curro's elder brother, had arrived with his wife, Lucia, and their young son, Pio. Nicanor's broad form towered over the crowd. His calm grey eyes bored into the troublemakers, challenging them. He carried an oblong chest made from a pale timber. The lid was meticulously inlaid with the carved head of a bear in a variety of wood. Its visage rose out of the timber slightly, its eyes, ears and the wave of its fur all accentuated by the ingenious use of different coloured wood.

'Are you going to dump his chest in the river too? I doubt it,' a caustic voice queried.

'This chest is a fraction of the size of the one Daniel threw out. *This* chest contains my tools. The very tools I used to make ready the boat. It is an example of my work and will stand me in good stead when we reach Matryan. We have not brought any excess or unnecessary baggage.' He took a deep breath, then continued sarcastically. 'It would be tragic to all die at sea because we couldn't fit enough supplies in, because we took someone's china with us instead.' *How can you be so damn shallow?* Nicanor silently fumed, running his hands through his sun bleached, sandy brown hair. 'You only need those things necessary to survive and start a new life. Taking anything more is foolishness.'

Grudgingly, they began re-sorting their belongings.

Jaime grinned at Nicanor, whispering, 'Now the real question is where is the barge? I'm not sure if even you can calm this lot if Isaura doesn't arrive with the bloody boat soon.'

Curro, who had been observing from the edge of the woods,

chose that moment to step forward with Elena. Nervous, she instinctively moved to Lucia and Pio's side. Curro, Jaime, Daniel and Nicanor entered the nearby mill and brought out their belongings from storage, all the while discretely listening to the bickering of the villagers, alert for any further escalation of tension amongst the group.

Pio had seated himself at his mother's feet and was absently playing his new wooden flute. Gradually his hesitant melody, the bleating of the milking goats, and the clucking of a few chickens were the only sounds to be heard. He looked up, acutely aware that his flute was unusually loud. Self-consciously he stopped, looking at the crowd of people gathered on the riverbank; standing, he reached for his mother's hand. Lucia drew him close to her, placing her hand protectively on his head.

'Where's the boat?'

'She's late.' People craned their necks from the end of the small jetty, fervently hoping to see the barge approach.

'Where is she?'

'Shouldn't trust her kind …'

Nicanor again appeased the crowd. 'Come, neighbours, be calm. We all know Isaura will be here. She's probably had her hands full this morning. We all know what Hugo is like, don't we?'

'Gods, she's not bringing him, is she?'

As Nicanor spoke, the barge rounded the river bend. A gasp coursed through the crowd; this was their first sight of it. The figurehead featured the graceful and muscular shoulders and neck of a horse poised and arched in play. The horse had large expressive eyes, slightly flaring nostrils and a full mane that was carved as if the wind was blowing its strands in graceful curves. The reflected light from the rippling water animated the carving to such an extent that its muscles appeared to move.

Originally, the barge had been designed purely for carrying cargo on rivers, being long, wide and of a relatively shallow draught. A small low cabin and galley was located at the stern of the boat.

There was also a series of oars along the sides, and a single mast with a square sail in the centre of the deck. A part of the tight space in the hold was fitted with special pens for small livestock, while the rest was to be taken up with barrels containing foodstuffs, grain and water. A section of the flat wide deck was covered with an awning.

Manning the tiller was a lean young woman of dark complexion and hair. Isaura's long hair was pulled back in a single braid; her green eyes missed no detail before her. She could see Curro and Nicanor waiting on the bank, Nicanor towering above his brother. Pio raced forward, waving at her excitedly, his shaggy brown hair bouncing up and down with the rest of him. Lucia quickly grabbed him, hauling him back from the river's edge. Her long brown curly hair became disarrayed by her tussle with her son. Just behind them the small crowd of villagers were already jostling one another.

Isaura smiled broadly, her eyes flashing reproach toward the crowd. 'Bet you thought I'd never make it.'

As the barge came alongside the jetty, she ran forward and threw the mooring lines to Curro. Trying to push the gangplank forward, her face reddened. 'A little help wouldn't go astray,' she grumbled.

Nicanor and Curro, grinning at her exertion, pulled the plank the rest of the way down with ease. Straightening up, she glared at them as she nimbly disembarked.

'Hey,' she croaked as first Curro, then Nicanor embraced her in a bear hug. 'I can't breathe.' Nicanor let go, setting her back down.

'What will your wife think?' Isaura said with mock indignation.

'His wife is just as glad to see you,' said Lucia, who hugged her together with Pio.

'Even you, Pio? I didn't think you liked girls.'

Pio stepped back, embarrassed. 'You don't count.' Lucia looked horrified. Isaura laughed, delighted.

Elena rushed forward, embracing her. Isaura stiffened, looking in surprise at an equally startled Lucia. She noticed Curro smiling happily at their encounter. *Clueless*, Isaura thought as she smiled back and returned Elena's greeting.

'I'm so relieved you're here,' Elena said, releasing her and stepping back. 'We all are. We didn't think you'd make it.'

Isaura's eyes narrowed briefly.

Curro frowned at the slight, hunched, balding form of Hugo, prone on the deck. 'Hugo?' The old man's chest rose and fell gently, while a quiet snore escaped the corner of his lips.

Isaura's expression became vacant. She shrugged.

'What happened?'

'Later. We have to go—*now*.'

Curro and Nicanor stared at her.

Isaura whispered, 'I went up to Mt Majula. I could see the enemy in the distance. They were burning everything as they went. Their army is huge. I've never seen anything like it. Their scouts were in the woods. I barely escaped.' She shuddered before continuing. 'We need to hurry. You know how they reward their troops.' Her concerned eyes surveyed the women and children on the shore.

'Ma,' Pio asked. 'Are the soldiers here already?'

'Hush, Pio,' Lucia said hastily. It was too late.

'What?'

'What did he say?'

'The enemy are here?' The crowd began to press forward toward the barge. Isaura and her friends were the only things blocking their way.

'Let us on.'

'Get out of our way!'

Curro rapidly unrolled a leather bundle, revealing several swords. Jaime and Daniel grabbed one each, while Isaura bounded onto the deck and grabbed her bow. She stood behind them, targeting the crowd.

Isaura let fly an arrow, striking the ground directly in the villagers' path. '*Stop!*' Her voice rang harshly across the crowd. She grinned wickedly while targeting them. 'Don't think I won't shoot again. Look at what I did to my own father. Why would any of you fare any better?'

The crowd halted.

Lucia impulsively grabbed the remaining dagger and sword and stood next to her husband. Her chest felt tight, she wasn't sure what she was doing.

Nicanor had never seen such a fierce look in her eyes. She was struggling to hold the tip of the sword up. Softly he said, 'Lucia, give me the sword.' Fixated on the crowd, she didn't hear him. 'Lucia?' Her eyes darted to him, the only sign that she'd heard him. He reached over. 'I'm going to take the sword.' Brusquely, she nodded, yet he struggled to remove her vice like grip from its hilt.

'Don't let them hurt Pio!' she said vehemently as she waved the dagger at the crowd. Some of the villagers shrunk back in shame.

Nicanor addressed them. 'We mustn't panic. If we work together, we'll finish quickly and be gone. If you panic, people will die. Just stay calm, we will all leave as planned. Let's load this boat—calmly. Curro, you and the others keep the peace.'

Isaura climbed onto the cabin roof, using the vantage point to continue her watch. She hadn't had this much fun since she was a child.

Disgruntled murmurs rippled through the crowd. Curro delegated men to load the boat. 'The rest of you—*wait*.'

Isaura kept a wary eye on their movements. Two men lowered their goods to others below in the hold. A surreptitious look passed between them. One of them lunged at Jaime, knocking him to the deck. Instinctively Isaura targeted the man's back, only altering her aim at the last second. Her arrow flew through the air. Its dull thunk was followed by an agonised roar. The second man froze as his friend rolled in pain, grasping at his thigh.

Jaime leapt up, waving his sword. 'Don't move!' He was stunned at the ease and precision with which Isaura responded.

The injured man stared in shock at Isaura.

'I warned you,' she said, keeping her own surprise hidden. 'Get on with it,' her voice rang out. 'Never forget I'm watching. Now move it!'

Curro and Nicanor looked askance at each other, brows raised.

Isaura remained at her post until the loading was finished. *Amazing how fast they can move with the right motivation.* Bitterness welled inside her. *The Zaragarians would be proud of me.* She jumped down to the deck as the villagers poured onto the barge.

A woman pushed past them and ran to the still moaning man. She helped him half upright, glaring balefully at Isaura as she did so. 'How could you?'

'Clan bitch!' The man spat at her.

Isaura felt a knot form in her belly. Before she could respond, an arrow hit him square in the chest. 'Zaragarians!' she yelled. 'Take cover!'

The woman screamed as he fell sideways. Isaura shoved her flat. 'You killed him!' she accused, slapping and scratching Isaura.

Isaura pressed the bow grip against her throat, pinning her down. An arrow thudded into the cabin wall behind them. The woman's eyes widened in understanding. 'Not me. You want to live? Shut up and stay down!'

'Move!' Nicanor shouted. He and Curro stood on the bank with their swords raised. A woman fell from the gangplank with an arrow in her back. The last of the passengers ran pell-mell onboard. More fell into the water as arrows struck them.

Laughing, three scouts stepped into view from the tree line. 'Dumb bastards.'

Isaura sprang up. Heedless, she took aim at the nearest scout. With a savage look she felled him. 'Who're the dumb bastards now?' she yelled at them, before loosing another arrow.

'That bloody girl!' a scout yelled.

Got your attention, Isaura thought. *Just keep them busy, girl.*

Curro and Nicanor shared a knowing look as Nicanor released the mooring line. They heaved with all their might against the hull of the barge. The gangplank dropped into the river. Elena screamed.

'Jump!' Isaura shouted. Nicanor and Curro plunged into the water. Frantically, she let fly another arrow, hitting one scout in the shoulder. *Two down.*

Everyone was sheltering behind the crates and possessions on deck. Isaura's side of the deck was now clear. The archer was targeting just her. She ran. An arrow flew behind her, whisking her hair on its way past.

'Get the damned sail up!' she hollered. The barge was slowly drifting out into the current. Knowing the archer would find his mark soon, Isaura dropped to her belly. An arrow flew overhead. She peered through the railing. *Where's Nic and Curro?* Another arrow hit the rail next to her head. She scrambled behind a crate.

'Throw us a rope!' Nicanor's voice drifted up the side of the hull.

'Nic?' Jaime and Daniel crawled to the far rail and peered down.

'Quick,' Daniel said. They dropped the rope's end over the side of the barge.

Another arrow flew over Isaura's head. *Bastard!*

Nicanor's head appeared at the edge of the deck. His eyes met hers. 'Isa, no!'

She stood up, aiming at where she thought the archer might be. She fired rapidly. She missed. *Damn.* Her next arrow merely nicked the scout.

Nicanor hauled himself flat over the railing. Curro's head appeared at the deck's edge. Elena stood up to run to him. Terrified she would be killed, he flashed a pleading look to Isaura.

'Shit.' Isaura sprang forward and tackled Elena to the ground. Her bow skittered out of reach. 'Stay down!'

'Let me go!'

'You'll get yourself killed. Stay *down.*'

Curro scrambled over the rail to the safety of the deck.

Elena glared at Isaura as she released her. 'Always between us.'

Isaura shook her head in disgust. She heard an arrow embed itself in the deck. Then another in the hull. She looked up. The sail was finally catching the wind. The sobbing of children filtered through the air. She looked back down at the families huddled around her. The barge was beginning to drift around the bend away from the village pier. No one was at the tiller. They needed to get into the main current—to the middle of the river. She peeked over the crate. Steeling herself, she ran hunched to the tiller and steered the boat further out. With each breath she waited for an arrow to strike her. None came.

Isaura straightened. 'You can come out now,' she said wearily.

Hesitantly, people emerged from their hiding places. Dazed, they stared at the arrows sticking out of the deck.

Nicanor strode over and embraced her. 'Isa, thank you. You saved us.' She nodded stiffly, saying nothing. He took the tiller from her.

Strangely lethargic, Isaura asked, 'How many did we lose?'

'Three boarding. On deck, I don't know.'

She moved off, surveying the deck and checking a nearby body. Absently, she murmured, 'Three more, including the one I shot and his wife.'

Jaime walked to her side. 'I can't believe you could do that.'

'You'd rather I hadn't?'

'Er, no. I just … I'm grateful, but …'

'You're welcome,' she replied sardonically. 'Help me retrieve these arrows.'

'What?' Jaime asked.

'I want my arrows back and I want any others stuck in the deck.'

'From the bodies?' His eyebrows disappeared into his hairline.

'Yes.' Observing his discomfort, she said, 'I'll get those. You get the ones out of the deck.' Shocked, he nodded gratefully.

Isaura tugged on the arrows. *Stuck.* She drew her knife and sliced down beside the arrow to free its head. Placing her foot against the body, she worked the arrows back and forth until she could pull them free, wincing at the slight sucking noise as they pulled clear. Casually, Isaura cleaned the tips on the clothes of the dead. She finished with the next body. Jaime hurried to her, handing her the arrows he'd collected. She put them in her quiver. It was then that Isaura realised that every eye on board seemed to be directed at her.

She raised her chin proudly and refused to look away.

'This is only the beginning. I don't have an endless supply of arrows. We may need every one we can get before this is over.'

Grimly, she stowed her bow and quiver in the cabin. Immediately she missed the feel of the smooth wood in her hand. She stared at her medical satchel. She'd never wanted to be a healer, but her fierce desire to pitch the satchel overboard stunned her. *I didn't even think to ask if anyone needed my help. How quickly I've broken the mould.*

CHAPTER THREE

THE breeze had died. The barge drifted slowly downstream for hours. The late afternoon sun beat down on the river, creating an oppressive, smothering heat. Willow tendrils rested languidly on the surface of the water, vaguely straying to the side with the gentle current. Not all the passengers were able to fit under the awning that had been rigged up on the deck, so they took turns in the shade, though there was still no escape from the heat.

Upon dusk a gentle breeze relieved the heat, and began to swell the sail and hasten their trip down river. They saw no other boats.

'You did the right thing earlier,' Nicanor said.

'I know.'

'They're not used to seeing women fight, that's all. It's one thing for them to know you carry a bow to hunt, but another to see it used like that.'

Hypocrites—the word was poised within Isaura, begging to be hurled at those around her.

'You just surprised them. Everything will return to normal soon, you'll see.'

Isaura kept her eyes fixed firmly forward. *I don't want things the way they were.*

Nicanor cleared his throat and changed the topic. 'What about Hugo?'

Her expression was shuttered. 'I succumbed to an overactive conscience.'

'By drugging him?'

'No, by bringing him.' Isaura's green eyes met Nicanor's and he briefly saw her torment. 'I wasn't going to bring him. In truth, I hadn't thought what I'd do. I suppose I thought I'd just have one final shouting match with him and go.' She stared at Hugo's sleeping form, her lips a thin line of disapproval. 'He was going on so. About how we'd be fine if we stayed.' She snorted. 'All I could think about was that army and how he *wouldn't* be fine. Then I thought of my mother and my conscience kicked me in the head.' She let out an exasperated breath and put her head in her hands.

Nicanor laughed. 'It's not that bad.'

'You've no idea.'

Hugo muttered in his sleep. 'No, no, no. Not the water, not the river … no.'

Isaura shuddered as she listened to her father's ramblings. 'Damn,' she groaned.

'Isa, how bad is he going to be when he wakes up?' Nicanor asked quietly.

She didn't answer directly. Instead, her voice took on a pleading tone. 'Nic, I couldn't leave him behind. He's the only father I've ever known.'

At daybreak Curro was manning the tiller. The breeze had picked up overnight, filling the sail, and the barge was making brisk time. Elena handed him a mug of tea along with a wedge of bread and cheese. Frowning, she glanced up river. He followed her gaze, noticing a large dark cloudbank had formed over the region of Mt Majula.

'Strange weather. The wind is from the wrong direction; the heat is insane. Storms almost never come in from the mountains, usually they go toward them. I don't understand it. Curro, I'm right, aren't I?'

'You're always right, dear, but you know that.'

'Here I was thinking you weren't listening.' She swatted him playfully.

'Stop worrying. What's to understand? The gods are favouring us. This breeze sends us on our way more quickly.'

'Mmm,' Elena said doubtfully. 'Should we pull into shore and wait it out?'

'No. We're safer on the river. The current should quicken when the Arunal river joins this and we might beat the storm,' Curro replied.

Within the next half hour the town of Arunal was visible. Plumes of smoke rose from parts of it. The breeze shifted briefly and the acrid smell of smoke wafted toward them. Faint cries and screams could be heard, and people could be seen running in panic through the streets.

Another barge, similar to theirs, was attempting to leave the river jetty. It was overcrowded with passengers and possessions. Burly armed men on the barge were trying to prevent more people from boarding as they hastily pushed off. They wore the uniforms of the city guard and were running those nearest through with swords, while three archers standing on the cabin picked off others in the milling crowd.

The passengers desperately attempted to man the oars in order to put more distance between themselves and the mass of people trying to board; however, the sheer number of people already on the boat hampered their efforts. There was simply no room to manoeuvre the oars into place quickly and they were still very close to the jetty. Passengers began throwing goods off the barge to make room to use the oars. Fighting broke out on the vessel as some people attempted to save their valuables. In the brawling, children and adults alike were knocked overboard. The air was filled with screams as those in the water struggled to regain the barge. Distraught mothers were leaning over the sides of the vessel, reaching out to their children in the water. Many jumped into the river to save their little ones. All the while, yet more people crowded down the jetty.

There was a resounding crack as the pylons gave way. The water was filled with frenzied people, each intent on reaching the barge at all costs. Some oars were now successfully in their locks, but the oarsmen's efforts were in vain, for many people had reached the boats and were clinging to the oars. Their weight caused the oar locks to tear away from the timber. Unable to maintain their grip, the oarsmen let them float free.

The archers, who had been shooting many of the mob before they got too close to the boat, had spent their arrows. Swordsmen were frantically stabbing those who tried to clamber onboard. Daggers sliced through throats, covering the defenders and the sides of the boat in crimson spray. For each one killed, another took his place or managed to board. The guards were overwhelmed and run through with their own weapons. Their bodies were casually pushed into the river.

Multitudes of panic-stricken people attempted to board the boat simultaneously, causing it to ride lower in the water on one side. With an aberrantly slow motion, the barge capsized. Briefly, the chaos escalated. Soon those in the water who had tried to rescue loved ones were tiring. The weight of their clothes, or the battle to calm and hold the one they rescued, was taking its toll. Some had made it back to shore, but others, with looks of fatalistic despair, lost their battles and disappeared beneath the waters. Some were trying to clamber onto the hull, but the boat was slowly sinking.

Lucia looked anxiously at Nicanor as Pio climbed into her lap.

'We can do nothing,' he said. 'We have no more room. Even if we did try to help they may swamp our boat and then all would be lost. Try not to look.'

Jaime and Daniel obviously wanted to help. Nicanor reached forward, clasping their forearms and shaking his head firmly. They subsided, yet the tears in their eyes clearly betrayed their distress.

Curro resolutely held the tiller, his face strained, his knuckles white as he stared at the chaos before them. Elena stood beside him, her face pressed into his shoulder to hide from the horrors before her.

'Is the enemy here already?' Elena murmured.

Isaura looked away, sickened by the chaos. Her face like granite, she replied, 'No. This is their own fault. Just like panicked animals.'

Elena glared at her, shocked. 'How can you say that?'

'How can you watch this and not know it?'

Elena, annoyed at the rebuke, was ready with a retort but Curro cut her off. 'Don't, Leni.' She glared at him. 'I know what you are going to say—don't.'

Red faced, she turned from Isaura and hugged Curro tightly. Still Isaura heard her say, 'Look at her—she's Hill Clan. Even the Matyrani don't like them, yet you defend her. You and Nic have always defended her.'

Nicanor leaned toward Isaura and whispered, 'Don't worry about Leni, Isa.'

'I never do,' was her too loud, too bright reply.

Just as they had reached the point where the two river currents merged, the breeze picked up again; quickly the barge left the city view behind. The smoke and screams faded with distance, leaving the river eerily quiet. They passed many smaller boats with one or two people on board, who seemed to have left in haste with no supplies. Their faces lacked all animation.

The sight of Arunal burning, the smell and the screams were etched in the villager's minds. Children clung sobbing to their mothers and fathers as their parents tried to soothe them. Pio was sitting on Lucia's knee, his eyes red and swollen. She rubbed his back gently and eased him into the crook of her arm, crooning to him and rocking him like he was a baby again. She felt sickened by what she had seen; it was taking all her will power to maintain a strong front. Lucia could vaguely hear Nicanor near her talking quietly to Jaime and Daniel and felt a wild need to feel his strong arms securely around her; to have him reassure her that they were safe, that he could protect them. Losing her battle, she began shaking uncontrollably.

Isaura leaned down at her shoulder. 'Lucia. Lucia?'

Lucia vaguely heard a noise. Isaura's face was level with hers. She was speaking to her—at least her lips were moving, but Lucia couldn't decipher her words. She shook her head, blinking rapidly, but it made no difference. Her vision took on an amber hue and she lost all focus.

Isaura caught her and lowered her to the deck. She bade Pio to sit near her.

'What's wrong, Isa?' His eyes were wide as he gazed at his mother.

'It's alright, Pio. She's fainted—that's all. She'll be fine.' She rubbed Lucia's hands, continuing to speak to her. Soon Lucia's eyes began to open and focus.

'What happened?'

'You fainted,' Isaura said softly.

Lucia looked embarrassed. 'Oh, I feel like such a fool!'

Isaura shrugged. 'No shame in it.'

Lucia felt strong hands around her shoulders as she sat up. Nicanor cradled her back in his arms. 'I'm alright Nic. I just feel like an idiot.' Pio snuggled in next to her.

Isaura left the family alone and quietly went to check on the others.

'How does she stay so calm?' Lucia asked Nicanor. 'For a girl who didn't want to be a healer, she's certainly convincing.'

'She's not calm, not really. Her mother taught her well. But we both know that's not enough for her—she's too restless.'

Lucia smiled. 'She just needs to find the right man, settle down and start a family.'

Nicanor laughed. 'I'm not sure that would work and I wouldn't mention it if I were you. I can't see a life of quiet domestic bliss suiting her.'

Lucia looked probingly at Nicanor. 'We taught her to fight when we were children. She even persuaded Curro to teach her what he knows about swordsmanship. The archery, she did that all on her own,' he added proudly.

Lucia looked horrified as she lowered her voice. 'You what? The archery she might have been able to get away with for hunting, but you saw how people looked at her after the fight.'

'She saved us.'

'Yes, but it singled her out as different. She doesn't need that. She already looks different. They don't need reminding of it.'

'You're not making sense. What would you have her do?'

'I don't know,' Lucia sighed. 'You know what would happen to her if the authorities found out. It's illegal for women to learn skill at arms.'

'Lucia, I'd be dead if it wasn't for her. What were we supposed to do? She was always in trouble as a child and we weren't always there to protect her.'

'What, so you thought you'd teach her to kill people?' she hissed. 'She's a healer, she's not supposed to *kill* people.' She gasped, surprised at herself. She looked around quickly, hoping no one overhead them.

'Thank the gods she did. Lucia, she only has Hugo as a father. She travels miles on her own visiting the sick and collecting ingredients. She has to know how to defend herself.' His voice grew a little more indignant as he added, 'It doesn't matter now, we're leaving.'

Isaura walked back toward the cabin, weaving between the villagers. Hugo's sleeping form was exactly where she'd dumped him. 'Father?' She gently shook him. 'Father?'

'Mmm,' came the groggy reply.

She shook him harder. 'Father!'

'What … Isaura? I was having a delightful dream. I felt like I was floating on the breeze.'

'Open your eyes and stay calm.' Hugo sat bolt upright, blinking rapidly and shading his eyes. Isaura grimaced as she said, 'You are floating—on a river.'

Hugo's eyes widened, he scrambled back against the cabin wall, tucked his knees to his chest and rocked back and forth. His breathing became more rapid; he spoke in gasps. 'You, you did this. You drugged me!'

'I couldn't leave you,' she said quietly.

'Yes, you could! I made it clear I did not want to come. Nor should you. I am a gifted healer. I would have been safe. My reputation is well known. My services would have been sought by our new rulers ... by the army. There will be so many wounded— there would have been great need for my services. I would have been safe. You would too, Isaura—you have enough skill to be useful.'

Isaura refrained from shaking her head in wonder at how deep his delusions ran. She didn't want to aggravate the situation. 'Father, the Zaragaria would have their own healers.' *You never leave home,* she silently derided him. *How on earth would anyone know your skill, or lack of it?* His eyes darted about the boat. She put her finger under his chin, drawing his face and attention back toward her. 'Besides, you've no guarantee they would not have killed us both for sport.'

Hugo continued on unabashed. 'Nonsense girl! They would have had great difficulty in finding our home tucked away as we were in the woods.'

'Father,' Isaura replied, trying to remain calm and relax her clenched teeth. 'The morning we left they were entering the other side of woods. Most likely they would have found us.' She sighed. 'We've been over all this before.'

'You should not have brought me,' he said indignantly.

'Do you want anything? A drink, or some food?'

'I am rather thirsty. Yes, I'll have a drink.' He sipped delicately at the offered water.

'Do you want to stand? Stretch your limbs and walk about?'

'Walk about!' he cried. 'It will take all my nerve just to stand, you foolish girl.'

Isaura was losing patience. 'It might not be as bad as you think. Standing will be good for your limbs. You can lean against the cabin and me.'

He muttered unintelligibly, yet held out his arm for Isaura to assist him. Rising stiffly, holding fast to Isaura's arm, he breathed deeply. 'Ah … yes … not so bad.'

'Father, open your eyes.' As he did so, he dug his fingers painfully into Isaura's arm and shoulder. She winced, but said nothing.

Hugo focused on the riverbank, noticing the trees seeming to pass quite rapidly. Reluctantly, he looked along the barge to the prow. 'So many people, Isaura. It's so crowded. There's not enough room,' he whispered in panic. He looked at the expanse of the river, listening to the water as it rippled along the hull. 'Oh my! Isaura, it's so wide. There is so much water.' Hugo's skin had grown pale and clammy. 'Isaura … I feel ill. You should not have brought me,' he whispered, burying his face in his hands as he sunk to the deck.

'Father—' Platitudes were useless, though she felt she should try. Instead, she said bluntly, 'If you are going to be sick, you'll have to hang your head over the side. No one wants to clean up after you.'

'Give me a bucket, you *cruel* girl.'

'No.'

He was turning green. She grabbed some rope, quickly tied it around his waist, then anchored it to a hook on the cabin wall.

'Hang your head over the side. You can't possibly fall in now. You'll be safe.'

He cast her a savage look as she turned and walked away. At the prow she leaned out over the water, inhaling deeply, hoping that the sight of her doing this would terrify her father. When she looked back he was leaning over the railing, being violently ill.

CHAPTER FOUR

THE storm clouds loomed over them, while the steadily rising wind carried a chill. Jaime and Daniel, usually buoyant, sat side by side quietly observing their friends and neighbours.

'Gods, Dan. Do you think this will work? I mean … it seemed like such a good idea in theory,' Jaime said in a hushed tone.

Daniel did not reply as his gaze roved first over their companions, then over the expanse of river before them.

'None of us really have any knowledge of sailing on a river or the sea,' Jaime continued. 'Who knows what will happen?'

Daniel looked squarely at his brother. 'At least we're alive. Not like those poor souls back there. We'll make it. I have to believe it … and Jaime, we *have* to act like we believe it. Look at them, just look at them. Doubt will be like a disease on this boat if we're not careful.' Jaime nodded, looking at his brother with a new element of respect and gratitude. 'Now *smile*, Jaime. People are watching,' Daniel said, shoving him impishly.

Jaime followed Daniel's glance to alight upon a pretty blonde. She stared at them pensively. Daniel smiled reassuringly at her; she gave a half smile in return, but her focus was on Jaime. Jaime frowned, looking down and away as he folded his arms on his chest.

'What in the world is wrong now?' Daniel whispered, stifling a laugh. 'It's obvious that Gabriela likes you. When are you going to do something about it?'

'You don't know that.' Jaime blushed.

Daniel groaned dramatically and rolled his eyes. 'Yes, actually, I do. Every time she has come into my shop for cloth, she asks after you. I kept hoping for months that she'd at least look at me. But she's just not interested. I even flirted *outrageously*,' he added in falsetto.

Jaime snorted in amusement. Of the two, he had always been the one who had no trouble attracting young women; Daniel was the shy one.

'I don't know, Dan. Well, you know I'm not ... ah ... inexperienced in this.'

Daniel was turning a puce colour, merriment dancing from his eyes. 'No, no ... definitely not inexperienced.'

'Oh, forget it!' Jaime snapped.

'All right, I'll let you finish,' Daniel said, raising his hands in appeasement.

'I've never had problems, but I've got no idea what to say to Gabriela. I just get near her and ...'

Grinning, Daniel said, 'Just say "hello", anything, talk.' He added solemnly, 'This could be your only chance.'

Jaime looked up sharply, then slowly nodded.

Daniel sighed and walked over to where Gabriela sat. Bending down he whispered to her, casting a mischievous look at Jaime's stunned face, before sauntering away to the stern.

Gabriela smiled at Jaime as she walked toward him. Hesitant, he returned her smile. His mouth was suddenly dry and his mind raced over what to talk about. 'Are you having a nice time?' hardly seemed appropriate.

Gabriela was alone on this barge. Her elderly parents had elected to stay behind, as had many others who were old or infirm. This was the time to take chances. She had nothing to lose. Too long she had watched him flirt with the girls of the village and listened to their tales of late night assignations. Sometimes she caught him looking at her, but he never seemed to want to pursue her. Sitting near him, she took a deep breath.

'Jaime, do you find me at all attractive?'

Jaime, beet red and nearly choking, stammered, 'Of course.' He'd never stammered in his life. His palms grew sweaty.

Her blonde hair was tied back in a loose ponytail. The brisk wind whipped stray strands of hair about her fair face, surrounding it with a slight golden aura. Her cheeks were rosy from the cold air. The combined effect made her eyes seem a more intense shade of blue.

'So why don't you talk to me?'

'I do talk to you!' he replied defensively. 'I am talking to you.'

'I suppose it's the wrong word. Jaime, I've seen you with other girls and trust me, those girls do *talk*.' He blanched. 'Why is it that you've got no problem with them?'

'You're not like those girls.'

'What do you mean?' Self-consciously she glanced down at herself, then raised an eyebrow.

He followed her gaze, his eyes lingering on her curves, and gulped nervously. 'I mean … you don't act like them. You're different.' *Damn*, he thought, *this is not going well.*

'How? You mean if I'd acted more like a coquette, you would have pursued me?'

'Well … um … er … You know I never really pursued those other girls … They flirted with me …' Flirt didn't quite cover it. 'I never really had to actually talk that much.'

Gabriela's eyes widened. He wasn't sure if she was angry, but then she suddenly laughed.

'They were never serious.' He wanted to say 'uncomplicated', but decided that was not going to help. 'They knew that too.'

Her eyes narrowed. 'Are you sure?'

'Oh yes, definitely. No promises were made.' He felt he was on solid ground now. 'They were harmless dalliances. They're all married now.'

'You've no idea, have you? I know you broke hearts. Those girls moved on because you never asked them to marry you.' He looked stunned. 'Not all girls risk their reputations for just a little fun.'

'To be fair, some had already risked their reputations before I came along.'

She gave him an arch look. 'You've never had to actually court a girl, have you? Well now you do. I'm not going to fall at your feet like the others.'

Jaime watched in dismay as she left.

Daniel's gut tightened as he watched this exchange. She was beautiful, all the more so because she seemed utterly unaware of it. He wanted to look away, but was transfixed.

Isaura joined Daniel at the stern, leaning against the railing with a faint smile at the edge of her lips. 'You know, Dan, you really are the brighter one. For all your brother's good looks, he really is as dumb as a stump sometimes.'

He merely grunted, trying to quell the small spark of joy at seeing the pair part and the stunned look on his brother's face.

Isaura patted his arm and gave him a rare hug. 'It will get better,' she said. 'I'm sorry, but I've got to save your dumb brother from himself.'

Daniel roused himself, grateful for her insight, returning her hug fiercely before she left him.

Jaime was just where Gabriela had left him, looking lost.

Isaura sat down beside him, giving his knee a gentle squeeze. 'You worry too much, you know that?'

Jaime, completely taken aback, stared at her as if she was a lunatic.

'You can charm the birds out of the trees when you have a mind to and yet you can't have a simple conversation with Gabriela without ...'

'It wasn't a simple conversation.'

'Jaime ...'

'Bloody ... damn it, Isa!' he said vehemently. 'When she is around, suddenly I don't know what I'm doing.'

'Clearly, Jaime. They say love scrambles the brain,' she said ruefully as he put his head in his hands. 'Look, here's my idea.' He groaned. Tapping her foot impatiently, she asked, 'Have you got any ideas of your own?' Jaime shook his head. 'Right then, listen up. See that storm bank? It's going to be pretty damn awful. Where's Gabi's stuff?

Oh yes, all the way over there near the edge of the deck. Not a good spot really; too exposed, too dangerous. Look at your spot, you've got the canopy and that covered cargo as protection. I'd say that's a much safer spot, wouldn't you? Go play the hero then and look after her. Everything will work out fine in the end.'

Jaime's face lit up as she spoke. 'Isa, you're a genius.' He scrambled to his feet, looking for Gabriela.

Watching him leave, she muttered affectionately, 'Dumb as a stump. My kingdom for a good-looking man who has a fully working brain.' If this absurd plan worked, then they really did deserve each other. Still, Isaura was pleased for Gabriela if it meant she would no longer be alone.

Jaime approached Gabriela, thanking the gods when the lightning flashed again. 'Gabi, this storm is going to be rough. I think … that is … would you like to move closer to Dan and me? It should be a bit more sheltered there. That is, we … I can keep you safe. You know, with the storm, and maybe the river might get rough too. You'd be safer with us.'

Gabriela stared at him, saying nothing. Jaime, scarlet, turned away.

Quickly she reached out, a soft smile on her face. 'Yes, Jaime. Yes, I think I'd like that.'

He nodded, relieved, and smiled tentatively. 'I would too.' More lightning lit up the sky, illuminating towering, roiling cloudbanks, but they hadn't yet heard any thunder. 'It's still miles away.'

'Yes, but look at the size of those clouds. Have you ever seen anything like it? What on earth are we going to do when the storm gets here?'

'One thing at a time. Let's just get your things, then worry about what *might* happen.'

>>—→

Nicanor awoke with Lucia and Pio sleeping soundly beside him. He heard a faint movement and noticed Isaura at the tiller. Gently he extricated himself from Lucia. She stirred. 'All's well. Go back to sleep.' She murmured something unintelligible and drifted off again.

He made his way to Isaura. 'Isa? Have you slept?'

She shook her head. 'I can't settle. Can't you feel it? The air is almost alive.'

'Hugo?'

'He complained so much he's exhausted himself—thank the gods.'

'Thank the gods?' Nicanor grinned.

'Didn't I tell you? I'm reforming; turning over a new leaf. I'm prepared to believe in any deity who will see us safe.'

Nicanor's sceptical look was her only reply.

The air was rent with a sizzle, immediately followed by an ear-splitting clap of thunder. They both ducked instinctively. Everyone woke up, cowering beneath their blankets and scrambling for more cover. A torrential downpour commenced, along with a gale force wind that screamed eerily through the trees on the banks. The sail filled and collapsed violently as the wind whipped around buffeting the boat.

'Maybe we should lower the sail?' Isaura suggested. It took several men to furl the single sail and tie it securely.

The canopy over the deck billowed wildly with the force of the wind and offered little protection from the driving rain. The children huddled closer to their parents. Flashes of lightning revealed terrified faces. Hail began to pelt down upon them and settle on the deck.

Nicanor took the tiller from Isaura so she could check on Hugo. He was awake and trying to claw his way along the deck around the side of the cabin in order to reach the shelter of its interior. Forgetting the rope still anchored him to the deck, Hugo let out a snarl as he reached its end.

Isaura moved toward him. 'Father, let me help.' As she reached down to aid him, he batted her away.

'Not you! You are the cause of all this.' He was still struggling forward, unaware of what was restraining him and growing more agitated with each passing moment.

'Father, enough, stop! I'll undo the rope so you can get in the cabin.' His feral eyes cleared momentarily. He looked down and began to untie the rope himself. She reached to help him; he snarled, lashing out viciously and swiping her across the face. His healer's insignia ring left a savage red gash from her cheekbone to her lip. Stunned, she sprawled backward and watched him crawl into the small cabin to hide from the storm. He had always been a petty, arrogant man, yet he had never been physically violent. Tears welled in her eyes, but she refused to let them fall. She berated herself for her foolishness—he would never change and, it seemed, she would never learn.

Isaura scrambled across the now slippery hailstone covered deck toward Lucia and Pio, who were huddled next to a crate near the canopy's edge. As she reached them, the canopy swelled upward and broke one of its tethering ropes. The rope swung about, lashing Isaura across her already injured face. She stumbled backward briefly as pain caused tears to stream down her face. Untethered at one corner, the canopy heaved further upward in the gale and threatened to come entirely loose. It was the only shelter on the deck.

Isaura launched herself forward to try to grab the flailing rope, missed and collapsed as her right leg slipped sideways on the hail. Pain seared through her inner thigh. She could not get back up. Lucia called out, but Isaura couldn't hear her over the wind. Two men grabbed the loose rope and were securing the canopy as she dragged herself across to Lucia. They locked arms and tucked their heads down, trying to shelter Pio between them. The hail felt like a barrage of stones. Isaura's wet clothing offered no protection, and her skin stung painfully wherever the hail hit. Abruptly it ceased, only to be replaced by steady driving rain.

The fierce wind propelled the barge down river with even greater speed. Flashes of lightning revealed the banks were further apart and the trees had thinned. The pitch of the wind altered; it was no longer a high howling, but a deep angry roar as it flattened the tall grass along the sandy banks.

Nicanor strained to catch a glimpse of the shoreline. He had no idea exactly where they were, or even how long had passed since the storm commenced.

The sound of the wind changed yet again. The grasses were replaced by tall reeds and bulrushes; it was as if thousands of spears were rattling, defying them passage. With one last onslaught the wind and rain ceased. The clouds began to disperse. The sound of the water lapping gently against the boat, interspersed by the odd whisper of conversation, was the only noise. Everyone held their breath, awed by the unexpected tranquillity and beauty before them. The moon was reflected in the calm waters of a massive lake.

The villagers grew excited. 'Where are we?'

'Is it the ocean?'

'No,' Nicanor said. 'I think it's Lake Runala.'

Standing by the mast, Curro was jubilant as he made to hoist the single sail.

'Curro, wait.' Nicanor grabbed his arm. 'Wait until dawn. We need to be sure of the river. We can't risk entering the fens.'

The sound of the unfurling sail woke Jaime to a pale grey, early morning sky. His legs were wet, cold and cramped, but he really didn't want to wake Gabriela. She had dozed off leaning against him and now his arm was draped protectively around her. He used his free arm to remove their sodden blanket. Underneath, his cloak was wet, but he noticed with satisfaction that Gabriela's was only damp. She was not tall and in her sleep had managed to curl closely in against him. Jaime had wanted to hold her for such a long time; he wished that she would just stay right where she was. He winced as he wiggled his toes in an attempt to get some feeling back in his legs.

Daniel chuckled. 'The trials one has to endure, eh?' *Lucky bastard.* Together they had sheltered Gabriela from the storm, yet somehow she had wound up in Jaime's arms. *I'm an idiot. It was never going to be me. Stop hoping for something that just isn't going to happen.*

Jaime tentatively placed his hand against Gabriela's cheek. She stirred and tried to snuggle deeper into his shoulder, fighting to stay asleep, but half her face was numb and her neck was incredibly stiff. She gasped when she realised someone was holding her. She pulled back and saw Jaime smiling down at her.

'Gabi—don't. It's so cold.' He repositioned himself more comfortably. 'Come.' He drew her toward him so that she leaned back against his chest. Jaime wrapped her cloak around her, then enclosed them both inside his own cloak and held her tightly. 'Better?' All she could do was nod, bewildered and content.

Curro took over the tiller from his exhausted brother. 'Nic, what do you think? The largest gap, directly across?'

Nicanor simply nodded. 'The current will tell.' Three quarters of the way across the lake the water's pull increased. The barge sailed gracefully through a wide gap between tall bulrushes and downstream as the river snaked its way to the coast. The calm surface of the water suggested a languorous pace, but the river was deceptively fast.

Minor chaos engulfed the deck as children ran to the front of the boat to lean over the railings, trying to be the first to see the ocean. Shrieks and squeals pierced the air as they were dragged back to more sheltered spots by the gaggle of fussing mothers, leaving Pio exposed, hugging the neck of the horse figurehead. His arms gripped the carved mane as he wriggled further out to peer between its ears.

'Pio!' Lucia barrelled up to the front of the boat, pushing past the disgruntled children being dragged back. 'Pio, get off there now!'

Pio looked back quickly, flinching. 'I'm going to be the first to the ocean.'

'Now, Pio! You will be the first to drown if you're not careful.'

Knowing he was already in trouble, he ignored his mother. *How much worse is it going to get? I've just got to hang on a bit longer.* The wind whipped his hair back. His cheeks were ruddy and his eyes watering. The barge dipped and Pio slipped sideways. Lucia gasped, too horrified to yell. Pio felt as if his stomach had flipped over. He clung tightly to the horse's carved mane and neck. Frightened, he started to inch backward. Lucia leaned over the bow, reaching out to grab him.

The barge rounded a bend in the river to a collective gasp. The dull grey light had given way to an early morning glow that illuminated a vista streaked with thin wisps of grey cloud and a horizon filled with the grey-blue ocean.

Pio looked with wonder at the vast expanse of water before him. 'Wow! Look Ma. Ma—I did it! I'm the first to the ocean.'

With the changing tide the barge continued to increase in speed. 'Pio! Get back here now.' Lucia's firm voice brooked no argument. Pio, glancing back at her face, immediately stopped crowing. He now knew just how much worse things could become.

Lucia hugged him fiercely as his feet touched the deck. 'Thank the gods you weren't hurt.' He winced as his mother's hand connected sharply with his backside. 'Now go and sit down.' Pio skulked up the deck briefly before darting to Isaura, who had not moved from where she had crawled during the storm.

'Isa, did you see?' She nodded. 'It was the best!'

'Look out—your mother is coming.'

Lucia glared at Pio as she pounded the deck toward him.

'Was it worth it?' Isaura whispered.

'Yep!' Pio whispered with a grin. Isaura flashed him a quick wink as Lucia dragged him away.

The barge continued to gather pace. As they approached another bend in the river, a massive old fallen tree lay entangled at its edge. Large branches protruded perilously into their path and Curro struggled to keep the boat away from it. The barge shuddered violently as it scraped over the partially submerged trunk and an overhanging branch rent the canopy.

The murky waters were deceptive. The river surface appeared calm, yet there were many odd little whirlpools and bubbles here and there signalling more underwater obstacles. The hull groaned as it fought against these unseen enemies. The river straightened and gradually widened. Curro relaxed, grinning at his brother. The ocean lay before them.

Smiling and cheering, the villagers hugged one another. The children raced forward again as the barge emerged into the ocean like a popped cork. Lucia and Nicanor stood silently embracing. *Now we just head up the coast and everything will be fine,* Lucia thought. Silence enveloped the barge as the sight of the vast grey ocean captivated them. Forks of lightning spiked from the retreating clouds, and in the growing light dense sheets of rain could be seen blanketing the horizon.

Nicanor shook his head as if waking from a trance. He looked back at the coast and was surprised at how far away it was.

'Why aren't we turning?' Nicanor strode toward Curro.

'What?'

'Why aren't we turning? We've got to head up the coast. Curro, you must turn us!' He saw the concentration on Curro's face and realised that he was trying to turn the barge, but it was having little effect. The currents were too strong. The coast was getting further away. He spun, racing down the deck, calling for help to put the oars into their locks. The villagers, ecstatic about reaching the ocean and ignorant to all else, clustered around, blocking his way.

Nicanor struggled to manoeuvre the first of the oars into place. Frustrated, he yelled, 'Get out of the way! Damn you, all of you get away!' Shocked, they remained immobile. 'Move, now!'

Daniel and Jaime hustled people around the deck. They recruited more men to help lock the oars in place and reposition some of the cargo. All the while the boat pulled further from the shore. Several men heaved on the oars on one side, struggling to aid their turning.

The breeze ebbed and then billowed the sail. Nicanor frowned, realising the square sail was hindering them. They were fighting against it and the current. He leapt up, calling for aid to furl the sail. Two men jumped to assist him, then darted back to their positions on the oars.

Muscles straining and red-faced, they barely kept the coastline in sight. Women took over from the men at rowing and at the helm. The breeze continued and a soft swell rose. Exhaustion began to overtake them. The oars felt increasingly unwieldy and with each swell of the ocean they continued to lose sight of land as nature insidiously conspired against them. When at last they collapsed, utterly spent, the coastline had long disappeared from view.

'What do you want us to do?' Jaime asked.

'We've got to rest,' said Curro.

Nicanor grunted in assent. He was wet with perspiration. His muscles were beginning to cramp from the prolonged exertion and his face was pale.

'We know which direction land is … if we rest and then take shifts again maybe we can make our way back?' Jaime suggested.

Nicanor wasn't sure it was going to be that easy.

CHAPTER FIVE

FRUSTRATION gnawed at Isaura. Her leg felt as if it was on fire. She could barely put weight on it. The laceration on her face had scabbed over, but if she opened her mouth a little it would split and slowly weep blood down the red, swollen side of her face. *Bugger, I can't do anything!*

Lucia was checking on Hugo and Isaura could hear his complaints clearly. She returned to Isaura, red-faced and fuming. 'Your mother was a patient woman. I'd forgotten what he was like.' Isaura heard the underlying accusation: *Why did you bring him?*

Embarrassed and ashamed, she replied, 'I'm sorry, Lucia.'

Lucia felt immediately guilty. 'Oh Isa, no … no.'

'Help me up? I'll deal with him.' Relief was clearly evident on Lucia's face. Isaura grimaced as pain shot up her leg. 'Let me lean on you. Once we get to him you don't have to stay.' She hobbled over to Hugo, tucked in the small cabin. He had not moved at all since the storm. Hoping to soothe him, she tried to take his hand as she sat on the bench seat. He snatched it away. The wild look he gave her shocked her.

'*You.* You couldn't even stay with me. Make sure I was safe, be here when I woke up. Instead a stranger cares more for my welfare than you do.'

'Lucia is hardly a stranger.'

'Where were you?'

'I had problems getting here.'

Hugo finally noticed Isaura's face pinched with pain, pale on one side, red and weeping blood on the other.

'You should know how to treat that. Or do you need *my* help?'

Ignoring this, she asked, 'How are you feeling? Nausea, dizziness? Would you like anything?'

Refusing to answer, he stared resentfully at the cabin wall.

'You obviously wanted me here, yet now you refuse to talk. Well, you should try stretching your limbs. Drink.' He grunted in assent, but remained where he was. 'Look—there's fresh water, bread, cheese, and apples. I can't get them for you ...' Still silence greeted her. 'You can ask Lucia ... or you could find them yourself.'

'That woman shows no respect,' he spat.

'Father! Lucia is a good, kind woman. You ...' His eyes narrowed. Isaura held up her hands placatingly. 'We've all got to get along. Come on, the boat's steady now. Now is the time for you to try to get your sea legs.'

'Sea legs! Girl—if it wasn't for you I wouldn't need sea legs,' he sneered.

Isaura sighed, pinching the bridge of her nose. She raised her eyes to his, playing the penitent. 'Father, you're right. I should have left you at home. I was trying to *save* you. I didn't realise how hard this voyage would be on you.' *The hard part hasn't even started yet.* 'I did it with the best of intentions ... your welfare at heart.' Isaura allowed the pain from her injuries to bring tears to her eyes, drawing a gulping breath as if to control her overwhelming emotions. She waited, praying she had not overplayed her hand.

Hugo blinked at her like an owl blinded by the sun. He cleared his throat and patted her wounded leg with the condescension due to a recalcitrant child. 'I was young once, child. We all make mistakes.'

Isaura winced, but victory was in sight. 'I am sorry. Try to walk about on deck, there are plenty of handholds.' His eyes narrowed again at Pio running along the deck. She took one last chance, pricking his pride. 'Everything is so easy at that age.'

'Hmf! Well, I am not so old.' Inhaling deeply, he rose shakily from the bench seat. With one hand braced on the cabin wall he proceeded through the door. He squared his shoulders as he went, while keeping a hand firmly on any fixture he could.

Isaura sighed; she hated manipulation, but could see no other option with Hugo.

Lucia eyed Hugo warily, then went to help him.

Overwhelmed with tiredness, Isaura bit back real tears and leaned back against the wall. She closed her eyes and drifted to sleep listening to the shipboard noises.

>>→

Isaura woke to a gentle touch on her shoulder. 'Isa, Isa, wake up.' Pio was standing beside her looking worried. She turned stiffly, but was unable to hide her pain. Pio's eyes widened. 'Isa, you're really hurt. You need help.'

'I'm sure I'll be fine in a few days, Pio, but I'd better do something about this leg to help it along, eh?' She smiled. 'Can you fetch my bag?'

While she waited, Isaura tried moving her leg. It took all of her concentration to do so and the movement caused a sharp stabbing pain high on her inner thigh.

Pio arrived with her bag and hovered in the doorway. It seemed he felt a sense of duty to help her, yet he still kept an eye on the other children.

Isaura chuckled. 'Pio, you don't have to stay. Go on with the others.'

Struggling with her leggings she momentarily wished she wore skirts. With her leg resting on the bench seat she methodically surveyed her injuries. Her outer thigh was deep blue-black where she had landed on the deck. Her inner thigh was ribboned with purple striations and there was a definite lump in the muscle high up in her leg. Absently she noted that her knee was also swollen. Opening a pungent brownish salve made from sunskiss, she placed some in a bowl and mixed in a small amount of a deep red salve made from bloodwort. Gingerly she applied the mixture to her bruises, braced her knee with a bandage and re-dressed.

Gabriela and Elena joined her.

'Isa, how are you?' Elena asked.

'Can we help?' Gabriela added.

Isaura looked thoughtfully at them. She rarely asked for help, but she knew Gabriela would if asked. If Elena chose to as well, so be it. 'Actually, yes please.'

Their voices radiated concern as they spoke in unison. 'What do you need?'

'Can you help me care for people?'

Gabriela looked confused, then slightly anxious. 'Isa?'

'I can barely stand. How am I to get to people?'

'They can come to you. Or we'll help you walk to them,' Elena said.

'I'm really not sure about this, Isa. What if I get something wrong?' Gabriela interrupted.

'You won't. You've nursed both your parents. You've never made mistakes. I trust you.' She smiled at Gabriela's pensive face.

Gabriela looked shamefaced. 'Isa, this is different ... If something should go wrong ... You'll recover soon. Let's just wait and see,' she finished hurriedly.

Elena added, 'Maybe Hugo can help?'

'Hugo is far more likely to poison someone than either of you,' Isaura snapped.

Elena tugged on Gabriela's arm. Gabriela looked apologetically at Isaura. 'Isa, I ...'

'Just go,' Isaura replied flatly. Disappointment and hurt sat like a lead weight in her belly as she watched them walk away.

Curro, Nicanor and Isaura examined the final tally of food.

'We planned for a few weeks at sea, a month at the most, on rations which were not generous. Isa, have you any idea how much we can cut the rations by?' Curro asked.

Hugo moved unsteadily toward them. 'Gentlemen, don't make any decisions without first consulting me. My wealth of knowledge, gained over many years,' at which point he looked condescendingly at Isaura, 'will stand us in good stead.'

Isaura raised her eyebrows, saying nothing. Hugo was now wandering the ship with more confidence, but he was prone to odd mood swings. This blend of simpering arrogance set her teeth on edge.

Curro replied, 'I was just asking Isa if she knew how far we could stretch the rations. But now that you're here we can have the benefit of your experience.' The sarcasm was lost on Hugo.

Hugo took the tallies, deep in thought. 'The original ration quantities were not ample to begin with. I feel that you could reduce them by a quarter or a third at the most.'

Isaura looked surprised. 'That's only an extra few weeks. We may need longer than that.'

'Surely not. Surely we will have sighted land by then. Some solution will have presented itself.' A slight edge of hysteria was creeping into Hugo's voice.

Isaura felt guilty for bringing him and imposing him on the others; paradoxically she felt guilty at the realisation that she would have felt little remorse if she had left him behind.

'We need to get more time out of the rations. What's the maximum we can get?' Nicanor asked Isaura.

Curro and Nicanor both turned to Isaura. 'At a guess we could halve it, maybe a little more. There's the animals ... They are consuming water, and fresh water is our most precious commodity out here. Damn! I don't know.' She ran her hand through her hair, eyes tightly closed. 'Water is our main worry. We will need to catch as much of it as we can. We're more exposed to the elements than I had counted on. Even a mild day seems too hot ... The nights are cold ... Then there's the wind ...'

'How *long*, Isa?' Nicanor asked with hint of impatience.

'Maybe three months with this many people.' Isaura was

pessimistic. 'Healing cuts and scrapes is one thing. I'm not …' She paused as Elena joined them.

Elena took one look at their grim faces and moved into Curro's embrace for reassurance.

'Isa?' Nicanor prompted.

Unable to answer immediately, she lowered her head while she battled to contain her emotions. *I didn't ask for this. You all expect some damn miracle.* She was on the verge of screaming at them. Instead she marshalled herself, raised her head and asserted, 'Kill one goat soon, the other later. The chickens can wait till we can't feed them anymore. Water must be conserved at all costs. We've got oats and barley, but they need to be soaked—that's a problem. There is limited supply of kindling for the galley stove …'

'Fishing,' Elena interrupted. 'We could make it a game for the children. It would keep them occupied and who knows, they may actually catch something.'

'We need to find containers to catch water in,' Curro said. 'And pray to Majula and Araceli that it rains sometime along the way.'

'Along the way to where? Aren't we going to try to get home? I can't survive on this ration. No grown man could. We'll all be dead …' Hugo began to panic.

Curro grabbed his arm. Bending forward he looked at him sharply and whispered, 'Isaura is as a sister to me, but you are *nothing*, old man. We have no need of your opinions. Do *not* spread panic.'

Hugo looked to Isaura for aid; she merely shrugged.

Elena cleared her throat. 'Everyone should be involved in these decisions.'

'No!' Hugo and Isaura both said.

Elena was shocked. She opened her mouth to speak, but Curro cut her off. 'They're right. Isa's right.'

Of course, Elena thought resentfully.

Hugo drew himself up, saying imperiously, 'We can't let the villagers interfere with a decision like this. Control must be maintained. If you have too much discussion or do not seem confident of your judgement then you will lose control and order with it.'

'Precisely.' Curro glared meaningfully at Hugo, who finally had the good sense to looked chastened.

'They have a right to contribute to a decision that affects their lives,' Elena persisted.

Isaura was resolved. 'They've already exercised that right. They chose to come on this voyage. Now we make the decisions. I never thought I'd say this, but Hugo is correct. You can inform them of the facts, but we must guide them toward this end. Let them think they have made the decision themselves.'

»——➤

'How can we live on this?'

'It's enough,' Isaura said flatly as she sat in the middle of the deck surrounded by irate villagers.

'For you, maybe.'

'We brought more food. Why should we have to suffer this ration?'

'I say let everyone eat their own supplies. Those who didn't plan ahead and bring more will just have to make do.'

'They brought all they could. Why should their lives be worth less than yours? Why should mine?' Isaura explained.

'Because you're not one ...' a man vehemently began before he was elbowed in the ribs.

'Ssh! You are our healer, Isa. You brought medical supplies. We ...'

'You need me,' Isaura finished drily. 'And when you don't?' The question hung in the air like a noose.

'You all agreed to come. You all agreed to share,' Lucia added defensively.

'Not this. We didn't agree to this. We agreed to go to Matryan. You've got us lost.'

'We need to keep trying to row back to land. We know land is in that direction.'

'Are you sure?' Nicanor asked.

'We're not trying to get back to the coast! You're just letting us get further and further away!'

Curro replied, 'We tried rowing for days, yet we are no closer to land.'

'We need to try again. To try harder! We don't need to lessen the rations. We can stay at full strength and make it back.'

Nicanor was blunt. 'I think we've drifted far off course. We can't row long or hard enough to make up the distance.'

A large man with greying hair stepped toward Nicanor, his furious red face only inches from him. 'No! We've listened to you and look where we are!'

Jaime and Daniel reached for their swords. Curro, looking like he wanted to rend limbs from bodies, stood beside Isaura. He heard Elena's harsh intake of breath when he left her side, but ignored her. Isaura would not be able to escape if a fight broke out; she would need his help.

Nicanor spoke calmly, though his fist was clenched and his shoulders tense. His expression urged Lucia and Pio to move out of harm's way. 'In days we have not been able to make it back to land. We are using up our reserves of strength when we should be conserving them. I think we should work with the current and wind. Row when we can and use the sail to speed us onward, and believe that the gods will see us to land.'

'What land? The only land we know of is back there!'

'We will find land.' Nicanor was resolute.

Daniel was ready to explode. 'What gives you the right to criticise our decisions? You had your chance months ago. None of you had a plan. None of you had any ideas for saving your families. You were happy enough to leave the thinking, the planning and the work to others, and *now* you want to complain!'

Curro placed a restraining hand on Daniel's shoulder and whispered, 'Let Nic handle this.'

Nicanor ran a hand through his hair, inhaling deeply, drawing up all the patience and resolve he could muster. He couldn't let this turn into violence only a few days into their voyage; they would self-destruct. He could see them fighting each other every inch of the way. Nicanor was determined these men would see reason—they had to. Abruptly he felt a wave of calmness sweep over him, his fist unclenched and his shoulders relaxed. He felt detached, yet more able to read the body language of those around him. He noticed the other man's eyes dart to a woman and child in the crowd; he saw the anxiety on their faces. He could read the man's fear that he had doomed his family and could see his uncertainty. Nicanor knew the path he must take.

'If we do as you say—if we don't ration our food, if we row and row—we use up our food and water fast. So we must find land fast. The current is against us. The wind has always been against us. Your course of action might, *just might* work, if we had more men and supplies. But more than half our number is women and children.'

Deliberately, he glanced at the man's wife and child, drawing his attention back to them. 'If we ration our food and follow the breeze and current, we give ourselves more time, we cover more area and we will increase our chance of landfall. More time gives us more chances. Gives *them* a chance.'

The man looked at his wife and child, his shoulders sagging as the fight left him. He nodded.

'We are all agreed then?' Nicanor's eyes roved the entire gathering searching for dissent. 'Now is the time to voice any other doubts.'

They dispersed, some shaking their heads despondently.

Nicanor whispered to Curro, 'Guard the supplies. Night and day one of us must be awake and the others should sleep with their weapons. Gods willing, we won't need them.'

'Gods willing … We seem to have a lot riding on the whims of the gods.'

'Yes, so now is not the time to lose your faith.'

Lucia stepped into Nicanor's embrace as he watched the disgruntled crowd return to their places. Lucia and Pio were his world. He would do anything to keep them from harm. Lost in his thoughts he realised too late that Lucia was talking quietly to him.

'Nic, Nic?'

He smiled apologetically.

'We can only do our best, and you have been doing it. They would already be dead if it wasn't for this plan. We'll survive. But right now I need you to do something for me.' He looked quizzically at her. She lowered her voice and continued. 'It's Isa. Pio is worried about her. After this, so am I. You heard them.'

'Yes, that surprised me too. How can they say she is not one of us?' He shook his head, trying to banish darker thoughts. 'Tell me Pio's idea.'

'He had a suggestion, a good one. Is there anything from which you can make a walking stick for her?'

'Yes. It's an excellent idea. She may need it as a weapon before long.' With Lucia still entrapped in his arms, he bent his head and tenderly kissed her. 'You know how much I love you, don't you?'

With a grin, she replied cheekily, 'Almost as much as I love you.'

He laughed. 'I suppose I deserved that. Lucia, can you keep an eye on Isa? Pio is right to worry about her and not just because of that lot. Something is wrong. Have you noticed how much she sleeps?'

'We will. But make the stick, it will give her back some independence. That might go a long way to helping her.'

He nodded. His wife was, despite everything, as practical as ever.

As he wandered off to set to his task, she thought, *And it will give you something to do other than dwell on what-ifs.*

CHAPTER SIX

GABRIELA stood at the ship's bow and laughed. The deck of the barge resembled a laundry house; clothes and belongings were hung or draped over ropes and cargo as they dried in the sun. People had firmly claimed their own spaces and set up home. She was still situated next to Daniel and Jaime. She felt guilty about Daniel. It was clear that her and Jaime's growing closeness was slowly torturing him, especially in the confines of the ship.

Gabriela felt a presence at her back before Jaime tentatively touched her shoulder. He smiled—something good had come from all this upheaval—they were together. He slipped his arm around her waist, placing a gentle kiss on her neck as she leaned back into him.

'I wonder how my parents are. If they are even still alive,' she said.

His arm tightened around her. 'Stop. They wanted you safe. Wondering is pointless.'

'All that time not thinking about the future. Now all we've got is time; at least some time.' She couldn't see his grimace. 'I feel guilty even saying this, but I feel more free now than I ever have. How on earth could I feel trapped by caring for my own parents? My parents who raised and loved me—who made sacrifices for me. I was relieved to get on this boat. Gods, I am so ungrateful.'

'Never, Gabi.' Jaime cupped her face in his hands and gently kissed her, wiping away her tears with his thumbs. She clung to him as she drew in shuddering breaths, attempting to control her sobbing. He enfolded in his arms, crooning to her. 'Gabi, just let go. Let it all out. Everything will be all right.'

Daniel sat beside Nicanor, as he carved Isaura's walking stick, yet his gaze repeatedly strayed to Jaime and Gabriela.

'That won't do you any good, you know,' Nicanor said quietly.

Daniel ducked his head. 'It's a bit hard not to.'

'Dan, she's not the girl for you. Oh, Gabi is sweet, pretty and honest, but she's not for you. She brings out the best in Jaime—he's matured, less selfish now. You've always been a joker like your brother, but you're more insightful, more serious; your jokes hide your deeper side. You need a girl who sees beyond the jokes into here.' He stopped carving and firmly pushed two fingers into Daniel's chest.

'Since when did you get so wise?' Daniel said.

Nicanor shrugged, returning to his to work. 'I just thought now you would be ready to listen. When we get off this boat, you make your own life.'

➤➤➤

Isaura leaned wearily on the railing where Lucia had left her. She found it increasingly difficult to concentrate. It took all of her energy to get around to help people, even with Lucia's aid. Angry and frustrated, her thoughts circled around her failure to help them; her mother would surely have done better. Isaura cursed her overactive conscience and sense of duty. She should have left years ago, but that smacked too much of running away. Isaura knew dwelling on such things was futile, yet there was no escape. Thank the gods she slept so much.

Pio bounded up to her, followed by Lucia. 'Papa made you a walking stick!'

Isaura reverently took the stick from him. Nicanor had carved it out of a piece of dark wood. The stick was just the right height and the hand piece was carved as the arching neck and head of a horse. Isaura was speechless, her eyes welled with tears. Pio, startled, looked to his mother for reassurance. Lucia nodded and smiled at him, then calmly enfolded Isaura in a hug. Pio grinned, trying to wrap his arms around them.

Lucia gently whispered, so Pio could not hear, 'Isa, it's all right. We love you.'

This was nearly Isaura's undoing. However, remembering Pio was there, she lifted her head, smiling. 'If not for you … thank you.'

Lucia hugged her a little tighter. 'Isa, for now, rest.'

'I can't. I need to replenish my bag.'

'We'll help.' Pio took Isaura's bag, carrying it with both hands. He led the way back to the cabin, turning now and then to watch her progress. Lucia walked beside her in case she fell. Each halting step increased her confidence in the stick.

'Keep going, Isa!' Pio grinned at her. For the first time in days she grinned back. By the time they reached the cabin, she was desperate to sit down.

'What do you need?'

'Everything,' Isaura replied with a sigh. 'Just pass me jars and I'll resupply the bag.'

Pio placed the bag on the bench seat next to Isaura. As he turned away the bag fell and vials, small jars and bandages littered the floor. A leather pouch poked out of the bag. Isaura's eyes darted to it protectively.

'Sorry, Isa!' While Pio gathered up the scattered contents, Isaura snatched up her bag and quickly shoved the pouch into the bottom.

'Never mind, nothing's broken. Can you pass me the ones on the floor? One at a time, and I'll fill them. Good boy. Lucia, can you get the supplies from that cupboard please?'

Lucia felt the weight of each jar as she returned them to the galley cupboard. 'Isa, how long will these last?'

'Not as long as we need. The moon flower will go first, since there's so much sunburn.'

'I'm not burnt,' Pio chimed in.

'No, you're not,' Lucia smiled. 'Not yet anyway.'

'Isa's not burnt either.'

'No, she's as brown as a nut.'

'It's my blood,' Isaura said calmly.

Lucia looked stricken. 'You know that's what they're saying?'

'But I'm brown too. Is it my blood? Isa, do we have the same blood?'

Isaura laughed. 'No, Pio, we don't have the same blood.'

'I'm so sorry, Isa,' Lucia whispered.

Isaura shrugged. 'It's not your fault.' She flexed her leg, wincing. 'One sore leg and I feel like I'm a hundred!'

'You need to rest.' They escorted her to her pallet near the cabin wall.

Pio plonked himself beside her with his flute in hand. 'Listen, Isa. I'm going to play for you.' Isaura carefully schooled her expression. Pio, uncharacteristically nervous, commenced to play very quietly and hesitantly. 'It's not very good … I'm not very good,' he said. 'But I want to get it right. I don't want to be laughed at.'

She smiled encouragingly. 'Just keep playing to me quietly until you figure it out. No one will laugh.'

'C'mon, let Isa rest.' As Isaura watched them leave, she pulled the leather pouch from her satchel. Opening the pouch, she drew out a small wooden box which had a lily carved into its top. Confirming that it was still sealed she discretely hid it again in the bottom of her satchel.

CHAPTER SEVEN

'LOOK out!' Pio raced to a gap in the railing and leapt into the air, curling up his body, wrapping his arms around his legs and hitting the water, bottom first. Peals of laughter ensued, followed by high pitched squeals and yells. Nicanor and Lucia leaned over the railing watching the antics in the water. A skinny figure swam up to the side of the barge, grabbed a rope and clambered onto the deck. He scrambled upright and moved out of the way as a petticoated figure followed him up.

'Ready?' A quick nod was the only reply. Together they ran hand in hand and jumped into the water, just as Pio had, to a chorus of cheers.

Squeals of delight and distant splashes roused Isaura. Grinning, she tried to struggle to her feet but could not rise. With a grunt of pain she sat back down with a thump. As she tried again, two sets of strong hands grabbed her under her armpits and hauled her up.

'Thanks. What's going on?' she said as Nicanor and Lucia helped her to the railing.

'No need to ask how your leg is?' Nicanor asked, concerned.

'A bit more rest and I'll be fine.' She watched the children's antics with amusement.

'At least they're enjoying themselves,' Lucia said, smiling at Nicanor.

'That boy swims like a fish,' Nicanor said.

Isaura turned her head in the direction of a plaintive bleat and saw the last of the goats being slaughtered further down the deck. Blood was being washed off the deck into the ocean on the opposite side of the barge from the children. She lowered herself to the deck and leaned against the railing. To stave off sleep again, she tried to concentrate on the shipboard sounds. Isaura could clearly discern the children, and beyond that an argument, then another splash further away. *More goat guts*, she thought.

Her mind drifted. Everything sounded so normal. They could have been at home in the village square. It was like this each time she lay down and closed her eyes to rest, almost as if she could hear every noise on board. Even the sound of the water was acute to her ears. Often she concentrated on the noises around her as a way to pass time, trying to guess what each was or who was talking. Usually she lost herself in the exercise and would drift into a dream-filled sleep. Letting the sounds wash over her, she remembered her home. Isaura felt something brush by her; her eyes shot open as she gasped. There was nothing there, yet she felt uneasy.

Lucia and Nicanor turned from watching the children. 'Isa?' they said in unison.

'Get me up!'

They looked at each other with concern, but quickly helped her. Isaura raked her eyes over the boat; everything seemed fine. People were resting or sorting their belongings. The butchering of the goat was finished and the deck clean. The children seemed fine, but she couldn't shake her unease. She looked at the water, and felt something brush against her again. 'I think the children should come out of the water.'

'Isa, they haven't been in that long,' Lucia said. 'They …'

'Just get them out. Get them out!' Again she felt something slide against her. 'Please!'

Lucia frowned. 'Pio! Time to get undercover.'

'*Aw … nooo …* Just a bit longer.'

'Hey, look at that!'

Nicanor, Lucia and Isaura looked further along the deck where several people were gathering to peer into the water. Nicanor quickly went to see for himself. As he reached the railing a massive fish rose out of the water and grabbed the floating innards of the goat in one bite. He paled at its size and the rows of deadly teeth he saw in its open maw. He could hear Pio pleading for more time to swim as he raced back up the deck, dodging obstacles.

'Pio, out now! All of you, out!' Nicanor boomed. Pio took one look at his father's face and hastened to climb the rope up the ship's side.

More ropes were thrown over the side to haul the children up. Parents were leaning over the railing to grab their young ones as they began to clamber aboard, all the while shouting, 'Quick, quick! Hurry!'

Once the last child was safely onboard, Isaura slumped in relief, sliding to the deck. 'What was it? What was wrong?' she asked Nicanor.

He didn't answer, just dragged a grumbling Pio to the other side of the boat. Lucia followed in his wake.

'Look!' Nicanor said to Pio. 'Do you really want to swim with *them*?' Pio's eyes bulged in shock. Several fish were fighting over the goat's remains, tearing it to shreds. 'We are lucky that they were too busy with this to notice you and your friends. No more swimming. Do you hear me?'

As Lucia dragged their son off to get dry, she stole an anxious look at Nicanor. 'How did she know?'

Nicanor shook his head. 'Later,' he said quietly, noting that Lucia was not the only one giving Isaura slightly untoward looks.

》》➤

Isaura felt an almost constant lethargy, yet she endeavoured to remain awake and alert as much as possible. She'd hoped that she would be so exhausted by the end of the day that she would have a dreamless sleep. It wasn't working. Each night as she relaxed and tried to sleep, the sounds around her would seem alluringly clear; she would lose herself in the sounds and then drift into her memories and dreams. Too often, she revisited the homes of the elderly they had left behind. She had provided them with what they needed, and for several people she supplied them with the only thing they had requested. 'Just in case,' they'd told her. Often she woke to the sounds of their voices and tears. Now, staving off sleep, Isaura surreptitiously watched Hugo sitting at what had become his favourite spot: on a small crate wedged between two larger ones. He had been uncharacteristically quiet. This worried Isaura, more than his moods and rantings ever had. She had no idea what to do with him.

Hugo shuddered at the endless blue desolation. The very sight of it had made his heart pound and caused him to break out in a sweat. The meagre water ration did nothing to slake his constant thirst. Isaura had cautioned him about staying out in the sun as if he were a child. His spot was shielded from most of the sun. Only a little hit his head and he'd tied one of his shirts around it for protection—he was only a little pink.

He had offered to help with deciding the daily ration since he had more experience than Isaura, but they didn't listen. She had refused his help to tend the misguided fools who volunteered to be on this miserable boat. *High handed girl! Well, no more offering.* He leaned against the crate, wrinkled his nose in disgust at the odour of unwashed bodies nearby, closed his eyes and dozed in the sun. Dreams he had not experienced for decades returned to haunt him.

Hugo was in a massive hall surrounded by people—sick people, rows of them lying on pallets or the floor. There was a sweet stench in the air. He didn't want to be there. He wanted to be in his garden. He loved his garden. He grew the best medicinal herbs and plants of all the apprentices.

He was shoved abruptly to the side as a body was carried out and dumped in a wagon. There were no medicines left; he'd spent days just placing cold compresses on patients, sponging the sweat and stink off them. He needed to get away from the rank mix of unwashed bodies, vomit and faeces. He stepped outside for air. The sky was black. Thick smoke rose from the many pyres outside the city walls; he was assailed by a different odour.

He and another young apprentice were taken to a large courtyard. Each entrance to the courtyard was flanked by two tall vases containing large purple lilies which emitted a cloying sweet scent. At one door, someone had placed a statue of Eloy, a famous Matryan hero who had chosen to sacrifice himself in order to save his comrades in arms. At the other entrance was a statue of Roldán, the guardian of the dead.

One of the physicians gave him a jug of purple liquid. 'Give everyone here a spoonful of this mixture. It will ease their suffering,' she said.

The other apprentice wrinkled his nose with disgust when he sniffed it. 'Love's lament … We're killing them.'

'They will die anyway. We need the room for others—some of whom can be saved. These cannot.'

Hugo was shaking as he took the liquid from her. The pain-filled moans had been consuming his days and haunting his nights. The stench pervaded everything. Even the drinking water from the fountain and the well had a black film from the fires coating its surface. He could not stand it any longer; he just wanted peace.

Many of the dying were barely conscious as he gently raised their heads and, murmuring encouragement, poured the tincture down their throats. Some were able to thank him and blessed him for his kindness; their small hope crushed him. Kneeling, he leaned forward and sobbed, drawing shuddering breaths which coated his soul with the stench of death. He just wanted to leave, but to where? Plague and famine had gone hand in hand. At least at the college there was still food to be had.

At last he rose to continue; a middle-aged woman was next. Her damp hair clung to sallow pustule-marked skin and her breath was ragged.

Hugo started to speak, but she raised a trembling hand to forestall him. Looking at him sympathetically she said, 'I know what awaits me … I'm sorry.' She shook as she tried to raise her head to drink. Tears streaked down Hugo's face. Amidst all her suffering she had felt sorry for him!

Hugo woke in fright, looking dazedly about him. He could still smell the fetor of death. He staggered to the railing gasping, for once not caring about the water, just trying to rid himself of that smell.

>>>—→

'But how did she know, Gabi?'

'I don't know and I don't care, Elena,' Gabriela whispered harshly. 'Nor should you.'

'I'm just saying, it's not normal. She's not nor—'

'Well, thank the gods she did know, Elena, or those children would be dead!' Disgusted, Gabriela strove to keep her voice low. 'Maybe that's just what this is, help from the gods. Who knows? But Isa is my friend and she has done nothing wrong. We should help her.'

'And why does she need our help?'

'She's unwell, her leg still pains her, she needs to rest.'

'All she does is sleep. When she is awake you all pander to her.'

'What is wrong with you? I let her down by not helping her and I'm ashamed that I did. I let my fear rule me, but what's your excuse? There's more going on with you than worrying about recriminations from the others if we help her and things go wrong. I see what you're doing. You sit and chat and whisper. All the while spreading poison about Isa. Why? What has she ever done to you?'

Elena's face twisted, but before she could say a word, Gabriela leaned close to her and vehemently continued, 'Don't speak unless it's about something else entirely. I don't know you anymore, Elena.' Gabriela spun away from her and stalked over to Jaime and Daniel. Her passage was marked by the gaze of many.

Lucia stood beside Nicanor, her arms folded, watching the animated discussion between Elena and Gabriela with interest.

Nicanor frowned. 'What was that about?'

Lucia shook her head. 'I can only guess, but it bears watching.'

Nicanor's lips brushed her cheek gently. 'But carefully, my love. She's family. Curro adores her.'

Lucia sighed. 'I know. You know I would never want to hurt him. Some things he'll have to see for himself.' She shook her head. 'Elena's never been this bad.'

>>>→

Curro had been watching his nephew practicing when Gabriela's disturbance captured his attention. He ruffled Pio's hair affectionately with a grin and a word of praise, then left to comfort Elena.

Elena watched Curro approach from the corner of her eye. Her hands gripped the railing with such intensity that her knuckles shone white. She forced herself to breathe deeply and relax her grip.

Curro slipped his arm around her waist. 'What's wrong? It's not like you to argue with Gabi.'

He hadn't heard them. *Good*, she thought. 'Nothing. I'm just tired, irritable and tense … We all are.'

'Mmm.' Doubt niggled at Curro.

'How's Pio?'

'Fine. His playing is improving, but I don't know how long he'll continue.' Elena looked enquiringly at him. 'His lips are getting too dry and chapped, just like the rest of us.'

She turned into his arms and burrowed her face into his chest as his arms tightened around her. She was learning to ignore the crustiness of their clothes and the smell of stale sweat. She could still smell Curro, *her* Curro. 'Gods, I miss this.' Her hands had slipped under his shirt and were gently playing along his back.

He groaned, lowered his head and kissed her. It didn't matter that he was exhausted, hungry and thirsty; she could still arouse him. 'I miss being alone. You're torturing me …' He gently extricated her arms from under his shirt. She immediately stiffened. 'Elena, don't be like that. I want nothing more than to touch you, to *be* with you

… It's just so frustrating.'

Reluctantly she nodded, her forehead resting against his chest. 'How's Isaura?' She hoped her tone of voice was neutral, but something about it alerted him and she felt a slight tension go through his large frame.

'Pio is keeping her company. He's like her sentinel. She seems to sleep a lot, but other than that she is no worse off than the rest of us.'

Elena bit her tongue. 'That's good.'

He sighed, embracing her more tightly. 'Elena, I married you. You are my wife. Not Isa, not ever. I have never loved Isa like that, ever.' She nodded, unable to look at him. 'Gods, I thought we were over this. You know I love you. Why is this surfacing again now? It's been so long.' He could feel her begin to shake. 'Elena, no.' He tipped her face up to his, wiping away her tears with his thumbs. 'Don't cry. *You* are my dearest, my only true love.' Her rained kisses on her face, her eyes and her lips. He held her face firmly, but tenderly, between his hands, forcing her to see the worry and love in his gaze; willing her to believe him.

She gave him a small tentative smile. 'I'm sorry. I just don't know what's wrong with me.'

CHAPTER EIGHT

ISAURA hobbled along the deck. The bruising had long gone, but her strength had not returned. The deep ache remained high in her leg along with a pulling sensation from torn muscles, but she forced herself to continue.

Pio carried her bag and walked beside her. She paused, leaning heavily on her walking stick.

Lucia caught sight of them and came to help. Placing an arm around Isaura's waist she assisted her forward. 'Isa, you need to rest.'

'I seem to spend all my time resting, when I need to check on people.'

Lucia helped Isaura sit on the deck near a little girl whose once fair skin was now red, raw and blistered. She had dark circles under her eyes.

Isaura looked at the girl's mother. 'No change?' She merely shook her head. Putting her hand on the girl's brow, Isaura frowned. She delved into her bag and pulled out several glazed jars. Removing the stoppers, she looked inside each with increasing frustration. 'Empty, all empty.' She didn't know why she even bothered to look. She dove her hands into her satchel, muttering, 'Maybe there's seeds?'

Lucia knelt down next to her, grabbing her hands to still her increasingly frantic searching. 'Isa.'

Isaura's eyes met Lucia's with a brief haunted, despairing glance that was gone with her next intake of breath. She put her hand on the child's brow again, then gently cupped her cheek in her hand. The girl's skin felt like paper. She sighed. 'There is nothing I can do. Susana was always frail.'

'Do something,' the mother implored her.

'I …'

'You are supposed to be our healer. Do something!'

'What do you want me to do?' Isaura snapped. 'I can't make it rain. I can't make food magically appear. She needs more of both; even that may not be enough.'

Pio said in a hoarse voice, 'She can have some of my water.'

Lucia gasped. 'No, Pio, she cannot.'

'Your son has more heart than you.'

'He can't …' Lucia sagged, looking miserable.

Isaura felt bone weary and helpless. She took the woman's hands in hers and looked her in the eye. 'Even if Pio did this—it would not help. Lucia, I want you to take Pio away, but if you could return in a few minutes that would be good.'

Lucia looked uncertain and confused, but did as Isaura asked.

Still holding the woman's hands, Isaura continued, 'Now, you have two choices.'

The woman looked startled, her eyes wide as she tried to pull her hands away. Isaura held them firmly, maintaining eye contact.

'You can leave her to die slowly—it may be today or tomorrow. Or you can end it quickly and peacefully with her in your arms.'

The woman wrenched her hands from Isaura's and slapped her hard across the face as Lucia returned. 'You are not a healer! We should have known better—bad blood will always come out. The two things your race is known for—magic and murder. Hill Clan witch!'

Lucia gasped. Isaura held out her arm and Lucia helped her stand.

'Find me if you change your mind.'

No one would look at Isaura, no one would speak to her. Even Lucia remained silent as she helped her return to her pallet.

➤➤➤

Elena reclined in Curro's arms on their pallet. She had never felt so tired. Her skin was nearly raw. Her eyes felt constantly as if they had grit in them; they hurt waking and sleeping. She was parched, hungry and dirty. Salt seemed to encrust everything on the ship, including her. Curro tenderly stroked her hair; his hands were so cracked and rough and her hair so dry and straw-like that they caught on her hair and tugged on her scalp. She had never felt so miserable and hopeless.

As they watched Lucia help Isaura, Curro whispered, 'Poor Isa.'

Elena felt a knife twist in her heart and her loathing deepened.

Hugo watched his daughter with dread, shuddering as he closed his eyes and drifted off into a fitful slumber. He awoke from his recurring nightmare sometime later to be assailed by the foul odour on the ship. In the chill darkness, he thought bitterly that there was no escape; in his dreams—and here—the stench of death still chased him. In the gloom he could just see Isaura being assisted across the deck by a thin man. Hugo sat up, watching intently as they stopped by a woman who was holding a child. Isaura spoke softly to her as she gently rocked and crooned to the child. She nodded, but did not cease her rocking. The man knelt and encompassed mother and child in his arms. Isaura drew a small leather pouch from her bag from which she removed a box of some kind. Hugo could not make out any more—he did not need to. He lay down, shaking.

By morning, the couple still held their lifeless child. The villagers were silent, there was not a breath of wind; it seemed the world had stopped to mourn the loss of this small life.

Unsure what to do, Nicanor and Lucia approached the parents. They roused the husband from his reverie and together they persuaded the mother to release her babe.

Isaura sat slumped on her pallet, clutching her bag tightly. She felt numb. *If any gods are listening, now would be a good time to get us out of this shit! Magic and murder. I have no magic ...* She weighed up the other—murder. *Oh yes, that was definitely true.*

Hugo approached her. Gripping her shoulder he whispered

accusingly, 'You have some love's lament, don't you?' Wearily she pushed his hand off, but he placed both hands on her shoulders. 'Tell me!'

'Yes.'

'Do you know what you are doing?'

'Yes.' She looked directly at him.

'What are you planning to do? Kill us all off to ease our suffering?'

'Don't be ridiculous.'

'Ridiculous, am I? You don't know the consequences … Your mother would have been ashamed to see this. She would never have used this … she … I'm glad she cannot see what you have become.'

'My mother? Who do you think taught me about it? Who do you think taught me to grow it in secret, to harvest and prepare it?' She glared at him.

Hugo reeled back away from her as if she had struck him. His eyes glazed as he muttered, 'Gods no … I can't believe it. You're lying. Oh gods … I can't see this again.' He staggered off.

Elena, ever watchful, followed this exchange. She looked thoughtfully at the grieving parents, then went to console them.

Hugo dreamed, always the same dream; always on waking he could still smell death. He saw the ill, prone bodies in his sleep and heard their moans; when he woke he still saw them. He glanced at Isaura as she was sleeping. She looked peaceful, guileless. He wished he could see her remain that way. Didn't she realise what would happen? He had seen all this before. He remembered how it felt to 'ease' the suffering of so many—he still suffered. He had tried to avoid thinking about it for so long.

Having fled the capital, unable to face anyone, he had made his way across the countryside. He avoided everyone until he chanced across Isaura's mother. She was pregnant and alone. They had both fled Matyran. She was not sick, but she needed help; he could help her. In the end they helped each other. Running from the plague they reached Arunabējar and Isaura was born in an abandoned cottage in the woods. That cottage became their home. *I saved two lives … just two out of so many.* Saved—there was the joke. Now he was back where he started, and Isaura was headed down the same path. By the gods, he wished he had not lived to see this. And her mother … how could she? He dozed again, succumbing to his dreams.

During the night he woke disorientated. Awareness returned, despair remained. He had wasted his life; he had not saved Isaura to see this happen. He had not saved himself to live through this again. He crept toward Isaura. She slept still. Her bag was by her side, her hand resting possessively upon it. He prodded her gently. She did not wake. He frowned. She looked frail; he'd never seen her look frail. Opening her satchel, he carefully managed to not disturb her hand. Very slowly he inched his hand into the leather bag. Gingerly he felt around until he found the small leather pouch. This was what he was looking for. With great care he slid the pouch out of the satchel and closed it again.

His cracked, stiff fingers fumbled with the small binding of the pouch, until he finally opened it and drew out the wooden box. His hands shook as he examined the intricate carving of the lily. Just a small amount was all he'd need; he knew it acted quickly. She'd suffer more if he didn't.

His face contorted, his eyes scrunched, but tears failed him; all he could do was shake. He took a small metal spoon from the pouch. Quietly, he removed the lid from the box, dipping the spoon into the contents. He had no water … It would still work without water, a little slower, but it would still work.

Trembling, he scooped some of the mixture into the spoon. As he moved it over Isaura's sleeping form he did not notice that his shaking was scattering fine particles of purple powder over the deck. He concentrated, trying to steady his hand as he moved it closer to her face. Her hair was coming out of its familiar braid, dark wisps of salt encrusted strands surrounded her tanned face, long lashes rested against her skin; she looked peaceful.

His breath became laboured. His hand hovered over her chest. He shook his head, suddenly appalled as clarity was bestowed upon him. *Gods, what am I doing? How can I?* Jerking back, horrified, he caused a curtain of the purple dust to fall toward his daughter and sprinkle over her blankets.

Hugo recoiled, shock and guilt warring for dominance across his countenance. He huddled near a gap in the railing, rocking back and forth, staring toward the water with the box clutched tightly in his hands. Eventually, he was still. Opening the box, he put his hand into the powder. Scooping some out, he stared in fascination at it. Suddenly, he put it in his mouth. It was bitter. It stuck to his tongue and inside his gums. His mouth was so dry that he couldn't swallow, yet still he could feel a tingling in his face, then a creeping numbness. Hugo tossed the box into the ocean and, finally at peace, he followed it.

CHAPTER NINE

'MA, Isa won't wake up,' Pio grumbled.

'Let her sleep, Pio. We're all tired … just let her sleep.'

'She's got purple stuff on her.'

'What?' Suddenly Lucia's lethargy vanished. She stumbled up and headed toward Isaura's sleeping place. 'Get your father.' Wide eyed, Pio ran to fetch Nicanor. Lucia stood immobile, looking down at Isaura's still form. There was a fine dusting of purple powder across her blankets. When Nicanor reached her, he stood transfixed with horror at the sight before him.

Lucia took his hand. 'Gods no … please no.'

Nicanor could not respond. He did not want to answer her, for speaking would confirm his friend's fate. Those nearby had clustered about; everyone looked at Isaura but no one dared move.

Pio's voice interrupted the silence. 'What is that purple stuff?' He knelt down, sniffing the air near the blanket. 'It smells strange.'

As he reached out, Lucia snapped, 'Don't touch it!'

He drew his hand back as if scalded. 'Why won't she wake up?'

'Oh, Pio …' Lucia choked out.

'Ma?' Pio looked in shock at the faces of the adults around him. 'Ma, she just won't wake up. She's not dead. Look, she's breathing.' By this stage he was kneeling by her head. 'Look!'

Lucia and Nicanor knelt down beside him. Sure enough, Isaura was breathing, albeit shallowly. They nodded their relief to those gathered around. Nicanor chuckled nervously, a dry hoarse sound, causing him to cough violently. Isaura did not stir.

'How do you suppose she got covered in that?' Lucia said.

'Let's just get it off her,' Nicanor replied. Curro pushed forward, ignoring Elena's restraining hand. Together he and Nicanor carefully folded the blanket inward and lifted it off Isaura.

'Throw it overboard,' Lucia said with revulsion. She examined her skin and clothing. 'I can't see any more on her. Isa?' She grabbed Isaura's shoulders, shaking her. 'Isa, Isa! Come on, wake up!'

Groggily Isaura opened her eyes, squinting in the bright sunlight. 'Uh, wha … what is it?' Her speech was slurred.

'Oh thank goodness! Isa, how do you feel?'

'Tired, like six shades of shi—' She looked at the crowd surrounding her. 'What's going on?'

'Isa, we were so worried. You were covered … that is … your blanket was covered in purple powder.' Lucia whispered, 'It looked like love's lament.'

Abruptly Isaura sat upright. 'What!' She peered at her hands, her torso, her legs, looking for any trace of the deadly powder. 'How?' Isaura looked frantically for her satchel. It had not been moved from its place beside her, but she noticed the clasp was undone. 'Someone took it out of my bag. Why?'

'Why indeed?' Elena's caustic remark carried like a tolling bell.

Lucia looked anxiously at Nicanor. 'Why would someone do this? Who would want to harm you?'

Lucia didn't think Isaura could look worse, but suddenly she did. She scrambled up frantically, lurched to the railing and began dry-retching over the side. Nicanor and Lucia caught her as she began to sag and eased her down. She leaned back into their arms, sweating profusely. 'Isa?'

'I'm fine, just tired, so tired … can't even think straight.'

As they held her, with Pio anxiously by their sides, Curro approached the gap in the railing near them to lower a bucket into the ocean. 'We'll set things to right, Isa. We'll wash any powder over the side so it's all gone. Don't think about it.' As he slowly hauled up the bucket, he noticed that more purple powder was visible at the edge of the deck. In a hushed voice he said to Nicanor, 'There's more here and a faint streak on the hull.'

With the deck cleaned, Isaura was settled on her pallet. Pio went to where Hugo usually slept, grabbed the bedding, took it back to Isaura, and covered her. Pio sat beside her, his arms hugging his legs, and kept vigil as she fell asleep again.

Lucia touched Pio gently on the shoulder. 'That's very kind of you, but you'll need that blanket later.'

'It's not mine. It's Hugo's. He won't need it—he's gone.'

The silence that followed this declaration was punctuated only by Elena's outburst. 'He tried to kill his own daughter!'

'No land, no food, no water! We pray every day. Still the gods do not answer.'

'Not all of us pray. *She* doesn't.'

'The boy said she doesn't believe.'

'Thinks the gods are "a load of old dog's bollocks" were Pio's words and that boy doesn't lie.'

'She offends the gods.'

'Her father knew best what to do with her.'

'She has lived among us all her life. She has helped us, cared for us. At the pier she …'

'Yes, at the pier she saved us.'

'How did she learn to shoot like that?'

'Hunting.'

'Hunting? Pah! You've been hunting for your family for years. Can you shoot like that?'

'But did you see her face?'

'She enjoyed the killing.'

'Then there's that poor wee girl … murder.'

'I tell you, her father knew best.'

Isaura woke in the night with Pio snuggled beside her. Carefully, she sat up without disturbing him. She moved gingerly to her hands and knees and used her stick to manoeuvre herself upright. A wave of dizziness washed over her. Sweating, she leaned back against the cabin while her head cleared. The chill night air raised goosebumps over her dampened skin.

She hobbled over to the gap in the railing where, fatigued by the short distance, she lowered herself down and dangled her feet over the side. The water gently rippling along the hull lulled her again as she rested her head against the rail. She'd always known Hugo was eccentric, but she'd never realised the extent of his problems. All the strategies her mother had for 'handling' him made sense now—she'd known how damaged he was. Her mother had never pushed him, yet Isaura knew she had the moment she brought him on this boat. *Did I drive him over the edge?* Thoughts tumbled around in her mind, but one always returned to the fore: *Was he really trying to poison me? Did he just spill it? Had Hugo found out about Gabriela's parents and the others? He can't have known—no one did.*

Staring at the huddled, sleeping forms of her friends who now surrounded her, Isaura thought back to when Nicanor had first broached his plan with her. When he'd told her, she'd jumped at it. She had an answer for every doubt and problem raised—she made it happen. She pushed them, just like she pushed Hugo. She questioned her real motivation—love or simply because she wanted to run away. Thankfully her friends didn't see things that way, because here they were, a bulwark of loyalty in a sea of treachery. Without them she feared Hugo would be right and if the truth about those they left behind were known, she'd be dead. Sorrow and regret sat poised, waiting for her to capitulate. She could agonise over the past, worry about whether her secret was safe, but not now.

It was so much easier to just follow the sounds, escape into the lullaby of the rippling water travelling the length of the hull. Isaura tried to focus on one ripple and follow it along the hull. Visualising it tickling the worn timber as it passed, she pursued it as it merged with larger currents and began to crest away in the distance. All too easily she slipped blissfully into her dreams.

A bird screeched, drawing her attention upward. *Funny*, she thought, *we haven't seen any birds in an age*. She strained to catch sight of it again, but it vanished into the sun.

'Isa … Isa, wake up.' Shielding her eyes with her hand and blinking hard, she could make out Pio's face staring intently at her. 'Why does everyone keep waking me up?'

'Because you are *always* asleep!' Pio groused. 'Besides, it's too hot here. Let's go back to your spot—and you could have fallen overboard!'

'Oh!' Isaura was startled. 'I must have been here all night.'

'I don't know, but you wouldn't wake up—again!'

'Everyone is sleeping a lot, Pio.'

'Not like you.'

She frowned as he went back to his parents, obviously cross with her. She lay on her back, staring at the sky, her feet still dangled over the side of the boat. Her eyes began to close again. *Pio is right, time to move.*

A howling gale buffeted the barge, causing it to bob and lurch erratically as a massive storm skirted around them. Each lurch brought with it groaning sounds. Anything that could hold water was on deck, held upright, ready to catch any rain. The villagers prayed. Curro beseeched his ancestors to intervene with the gods to help them. Finally the rain came as a deluge that lasted only minutes, but put inches of water in each container. A girl quickly grabbed a mug and began drinking greedily from it. Others began to follow suit.

Curro pleaded with them. 'We have to make this last. We're all thirsty—just drink a little.'

Villagers pushed the girl away in the rush to get to the water. She was sitting on the deck smiling, then she grabbed her stomach, groaned and vomited the water she had just consumed.

'See!' roared Curro. 'Drink only a little, or you'll be ill. We must ration it.'

The villagers were beyond reason. Daniel, Jaime and Nicanor hastily grabbed as many of the containers as they could and began tipping the rainwater into one barrel.

Lucia watched horrified, with Pio clutched to her, as the others pushed and shoved to get to the water. In the ensuing chaos, containers were knocked over and people tried to sop up water from the decks with their clothes. They sucked at the wet fabric, desperate for a taste of fresh water, only to scowl as the little they got was tainted by the salty grime on their clothes. Many sat on the deck, returning from frenzied joy to complete despair.

Curro's gut clenched as he watched their expressions of frustration, sadness, or vacant defeat. Gazes slowly turned toward Curro and his friends, who were armed and guarding the saved water.

'This water will be rationed to all. Starting with those who didn't just behave like animals. Anyone, and I do mean *anyone*, who tries to interfere will suffer for it.'

CHAPTER TEN

UMNIGA was old. Her long grey hair was braided back and her green eyes did not see as well as they used to. Her leathery, olive skin was creased with many wrinkles and deep crow's feet puckered the edges of her eyes. Despite this, when she smiled her aged appearance seemed to vanish. When she chose, her voice could remind listeners of some favoured friend, guaranteeing her an audience. Some days her bones ached and it took all her effort to rise. At these times her apprentice, Asha, would wordlessly place willow bark tea in her hand, ensure the room was warm and leave her be.

When her rheumatism was at its worst and she was unable to sleep, it was a joy to link with Devi, her guardian sent by Rana. Devi was a large barking owl. He had been with her since puberty, yet didn't seem to suffer the effects of age. Umniga could, almost effortlessly, merge her own consciousness with his, seeing the world through his eyes and experiencing the joy and speed of his flight. She could use Devi to communicate over great distances with the other Kenati: the priests and priestesses of Rana and Jalal, the keepers of Lore amongst the clans of Altaica. More often, like tonight, she merely wanted to escape her age and just take flight with Devi.

Lying down on her soft bed, she looked at Devi sitting in the open window. He rotated his large flat face toward her. Reaching out with her mind, she felt the instant recognition, welcome and connection. Her eyes changed shape, their size and colour mirroring those of Devi. Now she could see the world properly. The nightscape was no longer hidden to her. Even the smallest details stood out with a clarity that never ceased to amaze her.

Devi hopped off the window and took flight over the surrounding countryside. In the southeast they saw the town of Faros. Devi's mind flitted to thoughts of fat pigeons on rooftops and rats around the granary. *Not yet*, she instructed. *Later*. Umniga had no real desire to go to Faros, for she knew what she would find. It disappointed her that her clan had fallen so low and forgotten, or did not care for, the ancient ways. She felt little pride in her people when she saw Faros, and had not been there in years. It was a city of commerce, where avarice made new laws to oust the old. They had no time to honour the traditional ways—feasts, celebrations and the education of the young were neglected. Umniga concentrated her efforts amongst the country folk on the plains outside Faros and in the more remote areas of her clan's territory.

Normally they headed inland, toward the hills, yet tonight the ocean called her. Devi acquiesced grudgingly; there was little chance of a meal there. As they flew south, Umniga could feel Devi's powerful wings easily climbing, then the air current carried them and they glided. The full moon cast a wondrous luminescence over the ocean. Behind her the jagged cliff face rose to a distant point. Umniga savoured the peaceful rhythm of the beat and glide of his wings, but she felt a gentle yet persistent tug pulling them further still from the coast. She could not recall feeling any impulse as strong in all her long life. Just as Umniga was beginning to think herself addled for coming in this direction, Devi's thoughts of the epicurean delights surrounding Faros's granary emerged again.

'Oh, all right then, go on, fill your fat belly! I've no idea why we came this way.' As Devi banked, she noticed a shape on the horizon. She pulled his fixated mind away from thoughts of dinner, toward the object they had glimpsed. He made a disgruntled growl. 'You can eat as much as you want after this.'

Gliding down, Umniga could clearly see they were approaching a long, ungainly looking boat; much larger than the fishing boats she was used to. Everything about the boat was an oddity to her: the size, the shape, the square sail, everything except the figurehead. A magnificent horse rose from the timber work on which Devi landed. The carving delighted her with its meticulous attention to detail. Devi's sharp eyes revealed a crowded deck littered with sleeping people and possessions.

Many of the occupants were families; children slept huddled between their parents. Where had they come from? They had obviously been at sea for some time. The effects of exposure were evident—their faces, even in sleep, looked raw, thin, pinched and anxious. Empty barrels sat on deck, open to the sky waiting to catch rain. Umniga noticed a hatch that opened to a hold. Therein she saw some empty animal pens, tools, household utensils, pots and pans. They had brought enough to settle anew. Why? Had they fled from something?

Intrigued, she examined the passengers more closely. Most were fair with unusual hair colour—some blond, some red, many shades of brown, but none as dark as her people. 'I wonder ...'

Instinctively, Devi cocked his head to one side, causing the colours before them to fade. Slowly, other colours emerged as the auras around the people became visible. Scanning the passengers, she saw varying shades of brown and green, the odd flickering of blue; nothing unusual. Feeling disgruntled, she wanted Devi to leave, but he would not.

Instead he hopped along the railing until he was near a sleeping family. She waited. Suddenly a flash of red flicked through the aura of the small boy of about five, clutching a flute, as he stirred in his sleep. Immediately, Devi turned and flew to the stern of the boat. Umniga gasped. This girl against the side of the cabin—she was like a beacon. Her aura was stronger than the others, deep shades of brown, green, then fluctuating with streaks of violet and red.

Umniga's surprise was so great it broke her concentration, threatening her connection to Devi. Feeling the connection slipping further, she prayed to Rana and Jalal to help her. If she lost her link with Devi now so far from her body, she could not reconnect with it. She would be unable to navigate the spirit realm so far alone. As she struggled she sensed his surprise and fear for her, then, unexpectedly, she felt an irritated tug as he held their mental link until she regained her composure. Firmly linked again, but shaken, she looked on the girl without seeking her aura. Devi would not allow it again—he could feel her fatigue and would not risk her. The girl's appearance was different to the others, with much darker skin and long dark hair.

Isaura was sleeping on the deck in a sitting position, resting her back against the side of the cabin. She woke up, unsure of how long she'd slumbered, with a feeling that someone was watching her. Some *thing* was watching her. A large owl blinked before her. Isaura tried to focus, but struggled against her sleepy stupor. With fierce concentration, she emerged from her somnolence only to find that the owl was still there, its baleful eyes fixed on her.

However, Isaura could now also see a woman where the owl was. She shook her head, rubbed her eyes. When she next looked, the woman was gone; only the bird remained. She squinted and thought she could see the woman dimly again. Her figure was opaque— Isaura could still see the owl *through* her. *That's it, I've lost my mind.* Unable to resist the lure of sleep, she could not bring herself to care about this new development. It was easier to simply float in the comforting embrace of her dreams.

Umniga was startled. Devi hopped back instinctively. This girl could see her spirit form. She was sure that she could see her. Initially, the girl appeared stunned, so Umniga assumed she was untrained. The girl lost her struggle to remain conscious as her head fell forward. Umniga looked more closely and noted her wretched state. *By the gods, how long have they been on this boat? How much longer can they last?* She thought of the girl's aura and the gifts she must surely possess in order to see her, even though untrained and in such physical distress. *We were drawn this way. Is this the work of the Great Mother and Father?* Devi gave a soft growl. She smiled, her decision made.

>>—>

The sunlight blazing through the small bedroom window slowly roused Umniga. She didn't recall when she got home, or severing the link with Devi. Feeling impossibly ancient, she sat up, collected her wits and went in search of Asha. She found her working with rapid precision in their small garden. Umniga smiled, admiring the speed of Asha's movements. Asha stood up, aware that she was being watched and turned her small, oval face toward Umniga with a cheeky grin. Asha had been the youngest Kenati apprentice ever. Umniga had watched her grow from the frightened five-year-old she took on over seventeen years ago into a confident young woman.

'Finally, you're awake! Old one, you gave me a fright. You were gone so long last night, I thought you had left me.'

'Not yet, you whelp! Come inside. I've got to eat. I've much to tell you and I can't do it on an empty stomach.' Asha looked down at her half completed chore. 'That can wait. Come … come, we've got work do.'

Once inside, Umniga related the previous night's events to Asha. 'I want this girl … the boy too, but the girl—she's the one we really want!'

Asha's mind was racing. 'But Umniga, the last strangers who landed here were killed.'

'That was a long time ago, Asha. They were far from harmless. These are families, women, children … besides I only want the girl and the boy. I don't care about the rest. We'll enlist the help of old Deo and his sons; they can take their fishing boat out and bring those two back. We'll then smuggle them across to the Horse and Bear in the wagon. You get word to the other Kenati … it doesn't matter who. They'll all be at Bear Tooth Lake for the Harvest Festival. They'll tell the Horse and Bear lords what we're about.'

'Tell the lords? No one *tells* them what to do.'

'Well, this is sent by the gods—I'm sure of it. They must listen when we tell them that.'

'What about the Boar?'

'These two are not for the Boar Clan.'

'They are our clan.'

Umniga snorted in disgust. 'Do you think Shahjahan thought of that when he killed Juhangir? Our loyalty is to the old ways and Lore, and to those who honour it. The Boar stopped doing that a long time ago. Besides, they won't know.'

Asha nodded; although she could not dispel her unease, she trusted Umniga and was overjoyed to see the return of a hitherto long absent spark in the old woman's eyes.

'Don't you want to tell the others?'

'After last night, I don't think I can just yet.' A look of concern flicked across Asha's face. 'Come on girl. Get a move on. Call Fihr to you and let the others know. I'd get comfortable first if I were you. It's a long flight and then they'll just gab a lot at the other end.' Asha rolled her eyes melodramatically. Umniga chuckled as she made hastening motions with her hands.

'Yes, yes I know.' Asha's gaze became vacant briefly as she searched for Fihr. 'He's coming.'

Umniga was grinning like a child as she stood up and jostled Asha to her bed. 'Lie down.'

Asha began to laugh, carried away by her effusive energy. As she drew open the curtain that separated her alcove from the rest of the room, then laid down, an enormous sea eagle landed in the entrance to the cabin and crossed the floor to stand beside her bed. He had intelligent, dark eyes set amidst the snow white feathers of his head, along with a wickedly curved beak. Fihr puffed up his white chest and stretched out his dark wings as he settled beside her. She reached out her hand and he made a soft, deep sound as she reverently stroked his head and gazed intently at him. Asha was still. Fihr looked briefly at Umniga, then was gone. Umniga gently placed Asha's hand on the pallet and gave her forehead a kiss. 'Gods go with you, little whelp.'

>>→

Fihr's powerful wings pulled them rapidly higher, away from their little stone cabin nestled into the leeward side of a bluff that overlooked the ocean. To the east lay the delta of the Bear River, known simply as The Paw. The Bear River flowed from the lake at the base of the jagged, snow-capped, grey mountain range known as The Bear's Teeth. It was to this lake that they were headed. The area around The Paw was highly fertile and there were many small farms surrounding it. The small village of Galatan lay on this side of the delta, and on the other side, closer to the coast, lay Parlan. At this time of year, the crops having matured and been harvested, the ground was a nearly uniform brown, with the exception of the edges of the river and the small patches of household gardens.

Fihr levelled his flight, effortlessly working his way between air currents as they journeyed. Asha revelled in their connection.

Umniga had warned her of the danger of immersing herself too deeply into the world of her guardian. There was a captivating lure there, she'd said, in the brutal simplicity of their lives; those bonded with them could glimpse the harmony and power of Rana and Jalal. The danger was that some lost themselves in the bond. With Fihr, Asha was the master of the skies, powerful, graceful, strong—she loved it. From the moment Fihr had come to her as a child, she had not felt small or helpless.

Asha came from a remote farm near the lower part of The Divide, the large river that split Altaica in two. Her size, coupled with the poverty and lack of status of her family, meant that her clan had shown only disdain for her martial training. Traditionally, each child, with the help of the Kenati and the village elders, commenced education in Lore and martial training in many weapons. Sastravidya schools had existed in larger towns and training was conducted each week, or more often when work allowed. In the small villages and remote farms, this task was left to the families.

The Kenati regularly visited and the clan lord was meant to routinely send a Silahtar, an older warrior who was a weapons master, to supervise training. Between the Kenati and these warriors, the local populace had access to the ears of their lord. This was how it was supposed to be. This was how it was *not*.

Umniga and Juhangir, frustrated and angry at this neglect, began sending the children of those families who still practised the old ways to the other clans for their training. Slowly and discretely the influence of Horse and Bear grew, as they provided the aid that the Boar Lord had neglected. Finally, they took over all the land north of The Divide; war with Faros had ensued.

Fihr dived suddenly, plummeting toward the ground. Then, when impact seemed inevitable, he swooped wide and low, extended his talons and snatched a rabbit as it attempted to flee. A fierce joy pierced Asha. There was nothing more exhilarating than the hunt, this silent-winged death. She could sense Fihr's satisfaction with his kill. He sat in the nearby grass using talons and beak to tear into the rabbit, its soft grey fur no barrier to his fine natural weaponry. Together they feasted, glorying in the soft juicy flesh and innards. When his appetite was sated, she felt a gentle push against her presence as he disentangled her from their deep connection. Asha could not tell Umniga about this; she would not approve. She suspected this was the kind of 'dangerous' deep connection she had warned of.

However, Asha knew she was in no danger; she had never been in any danger. From the time she was a child, Fihr had shared the hunt with her, but it was he who initiated this and then released her. Travelling with him, within his presence, was like being home in a warm, welcoming, comfortable room, filled with affection. However, when he went to hunt or fight, he would open the door on the room and she could almost glimpse and feel an immense space and power, just before the sensations of the hunt overwhelmed her. All her attempts to fathom that initial vastness or hold any detailed or lasting impression of it were futile. Fihr protected her, he always had.

>>→

Fihr glided over Bear Tooth Lake through the glare of the last rays of the setting sun. Many tents were set up around the lake and members of the Horse and Bear clans mingled freely with those Boar Clan members who lived north of The Divide. Smoke from a myriad of small cooking fires rose into the twilight air.

The war between the allied Horse and Bear and Faros had not really ended—an informal truce existed. Or rather, the clans of Horse and Bear simply, boldly stated that they did not want any further land and would not seek more south of The Divide, but they would kill any trespassers.

The Boar Clan saved face by saying that they would not wish to rule a territory where the members of their clan, albeit sparse, had proved so treacherous and disloyal. That said, the celebration of the harvest festival in great numbers by Horse, Bear and their newest subjects was an affirmation of the change of rule and clearly showed the local's support of their new lords.

Asha and Fihr could see many warriors in the camps below, and had spotted a number of patrols along their journey. Throughout this crowd they searched for the other Kenati.

Eventually they located Anil and Suniti seated around a fire with Hadi and Munira. *Perfect, all together*, thought Asha as they swept low across the campsite to land near them.

Munira, the youngest apart from Asha, greeted them with a bright smile. 'Fihr, Asha, welcome.'

'Asha, why have you come? What is wrong?' Anil asked.

Asha could feel Fihr concentrating, then a slight surge of energy entered her as she projected herself before them. Knowing only the Kenati could see or hear her, she related Umniga's findings and decision. The other Kenati looked shocked; for many minutes no one spoke.

Finally Suniti said, 'Umniga is not prone to rash decisions, but …'

Hadi, the eldest after Umniga, silenced her with a wave of his hand. 'If she thinks this important then we must trust her and help her.'

'Umniga believes the hands of the gods are at work here,' Asha added defensively.

Lost in his thoughts, Hadi nodded. 'I'm sure she does, but *we* must talk to Lords Baldev and Karan.'

CHAPTER ELEVEN

'WHAT!' Baldev exploded. 'She's done what?'

Karan put a restraining arm on his friend. 'Tell us again, Hadi. Help us understand why the Kenati view this as so important, for neither of us can see why the fate of a group of strangers should be our concern. Our "truce", ' he grinned at this, 'is still only new and you tell us Umniga would bring these strangers into her clan lord's land, without his knowledge, and smuggle them to us. Why?'

Hadi raised his hands in a placating gesture. 'According to Asha, she does not want to bring all the people—just the boy and the girl— and she waits upon your permission to do so.' Karan snorted in disbelief at this. 'Umniga plans to sail out with a fisherman named Deo, retrieve the two and bring them back. She intends to smuggle them here under the guise of her regular rounds. The fate of the rest is in the hands of the gods; most likely they will die. I gather they are still some way out, without water and in no state to make shore.'

'Even if they do, Shahjahan will finish them when he finds out,' Karan concluded. 'You still haven't told us why.'

'There were too many coincidences that led to their discovery. Normally, they would not fly out over the sea, nor for so long. Umniga hints that she felt a compulsion to do so. On the verge of returning, she saw the boat, investigated and was about to leave when Devi noticed the girl and boy. The latent power in the girl was evident and unheard of in someone whom we believe is untrained. We are unanimous in our agreement; too many things aligned to bring this to our attention.' Hadi deliberately paused. 'There is something else—the figurehead of the boat is a horse. The gods have a hand in this.'

A scowl flicked across Karan's face. *A horse! It could just as easily have been a fish.* Karan looked toward Fihr, who sat patiently awaiting their decision, then motioned to a servant, speaking very quietly. Shortly the servant returned and gave Karan a bowl of raw meat. Fihr ruffled his feathers and moved from side to side in greedy anticipation. Rather than simply put the bowl down and let Fihr help himself, Karan grinned at him, his momentary anger forgotten, and hand-fed him tidbits, all the while talking to him quietly and praising his long, important flight. Karan pondered the problem before them, as he fed Fihr the last of the meat.

'Leave us,' Karan said quietly. The Kenati quietly departed.

Baldev frowned as he sat and stared at the fire. 'She can't possibly just smuggle out the two. How can she take the boy without his parents? Not if they are alive. To separate them … he'd remember. How can he be expected to grow up loyal, to trust us, to understand?'

'Agreed.'

'And the girl. They'll know. Killing … letting the others die is nothing, but if the gods have a hand in this, then how can we kill any of them? They may all have some part to play.' Silence. 'Karan?'

Karan shook his head in disgust. 'Correct. We have no choice but to save them all.'

Baldev nodded. 'But we will only take the two and their families.'

'Agreed—and we have no choice but to tell Shahjahan.' Baldev stared at him in surprise. 'There is no possible way to smuggle all of them overland without detection. I would not risk the peace for their sakes.'

'Aargh!' Baldev exclaimed. 'Peace exists because of our grace, not Shahjahan's. He'd never win.'

'I know, but neither of us wants control of his territory, so let's maintain the *peace*.'

'Damnation!'

'Exactly.' Karan had been reviewing strategy and tactics since the

Kenati had told them this news. If Umniga thought these two were important, then so be it, but in her excitement she had not thought through the ramifications of her plan. He could not blame her. In fact, he was pleased to hear of her enthusiasm and hope. Her clan had all but abandoned their Lore, and her clan lord had arranged the death of her fellow Kenati, Juhangir. She'd had little to hope for and it had slowly eroded the old woman's soul.

Karan shook his head. 'Umniga should have come north. She will not be safe if Shahjahan finds out we knew of this first.'

Baldev nodded. 'You and I have both asked her. While there are members of her clan in the south who still respect her teachings, she will not abandon them.'

'We must contrive a way that he does not discover she told us first and yet we must still get the two.' They sat for some time in silence. At last Karan continued, 'Perhaps we can manipulate him. They will land in the territory of the Boar, but the arrival of the strangers is important to all of us. We are *all* clans of Altaica. They are sent by Rana and Jalal, who do not discriminate between their children. For the greater good, at the will of the gods, we should unite as one and face this new event.'

'Or threat.'

Karan scowled. 'They present no threat, but why are they on the boat? No one would pack so many people on a boat—entire families, with enough possessions to start again—without good reason. What are they running from?' Baldev sat up, listening intently. 'We need to find out all we can from them, *all* the clans, to prepare. Rana and Jalal may be sending us a warning.'

'And Shahjahan can't ignore the gods.'

'Precisely. Also, we would be the vulnerable ones by walking into his territory; he will look like a coward if he doesn't let us in. He will look like a poor ruler if he ignores something that could hold such importance for all the clans.'

'Do you think he'll fall for it?' Baldev asked.

Karan shrugged. 'The old girl might be right, but we will make this work for us in other ways.'

'As long as Shahjahan believes it. Appealing to the minuscule love he may have for clan Lore may help.' Baldev continued, 'But I think, even if he doesn't believe it, he won't want to lose face when confronted with our *noble* intentions.'

>>>→

The following morning Karan and Baldev addressed the waiting Kenati. Baldev began, 'We will help these two and their families. The rest are nothing.'

'But,' Karan continued, 'they will not enter our homelands until we are satisfied they pose no threat and will assimilate.' He held up his hand, forestalling any interruptions. 'It is highly unlikely that they will speak our language or understand our ways. You must educate them. We must be able to communicate. Neither Baldev nor I will allow them into the Horse or Bear unless they understand the laws they are to abide by if they wish to remain with us. You know once they enter the clans there is no going back. They cannot leave. We will not allow them to betray us in any way. They will not take any information to our enemies.'

Baldev added, 'They will remain in a camp here at the lake, under guard, until we are satisfied with them. They may bring disease, so the further from our main homelands, the better.'

'It is your task to see to their education.' Karan outlined part of the plan he and Baldev had conceived. 'We will meet Shahjahan at The Four Ways; the early autumn rains have made Hunters' Ford impassable. Asha, you must tell him of the portentous news of the strangers' arrival. Make sure that he thinks we have all been told at once, and that he understands the deference we are showing him as a clan lord by meeting him at The Four Ways to seek his approval to enter Boar lands.'

'Why Asha? Why not Umniga?' Hadi asked.

'Asha is young, pretty and appears harmless.' He grinned at Fihr. 'Sorry, Asha. Shahjahan has no love for Umniga.'

The Kenati departed, leaving Baldev and Karan alone as they seated themselves near the fire.

'Do you think she can do it?' Baldev asked.

Karan shrugged. 'Asha? Easily. My spies tell me Shahjahan has ignored Umniga since he killed Juhangir, even though he hates her. Thinks she is a crazy old woman who few listen to—something she encourages, so he leaves her alone to do her work.'

'Cunning old girl. It's wise to keep her out of his sight.'

'Mmm. Getting into his lands will be one thing, getting out may be another.'

'Good thing we think ahead then.' Baldev laughed deeply as he clapped Karan on the back. 'We'll avoid the hornet's nest that's about to land on our heads, don't you worry.'

Umniga looked at the piles before her, making a mental tally of what she had gathered. Wicker baskets and sacks held foodstuffs, and she had several gourds filled with water. Her medical kit was full, as was Asha's, and a wooden box contained extra supplies for their kits. She had spent the day preparing for their journey, completing as many tasks around their little cottage as she could. She'd visited the local farm and asked them to tend the few goats and chickens they had while they were travelling. These were all the usual preparations she and Asha would perform before setting off for their regular rounds.

Umniga attempted to calm herself with the knowledge that no one would suspect her. All was as it should be. However, she had a tightness in the pit of her stomach, a sense of excitement and anticipation, which she felt sure must betray her secret. *Gods, you are a daft old woman, carrying on as if you were some silly young girl!*

She shook her head at her own foolishness, pushed herself to her feet, and proceeded to carry the provisions to the wagon. The covered wagon was a gift from Baldev and Karan to make her rounds easier as she grew older. It was sturdily constructed, with four large wooden wheels and solid timber sides which, when she was standing in it, reached to about her waist height. Bracketed into these sides were regularly spaced willow rods that bent over the tray of the wagon to form a domed roof. Further willow was woven across the centre of the dome and midway along its sides for several hand spans to strengthen its construction.

The Bear Clan was renowned for its carpenters and they had excelled themselves in this cleverly designed wagon. All the timbers were strong and light so that the wagon could be easily pulled by one horse. The interior featured cupboards, in a honey-coloured finely grained timber, which were intricately carved with a pattern of intertwined oak and willow branches. In the centre of each door, inlaid in many small pieces of variously coloured wood, were the images of either a bear, horse or boar. These cupboards came to only half the height of the wooden sides, creating narrow beds along the sides for Umniga and Asha. At either end was a small door, enabling dual access. The willow roof was covered with tough leather that was regularly waterproofed using a mixture of animal fat and beeswax.

After several trips to the wagon, Umniga felt exhausted. Her impatience had overridden her good sense. She thumped down the last load she could manage with an exasperated 'Oomf!' She chuckled. *The mind might be willing but the body is not.* Devi briefly woke and eyed her balefully from his roost under the lean-to. 'And you can just shut up too! I don't need a lecture from you. I know, I know—I'm old!' Devi gave a little bark, ruffled his feathers and went back to sleep. *Where is Asha? Surely, she should be back.* Umniga stomped wearily inside, slammed the door and sat dejectedly at the table as she considered the remainder of her supplies. 'Ach! Time for tea.' She sighed, lifted her head from her hands and rose to open the door in anticipation of Fihr's arrival: Fihr was too large to enter through a window. She prepared her tea and sat next to Asha's bed—waiting.

Fihr circled the cottage, gliding ever closer to the ground, until, with powerful grace, he landed in the doorway. His smugness overwhelmed Asha. Show off! she told him. She could feel him begin to leave her and panicked. Fihr! I need to be closer. I need to see my body. Impatience and slight scorn confronted her. Bewildered, Asha attempted to cling to her link with Fihr. Fihr, stop! He stopped, but refused to enter the house. Asha felt his irritation soften, and with this her panic abated slightly, only to be replaced with surprise as his presence housing and guarding her expanded. Again, Asha could not grasp how this 'door' had opened; it had never opened when they weren't hunting. She was acutely aware of her minuscule presence within an immense space. She waited, uncertain. Then another presence joined her; male or female she could not tell, but it dwarfed her. Her rising alarm was instantly quietened as she was embraced and taught. Images flowed into her mind, followed by reassurance.

As the presence withdrew, Asha experienced a sense of falling, then found herself again with only Fihr as her companion. He remained silent and subdued, yet gently prodded her to action. She concentrated, Fihr complied and she detected nervous excitement from him as her vision changed. Asha could now discern her own and Fihr's mixed auras, two slightly varying greens merging to create a more vibrant shade that appeared to pulse. From this, she saw a fine opaque thread of green leading into the cottage. Fihr fidgeted in anxious anticipation as he pushed at Asha. This was new—to follow the thread back to her body. *Give me a minute*, she thought. Fihr thrust her out of his mind.

Asha panicked, trying to reconnect with him. A wall of resistance met her. Dismay almost overwhelmed her, until she realised she was fine. Fihr's dark eyes bored into her. *Think, Asha!* She examined her form. Her image was an opaque green colour that matched her aura. Asha came to the realisation that this image was merely a projection of her consciousness; a shaping of her own power. She felt a pull upon her spirit a lure to simply travel, to see, to find another such power, to combine with it.

This was the danger Umniga had inferred, of travelling without a guardian. She spun around and looked at the thread, desperate to connect with her body, and simply 'walked'. As she approached the bed, she visualised the thread reeling in and her aura strengthened as it returned to her. Finally she 'lay' down in alignment with her physical form, experiencing a momentary disorientation as the two 'snapped' into place.

Asha sat up, grinning widely at Umniga who was sitting opposite her bed, sound asleep. She stood up quickly, was overcome by dizziness, groaned and sat back down. Fihr poked his head around the curtain to her alcove, fidgeting from side to side and making soft, low sounds at her.

Umniga awoke. 'Child, what are you doing? Take it slowly, you've been gone two days. You can't just get up and dance about, for the love of all that's holy!' Umniga sat beside her and rubbed her back. 'Just breathe slowly and deeply.'

'Umniga, you've no idea what I just had to do.'

'Mmm.' Umniga watched Fihr intently. 'Tell me.' Asha related her tale, unsure why, but omitting the other presence and its guidance. 'Smart bird that one,' was all Umniga said.

'How do the warriors do this? How do they bond and fight? I feel like I could sleep for an age now.'

Umniga chuckled. 'Their bond is different; perhaps not as deep. They do not travel as we do. Their guardians are given for a different purpose. The combination of skills from guardian and warrior has produced extraordinary feats, yet has great risk.' Both the Kenati were sobered by this thought. 'There are few born who have those talents and fewer Kenati who can do both. Wait here. I'll make you some tea with honey.'

When Umniga returned, Asha related everything that had happened at the lake.

'Hmf! Better he had not told him at all. I don't like putting you before him.'

'I will be fine. I understand why Karan and Baldev want this.'

Umniga shook her head. 'Well, I'm going to leave today. When you're rested you can help me get the wagon hitched and we'll load the rest of the supplies. I want to be on that boat without Shahjahan's men. Less likelihood that they'll kill them all at sea then. If Karan times everything correctly, then all the clans should arrive together when I return with the strangers—hopefully after. When you go to Faros make sure you are in full traditional attire. Maybe that will add to the sense of importance and remind Shahjahan of our history.'

CHAPTER TWELVE

THE old city of Faros lay behind strong walls and the citadel stood within these fortifications at the edge of a cliff. The original hill had been excavated and the citadel built upon it. The citadel rested upon a huge, steeply sloping dry stone wall laid against rammed earth. Its timber walls were plastered and, while not white, they appeared so against the grey of the massive stone foundation, the slate roof, and the dark timbers and shutters that surrounded the windows.

The outer city, beyond the walls, had developed over the years into a sprawling web of streets and alleys surrounded by houses of various shapes, sizes and construction—some large, some small, some clay brick, some timber, some reed and daubed walls. There was no consistency and no plan. In summer it was hot and dusty; in winter, cold, damp and muddy. Street drainage was either non-existent or comprised of simple spoon drains that ran out into the fields surrounding the town, or overflowed into the streets, turning some of them into rivers of effluent. Though it was not yet winter, Asha wrinkled her nose in disgust at the odours already wafting on the air.

The road leading to the old city had become the main thoroughfare. It was lined with stores and even on this cool autumn day the streets were crowded. The merchants in this street had laid timber boardwalks along their frontages in an effort to combat the oncoming winter mire. Spruikers loudly hailed passers-by, trying to encourage them into shops. Only the most affluent merchants were situated along this street. Many side streets branched from this one and how closely a store was located to this main street was a mark of the success of that business.

Fihr's cry rent the air as he flew directly down the main thoroughfare, his shadow darkening the unwary below. Surprised eyes followed his flight. A murmur of wonder travelled down the street, followed by a dreadful stillness as those eyes were drawn to the rider who travelled in his wake. Asha groaned inwardly. She was uncomfortable with the attention this calculated entrance was drawing, but she held her head high, managing to appear unconcerned. She smiled at the curious looks of the small children and returned the respectful acknowledgement of the older folk with a reassuring soft smile. Many looked once, initially uncaring, then again—clearly annoyed by the cessation of their trading.

Asha had worn full battle regalia, plus the traditional hooded cloak of a full Kenati. Her saddle was tooled along its edges with an intertwining pattern of oak and willow, which only the Kenati could display. The flaps of her saddle were embossed with a snarling boar's head. Her leather bow quiver hung from one side of her saddle; the arrow quiver hung from the other. Both featured the same willow and oak pattern, as did her hand-painted bow. A kalkan shield also hung from her saddle. Its fine canes were individually covered in green silk before being shaped into a circular shield with a spiral metal boss fixed into its centre.

She wore tan, sturdy, knee-length leather boots, whose tops were tooled with willow and oak and whose centres featured a boar's head. In the top of each boot were sheathed bone-handled daggers with silver pommels. Tucked into these boots were her loose, pale brown pants, over which she wore a light, long-sleeved, pale green woollen tunic. Protecting her torso was a shaped, boiled leather cuirass; on her arms were matching leather vambraces, both featuring a circular willow oak pattern around an eagle in flight. At her side hung a kilij with a silvery metal crosspiece and a katar. These weapons and armour were gifts from Lords Karan and Baldev. Over all this she wore her voluminous Kenati hooded cloak. It was a dense, yet soft woollen weave the colour of dry grass. This cloak was a recent gift to her, created by each of the Kenati elders upon the completion of her apprenticeship. Twining oak and willow bordered the cloak and a rearing horse and a standing bear were embroidered in its lower corners. A boar's head clasp secured the cloak around her neck.

Asha approached the barbican and curtain wall of the outer bailey. These were built upon a rammed earth foundation, faced with a dry stone wall, similar to the citadel. Above this foundation towered the barbican and the deep curtain wall, both of which were constructed of a mix of timber and stone. The timber had been originally rendered with plaster, to minimise the risk of fire. Towers and hoardings were built at regular intervals along the wall, all of which were peppered with loopholes. This structure had been built at the height of her clan's power and should have filled her with pride—it did not and she mourned its loss.

She could feel the curious eyes of the guards upon her. Asha had expected a mix of reactions to her entrance and appearance, but not the veiled hostility. Perhaps she and Umniga should have tried to maintain closer ties with the city folk. As she passed under the upraised portcullis and through the wall she could not help but eye the murder holes with trepidation.

Within the outer bailey walls lay the old city. It was here that the older, wealthier merchant families resided and there was a marked contrast between the buildings within these walls and those without. The street took a deliberately circuitous route to the inner bailey and was lined with large sturdy houses. The rooftops of these houses were designed to allow for the positioning of archers should the need arise and massive gates were constructed at the junctions of the side streets. This deliberate maze of streets and gates was designed purely to confuse and trap any attacking force. Having not been here since she was a child, Asha would have been lost, if not for Fihr's guidance.

These streets, while more orderly than the market street of the outer city, were far from deserted. She passed men, women and children in brightly coloured, well-made clothes. However, their curious looks quickly turned to casual disregard as they went about their business. The journey through Faros left Asha deeply disturbed. She had not really believed it when Umniga told her that most of these people cared only for privileged lifestyles and trade, not Lore.

At the barbican of the inner bailey she was stopped by two younger guards, who were surprised, sceptical and disrespectful when she stated who she was and that she needed to see the clan lord. Asha was losing patience and could feel Fihr's hostile and anxious mind trying to merge with her. She calmed herself as Fihr landed on her outstretched arm. Both she and Fihr gave them a scathing stare.

'Fetch your superior now! *You* do not stop Kenati.'

Under their combined glare, the young guards looked worriedly at each other until one disappeared hurriedly into the nearby armoury. He returned with an older member of the guard, who took one look at Asha and smacked the young man on the back of the head.

The older guard quickly approached Asha. 'Forgive them, mistress, they are young idiots. It has been too long since we have seen a Kenati in the city. Is Umniga with you?'

'No,' she said. 'I am Asha. I must see Clan Lord Shahjahan.'

He nodded. 'Mistress Asha, no visitor may bear weapons within these walls. I would ask you to please leave your weapons with me.'

'What? Does the clan lord fear his own Kenati?'

'Mistress, these are the orders of the clan lord. All those entering beyond here, who are not part of the watch, must leave their weapons in our safekeeping. I must obey.'

'This is outrageous.'

The older guard held up his hands placatingly. 'I'm sorry. I must. If you want to pass, then you must give us your weapons.'

Asha's lips drew into a thin line. The message must be delivered, she had no choice. She nodded tersely, dismounted and began to disarm. Handing her weapons to the young men galled her, though she took pleasure from their increasing consternation as the number of weapons grew.

The older guard was barely restraining his smile at their expense. 'Please wait here, mistress, while I put your things under lock and key. You will be escorted to the citadel.'

Asha rode into the courtyard of the citadel accompanied by the two chastened, now entirely respectful younger guards. She smiled. Umniga would be livid at this treatment. *Thank the gods she's not here.* They politely asked her to wait while they informed their commander of her presence. She lithely dismounted, waiting with what she hoped was an air of calm confidence. Fihr flew into the courtyard and landed on her saddle, ever watchful. The watch commander hurriedly emerged from a side building, knowing only that a Kenati was waiting in the courtyard. He stopped, transfixed by the sight before him. In the only sunlit place in the courtyard, a small, slender woman with short, spiky blonde hair stood at the shoulder of a dark palomino horse whose blonde mane and tail matched the hair colour of its rider. Poised on the saddle, glaring at him over the woman's shoulder, was a massive sea eagle. Light appeared to radiate from them; he shuddered at the contrast between this image and her grim surroundings.

'Asha.' He smiled as he greeted her. 'Well met.'

Asha grinned. 'Vikram. Well met indeed.'

Vikram shook his head. 'You shouldn't have come. You are not safe here.' Asha's smile faded. 'Why are you here?'

'I need to see Shahjahan.' Again he shook his head. 'Vikram, I have news of the utmost importance for Shahjahan. This news affects all of Altaica.' She briefly explained her purpose.

'You are not going in there alone. I'll come with you.'

'I don't want ...'

'Asha, I'm the captain of the watch. It's my duty to accompany you. Don't worry about me.' Together, they entered the stone keep. Quietly, with a wry grin, Vikram continued, 'You looked very impressive by the way. Staged beautifully.'

Asha snorted. 'If I had known you would be greeting me, I wouldn't have bothered.'

'You dressed the part too. I like it,' he said silkily. 'Wait here.' They had stopped before a pair of massive doors that led to the main meeting hall. 'Watch her,' Vikram addressed two guards, who had promptly come to attention, before disappearing down a side corridor.

Asha waited for what seemed like hours, during which the two guards remained impassively at attention. She wandered over to a window and stared absently at the courtyard. The timber window frame built into the stonework was weathered and, despite the fact that it had been recently re-oiled to preserve it, she could see that it was deteriorating, as were the hinges holding heavy wooden shutters. Frowning, she examined the courtyard more closely, noticing a patchwork of repairs, and more work to be done. She wondered at her surprise—why should the buildings not reflect the state of the clan? Asha could feel its slow death all around her.

She started as Vikram put his hand on her shoulder.

'Asha? My apologies, I spoke but you did not hear. Come. It took some time, but the chancellor has agreed to approach High Lord Shahjahan to inform him of your visit.'

'High lord?'

Vikram's expression soured. 'Much has changed.' He led her down several corridors, sparsely decorated with tapestries and ancient weapons. 'Ratilal calls himself "lord" as do others from amongst the wealthy families. Shahjahan is now "high lord". '

She looked at him, slightly aghast. 'Who decided this, Shahjahan or Ratilal?'

'Guess. Shahjahan puts up with it to pacify him and the restless *lords*. There are many who want revenge for the annexation of our lands north of The Divide.'

'Annexation. That's a nice term for it. I suppose it's better than saying they were outsmarted, outmanoeuvred and got their arses kicked.'

'Careful.' He continued in a soft voice, 'They think they can win and want to restore some glory to the clan.'

'Those days are over.'

He shrugged as they halted before a plain wooden door. 'You are to wait in here. I'll return presently.'

Asha entered the comfortably appointed room. A large rectangular table, surrounded by many comfortable chairs, was placed centrally and a fireplace dominated one end of the room. Above the mantel hung an ancient spear—a sinan—over which was mounted an enormous boar's head. Two longer sinan stood on either side of the fireplace in ornate brackets. *A dining room? No, a council room.* A map of Altaica hung, gaping, from one wall. There was a massive tear in it where someone had slashed the land north of The Divide. A series of shelves behind her held many scrolls of varying ages, and against one wall stood a side table on which sat a ewer and metal goblets.

Lost in thought, Asha did not hear the door open behind her. A firm hand landed on her shoulder, spinning her around. Ratilal leered down at her as he forced her backward against a wall.

'Asha, my, it's been a long time.'

She raised her hands to push him away, but he easily caught them and pinned them against the wall over her head.

'Mmm … I see you missed me. It's been too long.' He pressed himself against her, forcing his thigh between her legs.

She was effectively trapped—she couldn't even kick him at this angle. Heart pounding, she tried not to show her revulsion.

He smiled—a charming smile. A smile she was sure he used on many unsuspecting women, maids and girls. His tastes encompassed generations, sparing only the old from his favours. Ratilal was large and muscular, with very short cropped dark hair, a finely trimmed moustache, tanned flawless skin, and deep brown eyes framed by long lashes; he was astonishingly handsome. Bending his head into the curve of her neck, he inhaled deeply.

'Mmm, far too long. Nobody smells like you, Asha. Or tastes like you.' He ran his tongue along her neck. She turned her head away, shuddering. Ratilal laughed, delighted by her reaction. 'Gods, you're fun.'

Too many memories assailed Asha. She felt lost, small and alone again.

'Look at me.' Asha couldn't respond; she was too lost in her memories. Pinning her wrists with only one hand, he roughly grabbed her jaw, forcing her head toward his face. '*Look at me!*' He bashed her head back against the wall. The pain broke the spell of her past.

Asha blinked, trying to focus, to concentrate, and Fihr slipped into her mind. She was not alone. Asha narrowed her eyes at Ratilal.

'That's it, love. I want you here for this. It's no fun if you're not paying attention.'

'Leave me be, *Rati!*' she said vehemently.

His handsome features distorted briefly with rage, as he struck her across the face. 'How dare you!' Asha's face felt like it was on fire and her nose was bleeding. He held her throat tightly as he lowered his face to hers. Pausing, he stared at her lips, at the trail of blood that ran from her nose to her mouth, raised his eyes to hers, then grinning lasciviously, licked his lips. Asha's eyes widened in fury as he brutally kissed her, forcing her head back into the wall. She could feel his erection as he ground himself against her and licked the blood from her face. He moved the hand at her throat to grip her jaw harshly, then mauled her neck with his lips and tongue. As he grew more aroused he bit her.

Rage and hate burned through Asha's remaining fear. She shrieked as one with Fihr. Her pupils dilated and her eyes changed colour. Ratilal, oblivious, continued his assault by releasing her hands so he could paw at her breasts. Fihr shrieked again and power flowed through her. She lashed out, raking her nails across his face like talons, gouging his flesh from cheekbone to jaw. She could feel his torn skin under her nails and smiled triumphantly as blood dripped from her fingertips.

'*Bitch!*' he bellowed, thumping her head into the wall again, then pitching her across the room. She lay dazed and winded on the floor, her only thought was of regaining her breath. Asha could feel her consciousness fading, although she knew Fihr was still with her, trying to stop her passing out. Her sight dimmed, but she could still hear, and all she could hear were footsteps drawing near. She felt her face hit again and a great weight pinning her down.

Vikram followed the high lord and the chancellor down the corridor to the small meeting room.

'What in the name of the gods is going on?' Shahjahan growled as they heard the pounding of running feet from another corridor, followed by a piercing screech. They picked up their pace, reaching the door of the council room in time to see Fihr frantically gouging at it. Two guards slid to a halt near the door and were preparing to attack the enraged sea eagle with their halberds.

'Stop!' yelled Vikram.

'What is going on?' Shahjahan roared.

'That's Asha's guardian.'

Shahjahan needed no further explanation. 'Get that bloody door open. *Now!*'

Vikram approached quickly, trying to avoid Fihr. 'Let me open the damn door, bird,' he muttered. Fihr stilled, clinging to the door, rotated his head and glared at him. Vikram reached out, shaking, to flip the latch on the door. Simultaneously as he flipped the latch, Fihr dropped from the door to his arm, his talons almost piercing his thick gambeson. When Vikram thrust the door open, Fihr launched himself at Ratilal.

Ratilal had just punched Asha in the face and was pinning her down on the floor as he tore at the fastening on her trousers. Shahjahan and Vikram plunged forward. Fihr landed on Ratilal's back and tore a hunk of flesh from his neck. Ratilal reared up, bellowing and flailing his arms behind him, dislodging Fihr just as Vikram and Shahjahan reached him. Enraged, Shahjahan backhanded his son across the face with all his might, toppling him sideways to the floor. Vikram stood poised between Ratilal and Asha, hand on his sword.

Shahjahan looked at the two guards standing open-mouthed in the doorway. 'Well, get in here! Make yourselves useful. Detain my son.'

Vikram appraised his clan lord. He was red-faced and breathing heavily, his hands fisted at his sides as he restrained himself. Although still a large, powerful man despite his years, he was a shadow of his former self. Grief, age and indolence had taken their toll, but this was a spark of the clan lord of old. He hoped it would last.

Shahjahan knelt beside Asha's prone form, Vikram by his side. Ratilal was transfixed by Fihr, perched on the back of a chair, as he watched him devour the hunk of flesh he had torn from his neck. All the while Ratilal knew the raptor was taunting him, watching and waiting.

Asha's neck was bruised, showing clear finger marks. One cheek was swollen and red; one eye was blackening, swollen and closed.

'Asha?' Vikram said urgently. She groaned. 'Thank the gods.'

The chancellor, who had disappeared once the door opened, returned now with more guards and a medical kit. Shahjahan gently examined Asha's face and neck, causing her to wince.

'My apologies, child. I wish to the gods this had not happened to you. Can you move your arms? Legs?' Slowly, Asha did so. 'Can you sit up?'

'I'll need help,' came her hoarse whisper. 'I think some of my ribs are broken.' On either side of her, Vikram and the Boar Lord gently helped her sit up. She gave an agonised groan, leaning into Vikram, as the colour drained from her face and beads of sweat lined her brow.

'Easy, little one,' Shahjahan soothed. 'Damn it!' he exclaimed as he saw the blood and hair on the floor. He moved behind her to examine the back of her head more closely. 'This will need stitches.' He placed a cloth on the back of her head. 'Hold this,' he said to the chancellor. He stalked over to his son. 'Curse you, Ratilal! Why? You are no better than a wild beast.'

'She's Kenati. I didn't think you'd care.'

'What!' he roared and punched Ratilal squarely in the face. As he watched the blood pour from his son's shattered nose, he said through clenched teeth, 'I may have no love for the Kenati, but I still enforce the law and you know the law. You will be flogged for this. Get him out of my sight. Put him in a cell.'

Shahjahan knelt before Asha, taking her hand as the chancellor worked on her scalp. Asha struggled to remain conscious. 'Look at me, little one,' Shahjahan said. 'Don't think about what he is doing. Just remember your breathing and look at me.'

'Asha, I'm going to dab some bloodroot on this; it will be much less painful to work on for a little while. I need to shave some hair off, then stitch.'

Asha felt the chancellor gently dabbing a cloth on the back of her head, followed by a tingling sensation, after which she could feel very little other than the odd tug. She began to shake, tasted bile and resisted the urge to vomit as her vision went black. Resting heavily against Vikram, she heard someone say, 'Damn it!' She felt herself shifted slightly and a cloak placed around her shoulders and tucked in around her legs.

'Asha, come on—open your eyes. That's it, little one. Look at me. Now, Asha, you must tell me why you are here. Vikram has told me briefly, but I need you to tell me all. Come child, stay with me and talk. Focus.'

'First,' Asha croaked. 'Know this—I will never be without my weapons again, and if your son comes near me again I will butcher him like the animal he is.' She waited, realising she may have just overstepped. Angering him could risk her whole mission, though, at this point, part of her didn't care.

Shahjahan paused, looking closely at this young woman before him, battered and bruised, yet still defiant. He found no anger, just admiration. Finally, with a wry grin he said, 'If he comes near you again, you have my permission to do as you will with him. Your weapons will be returned to you and no one will take them away from you again. Now you must tell me why you have come.'

By the time Asha finished, her head was bandaged and she was sitting in one of the meeting chairs. Shahjahan had risen and was pacing before her, wearing a deep frown.

'Seems like a lot of damn fuss. We should just leave them there to die. If any make it to shore on their own, we can kill them and be done with it. The last time strangers visited us, gods know it was generations ago, they brought war; killing them was the best thing.'

'Umniga says there are families.'

'Umniga! Damn woman's been a thorn in my side for years!'

Asha smiled faintly. 'Many say that, my lord.' He barked in amusement. 'It is odd that she found them at all. Lords Karan and Baldev are concerned that they are fleeing something or someone. Perhaps the gods are warning us?' Her voice dwindled to nothing as the pain returned and fatigue overwhelmed her. This drew the Boar Lord's attention.

'Enough, Asha. You have done your duty. Now I must decide.' To the chancellor, he said, 'Have the chatelaine ready my daughter's room for Asha to stay in.'

'My lord?' came his shocked reply.

'You heard me. I'll not have her stay in the barracks. Vikram, assign two of your most trusted guards to her. If anything further happens to her I will hold you responsible.'

Quietly Asha rasped, 'I would feel safer in the barracks—more comfortable.'

Shahjahan glanced at her briefly and in that short moment she saw immense sorrow in his eyes. Quickly he guarded his look and said, 'Enough child, you will do as I bid and rest.'

>>—→

Vikram and the chatelaine helped Asha to the bedroom. She was increasingly groggy, shivering—despite still being wrapped in two cloaks—and needing Vikram's support to walk. He left two guards outside the door and helped her to the bed. Asha didn't notice much other than the large, soft bed. They sat her on its edge, Vikram's strong arm still around her. She rested her head against his shoulder and closed her eyes.

'Poor little love.' The chatelaine fussed and clucked as she removed Asha's boots and divested her of both cloaks. Vikram urged her upright as the chatelaine threw back the covers. Gratefully, Asha crawled onto the mattress, sinking into its soft, welcome embrace as she tried to find a position that would cause the least pain. The chatelaine pulled the covers over her, tucking them in snugly around her.

The chatelaine stared at Asha's swollen, mottled face. 'That bastard's been trouble since he was a boy,' she whispered fiercely. Vikram grunted in assent.

Asha opened her eyes, mumbling, 'Can you open the shutters please? Fihr …'

Vikram walked briskly over to the large window and threw open the timber shutters. Fihr flew into the room, landed on the bed end, looked down at Asha and made a low rumble. She smiled weakly at him, closing her eyes again.

'We'll have to keep waking her up for a while. We need to make sure she stays with us.'

'No need,' Asha said. 'Fihr will look after me.'

'Nevertheless,' the chatelaine continued decisively, 'someone should stay with you tonight in case you need anything. The bird can't help you up or get you what you need. Vikram, you must have things to organise. I will stay with Asha. You can relieve me later,' she ordered. 'Go on, be off with you. Hovering won't help her.'

Vikram bowed deeply and gracefully. 'Yes, mistress. I yield.' He held his hands up in mock surrender. 'I will return later.'

She laughed. 'Be off! Asha will be fine.'

'Chicken,' Asha muttered as he left.

'Rest,' the chatelaine ordered.

'You'd like Umniga,' Asha groused.

'Yes, I *do* like Umniga. We see eye to eye on many things. It's been too long since I've seen her.'

Asha did not comment, she had drifted to sleep. Fihr flew to the windowsill, ruffled his feathers and settled down, ever her guardian.

Vikram sat by Asha's bed, mulling over the day's events. The guards had no choice but to remove her weapons. He had no choice when he left her, yet he kept replaying events in his mind, wondering what he could have done differently. He stoked the fire and watched the flames. Unsure how long he rested there, he was roused from his reverie by a firm touch on his shoulder. Shahjahan stood over him.

'How fares our patient?'

'She's been sleeping soundly.'

He frowned. 'Have you been waking her regularly?'

Shaking his head, Vikram replied, 'No need—she said Fihr would keep her with us.'

Shahjahan looked thoughtfully at Fihr. 'I never realised, until today, just how important the guardians could be. Did you see those gouges on Ratilal's face? Asha's nails are short; they shouldn't be able to do that kind of damage.' Vikram said nothing, waiting. 'Things must change … Did you know?'

'I knew of the antipathy Asha felt toward him. I can only guess what caused it.'

Shahjahan was deep in thought. 'Get some rest, Vikram. Tomorrow my son faces his punishment. I want all the guard turned out to witness it.' He paused. 'You need to think about who your most loyal and trustworthy troops are. You will be coming with me when we meet Baldev and Karan. I need to leave this keep and Faros in good hands with people I can trust and I hope there are enough of those to bring some with us as well.'

'My lord?'

'We are going to meet the lords of Horse and Bear. That alone will chafe at my son. Aside from that, he is not going to like the other changes I intend. I've ignored the pretensions of him and his cronies for too long. They won't be happy.'

'Surely, you don't think …?' The clan lord simply stared at him. 'Yes, my lord.'

Shahjahan nodded, certain Vikram understood. 'Go, get some rest. Think on who to trust. I'll stay with her.'

Shahjahan stood by Asha's bed, staring down at her. Her face was a swollen mess of bruises. Anger welled up inside him again. Remembering her defiant words, he smiled, certain that she would do as she had vowed. She lay on her side, curled in a foetal position, hands fisted under her chin. Carefully, so as not to disturb her, he pulled the quilt higher. He could feel Fihr watching him carefully.

Slowly, he moved to the fire and sat, looking at the room in its flickering light. His chatelaine had maintained the room in pristine condition. She had not changed anything since the death of his daughter. Often he came to sit in here at night when everyone else was sleeping. Tonight, he berated himself for failing with Ratilal. He had always been a competitive, ambitious boy—something Shahjahan had considered admirable in a son destined to rule, but he had shown a callous, cruel streak on occasion. Once his hunt master had caught him tormenting a rabbit he had caught. He said he seemed to be delighting in discovering how much he could injure the animal without killing it. The hunt master had promptly boxed his ears, then lectured him on the ethics of a warrior and hunter. Unnecessary cruelty in battle, delighting in killing and causing pain as he had done, would not earn him respect, but disgust and contempt.

When told of Ratilal's actions, Shahjahan had taken a switch to the boy while reiterating the hunt master's message. He thought he had cured him of that tendency, for he did not hear of another such incident. He was a cocky adolescent, as many were. He and his friends were always together—always keen at their training, working hard, excelling at martial skills. They were treated no differently because of their rank. He had been proud of the victories Ratilal had achieved in the training bouts. There was many a young warrior sporting injuries that he heard were by the hands of his son in combat training. In hindsight he realised that perhaps he should have been more observant, questioned the instructors more closely. Had Ratilal been able to disguise his sadism via this means? What else had he, as a father, missed?

Vikram had indicated there was history between Asha and Ratilal; a longstanding hatred on her part. Scowling, he rubbed his face tiredly, leaned back in the chair, stretched his feet out before him and fell into a restless sleep, dreaming of his daughter.

Shahjahan awoke chilled. The fire had almost gone out. 'Blast,' he muttered as he put more logs onto it and coaxed it back to life. There was a rustle from the bed, followed by a quiet moan. He rose to check on Asha and adjusted the quilt around her again.

Sitting beside the bed, with the dream of his daughter fresh in his mind, he watched her sleep with a feeling of profound sadness. He had failed both of his children and his clan. Samia had been older than Asha. She had wanted to be a Kenati; it was *all* she had wanted. Desperately, she prayed to the gods to send her a guardian, so the Kenati would accept her. All youngsters learned the Lore and healing techniques with the supervision of the Kenati and Samia excelled at this. She had never been an overly confident or outgoing girl, but she threw all her energies into learning and praying. Her martial skills had not come easily; she worked hard just to become proficient—the bow being her weapon of choice.

Ratilal, for whom such skills came very easily, constantly teased her. At the time, he thought it was merely sibling squabbling. Samia redoubled her efforts, earning praise from him, her instructors and Umniga. She would visit the sick and help Umniga with her healing.

Shahjahan watched her quietly bloom; he was immensely proud of her dedication.

Yet Umniga cautioned him that the girl was growing obsessed with becoming a Kenati. She had reached puberty and no guardian presented itself; still she held out hope that one would come. It was odd—the more controlled and confident that Ratilal became, the more Samia seemed to want, and need, to leave and join the Kenati. As time went by she became more despairing. She begged Umniga to allow her to join the ranks of the Kenati, but the old woman refused. She seemed happy enough when she was away, but would mysteriously become withdrawn on her return. At this time Ratilal was the 'golden child', behaving as he should while Samia was slipping away.

Asha moaned and mumbled incoherently, then sleepily sat up, blinking her bleary eyes.

Shahjahan stood, bending over her in concern as he felt her brow. 'What's wrong, little one, what do you need?'

Asha did not recognise where she was. Flickering light revealed a large room, someone was beside her speaking softly. She moved, the pain in her ribs and head recalling to her the earlier events. She focused on the face beside her, astonished to see the clan lord.

'My lord?' she whispered hoarsely, still clearly a little confused and half asleep. 'My head hurts.' The last was said in a small, vulnerable childlike voice.

Shahjahan couldn't help but smile. 'I know. Scoot forward, I will put some more bloodroot on your stitches.'

Obediently, she did so. Slowly, the oddness of her situation dawned on her. Why was the clan lord looking after her? This was not what she had expected. He re-dressed her head, gave her water to drink and bade her lie down. Bewildered, she did so and fell into a dreamless sleep.

Alone again with his thoughts, he couldn't help but compare Asha with Samia. They seemed opposites. Samia had carried more weight, her face was more rounded, her hair long and dark. Asha, he knew, had never wanted to be a Kenati. She had wanted to remain with her parents, but Fihr arrived when she was a child and she had no choice. Samia found her reluctance to join the Kenati incomprehensible and aggravating. She described her as disagreeable, wild and ungrateful. When Asha became Umniga's apprentice, Samia withdrew emotionally even further.

One day he had found her lying in bed, curled up much as Asha was now, pale and apparently asleep. She would not wake. She was cold. He pulled back the covers and saw the blood. *Gods, the blood, so much blood!* And of her own doing. It had soaked into the bedding around her. He was a seasoned warrior, yet the sight of so much blood from his little girl felled him. He had blamed Umniga and the Kenati for so many years. His anger and grief consumed him. Yet, he grinned at the irony; here was Asha, in his daughter's room so many years later, and by his hand. He took one last look at her before returning to the chair by the fire and falling asleep.

CHAPTER THIRTEEN

THE courtyard was full, despite the early hour. All the watch and many of the wealthy who lived within the old city walls had turned out and stood facing a large pole with an iron ring near its top. Asha stood at the front of this crowd next to Vikram; her bandaged head and colourful bruises visible to all. Shahjahan stood beside a guard holding a short multi-tailed whip.

Ratilal, shackled, was escorted from his cell near the watch house to the pole. Once there, his shirt was removed and his shackles were unlocked and threaded through the metal ring attached to the pole, raising his arms high above his head.

'My son callously, brutally, attacked Asha of the Kenati. There can be no doubt of his crime, as he was caught in the act and the evidence of it is before you.' He paused. 'The law applies to all in my demesne, regardless of birth. Ratilal will receive twenty lashes. Let this be known where you will—I will not tolerate law breakers!'

Vikram felt a swell of pride—this was indeed the clan lord of old; maybe there was still hope. Shahjahan took the whip himself, causing a ripple of shock to course through the crowd. He gave it an experimental flick. Such was the silence that the clink of the small metal balls, which weighted each stiffened tail, could be heard clearly. Ratilal stood tall and defiant. His tanned, muscular back and shoulders were unblemished and taut. His father drew his arm back and flicked it forward in a deceptively lazy way, yet the whip flew toward its target.

Asha watched, appearing impassive, yet marvelling at how easily Ratilal's back began bleeding; each stroke bringing her immense satisfaction. The smooth noise of the whip steadily dulled as it became saturated with blood, the sound reminiscent of wet clothes being thrashed on a rock. The ground between him and his father was stained with blood that had been flicked off the whip as it swung. The first stroke left Ratilal's back red. By the final stroke his back was sliced, bleeding and bruised. Shahjahan remained resolute. A subtle pallor, the sweat on his brow and hardness in his eyes were the only indicators of what the task had cost him. He handed the whip to a guard. 'Remember this! The law is for everyone.'

He turned and headed into the keep where he met the chancellor. 'No Kenati will have their weapons removed when they visit here— ever.' He continued, 'The women who work here should have, at least, a knife always about themselves.'

The chancellor gave him an apologetic look. 'They have done so for many years, high lord.'

'I've been blind and a thorough fool,' he said, running his hand over his suddenly careworn face.

'You were grieving.'

'For too long. No, don't make excuses. I heard rumours about him, but no one came forward, no proof.'

'No, no proof.'

Once they were secluded in the meeting room again, Shahjahan bitterly ranted, 'Gods! It would have been better if Karan and Baldev had kept coming and taken Faros.' The chancellor looked shocked. 'Well, they could have dealt with him. If I was lucky, he'd have been killed in battle, or I would. Either way, he wouldn't be ruling the clan or I wouldn't have to worry. Oh, and enough of this "high lord" rubbish. I am simply clan lord and Ratilal does not deserve an elevated title—not him, not his cronies.'

'Yes, clan lord.' The chancellor grinned.

'Wipe that grin off your face,' Shahjahan huffed at him.

'Yes, clan lord.' The chancellor's grin grew.

'Now, we have to prepare to meet Baldev and Karan at The Four Ways. Ready wagons with supplies—plenty of food, water, blankets, some assorted clothing. Sounds like these people are in a bad way.'

'You are agreeing to let Lords Karan and Baldev in? With troops?'

'I have no damn choice. My son saw to that. I can't send Asha back to them in her state with a negative answer. Gods know what they'll think, or do. Aside from that, they may just be right about all this, damn them! Get everything ready. I want the wagons gone today. Asha, Vikram and a few guards can go with them direct to Parlan.'

Shahjahan entered Ratilal's chamber to see half a dozen of his son's friends hovering around the room. One of them was treating his back, if the litany of complaints issuing from Ratilal was anything to judge by. All conversation ceased upon his entry. He walked to the bed where his son lay face down. Ratilal coldly appraised his approaching father.

'Leave us,' Shahjahan commanded.

'No, they can stay.' The lacerations on his face made him wince as he spoke and his speech was clipped.

'Leave us!' They did not look to Ratilal, but hastily left the room.

'Cowards,' Ratilal sneered quietly at their departing backs.

'No. They know who is clan lord here.'

'What do you want?' came the truculent response.

'We need to talk.'

'You've done your talking already.'

Shahjahan ignored him, removing the cloth covering his wounded back. 'Did Niaz treat this?'

'Yes.'

'Are you sure he's your friend?' Ratilal moaned as he tried to turn his head enough to see the state of his back. 'Stay still. I will fix it.'

'What, have you got the whip with you? Going to finish the job properly?'

'Shut up. You gave me no choice and you know it,' Shahjahan growled. He retrieved salt from a well-stocked box of medical supplies and mixed up a strong salt water solution, then thoroughly bathed the gouges.

Ratilal hissed. 'It's already been bathed.'

'Not well.' Shahjahan smiled as his son groaned. 'I'm glad to see someone at least had the presence of mind to supply a kit for your use,' he said as he perused the contents of the box of medicinal supplies.

'Glad? The old woman left it and then scurried out like a cockroach. It was up to my men to help me.'

Shahjahan frowned at his use of 'my men'. He grabbed a salve of honeygold, scooped a liberal amount into a bowl, then blended in powdered duckweed. His hand paused over the bloodroot. *No*, he thought. *Let him hurt a little longer.*

'What are you doing?' Ratilal demanded.

'Honeygold salve mixed with duckweed—helps healing and stops bleeding. Your friends should have thought of this.'

'They hadn't finished.' Shahjahan began applying the salve to his son's lacerated back.

'Why are you doing this?'

'You are my son.'

'Didn't feel like that earlier. You whipped me like a common criminal.'

'You behaved like a common criminal. You know the law.'

Ratilal deflected this by saying, 'You picked an inopportune time to start caring about Kenati and being clan lord.' Shahjahan's pause in his ministrations gave Ratilal satisfaction in knowing that he had hurt him, but if he could have seen the pain and wrath on his father's face, he may well have given pause to his gloating.

'I have been wrong in my hatred of the Kenati. They were not to blame for Samia's death.' Ratilal stiffened under his hands. 'And I have neglected some of my duties. Regardless of that, you would have been punished. I have never neglected the law in this respect. What possessed you?' No answer was forthcoming. 'Things *will* change, Ratilal. Get used to it. We will resume our duties to the outlying settlements, and when I see Lords Karan and Baldev, I will talk about reinstating the games.'

Surprised, Ratilal tried to face him, but his father's large, firm hand on his shoulder restrained him. 'Be still, for the love of the gods, be still. I am nearly finished.' Ratilal grumbled, but laid quietly, his mind racing over this unwelcome turn of events. 'All right, slowly sit up. I'm going to need to look at your face.' Ratilal eased himself upright. 'Gods, that's deep! I can see part of your cheek bone. I'll need to stitch them.' Shahjahan carefully stitched Ratilal's face. 'It will scar. You won't be so pretty anymore.'

Ratilal snarled, pulling at his father's work, and scowled in pain. As if able to read his thoughts, Shahjahan suddenly grabbed his chin, forcing his son to look him in the eye.

'You will *not* go near Asha again. Do you hear me? Go find a willing whore, but never do this again. I don't ever want to hear even a whisper of such things again.' He resumed his stitching.

Ratilal, his mind still racing, put aside his anger. 'Why are you seeing Karan and Baldev?'

'*Lords* Karan and Baldev have asked to enter my territory.'

'They're already in *our* territory.'

'No. That is theirs now.'

'It was ours—they took it!'

'It's theirs—for now. If I had not neglected the people, they could not have taken it.'

'The people! Disloyal scum.' Ratilal was scathing.

'No! It is a mark of their loyalty that it took Karan and Baldev so long to annex the lands north of The Divide.' Shahjahan interpreted his silence to mean acquiescence, raising his hope that he could reach his son. 'Now, do you want to know why I am meeting them? Or have you heard rumours already?'

'How could I?' In truth, he had received information, but he had not given it any credence. He needed to hear it from the old man. He listened attentively as Shahjahan spoke while he continued stitching.

'This is perfect.' A cunning smile lit his face.

'How so?'

'Once they are in our territory they will be easy to kill. They will have fewer guards; they will be at our mercy. We can remove them, retake the northern territory and drive their clans back to the plateau and the Northern Forest where they belong.'

Shahjahan was silent, simply staring at him. 'No.'

'*No?*'

'I will give them safe passage. I will not break my word. They have not broken theirs.'

'Their word!'

'Son, make no mistake, the only reason I still rule here is because they did not want to. If they had wanted Faros, they would have taken it and we would never have been able to stop them.'

'No, we could stop them. We have excellent warriors.'

'They are better. How many would you sacrifice in a futile new war? We have lost the power, position, glory and honour of our clan, through stupidity and arrogance; not just mine. Over generations, we have forgotten and neglected our traditions. Traded old values for ones of lesser worth. We will not resurrect ourselves so easily. But from now on we will work toward it. These strangers represent a possible threat we must deal with together.'

'If they're a threat, kill them.'

Shahjahan shook his head. 'I doubt they themselves are a threat. Also, if the gods have brought them to our attention, it will not do to anger them by killing the strangers.' He paused, thoughtful. 'It's what they may be running from that I'm worried about. We need to find out about them.'

'I understand.' Ratilal nodded. 'If they have made it this far, then others may come too.'

The clan lord smiled at his understanding. 'Exactly. Be patient, son. We will return to our strength and reclaim our honour, but not your way.'

'I want to come.'

Shahjahan scrutinised his face carefully. Seeing nothing but eagerness, he assented, faintly hopeful that by having Ratilal work closely with him, it may not be too late to mould him into a better leader. 'Yes, but not to The Four Ways. Go directly to Parlan.'

'Why not The Four Ways?' Ratilal was petulant.

'I must tell them what befell Asha, for they will see her soon enough, and I do not want you there when I do.'

'I can look after myself,' he said, shrugging, thinking only of the opportunity it would provide him.

'Not in this state,' Shahjahan scoffed. 'Even if you were in fighting trim, Karan would gut you like a fish and Baldev would rip off your head and use it for a door knob because of what you have done. Let me deal with this and stay clear of Asha.'

Just when he thought he had made his son understand, Ratilal said, 'We don't have to meet them. I don't like them setting foot here. No one may follow the strangers. Or maybe not for a long time. We can build up our defences in the meantime. We don't need the others. The glory would be all ours.'

Shahjahan shook his head sadly. 'I thought you understood. Despite everything else, despite the fact that I think they are right—and remember, I am clan lord, not you—the moment you assaulted Asha you left me no choice in the matter. She came to me at *their* bidding. We cannot fight a war with them again, not so soon. I leave in the morning. You will not leave for a few days ...' He raised his hand to forestall his son. 'Because of your back. Then you will join me.'

Ratilal nodded. That would allow plenty of time to plan.

Shahjahan exited the room to be met by Ratilal's closest friend, Niaz, lolling in the corridor. Niaz drew himself up, nodding deferentially at the clan lord as he passed. He was ignored. His resentful glare followed the old man's back before he returned to Ratilal.

'Sit,' Ratilal instructed him. 'We have plans to make.'

>>>→

Shahjahan sought out the chatelaine. 'I've treated my son's wounds.'

'Yes, lord.'

'You left the medical supplies?'

'Indeed, my lord. His friends were there to treat him. I did not stay.'

'Could not or would not stay?'

'None of the other staff wanted to treat him. I would not force them. I would have treated him myself, my lord, but … I did not want to linger.'

'Gods, damn it! They're all scared of him?'

'They avoid him. Even his friends, debauched as they are, are not …'

'Has he assaulted any of the staff?'

Hesitatingly she replied, 'Once, just after Samia died.' Shahjahan groaned. 'We did not tell you at the time, because you had enough to bear.'

'Has it happened since?'

'No, my lord, not here. We thought he had learnt, after that, not to foul his own nest.'

'So someone dealt with him, yes? Barracks justice?' She nodded. 'Good.' The faint glimmer of hope he had experienced when talking to Ratilal was now almost quashed. He felt bereaved by its loss and wished he could cling to it. 'He will be bedridden for today. See that he stays that way for at least two more days beyond that. Take him willow bark tea and lace it with enough sleepsease to render him incapable of leaving until then. After that he can join me, but I don't want him interfering with my plans.'

'With pleasure, my lord,' the elderly woman smiled.

>>>→

Umniga's wagon rolled inexorably through the undulating slopes surrounding the delta. As she drove through the fertile farm lands, she received welcoming smiles from all, along with offers of a meal or bed should she choose to stop. Gratefully, she declined, but often was stopped thereafter so someone could give her a loaf of bread, cheese, apples, or anything small and ready to hand for her journey. The children invariably asked where Asha was, disappointed that they would not hear her stories.

Finally, she approached the small fishing village of Parlan. Colourful cottages dotted the lee side of a gentle rise along the grassy coast. She stopped her wagon outside a long, low, thatched cottage, around which were clustered other cottages like berries on a bush. All of them belonged to Deo and his family. His wife came out of the main house with a puzzled smile, followed by a small grandchild.

'Well met, Umniga, but we were not expecting you so soon.'

'Well met, Nada. I need Deo's help.'

'Come in and wait—they are repairing nets near the boats.' She bent to the young child, looking seriously into his eyes. 'Fetch your brother. He can see to Umniga's wagon and mule.'

'Thank you, but I really must speak with him first.'

Nada frowned, intrigued. 'I'll come with you.' She met Umniga at the rear of the wagon and slid out the steps for her. Stiffly she sidled down them.

'I'm getting too damn old.' When Umniga reached the ground, she pushed on her staff as she straightened her spine, twisting from side to side to un-kink her back. With determination, the two women headed off.

Deo sat with his sons mending nets, while some of their wives worked mending or making new fishing baskets. Others hung rows of fish waiting either for the smokehouse or for pickling. All of them wore wide-legged pants, along with thick-belted woollen tunics, embroidered along the collar, hem and cuffs. Some wore sturdy, mid-length boots in concession to the weather, but others still went barefoot. The women all had long hair tied back tightly or braided.

Deo watched the two old women approach from under his bushy

grey eyebrows, showing no sign that he knew of their approach. His daughter stopped what she was doing and waved gaily, calling out a greeting to Umniga. With his head remaining bent at his work, he scowled deeply. 'Bugger it,' he groused.

'You can't ignore me, you old grump,' Umniga chided.

'Umniga,' was all he said before he turned away from her and hawked a gob of spit on the ground.

'Deo!' Nada warned.

'Bloody interruptions, woman! I've got work to do and no one to help me.' Snorts of laughter broke out around him. He pursed his lips as he withheld his grin. 'You!' he said pointing his aged, coarse brown finger at Umniga. 'You are not due for a month.' He gave her a shrewd look. 'You look exhausted. What's wrong?'

'We must talk. I need your help.' He looked at his family, about to send them away. 'No—they can hear. I require *all* your help.' Umniga sat on a pile of nets near him and related the happenings of the last few days.

Deo frowned. 'You want to bring them here?' He looked toward the sea, thinking. 'No. We're not sailing that far from land sight. The weather is turning, soon the seas will get rough. I'm not risking my family for some stupid strangers, who may well be dead already. This is pure foolishness!' The Umniga he knew was practical, not prone to following whims; he wondered if she was becoming addled in the head.

Umniga was stunned. She quickly tried to regain her equilibrium. 'Sailing out of land sight will not be a problem. Devi will guide us.'

'They're strangers, Umniga. Why should we care? Who knows what dangers they bring with them. Who are they?'

'They are no threat to you or Altaica. They are families, women, children.'

'They could bring disease.'

'I saw no signs of disease, just exposure, starvation and lack of water.'

One of Deo's grandsons spoke up, eager for a diversion, for a chance of adventure. 'Grumpa, we could help. Devi and Umniga would not get us lost.' Umniga smiled at him, but Deo scowled, shaking his head.

'When I think of the odds of my finding them in the first place …' Umniga sighed. 'I need two of them in particular. Those two are special. I'm certain I was meant to find them. I've never been more certain in my life.'

Deo reappraised her then. 'You think the gods have sent them.'

His eldest son simply said, 'The weather will hold for a while yet.'

Nada, who had been listening quietly all this while, added, 'You *must* do this. There are children out there. How would you feel if it was our children, or our grand-babies? You must.'

'The clan lords will be coming here. They are in agreement about this.' *At least I hope they are.* 'You can leave early and have a chance of returning with them alive, or wait till the lords get here. They will not give you a choice and will be mightily annoyed if the strangers have died.' *Maybe.*

Looking at the determined set of his wife's jaw, Deo said, 'I suppose I'll get no damn peace and no damn work done unless I bloody well go. Fine!'

Under a cloudless sky, with the light of a full moon, they set sail. Devi and Umniga guided a dozen fishing boats. They'd stacked water skins and barrels, along with simple foodstuffs in the boats. Deo, ever cautious, wanted as many boats and men as were willing to come. It took longer than Umniga had wanted to organise extra boats, but she relented when Deo had said, 'I have not lived this long by being a fool. If you want my help, then I'm in charge on the water.' This way, he'd reasoned, they had spare crew to sail the strangers back on their boat, or use the fishing boats. He had finished by saying smugly, 'Since you know nothin' of the sea, I forgive you.' She could have smacked him in the face then and there.

Umniga was anxious and impatient, a state not helped by the fact that Deo was still being conceited, and her palms remained itchy with the desire to hit him. Who knew what condition the strangers would be in by now. *Delays!* Everything had seemed to take too long to organise and now the journey seemed interminable. She prayed to Jalal, for this was his domain, that she and Devi would find the barge again. She knew Devi would remember where it had been, but the likelihood that it was still there was slim. She just hoped that the others did not decide to return if it took longer to find the strangers than they had anticipated.

Devi landed on the prow near her. 'He has found them!'

The relief in her voice caused Deo to look at her sharply. 'How far have they moved since the last time you saw them?'

Umniga fell silent, staring at Devi. 'If anything they are a bit closer. Same direction, just closer.'

Deo grunted, nodding. 'Likely the current would have brought them to us anyway. Maybe this way we won't be too late.'

Nicanor stared, bleary eyed, at the steady rain; he thought he was hallucinating. The loud, yet hollow sputtering on the awning and the staccato taps on the decking were the most wonderful sounds he had ever heard. He looked around, his family was awake. He grinned at Curro, uncaring as his cracked lips split further. Pio lay on his back, his arms spread out and his mouth open, as his weak little body delighted in the moisture. A few people were sitting, too ill to move much, but Nicanor knew they must be feeling as relieved as he was.

When the rain ceased, there was no frantic rush for the water containers. He eased himself to a sitting position and reached for the small container nearest him. He took a swig, savouring it, feeling its soothing flow all the way down his throat. He took another, closing his eyes in appreciation and thanks. Had he been able to cry, he was certain he would have.

Nicanor urged Lucia to sit up a little. Holding the container, he encouraged her to drink.

She smiled feebly, taking two precious gulps. 'Pio?'

Nicanor crawled to their son. Pio rolled to his side as Nicanor approached, a beauteous smile on his face.

He took the container and enjoyed several swigs. 'I never thought water could taste so yum,' he croaked.

Nicanor heard Curro saying, 'Careful, not too much.' He was glad he could not hear Elena's cranky reply. He could see a few others drinking, but several had not moved. His gaze returned to Lucia and Pio. 'Go on, have another mouthful.'

'Isa needs some too,' Pio said. Nicanor, feeling guilty, looked at Curro. They both knew Isaura had not stirred in days. Together the three of them crawled the short distance to her. They tried to rouse her, but still she would not wake.

'Pio, there's no change.'

'But she must drink!'

'Pio,' he gently said, 'she's not waking up.' Pio glared at him, hearing the fatality in his voice, but unable to accept it. 'She's not waking up to drink, that's all,' Nicanor said, trying to mollify him.

Pio managed to raise Isaura's head onto his lap. He took the container from his father and tried to open her mouth and pour water down her throat. Still she did not wake. He tried again, beginning to rock over her, quietly repeating, 'Isa, Isa … Isa.' The water would not go down her throat. It was running out the side of her mouth onto the deck.

Nicanor felt helpless. He took the cup from his son's hands and wrapped his arms around him to stop his rocking.

'Enough, Pio. It's not working. Enough.'

Elena's hoarse whisper was clear. 'Stop wasting the water.' Curro and Nicanor both stiffened.

Curro looked both angry and apologetic. 'She's not herself.'

Nicanor grunted, livid with Elena, but unwilling to make his brother feel worse.

'Pio,' Curro said, 'if you spill it now, when she isn't awake, you will have nothing to give her when she does wake up.' He placed his hand on Pio's shoulder, giving it a squeeze before he returned to Elena, to whom he said nothing.

Nicanor and Pio tenderly placed Isaura as she was before. He urged Pio to return to his pallet, but he refused. Instead he lay next to Isaura and took her hand. His mouth and hands were still too dry and sore to play for her, so he recommenced whispering stories to her—stories of home, some old fireside tales, myths, tales of their adventures together hunting or fishing. When his repertoire ran out, he invented new stories. When, in his exhaustion, his voice dwindled altogether, he said the stories in his head and he fell asleep dreaming them. All the while, he would hold her hand. Sometimes he woke, with a sense of urgency, next to his parents, only to move back to Isaura again.

CHAPTER FOURTEEN

WHAT? I'm floating. Isaura panicked as she looked at the top of the mast. Instinctively she reached out to grab it. No hand. Where's my body? You're dreaming, idiot! She looked for her form, seeing only a slight haze in the air. Fervently hoping that she could control this dream, she concentrated on her appearance; as she did so her form became more substantial. Finally she looked as she should, albeit faded. She reached out to the mast, but her hand passed through it. Dread settled upon her. Wake up. She waited. She did not wake up. Don't look down. She looked down.

Below her lay her friends, surrounding her body. Stricken she looked away. 'It's only a dream, just a dream', became her mantra, broken only by silent pleas to awaken. Her face contorted in fear and grief as she steadfastly tried to look anywhere other than at the scene below her. She couldn't do it, she had to know. Her eyes were drawn inextricably downward. Concentrating, she put all her will into reaching them. Nothing happened. *Damn it!* She tried again to no avail. Everything around her seemed to blur, then coalesced, disconcerting and disorientating her. Suddenly, she was beside her body, staring at it.

She battled a rising wave of hysteria. *So this is death? Really? What were you expecting, Isa? Gods, now I'm talking to myself.* She tore her gaze away from her body to stare at the ocean in an attempt to regain self-control. The last thing Isaura could remember was seeing the old woman and the owl. They had seemed one and the same. *Oh good, I must have gone nuts before I died.* She finally quashed frenzy building inside her. *Well, this isn't paradise and it can't be the Underworld since Hugo's not here. Am I caught between, waiting to be reborn?*

It was said some people's spirits, at the whims of the gods, remained between worlds, waiting to be reborn as they had not led sufficiently virtuous lives in this life, so must try again in the next. *Lack of virtue—no denying that,* she thought bitterly. Others believed that these spirits belonged to particularly strong-willed individuals, and their rebirth was an act of defiance against the gods. *I should have paid more attention to all that religious twaddle.*

Isaura looked at Pio. *He's alive! What about the others?* She tried to move again. Nothing. She puzzled over how she had made herself move. What did she do differently the second time? *I was angry.* Was it due to the single-mindedness that came with anger?

Focusing solely on where she wanted to be, she managed to move. This time, she realised that it was not the world around her reforming, but that she coalesced at her destination. Isaura examined the boat's other occupants; they were in worse shape than her friends. *None of them will last long. Damn it! Even the Underworld would have been better than seeing this.* She had done her best, but it was not enough. Despondently she thought, *They'll die anyway. We've changed nothing, just prolonged it.*

Glancing back along the deck, she noticed a fine violet thread following the path she had taken and ending at her physical form. Without thinking, she effortlessly followed it, returning to her body. Isaura realised her friends, clustered around her, had formed a protective barrier; shielding her from the others. Gazing at them and the protective solidarity they offered, she felt the weight of her failure with profound sadness. *I can't do this. I can't watch. I can't stay here.* She focused on the top of the mast, and materialised beside it, feeling rather proud of herself.

The unhelpful view before her, in any direction, was of a vast grey ocean.

Her attention was caught by the same violet shimmer over the water that she had noticed on the deck. *It's the way I've travelled—the way home.* Drawn to it, she travelled the line with ease. Pausing, she turned toward the boat, which was now only a dot on the horizon. *Forgive me.* Running from her grief, she chose to embrace this new existence. She could return home. *You've spent all your time trying to leave, now you're running back?* Yet it had to be better than this. Perhaps her mother's spirit lingered too? What would she think? She grimaced. *Don't dwell, girl. Just go.*

Isaura concentrated on the furthest point that she could see of the thread and 'jumped' to it. At least she thought she had moved. The grey ocean offered no points of reference once she had lost sight of the boat.

An urge to explore pulled at her. The sun was setting over the ocean, firing the horizon with brilliant pinks and oranges, which then transformed into mauve and dusky purple. The colours disappeared higher into the sky as the ocean swallowed the sun. Mesmerised, she wanted to see more. *Follow the sun. Why not?* The pull at her consciousness, a delicious enticement that beckoned to her, called her to explore. Wavering, she heard music, a flute. It reminded her of Pio's clumsy playing. The pull upon her eased; its tendrils slowly released her. *Home. Go home.*

Looking for the violet shimmer of the thread, she realised with horror that she had already wandered from it. She had lost the line. Panicking, she spun around frantically searching for it. She managed to stop herself before she strayed further. *Calm down.* With no reference point she could overshoot it. *It hasn't gone. Think!*

The music lingered; concentrating on it calmed her. *Dusk is the hardest time to see.* In the purple light of early evening, just before the grey of night descended, she obeyed a compulsion to be still and thought about home. The purple deepened, then vanished as night encroached. The moon began to illuminate the sea. Isaura looked again and in the light of the moon and in the darkness, she found it. It glowed, and in doing so seemed more substantial than before.

Isaura paused, gazing at the estuary then along the coast. *I could go to Matyran like we'd planned. No invasion, no Zaragaria. See something new …* She stilled. She needed to know if they'd made the right choice. *Could they have stayed?* Her gut told her no, but still she needed to see what had happened to the village and to those they left behind. *What had happened to her home? I've all the time in the world to explore later.* Home first, she decided, never once looking back to notice that her trail was fading.

The fens, a maze of reeds and water glistening in the sun, lay below her. Tree-covered islands dotted its expanse. Thin sporadic wisps of smoke were the only indicator that people lived there. There was no destruction here. She doubted the Zaragaria would ever bother with the fens and that its inhabitants would not bother with the Zaragaria. The people who lived there were markedly different from the rest of the people of Arunabējar. They had more in common with the hill clans of Matyran, both being darker in skin and hair. Though they both spoke the common tongue, they had similar local dialects quite distinct from those around them. They both distrusted strangers and lived in near isolation. The villagers would have had no help from them.

As she approached Arunal, the outlying farmsteads and homes were in ashes. However, the riverside city was not filled with chaotic, panicking citizens. Screams did not pierce the air. The fires were out. The outer fortifications were in ruins at one point, although work had commenced on repairing them and the main gates. The city appeared remarkably normal, calm and ordered. The market was bustling with people all going about their business as if nothing had happened. She could see the darkly armoured Zaragarian officers wandering the stalls, smiling and inspecting the goods.

The wharf quarter of the city was also a hive of activity. The pier was being rebuilt on a grander scale than before. Organisation and control had been imposed by the Zaragaria. The harsh, abrasive sound of Zaragarian commands, abuse and the lash of enforcement randomly carried to her ears. *At least they're alive. Even this would have been better than slow death on the boat.*

Some distance from the city and the river, she noticed a freshly dug field. Filled with a sense of dread, yet compelled by it, she left the river to investigate. It was not entirely cultivated. The soil had been dug only in many long, wide rows. Clumps of white powder dotted the ground near the rows. At the head and foot of each row stood a stone marker, engraved with the image of a mountain beside a river: an ancient symbol of Majula and Araceli. The powder was lime. *Graves.* Isaura gazed at the rows in despair. *How many are here? Soldiers? Ordinary folk? Would we have ended up here? Maybe we could have hidden, just like Hugo said …*

She returned to the river and headed home.

>>—→

The soldiers had camped in the village. The earth still bore the taint of their presence. It was obvious where the horses had been kept, where trees had been felled for fuel and where those trees had provided many campfires. The houses were still standing, although they had been ransacked.

The first bodies Isaura came across were at the rear of a small outlying cottage. The animals had begun to feast upon them. There was little recognisable about them, yet Isaura knew who they were. She had helped them often enough. There had been no place for the elderly on the boat. Isaura thought of her final visit to them. She had offered them an escape from this fate; they had refused. They thought their age would save them. She urged them to take what she offered, just in case, and to hide deep in the forest. They never had a chance. Their throats had been cut and their bodies dumped like refuse behind their house.

How many others like this? Isaura found three more. One was behind an empty hen house with an arrow lodged in his back and a fat raven perched on his head, feasting. The other couple were in a ditch. The flies and dog alerted Isaura to their presence. The old man's head was caved in. The woman's stomach, to the dog's delight, was slashed open. There was something oddly compelling about it. She was fascinated by the incongruity between a village devoid of human life, and the vibrancy of the natural world surrounding it. If no one returned here, the village would disappear, but life would not. Isaura could feel its energy thrumming around her.

What about Gabi's parents? She hoped they had been spared this fate. Their orchard was some distance from the village, but it had not escaped the army. Soldiers had been camping under the apple trees. The house was bare. There were no bodies inside. The cold cellar under the house had been looted. A stone workshop built into the side of the hill behind the house and its adjoining cold room were empty. No apples, no barrels and no bodies. Where were they? They had been kind to her mother when she had first arrived and Gabriela's mother had helped birth her. She dreaded finding their bodies. Desperately she searched on. Hope blossomed within her at the thought that they may have survived.

To her surprise, she was beginning to feel tired; she just wanted to go home. There was no clear path to her cabin from here, but it did not matter—she had roamed these woods since she was a child. The moment she entered the forest she felt a sense of peace descend upon her. The restlessness and uncertainty that had been plaguing her since they began their voyage was dissipating. Sunlight filtered through the tree canopy, creating patches of mottled green interspersed with shafts of bright light. Ferns abounded, their tall fronds bowing their heads gracefully over moss-covered fallen logs and hollows. Small birds flitted amongst the undergrowth, their bright calls chorusing through the forest. It was a soothing balm to her sorrow. Here was life, abundant and vibrant. It beguiled her. *I'm not leaving. Not yet, maybe after I rest.*

A colourful finch landed near her and cocked its head. His bright, dark eyes appeared to look directly at her—inviting. He flew off. Isaura followed, delighting in chasing his path; it felt like a game. He would flit from branch to branch and dart under fronds. At each stop, he cocked his head in her direction, beckoning her on. She felt certain he knew she was there. She would catch up, then the game would begin anew. Finally, he dived near a pool of water to snatch up a larva and greedily gobble it down. She revelled in this simple primitive joy. All her cares were forgotten.

Everything here called to something deep within her spirit. It felt like the welcoming embrace of a friend, offering no judgement, just comfort; she desperately wanted that comfort. So much had happened. So many decisions she had made about the lives of others, choices she wished she had not had to make. The accusations of her father rang in her ears. *If he had known everything I did, would he have gone through with his plan?*

The finch was long gone. Isaura realised that she was drifting deep within the forest. *How have I come so far? I've faded.* She could barely see her limbs. Concentrating on her form, she managed to strengthen her image slightly, but it did not regain the definition it had first held. Isaura frowned. *Does it really matter? I just want to relax here, rest and not move.*

A stag wandered into view, paused and turned its magnificent antlered head toward her. *Pio would love this.* She knew what he would say and remembered his voice bursting with excitement the first time he had seen one with her. *Finish what you started, Isa. Go home.*

She struggled to maintain the faint hope that she may see her mother's spirit, but a desolate thought tortured her: *If she's anywhere it won't be here.* Travelling through the forest, Isaura put all of her will into ignoring the pull of the energy around her.

Isaura crossed the narrow, rutted track that ran through the forest to the next village. The grass that usually grew long between the wheel ruts was flattened and broken, as were the branches of the dense undergrowth directly beside the road—all signs of the passing army. Looking more carefully, Isaura could discern traces of someone's passing within the forest—scouts. Images of her home ransacked flashed into her mind. *Bastards. Did they find it?* It was still some way off.

The idea that it may not have been defiled by the Zaragaria cheered her and drew her focus away from the tantalising colours and sounds around her. Isaura encountered the path to her cabin where it meandered amongst towering, ancient trees. Their massive moss-covered boles were many arm-spans wide and the trunks formed graceful, sloping ridges that draped to the ground, anchoring them to life. Such was the size of these gentle curves that one could sit between them, reclining against the trunk on the soft earth, listening and losing oneself to the surrounding life. Isaura had often done so, letting the peace envelope her.

The path twisted and turned; with each bend the sound of the river would intrude, then recede. It was impossible to see the cabin until almost upon it. There was no sign of disturbance here. Nestled in a sudden clearing, the cabin looked just as she had left it. Peaceful. Home. Her memory restored her mother to the garden, raising her hand in greeting and smiling. With the rattle of seed pods, the vision dissolved. No one greeted her.

Isaura was alone as she wandered the small garden. The herb gardens had become unruly and the few remaining vegetables had gone to seed, their straggly drying stalks and seed pods making a dry scraping sound in the soft breeze. Her mother would have been horrified by its neglected state; even Hugo would have fretted over it. It was the one thing they tended together. Isaura couldn't bring herself to care any longer. It was no longer her duty. None of it mattered anymore.

She had shut the cabin up when she'd left for the barge, but the side shutter was now open. Frowning, she approached the window. It overlooked her parents' room. Her heart stopped. One of the beds was empty, but her mother's was not. On it lay Gabriela's parents. They were embracing each other, cramped on the narrow bed— lifeless. They had not been dead very long. Their skin appeared grey and waxy, a trace of purple stained their mouths. *The troops didn't get here. They didn't need to do this.*

Guilt threatened to overwhelm her. She tried to calculate their chances of reaching here undetected—slim given their age and condition. The likelihood that they would have wound up butchered like the others had been high, yet they'd made it here. They should have lived. She'd hoped for this to be a little haven, free from death, free from conscience.

If Hugo had been here they would have lived. If you hadn't given them the love's lament, they would have lived. Hugo's twisted visage appeared before her. 'Will you kill us all?' Her thoughts rebounded within her and each time they did she lost a little more of herself. *If you'd left Hugo behind, they'd all be alive.*

A great weight engulfed her as self-loathing wrapped itself about her spirit. *He was right—you didn't know what you were doing.*

Near the cabin was a huge old tree. It had lost the battle against age and lightning long ago. The top half had sheared off and its timber was broken and grey. The centre of the tree had burned out, leaving a hollow base that had been a perfect playing spot for a young adventurer. It was to this ancient soul she went. Entering its dark confines, she wished she could sit, lean against its charred walls, feel its rough texture and the smoothness of the ground. *Just let go … just … let … go.* Deep below her the tree began to stir to life

CHAPTER FIFTEEN

UMNIGA reached the barge by mid-morning. The large boat lay on the water like a bloated carcass. Its single sail was torn, as was the canvas awning over the deck. There was no movement on the deck. Deo hurled a grappling hook over the railing and several of the young men scaled the side. Umniga followed their rapid movements with envy.

'Don't worry, old girl. Neither of us is getting up that way,' Deo said, chuckling.

A rope ladder was rolled out over the side of the boat at the gap in the railing. One of Deo's sons leaned over, grinning. 'Come on, old timers. Up you get.'

Umniga scowled at Deo. 'I can see where that one gets his manners from.'

Deo laughed. 'Well, up you go, old girl.' Unmiga pursed her lips and clambered up with Deo behind her. 'I've seen that face before.'

'Deo—I swear if you touch my behind, I will kick you off this ladder into the water.'

'I wouldn't dream of it.'

Once on deck, Umniga could see the shock, dismay and disgust on the other's faces. Then there was the smell. She wrinkled her nose. 'Check who's alive.' She proceeded directly to the cabin.

'Get the water up here,' Deo quietly ordered before he followed Umniga. 'These the ones?'

'The girl and the boy.' She indicated Isaura and Pio, then snorted derisively. 'And their families.' The boy was next to the girl, holding her hand. Umniga held out her hand as Deo passed her a water bottle. She shook the boy and patted his face. 'Come on, little one, C'mon. Wake up.' Pio mumbled. She poured water on her skirt hem, then used it to wipe his face and eyes, clearing away the dirt and grime sticking his eyelids together. When he blinked disbelievingly at her, she grinned, lighting her wrinkled old visage with kindness. Raising his head, she tipped the water flask to his mouth, slowing him down as he greedily gulped. 'Slowly, slowly.' Pio could not understand her words, but her gestures made sense. He pointed to his parents. Deo nodded and took another flask to them.

Nicanor, now awake, was looking about dazedly. Deo held out the flask, but Nicanor's fingers fumbled at it, so Deo held it for him as he drank. Deo admired the man's self-control. Sunburned, chaffed, peeling and cracked skin, hollow-eyed and sallow—he looked terrible, but he only drank a little. Deo held up the flask, but he shook his head, indicating the woman beside him. Together they roused Lucia and she drank. One of Deo's sons saw to Jaime, Gabriela and Daniel. Umniga could not rouse Isaura.

Deo moved to Curro and Elena. Curro was attempting to sit up, but only made it halfway. Deo crouched behind him, propping him up. 'It's alright lad, you're safe. Here, drink this.' Curro looked puzzled, but Deo gave him his best gap-toothed grin while waving the water flask about. Curro nodded weakly and drank, smiling at the old man in gratitude.

Elena reached single-mindedly for the flask, determination etched harshly on her face. Curro tried to hold it for her, but Elena snatched it from him, succeeding in dropping it with her stiff, clumsy hands. She emitted an animalistic moan, scrambling for the flask as it skittered across the deck.

Deo reached it first. Uttering a harsh oath, he scowled at her and raised his hand toward her. 'Stop, girl.'

Dismay flicked across her face, anger quickly followed it. Her eyes lacked understanding. She remained fixated by the flask.

Deo smoothed the scowl from his face as he took pity on her. Kneeling before her, he said gently, 'It's all right. Just go slow.' She didn't hear. He held the flask out of her reach. 'Sl-ow-ly.' He enunciated each syllable, slowly and clearly, hoping the pace of his speech would make the message clear to her. The man with her, now sitting up on his own, spoke to her. She dragged her focus from the flask to him. He spoke again, softly, yet firmly. She nodded. Deo then held the flask up to her lips. She did not snatch it, but drank greedily. He began to withdraw the flask, worried she would make herself ill. Elena panicked, tried to snatch the flask and push him over. Curro restrained her, giving Deo a look of both apology and thanks as he left the flask.

Deo returned to Umniga, who was kneeling beside the girl. She had bathed her face and eyes and was now rubbing her hands. He had never seen such concern on her face. 'Damn it.'

'Is she …?'

'No. Not yet. I need Devi.'

Deo called down to his boat, now anchored to the barge. 'Wake up Devi. He's needed.'

'Ow! He just bit me,' cried a distant voice.

Umniga's fist thumped the deck. Just what she needed, cantankerous bird. 'Devi! Get up here before I decide you're more use as a feather duster.' An abrupt squawk followed before Devi landed awkwardly inside the cabin. He barked at her, ruffling his feathers and looking utterly indignant. 'Not long, my friend, then you can sleep. We'll make it nice and dark for you.'

Deo knelt beside Umniga. 'Give me a hand, will you?' He sat behind her supporting her as she merged deeply with Devi and slumped against him. Deo turned his attention to the girl. Although she was thin and dirty, she looked in better shape than the others, yet she appeared lifeless.

Umniga and Devi viewed the girl's aura. It was weak, the colours were muted. The flecks of violet and red were nearly non-existent. There was a very faint aura trail from her body. *She's travelling. Oh gods, no!* She scanned the length of the deck and about the barge. Desperation speared her. *Where is she?* She came back to her body and sat up, looking stricken.

'All right, old girl?' No answer.

'We're too late?'

'No, not yet … not quite. Not while she still breathes.' Umniga felt old and tired. The adrenaline that had spurred her thus far was dwindling. All this effort surely could not be wasted.

'You've got the boy,' Deo said. She nodded, pulling herself together. Pio was looking anxiously between them. She gave him a half-hearted smile.

'Yes, but I'll not give up the girl yet. We've got to get back as fast as we can.' She stood and surveyed the deck, surprised at the organisation quickly emerging from the chaos. The fishermen had lined up half a dozen bodies near the gap in the railing. The splash as they threw the first one overboard startled the remaining survivors. Some cowed, others cried out in indignation and tried to rise shakily to their feet. Though they were easily pushed back down on the deck, their hostility did not subside.

'Wait,' Deo called out before they could toss any more bodies into the ocean. 'Perhaps you should do something, old girl,' he suggested. She gave him a quizzical look. 'They are the dead and you are a priestess. Say a few words for their passing.'

'They're not our dead and they're not my concern.'

'Didn't you say Munira had brought you word from Lord Karan, that they were all to be saved? It'll be a lot easier if they trust us. Say some words, make it look like we care.'

Deo was right, she could not disobey her clan lord. 'You are the most gods annoying old sod I've ever met.' Umniga rose and made her way to the bodies. She made pacifying gestures with her hands as she walked among the survivors. 'Easy … easy,' she soothed.

She had no idea if Rana and Jalal would welcome these strangers or if they even deserved welcome. Perhaps they had their own gods—gods who had abandoned them. She knelt before each body and placed her hand upon their hearts. Umniga could feel the heated gazes of the strangers boring into her back as she muttered a quick prayer. 'May the Great Mother and Father find a place for you, and protect you—*alvida.*'

She stood, smiling warmly, facing the remaining villagers. Her real prayer was for their trust. The gazes that met hers were wary, but mollified. As the bodies were dropped over the side, Umniga walked among the survivors. She projected as much caring and calm assurance as she could while handing out more water and small amounts of food to reinforce the fact that they were here to save them. Soon they calmed.

Deo leaned over the railing to talk to his son, who was hanging from a rope inspecting the side of the ship. Clearly peeved, Deo spat in disgust. 'Let's look below and see what we've got on our hands.' The pair disappeared into the hold.

'Gods, this is an old tub! Who in their right mind would go to sea in this? It's got more patches than a quilt.'

His son grunted. 'They're all that's holding it together.'

On deck again, they inspected the mast and sail. 'Sail is useless; there's a crack in the mast too.'

'How long do you think they've been out here?'

Deo shrugged. 'I do know that they won't last much longer. It's not worth trying to sail this hulk back. We'll load them all on our boats—just them. No room for their things.'

'It'll be crowded.'

'We'll cope.'

The process of transferring the villagers from the barge to the fishing boats was laborious. They had to be lowered over the side via ropes. Only a few would fit on each boat; once one boat filled another took its place. Finally, only the group near the cabin remained. The men helped Gabriela to her feet. She protested weakly, fearful of being separated from Jaime.

Deo watched this with amusement, before turning to Umniga. 'You'd think they'd be a bit more grateful.'

Umniga moved forward and took the girl's face in her hands. 'Ssh,' was all she said as she held her. 'Ssh.' Umniga maintained eye contact with her and exuded calm. 'Ssh.' Gabriela, transfixed, stood quietly while the men prepared her to be lowered over the side. Her terrified eyes never let Jaime out of her sight. Once in the barge, Jaime held her protectively. Daniel followed, but sat apart from them, simply staring stoically out to sea.

Umniga next approached Elena, who shrank back from her. Umniga paused, then completely ignored Elena and gestured to Curro. He frowned. He would not leave without Elena. He was about to refuse, but the old woman gave a subtle shake of her head as she slid her eyes almost imperceptibly to Elena. Understanding, he allowed the men to help him to his feet. Curro struggled to bend to gather the rolled leather bundles he always kept near him. The man who had helped him up spoke gruffly and grabbed his arm, shaking his head adamantly.

At the look of consternation and bereavement that crossed the young man's face, Deo stepped forward. 'Wait. What is it? Let's see.' He calmly unrolled the bundles. Inside one were the tools of a smith, while the other contained swords and a dagger. Arching his eyebrow at Umniga, he said, 'We'll let the man have his tools, eh?' She nodded. 'This?' he continued, indicating the weapons.

'You keep them secure. The lords will want to see them.'

Curro watched this exchange helplessly, his anxiety patently clear. When he was given back his tools, he expelled a long, relieved breath. He looked hopefully at the weapons bundle, causing the old man to laugh and shake his head. Curro, grateful beyond words for his tools, bowed his head several times in thanks.

Elena watched as Curro made his way to the edge of the deck. *He's leaving!* He did not look back. Stunned, she did not move. Curro was determined not to appear weak before these people and managed to climb down the rope ladder; his tools were lowered to him. *He's going without me.* Elena's mind wavered between fear and panic. *Who are these people? How did they find us?* She shuddered. She didn't trust these people. Yes, they were helping them, but they looked so different; they spoke so differently. Nothing seemed to make sense anymore. Now Curro was leaving her without a backward glance. His head disappeared over the side of the boat. Hurt and anger at him flooded her mind. With a shriek she came to her knees and tried to stand. Her limbs failed her. She cried out again, then sobbed and tried to crawl along the deck.

Two young men approached her, gripped her upper arms, and dragged her to the edge of the deck. She did not resist, nor did she help them. All she was capable of was staring in disbelief at the spot she last saw Curro. At the edge of the deck, she began frantically searching for him, finding him already in the smaller boat. His encouraging smile faltered momentarily at the look of outrage and betrayal that flashed briefly across her face.

Deo and Umniga exchanged a meaningful glance. 'She'll bear watching.'

Another fishing boat moved alongside to take the remainder of the passengers—Nicanor, Lucia, Pio and Isaura. Pio was sitting with his parents, anxiously watching the others boarding the small boats. He was euphoric, yet his joy was tempered when he thought of Isaura. Would they take her? The first thing the old woman did was to come to him and Isaura, but she had not been able to wake her. Would they bother with her now?

Nicanor looked at Isaura, laying still on her pallet. *There's no hope. Pio needs to accept it. It'll be easier all round if he does.* Despite this, he could not give voice to his thoughts. These newcomers were clearly an answer to their prayers, yet he was intrigued and a little suspicious as to how they had found them. They were obviously prepared for a rescue and the old woman, clearly an authority figure, curiously had made straight for Pio and Isaura. Despite helping others, her gaze had repeatedly rested on them. *What does she want?* The old woman turned her smiling face upon him. He chastised himself for reading too much into the situation. The most important thing was that they were saved. These people could have killed them or just left them to die—they had not.

It was their turn to leave. Nicanor marshalled his strength to stand, but the old woman walked directly to Isaura, ignoring him. She fussed about her, issuing instructions to the men. The larger of the two put his arms under Isaura's neck and knees and lifted her easily.

At the gap in the railing another sailor waited on the rope ladder. Isaura was placed on the deck with her legs dangling over the edge. Her arms were bound behind the neck of the sailor on the ladder. Another rope bound her waist to him. This done, he slowly descended the rope ladder.

'Careful,' Umniga chided. 'Don't you drop her.'

'Just let them get on with it, old girl.' The rope groaned ominously under the strain of the weight. Two more men held the base of the ladder in an attempt to minimise its sway. Finally Isaura was left curled up in the bow of the waiting boat.

Pio was grinning like a loon, delighted that Isaura was being saved, when he knew his family had given up on her. One of the men came along, laughing at the sight of Pio's ecstatic expression, before scooping him up and carrying him toward the waiting boat. He was then lowered over the side, looking for all the world like he was having a marvellous time.

Nicanor shook his head in amazement. He had never known anyone as resilient or irrepressible as Pio, or who possessed such a well of fierce, natural joy. *Isaura*, he thought sadly. *Yes, Isaura had been similar when she was young.*

Lucia had been trying to remain awake, but her exhaustion continued to overwhelm her. He prodded her gently, drawing her attention to the approaching strangers. She took a deep ragged breath as she rubbed her eyes and drew herself up. Lucia was determined to get off this boat under her own power. She managed to stand, but dizziness overcame her and she toppled sideways. Strong arms caught her. The next thing she knew she was on board the other boat next to Pio.

When they came for Nicanor, he had a firm hold on his tool chest. He refused to let go of it as they helped him up. Someone tried to prise his hand away, but he shook his head vigorously. 'No!'

Umniga laughed. 'He has to be the brother of the other one. See what's in it.'

'Tools. Just tools. Carpenter?'

'Oh, just bring 'em!' Deo grumbled. 'I want off this stinking damn tub.' He ceased his complaints when he saw the lid of the small chest. 'Umniga, did you know about this?'

She stared in surprise at the depiction of the bear inlaid upon the lid. 'No. I only saw the figurehead. This just confirms my thoughts.'

Lucia sat huddled next to Nicanor with Pio before them. Umniga sat in front of them in the bow of the boat, her hand resting protectively on Isaura as she stared out to sea, deep in thought. Umniga felt a tug on her dress; turning she met Pio's hopeful face. He placed his hand on his chest and said, 'Pio.' She could not resist smiling at him. He had taken the initiative to introduce himself, despite the circumstances, something none of the adults around him had taken the time to do.

Placing her hand on her chest, she said, 'Umniga.'

'Um-ni-ga, Umniga.' He frowned as he voiced the unfamiliar sound. 'Umni,' he finished with a grin.

She pursed her lips in mock anger. 'Greetings, Pio.'

He copied her. 'Greetings, Umni.' Pio was not feeling tired anymore. He was buoyed by all that was happening around him. These people spoke another language, but already he had learnt a new word. He wanted to know the names of these others, but how to ask? Umniga watched the play of emotions across his young face—joy, followed by a slightly crestfallen look, then thoughtfulness. Clearly he wanted to ask something.

'Pio. What is your name?'

He frowned.

'Pio,' she supplied. She repeated the question, emphasising her facial expressions and voice modulation, trying to convey the question and answer. He smiled, suddenly excited, and repeated her words, but lost his phrasing halfway. On repetition he mastered it. Umniga clapped and the sailors cheered him.

Still sitting, Pio introduced himself to the man nearest to him, followed by a small bow. This became a game; the fishermen would approach him, repeat the phrase and exchange names. They taught him their traditional friendly greeting, in which they placed their hands over their hearts, lowered them wide and low, palms up and gave a slight bow. The touching of the heart, followed by upturned palms indicated that no ill will or threat was intended, and the bow indicated by baring the neck and removing eye contact that the individual held no fear of the person they were greeting. Pio's eagerness and trusting nature instantly endeared him to these men.

Umniga tapped his shoulder and gestured toward Deo. Pio warily shook his head. Deo sat at the tiller, wearing his usual dour expression.

Pio tried to cajole Umniga to teach him other words. Umniga shook her head, nodded toward Deo, folded her arms and stared out to sea.

'*Umni*,' came his small, pleading voice. Umniga remained resolute. The sullen silence continued between them, before Pio, with a deep breath, proceeded to make his way unsteadily to Deo.

Deo appeared engrossed in steering the boat and pretended not to notice him. Slowly, Deo turned his head, looking down his crooked nose at Pio. Pio drew himself up and introduced himself, determined to make his pronunciation perfect; he then gave a formal half bow. When Pio rose, he met Deo's severe gaze unwaveringly. Deo broke into a huge grin, proud of the boy.

Deo leaned forward from the tiller and extended his hand to Pio. Pio's eyebrows shot up; his courage deserted him. Deo took his hand and drew him forward. He stood Pio in front of him on a water keg, his arm steadying the boy. Once Deo proceeded to teach him how to steer the boat, Pio's reticence vanished and his eyes lit with excitement. As they steered, Deo continued teaching him new words. Soon, however, Pio flagged. Deo felt his knees give way and caught him, and he was returned to his parents.

Sometime later, Pio woke to see Umniga sitting in the same position, looking pensive. He sidled over with his flute in his hand, unable to resist the compulsion to be near Isaura and to play for her. Pio snuggled into Umniga's side and curled his legs so they rested against Isaura. *Wake up, Isa, please.* Umniga listened to his rough, hesitant playing and stopped him. She smoothed a greasy salve on his lips, then bade him continue.

With shut eyes she listened as she rhythmically stroked his head. The tune was rough and simple, but the salve soothed the pain of his cracked lips and his playing improved. Pio changed the tune, improvising slight alterations at first, adding little highs and lows to the melody, enhancing it more with each repetition until it became something altogether different. It swept her along, reminding her of the sweet new grass of spring, trees in bud bursting with life, the fresh smell after a rainstorm, the joy of childhood, and the safety of home. The entrancing tune ended with a plaintive trill of longing that beckoned her to return home. Its power stunned her. Umniga's eyes shot open with shock and her hand stopped stroking. Pio looked quizzically at her, yet, reassured by her slight smile, he resumed his playing. The crew were unusually quiet, each yearning for home. Deo caught Umniga's eye, his wonder and joy plain as he wiped his tears away.

CHAPTER SIXTEEN

BALDEV and Karan were camped near The Four Ways with fifty warriors each. They had been waiting for several days.

'What's taking the old bastard so long?'

Karan, unperturbed by their wait, smiled at Baldev's ranting. 'If you had been summoned … commanded to appear by your enemies, you would make them wait too. It's just a game to save face—to try to maintain power in the relationship.'

'Relationship? Maintain power? We could just ride in there and take over,' Baldev muttered.

'Of course, but we don't want to—even if he is rattling your gourd. Allow him his illusions.'

Baldev grunted.

'He'll be here.'

The Four Ways was a large lake at which was located the only bridge spanning The Divide. The Upper Divide flowed into the lake from the north and out at the east. The Farangine River flowed to Faros from the south-west end of the lake and the Mitta River flowed from the north-west end to the coast. Nowhere else was The Divide able to be crossed. In places the river was exceedingly wide; at others the northern banks presented a towering rock face. The Upper Divide originated near Gopindar, the home of the Bear Clan in the Northern Forests. It began from Falcon's Lake, where another smaller river, The Falcontine, diverged from it and headed west to the sea. Here, across the Falcontine and the very beginning of the Upper Divide, the river could be crossed relatively easily. Yet, as it dissected Altaica, it widened, becoming a vast expanse, moving sluggishly along until it encountered the lower rapids. Not far from these rapids lay Hunters' Ford. This name was almost a misnomer. The river could be forded here by horse, but only for part of the year. With the lowland winter, spring rains, then the snow melt from the north, the time remaining that the river was actually fordable was slim. Even when it was passable, there was a danger from deep shifting holes that could break a horse's leg.

Karan and Baldev both looked up as a sentry posted at the stone bridge reached them. 'My lords, Lord Shahjahan approaches.'

The two men led their horses to the bridge, the quiet chink of their chain mail and the soft nickers of their horses made the only noise. Both wore a zirh gomlek: a coat of mail and chain lined with red silk that buckled up over many narrow engraved plates, which protected their torsos, yet allowed flexibility. Engraved metal dastanas protected their forearms, and metal greaves the lower half of their legs. Upon their heads they wore crested zirh kulahs: round metal helmets with mail coifs that protected their necks and the side of their faces. Karan's zirh kulah was crested with a black feather and Baldev's with a brown. They each wore an ornate kilij and matching daggers. Baldev wore two throwing axes that hung from a belt at his waist; the blades were engraved with the roaring maw of a bear. Karan's horse bore his bow and arrows each in black quivers, embossed with a silver horse. The combined effect of weapons and clan engravings was one of beauty and menace.

Shahjahan approached leisurely from the head of a column of troops, stopping at the far side of the bridge. Baldev and Karan handed their horses' reins to the nearest guard.

'My lord?' the concerned guard asked. Realising that their lords were going to walk onto the bridge, the troops' tension heightened perceptibly; each stood taller, more alert, poised. None were happy about the risk as their lords waited in the centre of the bridge. Shahjahan rode forward to meet them.

'He insults our offer of trust,' Baldev muttered.

Karan shrugged. 'He's probably too old to get off and walk.'

Shahjahan stopped before them. His horse was tense and fidgety. Froth dripped from its mouth as it tossed its head and showed the whites of its eyes. Karan and Baldev watched calmly—this was a game. Shahjahan was very subtly agitating his mount.

'Baldev, Karan.' He barely inclined his head.

'Lord Shahjahan, well met,' Karan replied smoothly. Baldev merely nodded. *Gods, they're not much different*, Karan thought. *Neither of them are subtle.*

Shahjahan couldn't help but admire their courage. They were easy prey now. His horse stomped its feet and sidled around them. 'Damn horse,' he said without rancour, as it danced around Karan and Baldev to stand between them and their troops. This was followed by the restless sounds of the Horse and Bear warriors as they prepared to move forward. Their captains, at the fore, maintained control, holding up their hands, restraining the troops eager to protect their lords. Instantly, they stilled.

Having seen the enemy preparing to move, the opposing Boar troops surged forward. Their superiors did not stop them. Shahjahan glared at them, bellowing, '*Hold!*' He was disappointed that they had not shown the same discipline as their opposition.

Karan drew his attention. 'I think this game has gone on long enough, yes?'

Shahjahan frowned at him, red in the face.

'Do you really want to re-ignite the war?'

Shahjahan appraised Karan. *Just like his father, balls of steel and cool as ice.* He glanced back at his troops, walked his now miraculously calm horse to the same side of the bridge as his men, then dismounted.

Karan held out his arm to him first.

Damn, he's quick. Shahjahan grinned ruefully, grabbing his forearm in greeting and, not to be outdone, pulled him into an embrace. 'Well met indeed, Lord Karan!' He quickly released him to repeat the greeting with Baldev.

'How do you want to do this?' Baldev asked, irritated with the game and posturing.

Shahjahan surveyed their troops. 'You and your men can ride with me. It will be a good show of trust.'

Baldev snorted. 'And your own troops?'

'Oh, they can ride around us.'

'You mean encircle us, like bloody captives.'

'Captives? Never.'

'We'll ride at the head with you, and our troops in columns behind their leaders. You on the outside.'

Shahjahan shrugged. 'Fine, whatever you want.'

They had made good time and stopped to rest the horses at Karan's suggestion, but in reality he had seen the strain on the old clan lord's face. The three men sat near one another as they ate. Their troops had separated into resentful clusters, several of which remained close and watchful of their lords.

'You must know something,' Shahjahan began. Karan noted the Boar Captain nearest stiffen on hearing this. He and Baldev paused in their repast, waiting—wary. Shahjahan grimaced. They would not like this, but it had to be done, better now than later. 'Asha has been injured.'

Baldev tensed. 'How?' came his curt reply.

Karan waited, saying nothing, but vigilant of rising tension amongst all the troops.

Shahjahan licked his lips, appearing briefly angry, then contrite.

Unaccustomed disquiet filled Karan. He had never seen Shahjahan nervous; angry, bitter, ranting, rollicking with laughter— yes, but not nervous.

Baldev's frown deepened, and he put his hands on his knees in preparation to stand.

'Peace, Baldev, peace.' Shahjahan held out his hands. 'It was not my doing and, by all that's holy, I wish it had not happened, but it has. The perpetrator of the attack ...'—at this Baldev shot to his feet—'… has been punished and word of his shame spread.'

Karan watched Baldev carefully, as his hands fisted and he began to pace. Shahjahan's nearest guards began to move toward their master. He held up his hand, forestalling them without a word. Karan's troops, in their strategic clusters, were alert and ready despite the fact that they had not moved.

Not taking his eyes from Baldev, Karan asked, 'Who assaulted Asha?' He needed his suspicions confirmed.

Shahjahan's face contorted. 'Ratilal.'

Baldev was rigid; his silent condemnation of Shahjahan chilled the air.

Shahjahan looked even more uncomfortable, but Karan appeared unperturbed. Both were well aware that in his current state Baldev was more dangerous than if he were ranting.

'Where is she?' Baldev demanded.

'On her way to Parlan, with Vikram and his handpicked guards.'

Baldev glowered at Karan before stalking away from them, spitting out, 'Time to go.'

The wind whipped strands from Umniga's long grey braid about her face. It bit through her cloak, tangling it around her legs, while she walked beside Isaura's unconscious form as she was carried from the boat. The others had been taken to the Sastravidya Lodge. She knew Deo would ensure that they were fed, tended and guarded.

Glancing back at the ocean and the build up of dark clouds that had chased them homeward, she was grateful that they had returned safely. Deo's son looked back too. 'We were lucky the weather held. Rana and Jalal favoured us.'

'I am thankful for that. I can think of few things more miserable than being at sea in a storm, with *your* father.'

Nada approached her. 'We've plenty of simple, plain soup for the survivors. I thought it would be easier on their stomachs and gods know they need it.' Umniga, clearly distracted, did not reply.

'Umniga?'

'Hmm … Oh, yes—of course, Nada. It was well done. You know as well as I what they are likely to need.' She paused. 'Nada, can we take this one—Isaura—to your house first?' Nada frowned. 'I merely want to get her clean and examine her for injuries in privacy, then she can go with the others.'

'Of course.' Her relief that the girl would not be staying in her house was obvious.

Once Isaura was placed on Nada's table, Umniga cleared the room of everyone except Nada and herself. Nada watched as Umniga leaned heavily on the table, with her head bowed, muttering a prayer.

The girl needs all the prayers she can get. She's more dead than alive, Nada thought. *Why bother trying to save her? I suppose if we clean her up now, we won't have to do it later for her passage to the underworld.* Concerned, she placed her hand on Umniga's shoulder, to be greeted by worried, brimming eyes.

Umniga inhaled deeply, composing herself and patted Nada's hand. 'Come, let's see what's to be done.'

Carefully, they disrobed Isaura. They had to cut the lacing on her clothes as it was too stiff and encrusted with grime to be undone. Nada held the garments away from herself with disgust.

'I don't think we'll ever get these clean.'

'Burn them.'

'What will she wear?'

'You must have something old lying around that she can wear. Something that doesn't fit the boys anymore—anything?'

Nada stiffened. 'I'll find something,' she muttered as she walked off.

Umniga examined Isaura. *The girl must have been fit and strong before this or she might not have lasted.* She could see white striations on her upper inner thigh, but no bruising. Umniga picked up Isaura's hand, examining it, flexing her fingers, wrist and elbow, feeling the movement for any sign of injury. She continued this process on both arms, ending each by moving the arm in the shoulder joint. Umniga wrinkled her nose as she checked her scalp and her hands became entangled in the girl's hair.

'Anything?' Nada had returned with a bundle of clothes.

'Nothing yet, other than that scar on her face. I can't do anything for that.' Umniga walked around the table and proceeded to examine the un-scarred leg, commencing at her feet and working her way to her hips in the same fashion as she had done for her arms. She placed both hands on the girl's hip bones, pressed down gently, then moved to the side of her body with the scarred leg.

Shaking her head in consternation, she moved to the girl's feet and wrapped a cloth around the ankle of the injured leg for grip. 'Hold her shoulders. No, hands under her armpits. Yes, perfect.' Umniga gave an abrupt, vigorous tug on the cloth and leg. She then moved back to her hips and pressed her hands down on the girl's hip bones, nodding to herself with a grim smile when she was finished. Bending over the striations on the injured leg, she ran her hands over the muscles, concentrating on the sensations under her finger tips, seeking anomalies as she did so. 'Sorry little one, this will hurt,' she muttered as she worked her fingers, back and forward, vigorously into the tissue. She grabbed the muscle then gave a brutal push. Umniga massaged the area. Satisfied, she straightened and caught Nada's disbelieving gaze. 'What?'

'Nothing, but … I just think you might be wasting your time. Umniga, she looks half dead.' The wind outside, which had been steadily gaining pitch, sent a defiant blast whistling down the chimney, gusting around them.

'Only *half* dead.' Umniga despondent, prayed Nada was wrong. 'Will you help me clean her up?'

Nada nodded, apologetic. 'Who knows, maybe it will help wake her. The sensations, to know people are near …'

Umniga narrowed her eyes; she was too old to be patronised.

When they were finished, Nada tossed her wash-cloth into the bucket of water at her feet. 'That's as good as we can do under the circumstances,' she said. They were both looking at her hair with disgust.

'One of us has to wash it, before something takes up residence in it.'

'We could just cut it,' Nada suggested hopefully.

Umniga shook her head. 'I'll do it, but first I must get something from my wagon.'

With her cloak wrapped tightly around her, she made her way quickly to the small barn where her wagon had been stored. The world was becoming dark. Flashes of lightning illuminated the interior of the heavy clouds. She shivered. It was only by the grace of the gods that they were not out in this weather.

She returned carrying a box containing several jars and a fine paint brush. Deo's son had just left the kitchen, having carted in more water, and Nada was already washing the girl's hair. Umniga covered her surprise quickly, with a ready smile of gratitude. 'I thought you might have cut it after all.'

'I was tempted—I still am,' she said with distaste.

'Nada, thank you.'

Nada nodded brusquely in acknowledgement while continuing her work.

Umniga broke the wax seal on a glazed jar and picked up a fine paint brush. Dipping the brush into the jar, she began to paint henna tattoos on Isaura. She painted the traditional oak and willow pattern around her ankles, wrists and finally, when Nada was finished with her hair, around her neck.

'What are you doing?'

'Trying to keep her here. But this is all I can do for now. I need to mix more paste and let it sit.' She rubbed her forehead in worry. 'There's so much more to do; I need Asha.' The wind had continued unabated while Umniga worked, yet now it was subdued—waiting.

>>>→

Asha sat before the campfire, barely able to keep her head upright.

However, as Vikram dabbed bloodroot on her injuries, she became painfully alert.

He saw her wince. 'I'm sorry. I'm trying to be gentle.'

'I know.' The first night Vikram had treated her, when the guards had seen the extent of her injuries, they clearly had been angry. They had arranged the wagon so that the supplies of blankets and clothes formed a mattress on which she could sleep, rather than sleeping on the ground in a bedroll. Since then, she had not had to do anything other than eat, drink and ride; all of which were difficult enough. They took care of her horse, Honey, grooming and saddling her each morning and rubbing her down at night. She was grateful for their care, but it made her feel useless and ashamed. Once Vikram had finished treating her back, Asha awkwardly rearranged her shirt.

She hung her head, tears in her eyes. Āsim, the older guard who had met her at the barbican of the inner bailey, sat down beside her.

'Asha,' he quietly said. 'Hold your head up, you have nothing to be ashamed of. You're alive because you fought and you've left that bastard with a permanent reminder of your strength and his shame. Not everyone could do that.'

She chose to stare into the fire rather than meet his eyes.

'Head up. The guards were only staring because they couldn't believe you could ride all day in your state, let alone without complaint and little rest.'

Now she met his gaze with a puzzled look.

Across the fire a young guard spoke up. 'It's true.' Other voices from the semi-darkness murmured assent.

Vikram said, 'Asha, they are angry at Ratilal and Shahjahan. But they are *proud* of you.'

'Asha, we help you because you are one of us,' Āsim added. 'There is no shame in it. Every warrior … At least every warrior who has fought a real battle …' Here he eyed the young men scornfully, causing indignation to erupt around the campfire. '… gets injured at some point and his comrades help him. It is the way of things— there is no shame. We do this for each other. Now you have comrades to help. You are our Kenati, no matter what.'

Asha was still embarrassed, but deeply moved.

'Umniga has told you of the old tales—the tales of the Battle Kenati?'

She nodded. 'Every child learns of those.'

'Not anymore, at least not in Faros.' A fleeting look of sadness crossed his face. 'In you, Asha, we will see a Battle Kenati like the tales of old.'

We're not at war. Then Asha realised what he had said. *Battle Kenati? I'm not a Battle Kenati!*

Āsim saw her astonishment and gave her a crooked grin. Before she could question him, a voice carried clearly from across the fire. 'Tell us, Asha, of the old tales. Tell us of Tarun and Safa.' More voices murmured encouragement.

'Shut up, you lot,' Āsim interrupted, 'and I'll tell you of Tarun and Safa.'

Vikram passed Asha some kirfir, a potent spirit. 'Drink.'

'I hate this stuff.'

'Drink. Trust me, you'll sleep like a log.'

Her face registered disgust as she sipped some of the clear spirit.

Āsim cocked an eyebrow at Vikram. 'Well, pass it around, captain.' The flask passed between them all as Āsim began the tale.

'During the first clan wars, when the Boar Clan was mighty and drove first the Horse Clan, then Bear Clan into the north, there lived a brave warrior named Tarun—our clan lord's son. Tarun was young and headstrong, but unbeaten in battle. He could throw a spear and hit his target from further than any other warrior. Once he met the great Bear warrior Kuhlchan on the field of battle and, riding at a gallop, he threw his spear so hard it pierced Kuhlchan's gut, stuck out through his back, and jettisoned him from his horse.

'Without his spear, Tarun hacked and slashed at the enemy with his kilij from his horse. When his horse went down, he fought on foot, wading his way through the blood and bodies of those he cut down. His men struggled to keep up. Having cut his way through the remnants of the Bear guard, he reached the body of Kuhlchan. He pulled his spear from Kuhlchan's gut, then grabbed the fallen warrior's mighty axe, severed his head with it and mounted it, dripping blood, upon his spear, which he thrust into the air with such a scream that it rang across the battlefield. It stopped the fighting as all eyes turned toward the disembodied head. The Bear warriors were devastated. Those who could fled to regroup. Many were taken prisoner. That night the Boar Clan was jubilant. Tarun had ended the battle. The warriors celebrated.

'During the night a young female warrior of the Bear stole into the camp, unnoticed by all the sentries. Her name was Safa. Safa was small, blonde and tough—like our Asha.'

This was not part of the original story. Asha opened her mouth to protest, but Vikram's gentle pressure on her arm warned her not to.

'When Tarun woke the next morning, it was to find Safa in his tent looking down at him with contempt. "Mighty warrior," she spat at him. "So mighty that I could have killed you in your sleep." Tarun was speechless—a first I might add—then he was livid. He leapt to his feet only to fall over, cursing; Safa had tied his boots together.'

Quiet laughter rumbled around the campfire.

Āsim continued, 'He cursed. She laughed as she nimbly leapt behind him, grabbed a handful of his hair and wrenched his head back with her blade at his throat.

'He demanded to know what she wanted. Safa told him, "You will meet our champion in the valley north of here in the morning. If our champion wins, you will return our warriors you hold prisoner, and end your pursuit of our clans." Smiling she added, "The Horse are now with us."

'This was not what he expected, but Tarun thought he could not lose. Had he not already beaten their best warrior? "If we win, what then?"

'Safa told him Horse and Bear would forever be subject to his rule. "Do you agree?"

'She pressed the dagger a little more into his flesh. He had little choice.

'Safa did not trust Tarun as far as she could kick him. She ensured that the agreement be witnessed before his captains and warriors. Tarun agreed to her terms. He was angry and humiliated that so small a woman—a girl really, he thought—could get past all his men and make demands of him. Demands he was now honour bound to fulfil or risk being shamed as a coward and oath breaker.

'The next morning the clans met at the valley. It had a wide, flat bottom. The slopes at one end were lined with the combined clans' warriors. At the other the Boar Clan had assembled. In the centre of the valley stood the champion for the combined clans, partially surrounded by their warriors, creating a semicircular shield wall. Tarun met their champion on the field. A cohort of Boar warriors completed the other half of the shield wall. They were now locked into the arena by their own troops.

'An eagle's cry was heard above and it echoed across the valley floor. Tarun spat in disgust when he recognised the slight warrior before him. It was Safa. She sat astride a small horse, waiting, her bow ready, arrow nocked. Tarun urged his horse a few steps forward, adjusting the grip on his spear. Each watched the other, waiting. Safa feinted, darting her horse forward directly at him. Her horse spun to the side as he threw his javelin. It narrowly missed her. She controlled her horse with only her legs, firing behind her as she rode.

'The first arrow sliced the skin of Tarun's horse's rump, causing it to squeal and falter, but he urged it onward. The next glanced off his bronze helmet as he grabbed another javelin from the quiver hanging from his saddle, then another off his cuirass. Safa's nimble little horse avoided the spears. Tarun reached for another javelin, sighted and threw. It flew straight and true, but Safa swerved and it embedded in the shield wall. Her horse was tiring, but her next two arrows impaled Tarun's horse's rump, yet another its chest. The horse screamed in pain, staggered and fell. Tarun catapulted through the air, hitting the ground hard and skidding through the dirt. Safa spun back on her horse, shooting an arrow into Tarun's thigh before he could stand properly. His horse lay peppered with arrows. She dismounted beside it, slitting its throat to end its misery. "Ready to give up, *mighty* warrior?" she said.

' "You!" he roared as he broke the arrow shaft, leaving only a small protuberance from his leg. "What are you waiting for?" Safa taunted him. Enraged, he lunged at her with his kilij. He was a skilled swordsman. Even so, he still took Safa too cheaply. He did not know Safa was Kenati. The eagle was her guardian. Like Fihr is Asha's guardian.'

At this Āsim leaned forward, as if telling his audience a secret. Many had all heard this tale before, but Asha noticed the others all crowded in to hear what came next.

'What Tarun didn't know was that Safa was Kuhlchan's sister. She was Kenati, yes, but her training was done sparring with her big brother. He'd taught her how to fight a larger, stronger opponent. But there was more—they had a secret. Safa had all the skills of a Kenati, but she could merge with her eagle and still fight.

'Safa wanted Tarun angry. She would use his anger and cockiness to her advantage. She was not wounded and she was quick. He was a good swordsman, but she danced around him, dodging his sword; often only narrowly avoiding his sharp blade. His leg was bleeding and he was tiring. Seeing this, she'd attacked and as she danced, her sword flashed in the sunlight. Tarun now found himself on the defensive. Safa's blade, which had glinted wickedly at first, was now bloodied. She slashed at his arms and legs, until they were red from a thousand cuts.'

Asha snorted in disbelief, but upon Āsim's glare she restrained herself.

'Finally, she sliced his leg above the arrow shaft. The leg buckled. Listing, he struggled to remain upright. She kicked the broken arrow shaft sticking out of his leg. He toppled sideways.

'Her voice was as cold and hard as her steel. "Enough?" Tarun lashed out, attempting to grab her leg and make her fall. He was frothing at the mouth. The eagle landed on his head, digging its claws into his scalp, its wings flapping wildly before he dislodged it and it flew off.'

Asha paled at this description.

'Blood from his head wounds seeped into his eyes. He was having trouble seeing. Safa struck his face, her fingers now like talons, and she raked her hand down half his face and over his eye, blinding him.'

Āsim paused and stared meaningfully at Asha, who was now conscious of the awestruck gaze of the younger guards.

'He reeled back. Safa drove her talons into the slash in his injured leg and tore a piece of flesh from him and threw it to her eagle. Now her knife was at his throat. "Have you had enough, mighty warrior?" she said. He yielded and the clan lord honoured his son's promise. Safa, the first Battle Kenati, ended the first clan war.'

Asha could feel many eyes upon her. She quietly stood up, swaying a little. 'Gods, I hate kirfir.' She left the circle around the campfire, stumbling in the dark when an arm shot out to steady her.

She looked around to see Āsim. 'You really can't handle your grog, can you, girl?'

'I'm fine. My eyes haven't adjusted to the dark after looking at the fire,' she mumbled.

He chuckled. 'I see. Since you can't see straight, I'll just help you to the wagon.' She tried to shake her arm free of his grip, but could not.

She sighed and nodded. 'Fine.' Crawling into the back of the wagon, she drew her cloak about her, pulled its hood up and a blanket over her. 'Thanks,' she said quietly as Āsim turned away. Before he got too far, she called him back. 'Āsim, why?' He quirked an eyebrow at her. 'Why that story? And why change it? Safa didn't have an eagle, she had a gyrfalcon and I don't remember the bit about raking his face with her claws.'

'Asha, there are so many similarities between your tale and Safa's that a blind man could see them. So what if I changed the bird to match yours?'

'You made sure that they recognised the similarities. My hair colour, the bird …'

'Yes, and the scarring of his face. All the tales acknowledge that he came out of that battle permanently scarred. All tales grow in the telling. Asha, change is coming. I've felt it for a while, but now with these strangers arriving …' He shuddered, shaking his head. 'Change is coming. But our clan has already been changing for a while and not for the better. Umniga knows it and so do you. These young men that Vikram has here, they are all good young lads. Some are from the country, where you and Umniga have visited to teach and keep alive our old ways, but some come from Faros, where they don't know the tales or the Lore very well. They need something to believe in.' She stared at him, speechless. 'Don't look at me so, girl. How do you think legends are born?'

CHAPTER SEVENTEEN

ELENA had gone to sleep in Curro's arms, blissful, listening to the wind battering at the timber shutters of the lodge, grateful that they were not still at sea.

The survivors had been led from the beach down a narrow path amidst sand dunes to a small fishing village. The sand gave way to dirt and the path broadened to a street with a large white cedar in a village square. The buildings were rectangular, lower and longer than their own, with timber cut log walls and gable thatched roofs. The doors of each cottage were in the narrow end walls and were brightly painted as were the timber shutters. The gables protruded deeply over the doors to form a porch. There was a single trading post that was larger than the other buildings and had a shingled roof. Cottages were surrounded with well tended gardens, but there were few flowers—everything had been given over to the growing of food.

Figures appeared in the windows to close the shutters before the storm hit, and Elena could see their curious yet hostile glances directed at the bedraggled survivors. As they walked the shutters were drawn closed and the welcoming lights flicked out one by one along the street and surrounding slopes. Their attention was directed solely to the largest building that lay at the top of the street. Long, wide and imposing, Elena had heard the fishermen call this the Sastravidya Lodge; of all the buildings she had seen this looked the one most able to imprison them. A lantern hung at the front door, though she found its poor light no comfort at all.

Isaura was gone, probably dead. She could muster little sorrow for

Isaura, though she knew she had done her best. Maybe if Isaura had not wanted Curro or if she'd not been Hill Clan, they could have been friends, she mused. Elena's pity was for Nicanor and Curro, but she could console Curro and that made her exultant. Now she would not have to worry, she would not have to compete.

She woke fully as Curro's arm slipped from around her; she hastily reached out to grab him as he left her.

'It's all right, go back to sleep. They've brought Isa back. I want to see how she is.'

Isa! Through half-lidded eyes she saw Isaura being carried in the arms of a strong young man following Umniga, who carried a narrow mattress. Nicanor, Lucia, Pio and Curro gathered around as Isaura was laid down on the mattress in a corner, not far from them. Elena wanted to scream; she wished she could, or at least roll over and pretend that this was not happening. *Damn it!*

She rose and stood beside Curro, taking his hand and leaning her head on his shoulder. Elena felt indignation well up inside her at the sight of Isaura. She'd clearly been bathed, her hair washed and she was wearing clean clothes. Admittedly, they were old and patched, but they were clean. *More special treatment. Gods, does it never end?* Then the old woman covered her with an ornate cloak. Elena let go of Curro's hand and went back to her spot, from where she watched them hover about Isaura. *He hasn't even noticed I've gone.* Elena turned her attention to Pio, whose expression was full of concern. *He's my nephew, damn it. He never hangs off my every word.* She lay down, resentment consuming her, as the storm resumed in earnest.

Pio held Lucia's and Nicanor's hands. Isaura was back, but she was no better. He stifled a sob. Umniga covered her with her cloak, but spun to face Pio when she heard him sniffling.

'No,' she said, putting her fingers on the sides of his mouth and pulling them into a parody of a smile. He blinked, gulping to hold back his tears, understanding her tone. 'Hope,' Umniga told him. She guided him to sit beside Isaura. Pio's hands still held his flute, which she raised to his lips. Before he could begin she hummed the tune he had played on the boat, which Pio dutifully copied.

Lucia, confused, was watching Pio with concern and was about to interrupt. Nicanor reached for her hand, drawing her away.

'Come, it will resolve itself one way or another.'

'But, watching him, it's … She's giving him hope where there is none. It's not fair on him.'

Nicanor nodded, his expression sad. 'I know, we'll just be there at the end.'

Curro watched them leave, knelt down, placed a kiss on Pio's forehead and a hand on Isaura's brow, and briefly bowed his head. Only when he rose did he realise that Elena was gone.

Elena was curled tightly on her side. She felt Curro spoon behind her, brushing the hair gently from her forehead. He kissed her tenderly there, and pulled her into his embrace. She relaxed, but all she could think of was the way the same hand had tenderly rested on Isaura's brow.

>>—→

Umniga guessed the time to be nearly midnight. The henna paste had sat for long enough, so she grabbed it and headed for the Sastravidya Lodge.

Elena tried to listen to the soft breathing of those sleeping around her over the wind and rain battering down outside. Cautiously, she began to slide from under Curro's arm. He stirred. She waited, utterly still, trying to maintain the slow regular breathing of a sleeper, while her heart was pounding. Elena felt certain that someone must hear her. Nothing. She slid out completely from under his arm. His hand reached out to touch her back, then slid down to the floor. Elena lay curled on her side, waiting. He did not reach out again. Certain he was asleep, she sat up and looked toward where she knew Isaura lay. No one would suspect. It would appear as if she died in her sleep, just as everyone was expecting.

Peering through the darkness, she wondered if she could make it to Isaura without waking the others. She could barely see. Flashes of lightning through the cracks around the shutters provided brief fractured visions of the room. Most likely, she would stumble over someone and then what excuse could she offer for sneaking around in the dark? Was it worth it? Elena put her head in her hands. *What's wrong with me?* She tried to remind herself that Curro was with her; he married *her*. It didn't work, or at least not for long. Always there was this nagging doubt. *Stop it!* He said there was nothing between them; that there never had been. Elena moaned softly, shaking her head. *Why can't I stop?*

Elena lifted her head quickly, certain she heard a noise. She cocked her head, straining to hear it again. Unnerved, she lay back down next to Curro and snuggled into his side.

Umniga entered the lodge, silently cursing the storm as she struggled to keep a candle alight. By its minimal glow she trod softly, trying not to disturb the sleepers. Sitting beside Isaura, she undid the ties of the girl's wraparound jacket and shirt. Carefully Umniga began to paint.

The candle stub had burned low, so Umniga lit another. It had been hours since she began, but she was nearly finished. The storm had ended, yet she had not noticed. Rubbing her eyes and neck, she tried to ease the tension in her shoulders. Her old knees felt like they would never move again. A hand touched her shoulder and she jerked in fright. It was Pio's mother.

Lucia had watched the old woman enter, thinking she was checking on Isaura, and then gone back to sleep. When she woke, the old woman was still there and yet many hours must have passed; the pre-dawn light was filtering through the shutters and she could hear birds chirping nearby. Curious, she had risen and approached Umniga. Lucia could see signs of fatigue—the strain on her face and her obvious discomfort—so she began to massage Umniga's shoulders. It was then, with her head bent to her task, that she noticed what Umniga had been doing. She stared at Isaura in astonishment and her hands involuntarily stopped massaging.

Umniga patted her hand and gestured for her to sit. Still staring in disbelief, she sat like an automaton. Umniga chuckled, pleased at her reaction. Cheekily, she waved her hands in front of Lucia's face to attract her attention. Lucia blushed, but determined to make amends, she proceeded to introduce herself as Pio had instructed her.

Immediately on finishing her speech, Lucia again found herself staring again at her sleeping friend. Isaura's torso was covered in a henna tattoo of a tree—a weeping willow. The myriad roots of the tree covered her womb, her pubis and disappeared between her legs. The trunk extended to her breast bone, where divergent branches ranged over and around her breasts to the base of her throat and over her shoulders, with the tips of the branches ending on her upper arms. Leafy willow fronds hung gracefully from the branches. The upper ones entwined with the circular pattern Umniga had drawn earlier around Isaura's neck.

'Beautiful,' Lucia whispered.

Umniga smiled as she put the finishing touches on the tattoos. The willow fronds on Isaura's upper arms were drawn longer, until they merged with the pattern around her wrists. Finally satisfied, Umniga put down her brush. To bind the wrists, neck and ankles with the sacred symbols was not unusual; the tree, though, was a rare practice. She had only been told what it should look like when she was an apprentice; she had not drawn it before. She had endeavoured to make it as detailed as possible and it *felt* correct. As she had drawn, she had hummed Pio's tune and stopped thinking about the details of her painting. Instead, she felt how the pattern worked. The 'whole' had disappeared as she immersed herself in the small details; she was proud of her work.

'Beautiful,' Umniga repeated Lucia's word. It was clear by her tone what it had meant.

Lucia, still awestruck, was inexplicably almost moved to tears. She asked, 'Why?' in Umniga's tongue.

Umniga smiled sadly, sighing, wishing Lucia had the knowledge to understand. 'There is still hope, but we must be quick.'

Asha's party attracted a lot of attention when it finally reached Parlan. Guards from Faros were an unusual sight in the countryside. They were directed to the lodge, where they met Umniga.

After one look at Asha, a wave of fury coursed through Umniga.

'Who did this?' she spat. Gently, she examined Asha's neck. 'There's more, isn't there?'

Asha said nothing.

Instead, Vikram replied in a subdued tone, 'Her head, ribs, some bruises.'

'And where were you?' Umniga yelled, pushing him. 'Shahjahan?' Silence. 'No, or you wouldn't be here with him. Who?'

'Ratilal.'

'Bastard!' Umniga fumed. 'I'll damn well kill him for this.' The words that poured forth from her mouth as she pounded the ground before them astonished both Vikram and Asha.

After several minutes, Vikram began to smile. He glanced sideways at Asha, who remained rigidly straight-faced.

'Wipe that smile off your face, young man. What are you laughing for?'

Vikram shook his head, unable to form words.

'Are you finished now?' a gruff voice said.

'Āsim?' Umniga rolled her eyes. 'Wonderful! Will one of you please explain? Vikram?'

By the end of the tale she was calmer, having heard about Shahjahan's care of Asha and knowing that Ratilal had been punished. Though she felt execution would have been far more appropriate than whipping. She held Asha's face in her hands and said slowly and clearly, 'You did well, child.' Then she inspected the provisions they had brought. 'Excellent,' she muttered. 'It's about time the old goat got his head out from up his arse and acted like a leader.' She looked at Vikram. 'Well, you're in charge. They all stink, need to wash, need new clothes. We've kept them confined, except for the boy.'

'Boy?'

'You'll see. Anyway, now you're here you can sort that lot out.' She waved her hand airily. 'I need Asha now. Come on.' She took Asha's hand and led her into the lodge.

The noise outside and the arrival of soldiers had caused a flurry of anxiety inside the lodge. Asha and Umniga were the object of hopeful, nervous eyes. Several women approached them timidly, begging in their strange language. Umniga scowled and brushed them aside.

Asha wrinkled her nose in disgust. 'You were right about the smell. Why didn't you let them bathe?'

'I've had enough to do without looking after that lot. Besides, it was hard enough to get clean clothes for the girl, let alone the rest of them. They'd stink just as bad if they put their own clothes back on. Come on, we've more work to do yet. Let Vikram sort them out.'

'This is the one?' Asha dropped to her knees beside Isaura. 'How long has she been like this?'

Umniga shrugged, her disappointment clear. 'Too long.'

'What's wrong?'

'She's gone.'

'Gone?'

'Travelling.'

'Spirit walking?' Asha was astonished.

'Well, she hasn't got in a cart and driven off! Gods, girl, how hard did you hit your head?'

'How? She has a guardian?'

'No.'

'Shit.'

'Now, you understand.'

'It's not possible.'

'Of course it is—she's done it.'

'You looked for her?'

'Of course, but wherever she is, trust me, it's not nearby and her trail was fading.'

Asha plopped on her behind, staring at the girl dismally. 'All our efforts … What are we going to do?'

'What we can—the Ritual of Samara.'

Asha gaped at her. 'But it's only been performed once. Centuries ago. Do you know how?'

'Girl, we are all taught how. It's part of our training … We just haven't had to do it before.' Asha nodded dumbly. 'Now, I need your help with the rest of the tattoos. We'll need to get more supplies from the wagon.'

At this point, Vikram entered, accompanied by Āsim and some of the guards. A commotion broke out amongst those nearest the door. The women shied away. Those with children gathered them and huddled near their husbands. Vikram dropped a bundle of clothes and a bar of soap on the floor and pointed to the nearest male, who made no move toward it. He signalled to Āsim to bring the man forward. His wife began wailing and clinging to him, trying to prevent Āsim taking him; the man shook his head, resisting.

'Enough, Āsim. They're too scared to think.'

Curro stood up and proceeded to move forward. Elena made to grab his arm, but Lucia put her hand out, bidding her to stop. Nicanor joined him. Together, they moved forward to investigate. Vikram watched these two men step forward, obviously the only ones, he thought, with any form of courage. He smiled and nudged the pile with his toe.

Curro picked up the bundle and turned with a grin to the others. 'It's just soap and clothes. Come on, unless you've gotten used to smelling like you fell in the cess pit at the back of Standon's tavern.' He and Nicanor made to leave the building. Vikram raised his hand, stopping them briefly. He made sure everyone saw his gestures. He held up one finger and pointed to the men. Then he held up two fingers and pointed to the women. He repeated the gesture. Surely they would understand.

'Men first. Ladies second,' Nicanor said loudly as he and Curro departed.

Āsim made them stand in plain sight of those inside. Daniel and Jaime followed promptly. They waited a few minutes for the others to gain the courage to step outside. Slowly the remaining men emerged.

Deo was leaning against the wagon, peering into its contents. He whistled and one of his grandsons came running, with Pio straggling along behind. Hoisting his grandson up, he indicated the pile of clothes. 'See if those silly buggers in Faros put anything in for a boy. We'll make sure he gets first pick.' Pio reached his side and eyed the wagon curiously. The boy rummaged around and held up a plain coarse shirt. Deo gauged it for size and nodded, before it was dropped into Pio's hands. Pio was now on tiptoes trying to see in, but the wagon was far too tall. A jacket was raised. 'Not unless you want Pio to look like a pansy,' Deo said. Pants? No, too big. Skirt? Pio shook his head—definitely not.

A heavy hand landed on Deo's shoulder. 'Just what do you think you are doing, old man?' Āsim demanded. 'This is the clan lord's property.'

Deo jumped in fright. 'Just making sure the boy gets some decent clothing.' Pio had rushed to Nicanor, but still held the shirt tightly.

'Out!' Vikram directed the boy in the wagon. He jumped down and stood behind his grandfather.

Deo stiffened. 'We were simply looking for something for the boy. All we could find was that shirt. Didn't they tell you there were children in this lot?'

'Enough.' Vikram gestured to Āsim, who promptly climbed into the wagon.

'You've made a bloody mess,' Āsim grumbled. He quickly sorted out the detritus left in the boy's wake. He emerged with child-sized pants and a jacket. He leaned down, holding them out for Pio. With Deo's encouragement, Pio walked up bravely and accepted the clothes.

Pio bowed slightly, then formally said in Altaican, 'Thank you.' He stared at this big old man leaning down at him, whose eyebrows had risen so high they seemed to disappear into his hairline.

'This is obviously the boy Umniga has been letting roam,' Vikram stated blandly.

'Aye, commander,' Deo said. 'He's a good lad. He learns fast and he's done no harm.'

'Get the rest kitted with new clothes, Āsim. Then we'll take them to the river.'

As the men were escorted under guard to the river, Jaime asked, 'Nic? Do you really think we are going to bathe? They could just be taking us away to kill us.'

Daniel answered in a tired voice. 'Why give us new clothes then? Why feed us?'

Pio's hand tightened in Nicanor's and he piped up. 'They are helping us—that's all.'

'Jaime,' Nicanor said.

'Yes?'

'Shut up.'

⫸⟶

Inside the lodge the women waited; some were distraught and crying, some sat resignedly.

'Will they be hurt, do you think?' Gabriela asked Lucia.

Lucia shook her head in exasperation. 'They're *bathing* … How is that going to harm them? Look, if they wanted us dead, we would be.' She patted Gabriela's hand. 'It will be fine.'

Umniga and Asha unpacked their brushes and together began to remove Isaura's top.

Lucia glanced around at the other women. Many were absorbed in their own misery, but a few were keenly watching what the old woman and her friend were doing to Isaura; Elena sat amongst them, whispering. Lucia touched Umniga's arm, holding up her index finger. 'Wait?' Umniga nodded. 'Gabi, sit just there. I'll get Elena. If we all sit in a semicircle on this side, we can shield her from view.'

Gabriela looked with distaste at the gawkers. 'Absolutely.'

Lucia approached Elena. 'Leni, I need your help.' Elena remained mute. 'Elena, come with me, please?'

'What do you need help with, Lucia?' Elena replied in a saccharine tone.

Inwardly, Lucia was furious. She knew that Elena wanted her to say it was for Isaura, but that would draw more unwanted attention to the poor girl.

She reached out casually, yet took Elena's upper arm in a vice-like grip. 'Come, I'll show you—it will be easier.' Elena winced, but allowed herself to be towed along. Lucia whispered harshly in her ear, 'I don't know what is wrong with you, but I am sick and tired of it. You pour poison in their ears about Isa—I know it.'

'I haven't ...' Elena winced again as Lucia dragged her across the room.

'Don't lie to me!'

'I'm not ...'

'Pio can lie better than you.' Lucia sighed, frustrated and despairing of Elena. 'This will lead to your own downfall. By all that we hold sacred, stop this path you are on. You must stop!'

Elena was shaken. Lucia had never talked to her like this. Maybe she was right.

Umniga scowled, watching as Lucia brought another woman to join them.

'What is it?' Asha asked.

'I don't like that one. Her aura, it's dark, almost malignant. Take a look soon with Fihr. Tell me what you see.'

Elena saw the old woman scowl at her, then felt her bitterness rise again.

'Now sit here, like that,' Lucia instructed.

'Why?' came the sullen response.

'If you were in Isa's position, would you like everyone to see you like this?'

'I'm not and will never be in her position. There is something unholy happening here—the way they treat her—the special treatment,' she hissed.

'Your nephew has received *special treatment* from them too. Are you going to talk about him like this?' Lucia leaned in so they were nose to nose, before she said with open hostility and disgust, 'Just sit there and do not speak again.'

'I like that one though,' Umniga said to Asha, indicating Lucia. Now that Isaura was largely shielded from view, Asha and Umniga finished removing her wraparound top, loosened her drawstring pants and rolled her onto her stomach. 'Both trees must interlink.'

Asha nodded. 'I'm not sure where to start.'

'Just start at the base, her buttocks, and work up. Relax—it will come.' Together they painted an oak tree on Isaura's back. Umniga began humming Pio's tune and Asha joined in. The roots commenced at her buttocks, travelling across and down between her legs, where they intertwined with the willow roots. The strong trunk travelled up her spine to her shoulder blades, where it split into branches and a canopy that spanned to her neck, over her shoulders and upper arms, to mingle with the willow branches. Umniga pulled Isaura's arms to her sides and they continued the oak roots pattern across from her buttocks to her wrists, connecting with the willow. Asha continued the oak roots down her legs to her ankles.

'That's well done, we will have to finish the front likewise.'

Elena watched with horrified fascination as these strange women painted Isaura so carefully. Gabriela was transfixed and clutched Lucia's hand, as they quietly hummed the same tune as Umniga and Asha.

When they were finished and Gabriela could see the whole pattern of tattoos, she whispered, 'Magnificent.'

Without a word, only a look of disgust, Elena left them.

CHAPTER EIGHTEEN

BALDEV had said little since his earlier outburst and it was clear that he was impatient at their pace. Karan decided he'd had enough of his sullen anger. Baldev was at the river, refreshing himself and filling his water skin. Karan stood behind him, leaning against a tree, with his arms crossed.

Baldev heard Karan arrive—knew he was waiting. Determined to take his time, he stripped off his shirt and poured water over his bare torso, enjoying the chill water on his sore muscles. He dried himself with his shirt, before putting it on and turning to face Karan with a surprised look.

Karan scowled. 'Don't give me that. You knew I was there.' Baldev made to walk past him, but Karan grabbed his arm. He shrugged free. 'Wait.' Karan's voice, while calm, had an edge of steel to it. 'You can't keep acting like this. We must be unified and focused.' Baldev grunted. 'What is wrong?'

A look of fury crossed Baldev's face. 'Asha.'

'Asha?'

'Asha. It was *your* idea to send her there.'

'Yes, I wanted her there and it worked.'

Baldev gripped his friend's jacket and shoved him against the tree. 'She could have been killed.'

'Yes, she could have, but she wasn't. We both saw Shahjahan as the potential problem, but not one who would kill her.' Baldev growled and drove him harder against the tree. Karan continued, 'It was not Shahjahan who hurt her. *Neither* of us thought of Ratilal.' *I didn't think he'd dare in his father's house.* He placed his hands around Baldev's wrists and tried to force them away from him. 'Does she know how you feel?'

Baldev blinked, a little stunned, and let go. 'What? Ah … no.' He stepped back, ran his hands through his hair and looked sheepishly at Karan. 'Ah … sorry.'

Karan shrugged. 'Doesn't matter. But you must control yourself.'

'I want to get to her! We are going so damn slow.'

'You'll get there. This pace suits me—the horses will remain fresh.' Baldev scowled. 'Yes, be mad, but not like this. Keep your anger deep in here.' He tapped Baldev's chest. 'Otherwise you put her in more danger. If they think she is of personal importance to you, she will be at risk. That, and you are making our alliance seem strained.'

'I'll kill Ratilal one day.'

'Someone should, but not yet, not now. We have a chance here with Shahjahan to make a formal peace—let's use it. Long term, it could benefit everyone.'

Baldev nodded reluctantly. 'You're always right, aren't you?' Karan gave him a sardonic grin. Baldev continued, 'I don't know how you do it. Always cool, controlled, always analysing. I know you like Asha, you don't want her hurt, but you switch off. You have accepted what happened.'

'I am angry, Baldev, believe me. The fact that this happened at all, let alone in the home of her clan lord, is a disgrace, but Asha is a Kenati and a soldier. She knows her duty and the risks involved in combat.'

'This was not combat.'

'No, it wasn't. If she had been armed, things may have been different.'

'She should have been.'

'Yes, but have you thought about why she wasn't? Why is Shahjahan removing weapons from his own people who visit the keep? What has he to fear? And whom?' He gave him pause to think, before continuing, 'We need a formal peace, we need improved relations between our clans, so he can concentrate on putting his house in order. That will enable us to increase our spy network and that will benefit us.'

'Thank the gods you're my friend and not my enemy.'

A genuine smile lit Karan's face. 'You may drive me crazy, but I'll always be your friend.'

>>>—→

Gabriela was laughing as they walked back from the river. She was clean. Her clothes were clean. Clean and not hungry or thirsty! Three simple things she swore she would never take for granted again.

'Did you see the guards' faces when Umniga made them turn around? I still can't believe she did that for us—one little old lady.' Gabriela shook her head in disbelief.

'I can,' Lucia said, laughing. 'She's a little old lady with clout.'

'I don't think I could have bathed with them looking on.' Even Elena was smiling.

'I was contemplating jumping in clothes and all—just scrubbing the lot,' Lucia said.

Gabriela wrinkled her nose in disgust. 'Ewww!' Mischievous giggles burst forth. 'I was going to wash no matter who was watching.'

'Gabi!' Elena was scandalised.

'I couldn't stand the smell any longer,' she said, grinning. 'I doubt they could either.' She linked her arm in Lucia's. 'Oh, I feel so good!' she cried. 'Don't you feel good?'

Lucia nodded. 'Yes, but what's to happen now?'

'Now? Oh! For the moment I don't care. We're off that boat. We're away from war. We are safe. This is the chance that we were waiting for—that we were hoping for!'

Asha and Umniga walked behind the group, watching the interactions between the three closely. Lucia and Gabriela were buoyant; although Elena smiled she remained aloof from the others. If this woman wasn't happy now, when would she be?

Asha had been deep in thought, but now spoke. 'Umniga, the Ritual of Samara requires a male and female Kenati from each clan and the seeker.'

'Correct,' Umniga answered, although she was still distracted by the three women ahead.

'We can't succeed. Juhangir is dead. We have no male Kenati in the Boar Clan.'

'That's what the boy's for.'

'Pio?'

'Yes.'

'You think he's Kenati?'

'Yes. I'm still worried about how hard you hit your head, little whelp,' she said wryly.

'He has no guardian.'

'I don't think they have any understanding of such things where he came from. If they did, Isaura would have been trained.'

'And?'

'And? Well, he has only just arrived and he is still young. I'm hoping a guardian will present itself.'

'In time for the ritual?' Asha sounded sceptical.

'Maybe.'

'But he'll need one. He has no training … how?' Asha was despondent. They had gone to so much trouble and now more obstacles were in their way.

Umniga seemed nonchalant. 'Who knows? With a completed circle, maybe his presence will be enough.'

'How?'

Umniga frowned. 'Asha, I hope that it may be enough for him to sit in the circle with you and play.'

'Play?'

'Asha,' Umniga had slowed her speech as if she was talking to a simpleton, 'Pio will be a Kenati—a *Bard* Kenati. Of that I am absolutely certain. With a full circle and his playing, even without training, it might be enough.'

'*Might?*'

Umniga's frown chastised her. 'We can only try,' she replied, shrugging. They walked in silence for a while.

'A Bard Kenati?' Asha said in wonder. Umniga nodded. 'We have not had a Bard Kenati in generations. You are certain?'

'Oh yes. I think he is the only reason the girl is still alive.'

Asha's eyes widened with sudden understanding. 'He's anchoring her.'

She nodded. 'I don't think we have much time though. We need to get her to the others and perform the ritual as soon as possible. I would like us to leave with her and Pio in the wagon now, but the situation is, as always, more complicated by the clan lords. If I overstep, I could ruin everything.'

'Yes, well, we could just take them—Shahjahan wouldn't know.'

'Possibly, but the families …'

'It's too many.'

'And too far.'

'We could ready the wagon anyway. Vikram may help.'

'Vikram is a good man, but you misjudge his loyalty. He will not disobey his clan lord and should he do so, Shahjahan would flay him and his men.'

'He doesn't have to know.'

'They'd know, the others would know. Too many to keep it a secret. We'd have to get them to come quietly without their guards knowing and without their friends; their friends may object. That will be our last resort. No, we just have to wait. If I know the lords, they'll be here very soon.'

➤

Shahjahan had not ventured far from Faros for a long time—too long, he realised, from the reaction of his people as they travelled along. Ratilal and some of his generals had been out in the countryside on various unsuccessful missions to try to reclaim their lost territory. The further from the capital they travelled, the less friendly became the greetings and observation of the group. Initially, children had fled at the sight of the soldiers. Workers in the fields remained, but were obviously on alert. When they realised that it was Shahjahan and the other clan lords, their wariness dropped, but there were no smiling faces.

Shahjahan had plenty of time to think as they rode and his anger at their reactions had faded. He compared their reactions of today with those he remembered from years ago; he did not like the comparison. Gone was the joy at seeing a procession from Faros, what replaced it was trepidation. He was relieved and grateful that neither Karan nor Baldev commented on their reception. As they progressed, word seemed to have travelled ahead to the villages they passed through that *he* was coming, and they saw more smiling faces amongst the older members of these communities, but too many were still wary.

When they reached Parlan, all the villagers gathered at its entrance. Shahjahan stopped and dismounted as Vikram approached him. The villagers gave the formal greeting gesture commencing with their hands on their hearts, followed by a low bow as they moved their hands wide apart, palms up. Karan and Baldev remained mounted, not wanting to detract from the greeting to Shahjahan.

'Clan lord,' Vikram began. 'You have made good time. The strangers are in the lodge.'

Shahjahan nodded in greeting. 'People of Parlan. It has been too long since I have travelled so far from Faros and I am honoured by your greeting. I'm sure that you have heard, nevertheless I shall tell you, that lords Karan and Baldev ride with me to investigate the strangers we found at sea. In this, the clans are united.'

Karan and Baldev dismounted and faced the villagers, greeting them as formally as they had Shahjahan.

'Come, my friends—let us see what we are dealing with.'

Now that they had done all they could for Isaura, Umniga and Asha were tending to the other villagers. It was an easy task now that they had food and water in their bellies—miraculously all that remained to do was some simple healing. They paused, looking up at the sound of approaching voices.

'The clan lords,' Asha murmured. Umniga nodded.

Asha began to move toward the door, but Umniga restrained her. 'Just wait, let him come.'

'He's our lord.'

Umniga's face soured. 'As you will.' She moved to Isaura and her friends and waited.

Asha greeted Shahjahan formally at the door. 'High …' she corrected herself, 'Clan lord, welcome.'

Karan and Baldev looked at each other with brows raised. They had heard this salutation slip from several of the Boar guards, who had also hastily corrected themselves. Karan thought, *Why 'high lord'? Has someone else the title of 'lord'? Ratilal?* They would need to expand their network of spies. He broke from his reverie as he heard Baldev emit a low growl.

The sight of Asha's bruises made Baldev furious. At her furtive glance, he attempted to wipe the scowl from his face and control the emotions roiling within him. He did not want her thinking he was angry with her. His fury quickly changed to relief that she was alive and obviously healing, though he fought the powerful desire to simply embrace her and take her away. She would think him insane. She had no idea how he felt.

Shahjahan began talking to Asha and moving through the survivors. Baldev was still marshalling his emotions and had not really heard what was being said, when Karan nudged him, then grabbed his elbow and led him along whispering, 'Focus! You give too much away. If you lose your temper now we are done for.'

As they walked through the group, Asha was describing the strangers' state of health and what had been done for them so far. Vikram added only that so far they had presented no threat whatsoever to the Altaicans and that, due to the language problems, they had managed to discover only a little about them. It was clear that these people were not rich—the clothes they had been wearing when found, although well made, were sturdy and simple; their skin bore the callouses of working men and women. They knew that two men were a smith and a carpenter and the unconscious woman was some sort of healer. The lords listened quietly while they surveyed the still bedraggled people before them, finally stopping before Umniga.

Umniga gave only half of the formal greeting, merely bowing perfunctorily before Shahjahan. Karan saw Shahjahan narrow his eyes at Umniga and prayed to Rana and Jalal that these two would deal peacefully with each other and that Umniga would not lose sight of their goal.

'Well met, Umniga.' Shahjahan countered her with scrupulous courtesy and a full formal greeting.

Umniga's eyes were hard as she was forced to reply, 'Well met, Clan Lord Shahjahan.'

Pio was sitting at her feet beside Isaura. Upon the entrance of the three large men, he had stopped playing his flute. Now he looked between the old man and Umniga with worry. Umniga was angry. The old man looked annoyed. He felt the tension between them build like static in the air before a storm. Suddenly, he stood. Gripping his flute tightly, he stepped forward between them. Nicanor moved to grab him.

Vikram intercepted Nicanor, his hand on his sword. The old man's eyes snapped from Umniga to Nicanor, then to Pio. Pio gripped his flute so tightly he was afraid it would break. Silently he gave it to Umniga. He drew a breath and introduced himself as he had been taught.

Shahjahan appeared stunned and said nothing. Umniga's lips were twitching in amusement at the look on his face. Baldev laughed uproariously and couldn't master himself to respond. Karan's eyes twinkled with amusement as Pio began to look worried and back away.

Karan bowed low to Pio and returned his formal introduction and greeting. He winked at Pio as he stood. 'Baldev, I'm not sure who is scaring him the most—you braying like a donkey, or Shahjahan.'

Shahjahan, rueful, laughed at Baldev, before returning Pio's formal bow. 'If only I had a company of warriors as brave as this boy.'

Baldev's laughter ceased, though following Karan's example his grin remained fixed in place as he bowed to Pio. 'Well met, little man. Let's hope they all have such stout hearts.'

'Pio.' Lucia, clearly unimpressed with her son, was holding out her hand, beckoning him. He went quickly to her and she grabbed his hand and hauled him against her side, eyeing the men warily. Nicanor moved beside them protectively.

'They don't look like much. Do you know why they were on the boat?'

'Not yet, my lord. We have been occupied with other tasks.'

'I hope this wasn't a waste of time. Come, we'll talk outside.' Shahjahan spun on his heel to leave.

'My lords, there is something you should see first,' Umniga said, interrupting their exit.

Shahjahan frowned. 'You are not in charge here, old woman.'

Umniga bit back a retort before smoothly continuing, 'Nevertheless, Lord Karan and Lord Baldev may want to see this, and by your grace they will.'

Shahjahan nodded tersely before she led them to Nicanor's tool box. Baldev examined the bear carving closely. 'Fine work. Which one did this?'

'The *boy's* father, Nicanor is his name.'

Shahjahan cast an appraising glance at Nicanor. He did not fail to note the emphasis in Umniga's speech. He was certain that there were more plans afoot than his.

'The other one, his brother—Curro—has the tools of a smith. The boat's figurehead was a horse.'

'Enough, Umniga,' Shahjahan warned.

'Shahjahan, perhaps we could try to find out now why they were on the boat, before we confer?' Karan suggested.

Nicanor and Curro tensed as the three lords approached them and their family and friends sitting nearby. Jaime protectively moved Gabriela slightly behind him. Daniel, however, sat disinterested to the side.

Baldev gave a toothy grin, trying to look harmless, and held his hands out palm up. The effect was unsettling at best.

'Umniga, they know you. See what you can do,' Shahjahan ordered.

'I'll try, but it will be a pantomime, I expect. They only know a few words and nothing useful at that.' She pointed at Nicanor and Curro, then gestured to indicate all of them. She made an undulating sideways motion with her hands to indicate the ocean and then looked at them raising her hands in query. *Please gods, let them understand.*

They were too focused on the lords to respond. Umniga scowled, huffed in frustration at the three men behind her, then returned to her task. She grabbed a bucket of water nearby, dunked her finger in it and drew a crude boat and waves on the earthen floor.

'Oh!' Lucia exclaimed. 'Of course. They want to know why we were at sea.' Lucia drew stick figures of people, lots of them. Then she drew a sword, gestured to indicate all the figures. She pointed repeatedly, alternating between the sword and each figure. Finally, she arranged her face into a terrified expression, touched the sword, pretended it impaled her and died theatrically.

'Now, we must talk,' Shahjahan said quietly.

Umniga cast a subtle glance at Karan, indicating Isaura and Pio, before she followed him out.

'You should have been a travelling player, Lucia,' Daniel commented dryly. 'Their theatre companies always did like shameless overacting.'

She made a face at him. 'Well, it worked, and I didn't see any of you coming up with anything better.'

'We were too busy enjoying the show,' Nicanor said as he gathered Lucia and Pio in his arms. 'And please, by all that's holy, stop introducing yourself to everyone, Pio!'

'I think we just saw who's in charge,' Curro murmured as Nicanor sat next to him.

'Mmm. Did you see the way they looked at Pio and Isa?' Nicanor asked.

'Yes. You think they want something from them?'

'I don't know. There's nothing we can do until we know more, even then I doubt we'll have much say in anything.'

'They have only helped us,' Gabriela offered from where she sat nestled in Jaime's arms.

'Yes, but they helped Isa first, then Pio,' Elena said. 'Haven't any of you noticed that Isa is always their primary concern?'

'Isa is in a worse state than the rest of us—*that* is why.' Lucia's voice was fierce. 'There's no other reason, Elena.'

'Asha,' Karan said. 'These people have been fed and given new clothes. Did the villagers of Parlan supply this?'

'The clothes, most of the clothes, Lord Shahjahan delivered via us, along with food, but the people of Parlan had fed them already, Lord Karan.'

'We have brought supplies too.' He summoned one of his captains. 'I will make sure that my men restock the villagers' stores.'

'And, no doubt, make sure they know it is from you,' came Shahjahan's sarcastic tone. 'None of your games here. We need to talk.'

Karan ignored him and instructed his captain to deliver the supplies.

'Let's walk down to the beach. I've always liked the sound of the ocean.'

Karan snorted at Baldev's uncharacteristically mellow remark.

Shahjahan led the way.

'Your mood has improved,' Karan said.

'I just needed to see Asha.'

'At some stage, try to actually talk to her and tell her how you feel, rather than just *see* her.'

'You're not one who should be giving advice about women.' At this Karan merely grinned.

They caught up to Shahjahan, who was talking to an old man sitting by a workshop, nestled into the grassy dunes near the beach. 'This is Deo,' Shahjahan tersely stated by way of introduction. 'He led the rescue of our strangers.'

'Well met, Deo.' Baldev smiled. 'You have our thanks.'

Shahjahan scowled, wishing these two would stop ingratiating themselves with his people. 'Deo said we should walk over there to the rise—that there is something we should see.'

When they crested the rise they realised what Deo meant. Wrecked on the rocks at the headland was a boat. Its side was impaled upon a large outcrop of rock, being pounded by the waves. Each one further stabbed its rapidly breaking hull. With the surge and wane of the current, the boat would waver from side to side. Slowly it came to rest at an ungainly angle on the rocks, until the figurehead sat half submerged. Its rearing horse appeared as if it was struggling valiantly against drowning.

Karan understood Umniga's reaction to the horse. As he watched it struggle, a visceral tension filled him and he shuddered involuntarily. None of the men spoke, yet they turned away as one.

'We want the boy and his family,' Baldev said.

Shahjahan raised his brow, he was not surprised. 'You and they are in my territory.'

'You saw the figurehead and the box.'

'It doesn't change anything.'

'We don't care about the others. They are yours.'

'At the moment they are all mine,' Shahjahan countered.

'Now who is playing games? What do you want?' Karan

demanded.

'A formal peace agreement.'

'Only on the same terms on which it now stands.' Karan continued, 'We hold north of The Divide, we will not enter your lands save with your permission. Your clan members south of The Divide will not venture across the river into the north. You and your issue will make no hostile incursions into what is now our territory.'

Shahjahan had expected no less. He would not have given up the land, why would they? He countered them with, 'Some will have relatives in the south. You will never allow them to meet?'

Karan shrugged; he knew this game.

'I want a resumption of the quarterly trade fair between our clans. That will allow families to meet and benefit us all.'

Karan looked at Baldev before speaking. 'An *annual* trade fair.'

'Karan, you test my patience!'

'Annual.'

Shahjahan scowled. 'Done, on one more condition.'

'What?'

'We also resume the annual games between our clans.'

'They will be held at the same time,' Karan said. 'At The Four Ways as they used to be.'

'Agreed, but alternating each year between the north and south side of the bridge.'

Karan and Baldev moved away to quietly discuss the terms. 'He's asked for almost exactly what we thought,' Baldev said.

'And for what I hoped,' Karan replied.

'The trade?' Baldev asked, to which Karan nodded. 'The games?'

'That I hadn't foreseen. Are you happy for them to resume?'

'They'll lose,' Baldev said with delight.

'You are such a child sometimes, you know that? I take it that we are in agreement,' Karan said affectionately.

'Yes, I'm happy for them to go ahead. One event for both will be easier to control than several.'

'Exactly. Closer ties will provide the opportunities that I seek.'

They returned to Shahjahan. 'Agreed. You will have your formal peace, an annual market and the games. We will have the boy and his family.'

'None of which you were not prepared to give already, eh? Well, it is done. Let us pledge it before the Kenati and the village as witnesses.'

'I will also draw up an agreement; Asha and Umniga can formally witness it,' Karan finished.

'You will not take my word before witnesses as is traditional?'

'It's not *your* word I'm concerned about.'

CHAPTER NINETEEN

WHEN they returned to Parlan, the village was in a flurry. As the clan lords walked past the houses, they noticed worried glances from some of the villagers.

'Damn it!' Shahjahan cursed. Outside the lodge was a contingent of soldiers. Ratilal had arrived.

Baldev's entire frame stiffened and his fists clenched. Karan placed a restraining hand upon his arm, diverting his attention and cast him a warning look. Baldev drew a deep breath and regained his control, only then did Karan release his arm.

The warriors of Horse and Bear appeared to lounge under the white cedar tree in the square, yet they were acutely aware of the altercation at the door, the locations of their enemies and the return of their lords.

The three men marched up to the lodge where Vikram was half blocking the door.

'Bring them out,' Ratilal demanded.

'Ratilal …' Vikram began.

'*Lord* Ratilal.'

Inside, Daniel watched the door of the lodge intently. Jaime joined him; it was the most animated he'd seen his brother in weeks. 'Any idea what's going on?'

'Of course not,' Daniel bit out. Jaime had been trying to engage him in conversation since they were rescued; it was irritating. He tried to talk to Jaime the way they used to, he tried to joke and be lighthearted, but the words never came out the way he intended. He knew he shouldn't be annoyed, but he couldn't help it. Jaime was happy, he was not. It was that simple. There was no escape from the happy couple. He prayed that the men in charge would decide what to do with them soon, for he was beginning to hate the sight of Jaime and Gabriela.

Daniel took a breath and tried again. 'All I can tell is this one is new and, judging from Vikram's posture, he doesn't like him one bit.'

Following the commotion at the door, Lucia looked up anxiously. She shuddered, whispering to Gabriela, 'I don't like the look of that one. Look at his face, those scars.'

Ratilal saw her look at him and leered coldly, which turned into a grimace as it tugged on his facial stitches. The look lasted only seconds, but Lucia felt a chill run down her spine and was thankful he broke eye contact as the other leaders approached.

A large calloused hand landed heavily on Ratilal's shoulder. 'Ratilal, good to see you up and about. A word, son.'

Wincing, Ratilal cast a scathing glance at Vikram, but followed his father away from the lodge door.

Baldev glared at his departing back before moving with Karan to Vikram's side. 'Where is Asha?' he urgently asked.

'With Umniga in Deo's barn. They're restocking her wagon. Her guard is there too.'

'*Her* guard?'

'Those who travelled with her. Most consider themselves her guard now. The moment Ratilal arrived they discreetly went to her.'

'Excellent.'

'What did he want?' Karan asked.

'To drag them all out and inspect them like animals.'

Baldev and Karan shared a knowing glance. Their captains had materialised beside them. Karan took his aside and whispered to him, 'Split some men off to help Vikram protect these people. Your primary task though is the safety of the boy, Pio, his family and the unconscious girl.'

'What of her family, my lord?'

'From what little I have observed, the boy's family may well be hers, but watch to see if any others show an interest in her. Do whatever it takes to keep them safe and out of Ratilal's clutches.'

Baldev and his captain joined them. 'You will have some of my men too,' he began. 'But you must all tread gently; it appears they have run from an enemy—they are scared. Guard them, and befriend them if you can. We need them to trust us.'

The captains nodded, but before they departed, Karan spoke again. 'Remember, whatever it takes.'

The two lords returned to Vikram. 'You will have help,' Baldev said.

'Lord, we need none.'

'No, Vikram. This is not optional,' Karan insisted. 'I gather the men you chose to accompany Asha—you trust them completely?' Vikram nodded. 'How many of those that came with Shahjahan do you trust?'

Vikram paled, pursed his lips, but said nothing.

Karan spun about and Baldev fell into step beside him. As they strode off, Karan said, 'We need to see the Kenati, *now.*'

As Ratilal left with his father, Lucia suddenly realised that she had grabbed Gabriela's hand in fear and that Gabriela was now speaking to her.

'Lucia, what is it?'

'Didn't you see him?'

'Who?'

'The new one at the door.'

'Not really,' Gabriela mumbled. 'I was watching Jaime and Daniel. Do you think things will ever be the same again?

Lucia, still shaken, said bluntly, 'No, never.'

Gabriela let out a small groan, recalling Lucia to herself.

'I'm sorry—I was still thinking about that man. Gabi, Daniel needs time. He will find someone else eventually, but give him time. There is nothing you can do.'

'I wish Isa was awake,' Gabriela said wistfully. 'She'd think of some way to fix this.'

'She'd certainly have something to say, but I don't think it would be any different.'

➤➤➤→

Asha was tense, angry and pacing. 'I can't stay hidden! We've work to do.'

'Yes, you've work to do, both of you, and a lot of it,' Karan remarked as he and Baldev entered the barn.

'What do you need?' Umniga asked as she poked her head out of the wagon. They explained the peace agreement. 'I'm not a scribe,' she grumbled. 'I don't carry parchment, quills or ink.'

'That's not the work you have to do. I brought those.' Karan said. Baldev raised his brows in surprise. 'You will just have to witness it. We will do both the traditional swearing before the village and witnessed documents for each of us.' Umniga opened her mouth to speak, but Karan cut her off. 'No, you need to determine exactly who the boy's …'

'Pio.'

'Who Pio's and the girl's family are. We have assigned guards to them. The guards will need to know who their families are. Umniga, Asha, we need these people to understand they are ours now and will be coming with us. Make them think that we are their friends and will protect them. It will be easier if they come willingly.'

Umniga nodded. 'Of course, but I need to get the girl across the river to the other Kenati and I need to do it soon, or she will die.'

'Then you need to start working—go.'

'You lot,' Baldev growled at the guards. 'Don't let Asha out of your sight.' They left, but not before Asha cast a puzzled look over her shoulder at him. 'I'd be a lot happier if she could have stayed in here,' he grumbled.

'Ratilal won't try anything now.'

'I am going to kill him,' Baldev ground out.

'Come on, let's get this agreement finished.'

'Finished? Don't you mean started?'

'I have half of it already written.' Karan grinned. 'We just need to add the games and the fair and it will be done.'

Baldev shook his head.

'What?' Karan said. 'Can't a man be prepared?'

Shahjahan stood with his arms folded, waiting for Ratilal to speak. Instead, Ratilal turned defiantly from his father, maintaining a sullen silence as his resentment mounted. Shahjahan broke the silence. 'You are not here to order my men about. You are here to learn.'

'Vikram was disrespectful,' he ground out.

'What have you done to warrant his respect? Or the respect of any warrior?' Shahjahan was scathing.

Ratilal felt as if the whip had struck his back again. *I have proven my skills. I am your son. What more do I have to do?*

'Next, you are not to use the title of lord. There is only one lord here—me.'

Ratilal's jaw was clenched, but he bit out, 'It seems to me there are two other lords here as well and *they* seem to be in control.'

Shahjahan spun him around and slapped him across the face, opening his scabs and making them bleed. 'Grow up, watch and learn. There may still be hope that you will make something useful of yourself.' Shahjahan all but spat at him before turning on his heel and marching back to Parlan.

Baldev instructed his warriors to be ready to leave once the treaty was signed. Neither he nor Karan wished to linger in this territory. He was thankful that Ratilal had stayed out of his way; killing him would be entirely satisfying, but would not help peace. *Perhaps I can arrange an accident for him?* Thinking about it some more, he realised that Ratilal had disappeared for a few hours, then remained by his father's side—observing, seemingly contrite and dutiful. Perhaps the old man had finally reached him. *No, I don't believe that for one second.*

Baldev had been observing for some time since *their* strangers had been encouraged to leave the lodge and sit under the large tree that dominated the square, where the guards had extra rations for them. Asha was with them, smiling, encouraging them to relax. The guards attempted to mingle with the strangers and appeared at ease, but Baldev knew they would be ever watchful.

Asha felt Baldev's scrutiny even from a distance and decided to talk to him. Umniga had always visited the Bear territory regularly. When they were young, Asha had trained with Baldev at Gopindar's lodge. He was always friendly, never patronising and helped her in anyway he could, but then so did the other young warriors.

They'd all regularly relaxed at the local tavern. She remembered one drinking game after which she'd learned to loathe kirfir—she'd never had such a hangover in her life. Baldev had snuck her back to his father's citadel and taken care of her until she was sober so Umniga wouldn't find out. After that night he had thrown intense looks her way and she wondered what on earth she'd revealed in her drunken ramblings.

Then his father died, suddenly he was clan lord and everything changed. The boy she knew had been consumed by the role of clan lord—she prayed that boy, *her boy*, was still there. Sometimes, like now, she caught a glimpse of something beyond the gruff role he'd assumed. As she approached him, she hoped she was right.

His smile was unguarded. 'Asha?'

'I just came to tell you it seems to be working.' She paused, uncertain, embarrassed, sure she was telling him what he could see plainly himself, but she kept talking, willing herself to get over her nerves and ensure the conversation continued. 'They were very wary at first, but then glad to walk out.' *I must sound like an idiot.* 'We have been trying to talk with them. We've been teaching them words …'

Overcoming his own case of nerves, Baldev cleared his throat. 'How are they faring with that?' They both watched Pio go back to the lodge door and peer in briefly before returning to the others.

Asha laughed lightheartedly. It amazed and delighted Baldev that she could still do so. 'He'll be checking on Isaura.' Baldev frowned. 'The girl,' she explained. 'Little Pio is a wonder. He seems to simply absorb the new language; his curiosity and thirst for knowledge runs rampant, along with the rest of him.'

Baldev grinned. 'You like him?'

'Oh yes! He'll be fun to teach. You know Umniga thinks he'll be a Bard Kenati?'

Baldev shook his head, mesmerised by her expressive face. He knew she would have to return to the others soon, but he longed for her to stay beside him. 'Once we are in the North, you and Umniga will have a lot to teach them. You will have to stay put for a while to do so.'

She glanced sharply at him. 'Of course, if you command it.'

'It is not a command, just a wish,' he said very softly.

Asha blushed. He had never seen her blush, and it took a moment before she could meet his eyes.

'What did those left behind do when you took the others out?' He hoped a change in conversation would alleviate her embarrassment.

'They wanted to come, but we stopped them.'

'Good.'

'I fear it will drive a wedge between them and their fellows. They were clearly resentful.'

'That is good, Asha. It will mean less trouble for us when we leave with them. Remember we don't want the others.' She stared at the ground, obviously feeling guilty. 'They are Shahjahan's responsibility.' He wanted to take her hand and raise her face to his, but Karan's warning rang through his mind. He would not risk her by revealing here how deeply he felt. *There will be time later.* 'Asha,' his voice held a quiet anguish that made her look at him with concern. 'We couldn't take them even if we wanted to. We would never have reached a peace agreement if we wanted them all.'

Asha stared at him, feeling the emotion he put into her name like a ripple of warmth along her soul. Baldev looked apologetic when he broke the sudden stillness between them.

'Does the girl Isaura have family?'

'No, just these ones, her friends.'

'Where did Umniga go?'

'Karan summoned her.' Another silence ensued, this one awkward. Baldev cursed.

'Baldev? I mean, my lord?'

Baldev scowled at the term—a reminder of duty and opportunity lost. 'You do not have to address me as lord. Baldev will do.' His scowl deepened and he took a great breath before continuing softly, 'Asha, there is much I would tell you … much I would say to you, but I cannot here amongst my enemies. Just know this, when I heard you had been attacked, I was enraged. I felt as if a great weight had seated itself upon my chest and I have never been more relieved in my life to hear that you lived, save when I saw you again.'

Asha grinned—she couldn't help it. Suddenly everything felt right. She began to reach out to him, but stopped herself.

He nodded. 'Later … we'll talk later. Go back to the others.'

Shahjahan had ordered tables set up around the square and all the extra food he had brought to be given to the villagers of Parlan for a feast that night in celebration of the peace treaty, with a promise that any extra food used would be replaced from his personal stores. Several spits were turning—some with hogs, others with goats. Pio and the other children had been regularly checking on the progress of the roast all afternoon until they were finally sent on their way by a fierce-faced Nada wielding a wooden spoon.

Lucia and Gabriela had approached Nada, hoping to help with

preparations. Although they still tired easily, they had both needed something to do, and felt a need to help and show their gratitude to these people who had rescued them. Curro, Nicanor and Jaime had helped the men set up in anyway they could.

It was now near dusk. The locals of Parlan were gathering and guards intermingled with the crowd. The rest of the strangers had been allowed out of the lodge, but Elena found she could no longer enjoy their friendship; after witnessing the special treatment Elena and the others received, they were suspicious and resentful of her. Elena joined Lucia and Gabriela, suddenly desirous of their company.

'They hate us,' Elena said.

Lucia said wearily, 'They don't hate us. They are just scared. Worried what singles us out, and not them.'

'That's easy,' Elena muttered.

Lucia glared at her. 'Watch your tone, Elena. Or you can go back to them.'

'At least Daniel has come out now,' Gabriela said with relief. Now that everyone had exited the lodge, he had no choice but to join them.

Karan peered through a crack in the barn wall. He heard Umniga stir behind him, then join him at his side. He raised an eyebrow in question at her.

'They are there,' she said.

'Good.' He moved away from the wall so she could take up his position and look through the crack. Her lips pursed as she saw Baldev and Asha.

'Leave them be, old one.'

'She has a duty to perform.'

'So does he, but leave them be. Her duty and his are not incompatible.' Umniga ignored him. He put his hand heavily on her shoulder and pulled her away from the spy hole. 'Umniga, I mean this. Do not interfere with them. Let things take whatever course they will. Let them fall in love.'

'Spoken so well for someone who has never given his heart to anyone.'

'Listen to me now. Baldev and I both had our duty drummed into us when we were children. We have lived our entire lives by doing our duty. In this, we will have freedom. I know you better than you think. You would have us marry and breed for lineage and talent, not love. But if you interfere with them, you will no longer have my support, but my enmity. In this, I will not be denied.'

'You mean this?' She was wary, but sceptical.

'Umniga.' His tone brooked no argument and had taken on a sharp, hard edge. She could feel steel against her throat, yet his sword was not drawn. 'I grant you leeway in your address, because of your age and service, but remember this—I am clan lord, not you. Do not play games with Asha and Baldev.'

She felt the pressure against her release. 'You are more like your grandfather than you know.'

Karan grimaced. 'Obey me in this. You are very good, old woman, at reminding us of the will of the gods; we are here because of it. I have risked my men because of you. Did you ever think that this, between Asha and Baldev, might be the will of the gods too? Remember your true role.'

At this, her head snapped up and her eyes flashed in anger. 'The gods have their own agenda—one that we are not privy to.'

'Asha's path does not have to be the same as yours. She can still fulfil her duty. Leave them be. Let them be happy.' Karan slipped from the barn.

Umniga, thoughtful, took a last look through the crack at Asha and Baldev, tears in her eyes. She watched Karan's departing back, smiling through her tears. Perversely, she felt proud. How had he gone from boy to clan lord so quickly? She had been treating him as if he was still a green young man when he wasn't—not at all. He was a clan lord to be proud of, like those of old. She suspected he had talents she didn't know about, talents he'd kept hidden. *Cunning one.* She found herself chuckling. *He put me in my place. And he was right to do so.* She was still smiling as she left the barn to join the others.

CHAPTER TWENTY

THE Clan Lords had made their pledge for peace before the assembled villagers and guards; now they took turns to sign the copies of the treaty. The observers cheered loudly at the end of the oaths, proud that their little village was host to something so momentous. However, they were solemn as they craned their necks to see the signing. This was a new notion to them. Someone near Deo muttered, 'Why are they doing this? Don't they trust our lord?'

Deo cast them a disparaging look. 'I'll bet my life it's not our lord they don't trust.'

Quizzical, the man near him leaned down to whisper, 'What?'

Deo rolled his eyes. 'Ratilal. Would you trust him?' There were murmurs of assent from those near him.

Nada thumped his arm. 'Ssh! You'll be heard.'

The signing was complete. Three copies of the treaty existed, one for each lord.

'Now,' Shahjahan announced, 'let the feast begin.' Aside he said quietly to Karan and Baldev, clapping his arms on their shoulders, 'I know you two wish to be gone, but we must be seen to cement this in celebration together.'

'We will stay for a few hours, then take our leave,' Baldev replied.

Barrels of mead and ale were tapped. Local musicians had gathered and began the Ristandia. It was a dance that always opened every celebration night. All the couples held hands and danced in a circle, before the circle came together in the centre and moved back. The couples then paired off to dance, arm in arm until the close of the music where the circle was joined and the danced finished as it had begun. Most of the locals and not a few of the soldiers were dancing; those who were not were clapping and stamping time on the sidelines. The strangers were smiling and clapping, but not dancing.

Karan approached Nicanor, inclining his head slightly toward him, and held out his hand to Lucia. He kept his eyes on Nicanor, clearly seeking permission. Lucia took a step back smiling, but shaking her head.

Nicanor grinned at her. 'Go on. We've got to mix.'

Lucia took Karan's hand and found herself whirled around in the dance. She was worried about missing the steps, but quickly realised that they were not unlike dances at home. Once or twice she misstepped, but no one seemed to notice, or Karan covered for her. Karan watched as the strangers slowly joined in the dance. Though none would dance for long in their still weakened state, at least it was a beginning. He knew that Lucia was tiring and, his purpose served, he returned her to her husband.

'Well,' Nicanor said, laughing. 'You did enjoy yourself after all.'

Lucia, breathless, replied, 'Yes. It seems one country dance is just like another.'

'A dance for me?'

'Oh Nic, I haven't got it in me. I need a rest.'

With good humour, Nicanor embraced her. 'Next time, my love,' he said as he kissed her brow. 'There will be a next time. I think everything will be fine now. I feel good about this new land.'

Karan stood beside Baldev. 'Not dancing?'

Baldev snorted into his ale, sending foam flying. 'I have my pride, and falling on my arse in front of this lot would do nothing for it.' He glared as Vikram tried to encourage Asha to dance.

'Careful, you'll break the handle off that tankard if you hold it any tighter. I don't think your pride will cope too well covered in ale either.'

Baldev growled something unintelligible.

'He just wants to dance.'

'She's not up to it.'

'Come on.' Karan grabbed his arm and hauled him off. 'Let's make sure that the men are still organising to leave.'

'You know they are,' Baldev glowered.

'Yes, but if we keep standing here you will make an arse of yourself one way or another—that won't endear you to Asha.'

Karan was proud of his men. They had all participated in the celebration in some way, but had fulfilled their orders to the letter— be seen to celebrate, but remain watchful. He had expected no less. None over indulged in alcohol, but he could not say the same for Shahjahan's men. Vikram and Āsim had kept a tight rein on Asha's guard, but half the others were drunk. What worried Karan was that fewer of Ratilal's men were in the same state.

He had intended to leave earlier, but Shahjahan had wanted to discuss the games, and this had led to him reminiscing. Karan had enjoyed his tales of bygone days and let him continue for a while, but now they must leave. He went in search of Baldev and Umniga.

Pio lay asleep on the side of the grassy slope near the beach with his new friend. They had left the celebration armed with two large tankards of mead and a plate piled with food. Having devoured the food and mead and spent time chasing rabbits, they had then gone back for more food and ale. Though satiated, they made themselves finish the ale. After all, they had gone to a lot of trouble to procure it—they should finish it. The pair had lain down, giggling at the stars. When the stars began to spin, they had closed their eyes. Moaning, they realised that this did not help—they still felt like they were spinning. Pio had sat up. He felt worse, so he had lain back down, shut his eyes tightly and prayed.

Lucia was frantic. 'Pio is gone! I can't find him anywhere!'

'Last I saw he was with the other children,' Nicanor said. He was worried but he wouldn't let Lucia see it. 'He has plenty of common sense. He won't go far or get into trouble. He's probably with Isa …'

'Nic! Don't you think that was the first place I looked?'

Lucia marched up to Karan, who was talking with Umniga. She reached out to touch his arm and get his attention. Remembering who he was, she quickly dropped her arm and waited. They both turned to her. 'Pio?' was all she got out.

Annoyed, Karan bit out, 'Find him, Umniga. We need to leave. We have delayed long enough.'

Umniga took Lucia's hand and went to Nicanor. She saw Asha and waved her over. 'Pio has wandered off.'

'Last I saw he was with one of Deo's grandsons.'

'Wonderful,' Umniga said sarcastically. Devi landed on her outstretched arm. Umniga bade Lucia and Nicanor to sit with her. Asha stood behind her protectively as she connected with Devi. Bewildered, Lucia watched the brown owl fly away.

'Pio,' Asha said, pointing in the direction the bird went.

'That bird is going to find Pio?' Lucia asked dubiously.

Curro and the others joined the group sitting on the grass. 'No luck,' he said. 'We can't find him anywhere nearby. The soldiers haven't seen him and won't let us leave to look further away.'

Lucia gave a slightly hysterical laugh. 'Oh, it's fine, really. The old woman's sent a bird to find him.'

About ten minutes later, Karan and Baldev appeared. Baldev was furious. He had just berated his captain for losing one little boy. 'Have you found him?'

'Not yet. Devi is looking,' said Asha.

Karan nodded. 'You have a little longer. Shahjahan has apparently wandered down to the beach to clear his head. We must wait for his return.'

Umniga held out her arm as Devi gently landed upon it. 'They are asleep in the dunes near the beach, at the back of Deo's hut.'

Lucia could hear the amusement and relief in Umniga's voice. 'Pio?' she ventured with a hopeful smile. Umniga nodded and patted her hand.

'I'll go,' Asha said. As she turned to leave, Nicanor stood to follow her. Karan shook his head, restraining him.

'We'll go,' Karan said. 'We might see Shahjahan and take our leave of him.'

'I would still like to come, my lords,' Asha offered. 'He knows me better than you. You may frighten him.'

'I have no objection and I'm sure Baldev doesn't either.'

Together they made their way through the dunes to where Pio and his friend lay. Asha knelt down beside the boys and gently shook Pio.

He moaned, sat up and promptly leaned into Asha's arms. 'Oh Asha, I don't feel so good.'

Baldev looked at the plates beside them and the empty mugs as he woke the other boy. 'Come on, wake up.' He shook him firmly. The boy groaned and rolled into a ball. Baldev uncurled him and held him up. 'Here, drink this—it's water.' The boy shook his head. Baldev grabbed his chin, holding his face still. 'Drink it. You'll feel better.' The boy nodded and drank, then emptied his stomach near Baldev's boots. 'Watch where you aim, boy.' He handed the flask to Asha who made Pio drink.

Karan stepped back, just in case. He picked up an empty tankard and addressed Deo's grandson. 'How much have you drunk?' The boy, still retching, held up two fingers. 'Between you?'

He shook his head. 'Each.'

Asha looked grim. 'Drunk? Idiots! Wait until your mothers get hold of you.'

'Let's get them back.' Baldev stifled a laugh as he lifted the boy.

'It will be easier to go past Deo's workshop, up the beach, then onto the path,' Asha offered. 'Follow me.'

Karan picked up Pio and they began to make their way back to the celebration. As they neared the top of the last dune, Asha froze at the sound of voices, dropped to her belly and wriggled up the slope to peer through the grass at the top. Karan stopped, suddenly tense and alert. Baldev was instantly still. They lowered the boys, indicating that they should remain there. Wide-eyed, the children obeyed. Quietly, Karan and Baldev joined Asha, leaving Pio and his friend crouching at the base of the dune, feeling vulnerable yet curious. They crawled silently to Asha. Annoyed, she signalled them to silence and to stay down.

>>>—→

Shahjahan stood on the beach, the waves gently lapping against the shore. The fierce storm they'd endured on the journey here, followed by the wrangling over peace and organising the future of these new members of his clan, had left him weary to his core. The lull of the waves had always soothed him in the past and it did so now. He was pleased with the outcome they had reached and, while he had never felt so old, he felt as if a veil had been lifted from his eyes and a shadow from his heart. There was much work to be done, and he had many plans laid out already in his mind. For the first time in many years, he felt like leading.

There was a halo around the moon, a sure sign of a cold night and rain to come. *I should head back. I've kept those young lords waiting long enough.* He chuckled, gaining some satisfaction knowing Karan and Baldev would be champing at the bit to be off. Turning to leave, he spotted a figure who had just stepped from the path between the dunes. It was Ratilal.

'Well met, my son.' Ratilal said nothing. 'We have had a good day's work and you were most helpful with the future placement of the strangers.' Still Ratilal did not speak. Instead he looked out to sea. 'Come now, what is wrong? Why do you not speak?'

'What is wrong?' he repeated his father's words quietly at first, then louder. 'What is wrong?'

Shahjahan scowled at him and opened his mouth to speak, but Ratilal cut him off.

'Surely you cannot be so blind? You have given them what they want. We do not have our lands back.'

'We have been over this already. We need stronger ties with them while we rebuild our clan and our army. Trade will resume, as will the games.' At the mention of the games Ratilal looked interested. 'All this will benefit us. We need to reconnect with our traditions, reclaim our identity and pride. While we do this our people will have peace.'

'Peace! Reclaim our pride? How? With the Horse and Bear ruling lands that are rightfully ours? With our clan relegated to inferior status, begging them for trade?'

'I told you, it will take time to rebuild ...'

'Years! This will take years.'

'Listen to me, boy. These strangers have fled an enemy, possibly a vast enemy by the looks of it. The clans must be closer, so we can work together if we face a threat.'

'What threat? From them?' Ratilal mocked. 'You are not seriously worried about the enemy *they* ran from, are you? They barely made it here, I doubt anyone else will.'

'Ratilal ...'

'No, do not patronise me! Even if such an enemy were to reach here, we would be able to defend ourselves. It is your lack of leadership, your folly, your weakness, that has led us to this pass.'

'Remember your place, boy!'

'My place? How could I forget? You are always so good to remind me. All my life I have tried to please you, but no, you always preferred Samia. She could do no wrong.' Spittle flew from his mouth. 'I was always made to feel the lesser child. It never mattered to you how I tried, or how you hurt me. It was always *her.*' He paused, drawing a ragged breath. His hands were fisted by his sides, his control thinly holding.

'She did no wrong,' Shahjahan retaliated. 'You ...'

Ratilal laughed in scorn at this. 'Oh yes, *me.* Do tell me again my many faults.'

'You have only ever been impetuous, angry and ill-disciplined. I hoped you would learn patience. If only you would have learned patience and prudence.'

'Patience, prudence!' Ratilal hissed.

'Yes. You have many admirable qualities, boy, but without those two you will not make a good ruler.'

'Oh, here we have it, you patronise me again, old man. You would counsel patience and prudence while others rule in our stead north of The Divide. You, who were too weak, who let your grief consume you like a woman, until we were left with not a clan lord but with a mere shadow of one, and a ball-less one at that.'

Shahjahan stepped closer to Ratilal, slapping him savagely. 'How dare you! You will never be clan lord. I will have a contest for my ...' Shahjahan looked down in amazement at Ratilal's dagger sticking from his belly.

Karan and Baldev were poised to move, to come to his aid, but with amazing speed Ratilal whipped the dagger out of his gut and stepped behind him. He seized his father's neck, pushed aside his head, then drove the dagger into his neck. Karan was certain he saw Ratilal smile as he flicked it sideways, almost casually, before withdrawing it.

Shahjahan toppled forward, clutching futilely at the gash as his blood pumped out.

Karan and Baldev subsided; there was nothing to be done now. The boys held Asha's hands. They were trembling, but utterly silent.

Ratilal walked around his father seething. 'I will be high lord of our clan. I will regain our territory. Now that you have served your purpose, you can join my dear departed weakling of a sister. She too had only one use.' Wistfully he continued, 'I miss her sometimes ...' He bent down, speaking directly into his father's ear, gloating. 'She had a lovely body.'

With these words the life left Shahjahan's eyes. Ratilal departed as quietly as he had come. Baldev looked at Asha. Even in the moonlight he could see her pain and anger. He reached over Pio and squeezed her shoulder.

Karan's face held a fierce sadness. He knew he should not linger, but it galled him to leave Shahjahan without the ritual words being spoken. Karan strode across the beach and knelt beside the clan lord's body. He closed Shahjahan's sightless eyes, angry at the startled expression frozen on his face. The hairs on the back of his neck rose as he whispered, 'I'm sorry this happened to you—after everything you have endured. May Rana and Jalal guide you and protect you on your journey. May you find peace and happiness in the next life—*alvida*.' The tingling on the back of his neck subsided; he was alone.

Karan rose to join the others, then heard the chink of armour. Niaz, Ratilal's confidante, with half a dozen guards, stepped from the path onto the beach. A slow, cunning smile crept across Niaz's face.

'He has attacked the clan lord. Get him!' He pointed at a young warrior. 'Return to the village, raise the alarm.'

In an instant Karan weighed the possibility of fighting them. If he did, Baldev would help. Asha would have to get the boys back to safety alone. The risk of their exposure was too great. He ran, making sure they could follow him.

Niaz looked at Shahjahan's fallen body, then joined in the chase.

Baldev said to Asha. 'We've got to get back to the village now.'

'What about Karan?'

'He'll be fine,' he replied tersely. 'Boys, smarten up. Time to move, as quickly as you can and quietly. Keep moving, I'll be back.' Baldev sped off after the returning soldier. Despite his bulk and the deep gloom between the dunes, he moved surely and silently. The young man was running without care, making enough noise for Baldev to track him. Baldev tried to remember the way the path lay from his walk earlier in the day. Praying he was correct, he veered off to the side, crested the dune and spied the path running along its other side. He was now ahead of the runner.

Baldev concealed himself beside a low lying scrubby bush and waited. The sound of sand underfoot grew louder. He could hear rapid breathing. *Wait ... wait ... NOW!* Baldev thrust out a leg, tripping him. The soldier had no idea what he had fallen over. Baldev was instantly upon him, wrapping his massive forearm around the front of the young man's neck. He struggled, but was unable to cry out. On his side, he continued to fight to escape, but Baldev wrapped his legs around his lower body, further hindering his efforts. Baldev applied steady backward force with his forearm, while using his other arm to force the soldier's head forward, throttling him. The young man's struggles quickly lessened in this vice-like grip, until they ceased altogether. Shoving the body away from him, Baldev rose and dragged him off the path. Then he caught up with Asha and led the way back to the village, with Asha bringing up the rear.

Pio felt ill. He wished they had not drunk the ale, or the mead, but it was more than that. He had never seen someone murdered; it was so quick, so easy. He would never forget the hate in that man's voice. He was frightened and worried and he wanted his father and mother terribly. Pio knew they must be stealthy, but felt certain his clumsiness, thanks to the alcohol, would be heard.

'Baldev,' Asha whispered. He waited. She knelt and encouraged Pio to climb on her back, managing not to show her pain as his slight weight pressed against her bruised body. *Don't think about it, just get out of here.* Baldev carried the other boy.

Pio was astonished—Asha was stronger than she looked and they moved at a faster pace. When they reached the outskirts of the village, Baldev and Asha put the boys down.

'Find your grandfather,' Asha directed the other boy. 'Tell him what happened, but tell no one else.'

'Tell Deo to be careful. If Ratilal suspects any of you know the truth, you are dead,' Baldev finished. The boy nodded and disappeared.

'Baldev, I'll take Pio back. Make sure he understands …'

Baldev reached out and pulled her to him, kissing her ardently. 'I'll see you again. Take Pio to his parents. They'll know something is wrong. Let him tell them, but they must keep quiet. Then find Umniga—she knows what to do. The pair of you hide until later.'

'Later?'

'Trust me. Find Umniga.' He kissed her again and slipped into the darkness.

'Pio.' He looked at her wide-eyed. She pointed in the direction they came from and placed her finger on her lips. 'Ssh.' He nodded. She took his hand, straightened up and smiled broadly, encouraging him to do so too. *Oh, good boy*, she thought as Pio followed her lead and plastered a grin onto his face. Together, they walked through the village.

Asha was not sure what she expected—an uproar perhaps? However, Parlan was quiet. There were a few revellers left, but most people were calmly packing up the tables. She walked to the door of the lodge, where she could see Nicanor and Lucia waiting. Asha urged them all to sit and smiled indulgently at Pio, laughing as if she'd just caught him at a prank, but the tight lines around her eyes betrayed her tension. Pio tugged on her hand, wanting her to release him so he could run to his mother, but Asha held fast. He looked at her and, reminded of the need for caution, kept walking at a sedate pace. His hands were sweating, and he looked frightened, but Asha hoped that to any observers it would merely appear as if he was worried about parental chastisement.

Lucia swept him out of Asha's hands and into her arms. 'Where have you been? Ugh! Pio, you smell of ale!' Nicanor leaned forward, sniffed him, and wrinkled his nose in disgust.

Asha ushered them inside the lodge. She saw the Boar and Horse guards assigned to them. She needed to go pass them the news, so she held up her finger to Pio indicating for him to wait.

Nicanor questioned his son. 'How much did you drink?'

Pio looked guilty, darting his eyes to Asha as he stalled for time. 'We were just having fun. Then we got hungry and thirsty.'

'I asked you, how much did you drink?' Nicanor was watching Asha speaking intently with the guards who had been with them all afternoon. When they quickly dispersed, Asha briskly entered the lodge, followed by Vikram and Āsim. They ushered Nicanor, Lucia and Pio over to Isaura where the rest of the group had been waiting.

Asha urged them all to sit and smiled indulgently

Nicanor was filled with foreboding. He asked Pio very softly, 'What happened?'

'We did drink too much …' Pio mumbled, not meeting his father's gaze.

'Pio, what else happened?' Pio looked at Asha, confused at how to respond. 'Pio—look at me, I am your father. What else?'

Pio was torn. He wanted to tell him, but Asha wanted him quiet.

Nicanor was angry and extremely worried. Pio had always told the truth. Now he was denying his father—waiting upon permission from a stranger to speak. What had happened to his son?

Asha leaned forward, took Pio's hand and nodded at him to speak.

His hushed voice answered, 'We did eat and drink too much and fell asleep. Then Asha, Karan and Baldev found us. My friend threw up.' He paused, not wanting to recount what happened next.

Lucia could see him struggling to speak. She put her arms around him to soothe him. 'And?'

'And they were going to bring us back, but we heard voices. Angry voices. We hid and watched. It was that old man, Shahjahan, and a younger one. The nasty looking one who you saw at the door … He killed the old man.' Lucia stifled a gasp. 'Karan went to the body. I don't know why. But when he was coming back, some men saw him. They yelled and chased him.' He looked at the adults around him plaintively. 'They must think he killed the old man, but he didn't. Ma, Pa, he never did.'

There was shocked silence for a few minutes. Then each adult began to speak.

Asha thumped the floor, attracting their attention. 'Enough. Ssh, ssh.'

'What does she mean, "ssh"?' Elena was shocked. 'Someone's been murdered.'

'Yes,' Curro said through clenched teeth. 'And Pio has seen it all.'

'Think, Elena.' Jaime continued quietly, 'What do you think will happen if the wrong people find out that he knows?'

'Elena, we must not let anyone know,' Gabriela urged. 'Asha is trying to help us. We must go about as if nothing has happened.'

'Other than my son getting drunk,' Lucia added.

Asha listened carefully to this exchange. Convinced that they would remain quiet, she left with Vikram and Āsim.

'Where is Umniga?' she asked them.

'Here.' Umniga had been sitting under a tree, waiting. She stood at their approach. 'You two should go,' she directed Vikram and Āsim. They did not leave. 'Asha will be fine with me. But you do not want to hear what I have to say—at least not yet. Go on.' She waved them away.

'As yet, Niaz has not returned. No one knows what happened.' Umniga snorted. 'Fools. I don't know why they haven't raised the alarm.'

'We should hide Isa and the others,' Asha said.

'No, that will just bring them to Ratilal's attention. We wait, Asha.' She whispered in her ear, 'Now hide. I'll come to you. I don't want Ratilal to see you.'

CHAPTER TWENTY-ONE

KARAN wove amongst the dunes. He could hear his pursuers clearly. This section of dunes was covered in clumps of long feathered grass. Karan crouched on the side of a dune between two clumps of grass, ensuring their feathery tips fell back naturally over him. A pair of guards ran past, disappearing into the dark. A third followed along behind them, more quietly—cautious. Karan had heard others talking off to the side somewhere. *They are green.* He waited for the last one to pass his hiding place. Stealthily, he rose and moved forward. He was gaining on the cautious one, his dagger poised. A soft breeze blew. The grasses rustled. His quarry spun, nervous, and saw Karan almost upon him. Karan pounced as the man opened his mouth to call out. He knocked him to the ground, hand over his mouth, gagging him, then drove the dagger into the base of his neck near his collarbone. Casually he wiped his blade clean on the dead man, before moving on.

Karan needed to get back to the village, to meet with Baldev and leave. He crept between the dunes, avoiding the pale moonlight and keeping to the gloomy shadows as much as possible. He was heading in the general direction from which he had come, but trying to travel diagonally through the dunes to save time. He had not heard the noisy two who passed him again, but knew that at least six guards had been with Niaz. Karan came to an open expanse between the dunes—too exposed. *Where are they?* He crawled on his belly through the vegetation to the rise of the dune nearest him. At the rise, he could see across the expanse and down the other side of the dune. *Nothing.* He waited.

Two cautious figures entered the shallow vale below him. Swords drawn, they walked its length, increasingly wary as they reached the exposed ground at the end of the dune. Concealed by the end of the dune, they lay in wait for him. Karan doubted he could slip away behind them, but his options were limited. If he had his bow he could pick them off, then make for the village. It was not far. He could see the light from the fire that had burned outside during their celebration. He could probably kill one of the waiting soldiers with a dagger throw, but a sword fight with the other would attract attention.

Karan slid over the side of the dune, attempting to slip away unnoticed behind them and find another way across to the village. They turned and saw him, surprise in their eyes. Before they could cry out two arrows sliced through the air and embedded themselves in their chests. Two of Karan's men stepped out of the dark in the direction he had intended to go. Devi glided silently past them, wheeled and headed back to the village.

Niaz stumbled over the man Karan had killed in the dark. 'Damn,' he muttered. Wandering around in the dark alone, he realised he was just as likely to be picked off by Karan as he was by his own men. *Why have more troops not arrived from the village? They should have by now.* He wavered. *Ratilal would be furious if the planned messenger didn't arrive. Karan may well make it back and escape.* There was not much choice—risk death stumbling blindly through the dunes, or return, raise the alarm and face Ratilal. He'd have to go back and raise the alarm or the entire plan could fail, then he would be dead.

Karan and the two men, aided by Devi, quickly made their way back to the village. Hidden between two buildings, they viewed the scene before them. The villagers were tidying up after the celebration, a few men still sat talking around the fire; all seemed normal and calm. Boar troops lingered amongst the locals. There was no haste, urgency, or tension amongst those they watched.

'We're still in luck,' Karan said. 'Follow me. Be calm.' They moved through the shadows and blended in with the crowd. Outwardly, he appeared relaxed as he returned the greetings of the villagers, but his heart was pounding. Karan could feel the adrenaline pumping through his veins. The short walk through the crowd seemed to drag on. Finally, they reached the spot just on the outskirts of the village where both the Horse and Bear warriors had bivouacked.

The men were ready to ride. Baldev greeted him and calmly handed him the reins of his horse, Mirza. 'Good to see you back.'

'Good to be back.' Karan looked at the calm village. 'I assume you are responsible for this.'

'Ratilal's messenger never made it.'

'The others?'

'All back safe and sound. Asha is hiding, and Umniga has gone to join her,' Baldev said as Karan mounted. 'How long do you think we'll have to wait?'

In the distance Niaz ran into the village, shouting, 'Our clan lord! Our Clan Lord Shahjahan is dead!' On cue Ratilal appeared. 'My lord! Your father ...' A crowd began to gather around. The Boar guards were on alert.

'What is it? What has happened?'

'I'm sorry, my lord. Your father has been slain. Murdered!'

'How? By whom?' Ratilal demanded.

'My lord, it was Lord Karan. I saw him with my own eyes, as did the guards who were with me. He ran, and we pursued him.'

'How long ago?' Ratilal was livid.

Niaz gulped. 'It was some time ago. I sent a messenger back immediately. I fear he is dead.'

'If he is, then Karan had help. He and Baldev always work together.'

'My lord, I returned as soon as I realised the messenger must not have arrived.'

'Where are your men?'

'Still scouring the dunes, my lord.'

Ratilal's eyes glinted cruelly. He was displeased. They had taken too long. Karan may have escaped already. Every delay could ruin his plan. 'Rouse the men. The Horse and Bear have murdered Clan Lord Shahjahan. They have breached the peace treaty. This is war. We must avenge my father!'

'Hail, Clan Lord Ratilal. Hail, High Lord Ratilal,' Niaz chanted. Ratilal's soldiers heartily chorused this. The bewildered villagers of Parlan mimicked the words and hastily departed. Boar warriors raced off to pass the news, and to ready themselves for combat.

'High lord,' Vikram said as he presented himself.

'What?' Ratilal knew Vikram had been fiercely loyal to his father, but questioned whether his loyalty lay with the office or the man.

Vikram knelt before him with his head bowed. He held his sword flat in both hands and raised it before Ratilal. 'High Lord and Clan Lord Ratilal, I swear to you on my sword, my loyalty, my life, I will bring the murderer of your father to justice. I will avenge his death.'

Ratilal was flattered, though wary. This was a formal, binding declaration and the first he had received. Vikram would not break this oath lightly. To do so would cause not only the loss of his honour, status and possessions, but more likely the loss of his life. He was not sure he could trust him, but he was an experienced commander and Ratilal was smart enough to know that he would need all those he could muster. Besides, if Vikram was truly loyal then his obvious devotion would shore up the loyalty of others.

'Rise, Vikram, it was well said. But you and your men can serve me best by staying here and guarding those strangers.'

'My lord, we would prefer to fight with you.'

'You will remain here.' Ratilal was stern.

Vikram nodded. 'What would you have me do with them?'

Ratilal's first thoughts were to have them all killed. However, it was thanks to their arrival that he was now clan lord. *Perhaps the gods sent these strangers for this purpose?* In which case it would not do to anger them. If he was kind to them and resettled them, they would be unswervingly loyal. He would be responsible for their salvation.

'Your orders from my father were to discover their skills and resettle them around Faros; those orders still stand.' Niaz rode up with Ratilal's mount. 'I will leave some more men to help you.' *And to watch you.*

Karan and Baldev could hear the commotion at the other end of the village. Mounted, they waited.

'It's taking them long enough.' Baldev sounded bored. Their men laughed.

'Don't worry. You won't be bored for long.' They could hear a distant rumble growing closer. 'Ready for it,' Karan commanded. By the moonlight they saw the Boar warriors galloping toward them. Baldev spun his horse and raced off, followed by their combined troops.

Karan stilled Mirza. 'Calm now, boy. Just wait.' Ratilal was in the lead. Karan smiled, drew his bow and let fly one arrow. It skimmed past Ratilal, embedding itself in a warrior behind him who fell from his horse and was trampled by those following. Karan waved and smiled at Ratilal before spurring Mirza away.

Ratilal, goaded to further fury, screeched, 'After him!'

Mirza galloped on a free rein until he caught up with the others. The Horse Clan's mounts were exceptional. The hills naturally toughened them, they were well fed and kept at the peak of fitness. Their warriors had been chosen for this mission based on their experience and the stamina of their horses.

Baldev had set a good pace, fast enough to stay ahead, yet allow the enemy not to lose sight of them, and one that could be sustained. Karan merged with Mirza. The horse's superior eyesight picked out the road more clearly than Karan was able to and allowed him to see behind him. The horses before him parted and they moved their way to the front where Baldev led the group. Baldev nodded in greeting as Karan passed him and galloped further into the distance.

Mirza was maintaining a ground-eating pace. The edge of the Eastern Forest was now on their right and its ancient giants towered over the road. There was an old track, seldom used, that diverged from the main road to Parlan and headed toward Hunters' Ford. The entrance was hidden, partially covered by the slightly weeping branches of some sheoaks; there was a massive cherry pine opposite. Karan was looking for it with each stride; it should be nearby. *Soon,* he told Mirza. However, Mirza was already slowing. His thoughts scolded Karan, reminding him that he knew perfectly well where the turn was. Mirza puffed, snorted and tossed his head. *Point taken, my friend.* Karan leaned along his neck as they trotted under the branches of the sheoaks. They wandered a short distance before a warrior stepped out from cover, blocking their way.

'Well met, my lord,' he said. Others filtered out of the undergrowth to join them.

'Well met indeed,' Karan replied as he leapt from Mirza's back. 'Here, wear this.' He removed his cloak and gave it to the warrior. They were a similar height and build with dark wavy hair.

Munira, the Kenati of the Horse Clan, stepped forward. 'All is in readiness.'

Karan took his bow from the saddle quiver. The warrior mounted. Though an experienced horseman, he looked a little wary. Mirza snorted, pawed the ground and tossed his head.

'Be nice,' Karan told him as he stroked his nose. 'We'll be together soon. You cannot come. You must be seen, darkling. Everyone knows who you are and that only I ride you.' Mirza lowered his head to Karan's chest, snuffling gently. Karan looked up at his replacement. 'Go,' he said. 'And may the gods go with you.'

The warrior gathered up his reins firmly to turn the horse. Mirza baulked, pawed the ground and shook his head.

'I wouldn't bother with those. You'll just make him mad.'

The warrior quickly loosened the reins and Mirza spun about before trotting off.

'I'd hang on, though, if I were you,' Karan murmured at his departing back. 'We need to get going while Ratilal is focused on attacking the others.' Karan turned and led the others at a forced march across country, back toward Parlan.

CHAPTER TWENTY-TWO

KARAN and his warriors travelled the most direct way to Parlan—sometimes using the road, sometimes going across farmland. Having crested a rise in a field, they paused for a brief rest. Everyone was silent, listening intently and trying to peer into the depths of night for any sign of the enemy. Instead, an eerie quiet greeted them, as if the world were waiting with bated breath. Loathe to break this shield of silence, they travelled on.

On the outskirts of Parlan, while his men rested and waited, Karan went with two scouts to determine how many, if any, guards were left in the village. They separated at the rear of the lodge, with the scouts moving to the opposite ends of the village and where the Boar Clan warriors had bivouacked. Karan crept forward and peered through a crack in the timber shutters. Two lamps burned within and by their dim light it appeared that all the refugees were still inside the lodge. *Good.* He inched his way along the side of the building, staying back from the corner. He could hear voices—Vikram and Āsim. Karan moved back the way he had come, then circled around the village. He wanted to reach the barn and hopefully find some sign of Umniga and Asha; it would also enable him to view the front of the lodge undetected.

Karan had to move carefully, for there was limited cover. The village itself was not densely populated, there were few houses and few large trees. In places, the low scrub that dotted the dunes afforded some cover; here he was able to move quickly and stealthily. He waited, crouched behind such scrub, as some troops whom he didn't recognise filed past. *How many has Ratilal left?*

Karan was now at the end of the village and there was no more cover. He surreptitiously leaned around the bush to see down the centre of the village. The fire in the square was still burning; more soldiers were loitering around it, under the tree.

Karan edged carefully backward, then skirted well around the small village. He expected patrols around its perimeter, but encountered none. He would not tolerate such laxity amongst his own men. As he stole through the undergrowth near the rear of the barn, the hairs on the back of his neck rose. He froze. He was being watched. Cautiously, he peered around. Karan's ears strained to catch any sound. He looked up, then smiled. Perched, silent, ever watchful, on the top of the barn, was Devi.

Karan darted, half crouching, from his hiding place to the barn wall. He looked down the length of the barn and could partially see the square, the lodge and the guards. Karan needed to get inside the barn, but he had known he could not slip in the front doors. As he turned his attention to the rear wall, several planks next to him moved.

'Give me a hand?' came Asha's frustrated whisper. Grinning, he pulled slowly on the vertical timbers, levering them up and loosening their nails. They swung up enough for him to crawl through.

Karan clasped her arms and hugged her to him. 'I'm very glad to see you unharmed, Asha.' She was speechless. Karan was not prone to outbursts of emotion. He released her, smiling warmly. 'Baldev will be even more happy.' Asha blushed and looked away.

Umniga was preparing the body of Shahjahan. He wore a crown of willow and oak, leafless and dry, on his head. His hands and face were adorned with his clan's symbols.

'I thought you were hiding. How did you do this? How did you get him?' Karan asked sternly.

'Asha was hiding safely. I just waited until that bastard Ratilal and his men were gone. Then I walked out and told some of those left to get the body so I could prepare him for his final journey.'

'Umniga, you were careless … and lucky.'

'Pah!' she spat. 'They objected, but Vikram was out there and he retains at least enough honour to command them to do that. Shahjahan may have been a cantankerous old dog, but he wasn't always. He deserved a better death than this.'

'Yes, yes he did … I said the words, Umniga.'

'I thought so. Was that how you were seen?'

He nodded. 'Tell me, why so vehement toward Vikram?'

'He gave his oath to Ratilal!'

'Did he indeed?' Karan was deep in thought as he peered through the crack in the barn doors. Most of the troops still seemed to be either guarding the lodge door or huddled around the fire in the square. 'I count about a dozen men that Ratilal has left in addition to Asha's guard.'

'How many are still her guard?'

'We'll soon discover.'

>>——→

Asha and Umniga walked from the barn toward the square. Asha kept telling herself that Ratilal was gone, but she could not help her anxiety. The men Ratilal left behind were clustered around the fire. They nodded and smiled at the men they passed, a few returned the gesture, but many ignored them. Vikram and Āsim met them outside the lodge. The other members of her guard were nearby.

'Should you be here?' Vikram asked.

'Why? Am I unsafe?' *Now that you have given your oath to Ratilal.*

'No,' came Āsim's firm reply. 'You are not. We can protect you from that rabble if need be.'

A moment's silence ensued. Vikram scrutinised them before scanning the darkness intensely. For a moment Asha thought he must have suspected something was afoot.

'Ratilal left no orders regarding you, either of you. For the moment you are, as you have always been, our *honoured* Kenati.'

Āsim stiffened at his tone. Asha's guard were listening; they bristled and moved closer, looking bewildered at Vikram.

'What did you expect? Shahjahan is dead. Ratilal rules. Only a fool would oppose their clan lord, and I have given him my oath.' Hostile grumblings followed this announcement.

'Asha, come,' Umniga said stiffly before she pushed past Vikram into the lodge.

'I can't believe this. What is he doing?' Asha whispered.

'Believe it. I told you not to test his loyalty. Vikram is loyal to himself and his clan lord. He may not like Ratilal, but he will follow him.'

The headlong gallop down the road to The Four Ways was dangerous at night. The cloud cover had thickened and moonlight was intermittent, making it increasingly difficult to see any potholes and ruts in the road. Baldev's horse had stumbled several times, but, surefooted beast that he was, he had not gone down. Mirza was now beside him and Baldev grinned at his new rider, who looked slightly awestruck and a little terrified. Baldev estimated that they had travelled far enough from both Parlan and the old track to Hunters' Ford. The horses were blowing hard and needed a rest; at some point they would have to find a suitable spot to stop for a few hours. He slowed his troops as they entered a short, straight stretch of road that ran along the base of a small, narrow, rocky valley.

'Spread them along this section,' Baldev said to his captain. 'I want archers concealed up in those rocks—now. We'll cause some chaos, then make off. Have a couple of riders wait in sight as bait.' Men leapt from their horses to obey, scrambling urgently up the slope to cover. Baldev and the most of the others, along with the riderless horses, cantered out of the valley and hid beyond the final bend in the road.

The captain returned at a gallop. 'It's done. They're coming.' He and Baldev dismounted and scrambled up the last ridge to watch.

Ratilal was still furious. The delayed message had cost him dearly; Karan and Baldev were escaping. Instead of having them in his grasp, he was racing through the night to catch them. Sometimes they had seemed to be gaining on them, only to be eluded at the next turn. The horses were tiring. They were slick with sweat and foam had formed on their necks and sides. Heedless, Ratilal urged his men on. Eventually they must catch the others; they couldn't be that far ahead. Moonlight broke through the clouds as they rounded the next bend, illuminating the straight road before them. 'There!' he shouted. 'We nearly have them.'

He urged his horse forward. Halfway along the straight it stumbled and fell, tumbling head first into the dirt then somersaulting onto its back. Ratilal was jettisoned out of the saddle. He flew through the air, his arms out before him, landed heavily and skidded on his belly along the road. Completely winded and dazed, he desperately tried to inhale. Instinct made him haul himself onto his hands and knees. He felt a dull stab in his palm. His movements felt sluggish, as if he was wading through molasses. His vision was failing; filled only with whirling pinpricks of red.

Ratilal groaned, still struggling to regain his breathing. His hearing was dulled, but he knew he was making animalistic sounds as his body desperately sought air. At last he drew one shuddering breath, then another. Time appeared to move slowly, yet as his senses returned, he realised little time had passed. With the clearing of his head came the sounds of screaming horses and men. Still on hands and knees, he looked around to see the road littered with the bodies.

His horse lay dead, ten feet or so behind him. Another horse must have collided with it and now lay half sprawled over its rump, also dead. Men, thrown clear as he was, were on either side of him. Some were clearly dazed and striving to regain their wits, others lay unmoving. Beyond him, horses who must have jumped the bodies were limping; most were panicked. Those still riding were frantically bringing their mounts under control.

Ratilal heard a dull whoosh, then a whump as an arrow embedded itself in the ground near him. Still dazed, all he could do was stare at it stupidly.

'My lord? Ratilal?' Niaz's face filled his vision, before he hauled him upright and dragged him away. 'We must seek cover.'

'Aargh!' Something pierced his boot and foot.

'Caltrops!' Niaz shouted as he shoved Ratilal down behind the belly of his dead horse. Whump! An arrow implanted itself in its carcass as they dived for cover. Blood trickled down Ratilal's face from a gash on his forehead. He raised his hand to wipe it away in irritation, but Niaz quickly grabbed his arm. 'No, my lord, look!' A metal spike was sticking out through the top of his hand. Turning it over he noticed the three other vicious spikes underneath. 'Can't you feel it?' Ratilal shook his head, causing blood to drip into his eyes.

He held his hand out to Niaz. His tongue felt thick and useless. 'P, p, pool … it … oout,' he managed with difficulty. Niaz gripped Ratilal's wrist and concealed his hand from view. He pulled the caltrop firmly and quickly. Ratilal groaned at the sucking, tearing sensation, grateful to his current stupor for the dulled pain.

Niaz nudged a nearby body. When the man didn't move, he cut the cloth of his pants, tearing a section off and wadding it in Ratilal's palm. 'Hold this, my lord.' With another section he wiped the blood from Ratilal's eyes.

Dimly, Ratilal remembered standing on something. *Shit!* His hand and head were beginning to throb; the pain brought him out of his daze. He elbowed Niaz, who was peeking over the side of the horse, assessing their position and status. Niaz slunk down, grim-faced.

'Th … therors.' Ratilal scowled and ran his tongue around his mouth, before trying again slowly. 'There's … one … in my … foot.'

Niaz slid down on his belly and wriggled backward to examine the foot. He grabbed the caltrop and looked apologetically at Ratilal. An arrow found its mark in the corpse near them. Alarmed, he wildly yanked the caltrop from Ratilal's boot, before wriggling in close to the horse. Ratilal hollered in pain. 'Sorry, high lord. There was no easy way.'

Ratilal glared at him, though he nodded. 'Status?'

Niaz shook his head. 'I can't tell exactly. The moonlight's too fleeting and when there is enough to see by ...' Another arrow whizzed overhead, followed by the dull thump of a body hitting the ground.

'We can't stay here.' Ratilal waited for the moon to slip behind a large cloud, then slid to the shoulder of his fallen horse. Lying flat and perfectly still, he peered over its neck into the darkness, waiting. The cloud passed and the moon revealed the road before them. The men he had earlier seen trying to control their horses were now dead or dying, as were many of their mounts. The remaining horses had either bolted or stood in a frightened, shaking cluster beside the road.

A distant, plaintive whinny drifted on the night air from the direction they had come. One of the terrified horses broke away and led the others in a panicked dash toward its calling friend. Some were able to run freely, others tried brokenly, their fear the only thing propelling them on woefully injured hooves. They were headed directly toward Ratilal. He rolled across to Niaz, both of them cowering close to the belly of his horse, as the first flew by him. Several followed; he prayed the uninjured ones would not impale themselves on caltrops in their flight.

'Bloody bastards!' he spat. 'When the moon is covered again, we'll make our way toward the rear. Check who's alive. Get as many as we can out of this damn valley.'

Baldev watched the chaos unfolding beneath them with grim satisfaction. 'I hate caltrops.' His captain said nothing, they both knew it was necessary. 'Get the archers out when clouds cover the moon again. We're leaving.'

CHAPTER TWENTY-THREE

RATILAL, though limping badly, walked amongst his men, giving orders to those who remained able-bodied regarding the care of the wounded. He refused aid for his injuries, making certain that his men knew that their commander regarded their welfare as paramount. He promised revenge for this cowardly act that had laid them low. Ratilal controlled his rage and pain, determined to prove his strength and resilience, yet in his heart and mind he felt a burning black fire that he longed to surrender to. He swore that he would hunt down Karan and his dog Baldev, and mount their heads over the main gates of Faros. He would annihilate their forces, and enslave those left. He had a vision of a new kingdom. Under his rule, they would not only regain their lost glory, but surpass it.

Ratilal paused beside two young men who were situated a little apart from the others. One was prone and the other held his hand, yet was wounded himself, with one arm resting uselessly across his lap. Ratilal sat beside them. 'Your friend?'

The young man nodded, replying distractedly, 'Yes, my lord. Forgive me, *high* lord.'

'There's nothing to forgive. The title sits new and unfamiliar with me as well.' Ratilal reached out with his good hand and felt the brow of the prone man. 'Has anyone looked at your friend?'

'My brother … Yes, but there's nothing to be done, high lord. His horse … it fell on him. He couldn't feel his legs when I found him. I dragged him here with my good arm, but since then he's just faded. I think his insides are damaged.'

'I'm sorry. My need for vengeance upon the loss of my father has led to this. I am honoured by his sacrifice …'

Niaz approached with an older warrior and interrupted him in an urgent tone. 'My lord.' Ratilal quirked his brow at him. '*High* lord, we have assessed our losses.'

'In a moment, Niaz.'

'High lord, we …'

Ratilal's face grew rigid as his composure slipped; he held up his hand imperiously. 'Later. First you can assist me best by helping me tend to this one's injuries.'

'What of your own injuries, high lord?'

'Later.'

'My brother?'

With a dismissive flick of his head, Ratilal indicated Niaz should check the youth.

Niaz saw through Ratilal's games. He knew Ratilal did not care for the life of the fallen warrior and was surprised by the distaste he felt toward his friend at that moment. Niaz assessed the prone figure and shook his head.

'He's gone,' Ratilal said sympathetically. 'Now, we must help you.'

The young man was rendered mute by the knowledge that his brother had slipped into the afterlife without him even noticing. A look of dismay crossed his features.

Ratilal didn't think he could tolerate it if this whelp cried. He kept his temper in check, as he was now aware they had an audience. 'He is gone now, with Rana and Jalal. There was nothing to be done, but you were with him, holding his hand, comforting him, which is more than many of us get. Now Niaz and I will tend to you.'

'Thank you, high lord.'

The warrior smiled half-heartedly, trying to be stoic before his lord. 'In truth, high lord, I don't know what I've done, other than the forearm is broken.'

'You must be tough, lad. I think this shoulder is dislocated.' Ratilal thought for a moment. 'Give me some arrows,' he ordered Niaz. 'Bind several into two lots. We'll use them as splints.' While

Niaz worked he explained, 'This is temporary. We will treat your arm properly when we are out of here. I regret that I have nothing to give you to ease your pain.' He proceeded to splint the forearm. 'Damn, Niaz. I can't quite use my fingers properly.' He ruefully held up his injured hand for all to see. 'You'll have to help me.' Niaz dutifully bound the arm. 'Now, for the shoulder …' Ratilal gritted his teeth, putting his hands in place.

'High lord, I shall do that for you.'

Ratilal cursed, but nodded. Niaz loosened the young man's cuirass, managed to put his hand under the outer tunic and felt the shoulder, grimacing as he did so. Ratilal made a show of checking the shoulder himself before allowing Niaz to commence. Even then he pretended to correct the position of his hands before allowing him to continue. 'Watch me,' he told the young man. 'Not Niaz. Do not take your eyes from me.' The young man's body jerked as Niaz popped the shoulder back in. 'Well done indeed!'

'Thank you, high lord.'

'No need, we are all warriors together and must help each other.' There was a murmur of assent from those present. 'Now, Niaz, you may report.'

'High lord, perhaps …' Niaz began in a near whisper.

'You may speak freely before my men. We have no secrets and they will likely already know what you are going to say.'

Niaz cleared his throat. 'High lord, we have lost half the horses. A quarter were killed in the falls, and the rest are badly lame. It is difficult to tell in the dark, but …'

'Many will not recover.' Ratilal allowed his frustration to bubble to the surface in his righteous indignation.

Niaz nodded, half bowing. 'Half the men are either dead or wounded. Some in falls, some by the enemy arrows.'

'The enemy. Yes, they are our enemy, make no mistake. I warned my father of this, yet his generous nature denied it. He wanted peace. They betrayed him.' His gesture encompassed his depleted forces. 'Look what they have wrought now. Barbarous! Too cowardly to fight us openly.'

'High lord, your orders?' Niaz asked.

A keen young voice spoke up. 'We can still pursue them. There are enough of us able, high lord. We can still stop them.'

Ratilal smiled indulgently at him, appearing to consider his words carefully. Many of the younger warriors waited eagerly. The older ones stood at the edge of the crowd, waiting, saying nothing, yet knowing the stupidity of another heedless pursuit in the dark. They were not interested in glory, but in what the next few moments would teach them regarding their new clan lord. Ratilal longed to chase the enemy down and personally gut them, but he could see the folly in this. Their headlong, careless pursuit was precisely how they were ambushed.

'No. I will send two scouts out to keep track of them and report back to me. The Four Ways is the only nearby way across The Divide and they must rest before they reach it. I will not risk another ambush in the dark. They have shown us the level they will stoop to. We need to get these horses and men tended to and this is not the place. I want two riders to return to Parlan and fetch the wagons left there; we can transport the wounded in them. Bring those two Kenati, they will have extra supplies and can tend the men.'

'The horses, high lord?'

'Find the nearest farm. In the light of day, we'll get the horses and men there and treat them properly.' He singled out two soldiers. 'You and you—to Parlan, now. I need two scouts.' The earlier eager youngster and his friends stepped forward. Ratilal chose the one who had spoken. 'You get to show your mettle. But I want you with an experienced hand.' He chose a seasoned warrior, placing him in charge. 'You,' he pointed to the younger man, 'listen. He has seen many more battles than you and survived. Do as he says—you will live longer. Both come with me.'

They approached the opening of the small valley, yet stayed hidden in the shadows. To the warriors on watch Ratilal asked, 'Any movement?'

'None, high lord.'

Ratilal nodded, deep in thought. 'Why haven't they attacked us? We are vulnerable.'

'Perhaps—the caltrops, high lord. Once scattered on the road, they would not be able to get their own horses through without risking them.'

'They could have come on foot, along the sides of the hills.'

'Begging your pardon, high lord, but our archers would have seen them—now that cloud is gone and the moon is fully out. The rock cover would only hide a few, not a whole force. Maybe it would have been too risky. They've got too far to get home if they had many wounded and none to ask for aid in this land.'

Ratilal nodded. 'Doubtless, you are correct.' *So they just wanted to slow me—why?* He could not shake the uneasy feeling that he had overlooked something. He stepped out into the moonlight, certain the enemy was gone. He heard the objections of his men with grim satisfaction as he walked further along the road to the far side of the fallen horses. Reaching them, he theatrically raised his arms out wide and bellowed to the empty night. 'Well! I am here! Shoot!'

Niaz walked up beside him. Ratilal looked at him smugly, knowing he had just given his men a good show. His back to his men, Ratilal pulled a metal flask from inside his tunic. 'Good thing this couldn't break.'

Niaz did not care for shadebell tea. His disapproval must have shown.

'Wipe that look off your face. I know what I am doing. This and the bloodroot are the only things keeping me upright and on a horse.'

'How can you stand the taste?'

'Honey and lots of it. I'm only sipping it.'

'You know you can't take it for long.'

Ratilal glared at him. 'Once the marks of my father's *love* are healed, I'll stop. Get the men to clear a path through this shit for the scouts.' He dismissively indicated the bodies of horses and men. Niaz moved to obey. 'Oh, and keep the caltrops they clear. We will have our revenge.'

➤

Karan and a few men entered the barn via the loose boards in its rear wall. Umniga and Asha waited inside. Honey was saddled and Umniga's mule was hitched to her wagon.

'We've emptied everything out to make it lighter,' Umniga said.

'Good.'

'How do we do this?'

'I need you two to go out there and attempt to take the strangers away.' Asha looked disconcerted. 'My men are in position, all will be well. I need to see who will side with you. If your guard follow you, things will go much easier.' He motioned his men into the wagon, then followed them.

Asha opened the doors and led Honey out, with Umniga following in the wagon behind her.

Vikram tensed as the two women approached. 'Be alert,' he instructed the soldiers nearest to him. 'You lot over there,' he bellowed at Ratilal's soldiers lounging around the fire and under the tree in the square. 'To me!' The command in his voice snapped them out of their lackadaisy and they hastened to the lodge. He trusted his instincts and if he was right, two split forces was not what they needed right now.

The wagon halted before the lodge; Umniga clambered down, using her staff for balance. Asha looped Honey's reins over the saddle and the mare stood patiently waiting.

'Asha, Umniga, are you leaving us?'

'Yes, but not just yet,' Umniga said. 'We've come for the villagers who Shahjahan agreed could go to the Horse and Bear.' Āsim, flanking Asha, gave a subtle hand signal and Asha's guards dispersed amongst the others.

'Shahjahan is dead.'

'Nevertheless, I think he would want his wishes carried out. Wishes he felt strongly enough about to formalise in a binding peace treaty.'

'The peace treaty,' his words dripped sarcasm, 'was broken by Karan and Baldev the moment they murdered Clan Lord Shahjahan. It no longer stands. These strangers are the property of High Lord Ratilal.'

Asha wanted to scream. *What has happened to you?* She moved forward to push past Vikram and enter the lodge.

'No!' Vikram barked, as he shoved Asha back.

Āsim leapt to her side, pulling her back, sword drawn. Ratilal's men drew their weapons to confront him, only to engage with Asha's guard. Karan and the others vaulted from the wagon to fight Ratilal's men. The rest of the Horse warriors poured forth from between buildings, surrounding their enemy. Swords gleamed dully in the moonlight, as the clash of metal filled the air.

Umniga swung her staff with a speed and skill which belied her age. She grinned widely as she thundered her staff into knee caps and bellies, then finished with crashing blows to backs and skulls as her opponents fell. She looked for Asha, finding her on the edge of the battle. Āsim was disarmed and Vikram was closing on him. Asha stepped between them and fought Vikram savagely. Fihr screeched indignation, but did not have the room to help her in the crush. Her blade flashed. Vikram grunted as she cut him and he doubled over. She stepped back, unable to place a killing blow on her friend.

'Vikram, yield.' He did not answer, but his sword fell from his hand. Asha moved toward him. 'Vikram?' As she moved, he lunged toward her, felling her. Her ribs screamed in protest as his weight bore down on her. Then Asha felt the unforgiving point of a dagger against her throat as he hauled her up before him.

'Stop!' Smiling cruelly, he continued, 'That's it. Now drop your weapons.' No one moved, but every eye was upon him. 'Do it!'

Karan nodded to his men. With deliberate slowness Karan bent his knees and began to lower his sword to the ground, never taking his eyes from Vikram, but not yet letting go of his sword. They glared at each other. Slowly Karan's men did the same thing. Ratilal's men relaxed slightly. Vikram's eyes darted around the crowd, and he licked his lips nervously.

Asha could feel the blade at her throat tremble. 'You don't have to do this,' she whispered.

Umniga stood in the shadows, watching, waiting. *Soon.*

'Yes I do, shut up,' he hissed back. The moment he spoke, Umniga sprang out of the dark wielding her staff and cracked him across the skull. Vikram dropped like a stone.

Karan, his men, and Asha's guard rushed upright and resumed the battle. As more of Ratilal's men fell, the fight went out of the remainder who, with their leader gone, surrendered. Vikram moaned as he regained consciousness, only to have Asha's guard descend upon him. They spat on him and kicked his prone form. Āsim hauled him to his feet, punched him and dragged him to the wagon wheel. He propped Vikram against it, before proceeding to pummel him repeatedly.

'Enough!' Karan ordered as he put a restraining hand on his arm. 'Āsim, enough. Bind them, then throw them in the lodge.' He bent and casually cleaned the blood from his sword on the clothing of the nearest corpse.

Karan addressed Asha's guard. 'You have upheld the values of your old clan lord by choosing to protect Asha, for which I honour you. But, you have now attacked your fellows; Ratilal will not tolerate this. He is corrupt—evil. You need to know that he killed Shahjahan. Asha, Baldev and I all saw it happen. We could do nothing. We watched Ratilal gloat over his father as his last breath left his body. I could not leave Shahjahan without saying the words of passage over his corpse; when I did so Niaz conveniently appeared to catch me. It was all carefully orchestrated by Ratilal. He does not want what Shahjahan wanted. He does not want the clans united. He does not want peace. He will be nothing other than a perversion of what a clan lord should be.' Karan watched them process this information. He could see that they readily believed it. They had, after all, witnessed the result of his brutal attack on Asha. 'You have a choice: face Ratilal, or come with us and continue to act as Asha's guard. You will not be asked to fight against your own clan, save in defence of Asha or Umniga—*your* Kenati.' He paused. 'There is little time, you must decide now.'

Āsim stepped forward. 'I am with you.' He placed his palm on his heart, before turning it into a fist: an ancient symbol of fidelity amongst warriors.

Almost as one the rest of Asha's guard moved to join him, mimicking his actions. 'We are with you.'

'And glad I am of it,' Karan said with a genuine smile. 'Asha, Umniga, come.' Karan strode into the lodge, proceeding directly to Isaura. He scooped her up, frowning at how light she felt. Looking at Nicanor and Curro, he ordered, 'Come,' before leaving without a backward glance. Karan climbed into the wagon, cradling Isaura to his chest, taking care not to bump her in the confined space. Carefully, he placed her on the remaining bed and covered her with a quilt Umniga had left. Karan looked at her gaunt face before he left. *I hope you're worth it.*

Nicanor, Lucia and Pio were the first to leave. Pio, confused and frightened, stared at a bound, gagged and bloody Vikram before Nicanor urged him on. Elena, frightened by the fighting, dragged her heels. She stopped near the entrance looking in dismay at the injured soldiers being hauled into the lodge. Curro took her hand and towed her onward, but the sight of the dead outside halted her again.

'Curro, I don't know that we should go with these people.'

Gabriela was behind her. 'Well, I am going. These men,' she nodded at those tied up, 'are under the command of Ratilal. Remember Asha? Remember her injuries? He did that. You are crazy if you want to stay anywhere near him.'

Lucia concurred, remembering his callous eyes. 'He is evil,

Elena. You can't stay.'

She nodded but didn't move, so Curro picked her up, strode to the wagon, and dumped her in the back.

Upon hearing Lucia's words, and having witnessed the fighting, the other survivors made moves to leave. Karan barked out a command. His men swept into the lodge, their imposing presence forcing the others to remain.

Looking back, Jaime realised that Daniel was not with them. Daniel remained sitting, trying to appear impassive but failing miserably. Jaime returned to him hesitantly, instinctively afraid of the outcome. 'Daniel?'

Daniel's eyes were tear-filled, his face twisted. He was about to crumple, but he schooled his features, avoiding Jaime's gaze. 'I can't.'

'Can't?'

'Won't. You two go. You deserve to be happy, but I can't stay to watch it. It's eating me up inside. I'll never get over her if I have to watch the two of you. I need to find my own way.'

'It's not safe. What if ...'

'It's not safe anywhere. I'll take my chances. I don't think one weaver offers much of a threat to this lot.'

Umniga, hastily treating some of the wounded, bound warriors, paused in her work to watch this exchange. She noted Karan was also watching with keen interest from the door. He caught her look, cocked his brow, and gave her a wry grin. *He has plans within plans*, Uminga thought. *What will he want with the boy?*

'Umniga, Asha. We go now.' Umniga dropped her bag at the feet of the stranger nearest her, taking the time to indicate the bandages within and point to the wounded men. The stranger nodded and proceeded to bind their wounds.

Jaime and Daniel were frozen in a tableau of grief. Karan regretted having to interrupt their farewell, but placed his hand on Jaime's shoulder and urged him on.

Umniga saw the look of devastation that crossed Daniel's face. Her heart went out to him. Impulsively she went to him and embraced him, saying softly, 'May the Great Mother and Father guard and guide you. May you find happiness in the light of their blessing.' Daniel had no idea what Umniga said, but he melted into her embrace with a sob. Gently, she disentangled herself, put her hands on either side of his face and pulled it down to place a soft kiss on his brow. 'Be well, young one.'

Karan remained near the door as his men filtered out of the lodge. Vikram was on the floor propped against the wall near Karan's feet. His face was bloody and one eye was swollen. Karan scowled, grabbed his collar roughly, put his lips against his ear and said, 'I'm sorry. It was necessary. Forgive me.'

Vikram's eye acknowledged the truth of his words, but his face remained savage, just as Karan never let his look shift from one of loathing, despite his speech. Karan shook him, then spat on him and left.

CHAPTER TWENTY-FOUR

KARAN was feeling very pleased with himself—everything was going according to plan. Thanks to Ratilal's men, he and his own men were now all riding, as were Curro, Nicanor and Jaime; while their women and Pio were in the wagon driven by Umniga. Devi was aloft, scouring the way before them, alert for the enemy. Fihr was perched on the wagon seat beside Umniga, while Asha rode alongside them. He thought about the training that would await the strangers. It would not take long to put some skill on the men; they were strong and not unfit. Of the women, he was not so certain. They looked soft and weak, it would take a long while; all he asked was that they were willing. If not … Even Asha's guard, while Vikram had chosen them well, would need their skills honed before they would be a match for his men.

Karan flashed Āsim an open friendly grin. 'They'll not know what's hit them.'

'My lord?'

'Āsim, you have known me too long to call me anything other than my name. But I am referring to their training, which you will help with.'

'Once, Karan, I could have put them to shame, but I have been tucked away in Faros with soft living too long. I have forgotten the rigours of my training with your father.'

'I am sorry you were exiled from us for so long, but you were invaluable.' He paused. 'You still are.'

'And Vikram?' Āsim said.

'He still has a task to perform.'

'Thank the gods he thought to call all Ratilal's men together. If they were split, some may have got away and warned the others.'

Devi, screeched. Umniga sat bolt upright. 'Someone is coming!'

'You lot, with me. The rest of you and the horses, into cover. Asha, you too—it could be Ratilal.' Karan quickly dismounted with a few men.

The outer edge of the Eastern Forest was only a short distance from the road, and it was to this that the main force moved with all speed. Fihr took flight and joined Asha. The wagon, however, could not do so. Karan and his squad flattened themselves in a slight ditch that ran beside the road. The long grass that verged it and the road sheltered them. Tense, poised, they waited.

The women in the wagon began whispering anxiously. 'Ssh!' Umniga hissed at them. She drew the cover across the doorway, nodded to Lucia to do the same for the rear door, then passed her a dagger. Lucia took it with a determined look and immediately drew the rear cover closed. Umniga smiled. *The woman has more grit than she realises.* She moved her staff across her lap and waited. She did not have to wait very long before two horses came trotting along the road.

Their riders stopped beside her, with their horses blowing hard, grateful for a moment's rest.

'Umniga, we did not expect to see you on the road. Why are you not in Parlan with the refugees High Lord Ratilal left under your care?'

It was an honest enquiry, but edged with the slightest bit of distrust. Lucia tensed; understanding the edge of suspicion in their tone, her hand tightened on the dagger. She shared a determined look with Gabriela, who nodded, signalling her desire to help.

Umniga took umbrage at his tone. 'What kind of fool do you think I am, you whelp? Do you think that I would see my clan lord'—she rebelled at the term 'high lord'—'disappear into the night, chasing the enemy, without keeping an eye on him? How dare you! I have served this clan longer than you have been alive, boy. I know my duty. Did you think I would not know that the clan lord needed me?' Devi chose this moment to land on the roof of the wagon and turn his own baleful glare on the two abashed soldiers.

'How did you know?'

'Devi has shown me. Do they teach you nothing in Faros? You are delaying my journey to our clan lord—he will not be pleased.'

'Our apologies, mistress,' came the contrite reply.

Umniga sniffed, still glaring. 'You were headed to Parlan?'

'Yes, mistress, to fetch the wagons for the wounded and any supplies we could muster.'

'Too many dead,' she guessed with sorrow.

'Aye, mistress. Too many men and too many horses. They used caltrops—we rode at a gallop straight into them.'

'The bastards!' she said vehemently. 'Off with you, get those wagons. We'll be needing them. Asha is there with the strangers, she will help you. And take care of those horses before they drop, or you'll be walking there and that will be just one more thing to annoy the clan lord—trust me, you don't want that.' She gave them a sly smile as if taking them into her confidence. 'Boy's got a worse temper than his father, and that's saying something.'

She watched as they disappeared down the track. 'Follow them,' she said to Devi. 'Let me know if they come back.'

Umniga shoved her head in the rear of the wagon and chuckled—the others, who had been holding their breath in fear, inhaled collectively. When she turned back and gathered up the reins to move off, Karan was already beside them and the horses and men were returning from cover.

'You never even raised a sweat. Old one, you take some beating,' he said.

'Looks like Baldev's been busy,' was all she replied.

'It was necessary,' Karan said soberly. 'You want these people? Then it was necessary. Don't forget for an instant that this is war and that it's not Shahjahan we're dealing with, but Ratilal. There will be no mercy from him.'

The horses passed between the greenery of the hidden entrance, but Karan knew they would not get Umniga's wagon past the low hanging branches that obscured the way to the ancient, overgrown track to Hunters' Ford. Umniga beckoned the women out, after which Karan climbed in and went to Isaura. He scooped her up easily and exited the wagon.

'Get rid of the canopy. Then maybe we can get it out of sight.' He carried Isaura through the hanging branches of the sheoaks and deposited her on a soft bed of pine needles further down the track with her friends, before returning to the wagon.

Umniga spoke softly to her mule, Nasir, still in the traces, while one of Karan's men used a war axe to quickly hack through the willow uprights on the canopy, which was then deftly collapsed into the wagon tray. Nasir kept a watchful eye on the commotion behind him. His ears flicked back and forth as he listened to Umniga and the men to his rear. He never once appeared unduly frightened by their activities, but when the canopy was folded up, he gave a soft snort of satisfaction that they were finished.

'He's a good fellow,' Karan said affectionately, patting Nasir's neck.

'I'll be sad to leave him.' Nasir's ears flicked forward at this and he nudged her firmly as if in distaste.

'My lord, we are ready.'

'When we pull the branches away, lead him forward.' Karan and his men managed to pull back and lift the larger branches out of the way as Umniga led Nasir through the trees. She moved the wagon slowly, for the tree limbs still rested on its timber sides and scraped their way along them. As the wagon moved, the men endeavoured to protect the branches from breaking; they did not want any obvious sign that they had passed this way. Ratilal was bound to discover their scheme, but they were certainly not going to leave him any clues.

Behind these massive trees towered a few great pines—guardians of the path. Their combined canopies blocked out much of the sunlight during the day, and little moonlight entered at night. With so little light, and the soft thick springy mat of pine and sheoak needles, there was no undergrowth until beyond the pines. It was a perfect spot to conceal the wagon.

Umniga led Nasir forward as far as she could, then began to unharness him, leaving his bridle on and cutting the driving reins to a shorter length, before leading him forward to join the horses.

Karan and the others pushed the wagon further into this dim enclave until it abutted the trunk of one of the pines. Karan carried Isaura as they led the horses under the low-hanging branches of the pines.

Nicanor usually found forests tranquil places, yet the pine scent that should have been reassuring and calming to him was not. He did not know if it was just his nerves, or the adrenaline of this escape, but he was uncomfortable. This dim, eerie world was too quiet. At home there were many night noises; here, there was not a sound. The horses made no nickers or nervous snorts in the dark, and their footfalls were completely muted by the needle bed. Above all loomed the feeling that he was being watched.

Once past the pines, the forest thinned and moonlight filtered through the trees in flickering gasps between cloud cover. The warriors remounted the horses, with Karan in the forefront, carrying Isaura before him. Curro and the others were encouraged back onto their horses; their women were lifted behind them. Jaime winced as he mounted, earning a grin from the others. Back home, only the farmers had horses for field work. Curro, as a smith, had handled them and Nicanor had a mule to pull timber from the forest. None of them were used to riding; their inner thighs were raw and they had been glad of the chance to stretch their legs. Pio was lifted behind Asha onto Honey. He turned around and shot his father a gleeful look as they followed along. Lucia said nothing, but Nicanor could feel her shaking her head in disbelief.

Pio resisted the urge to talk. He had so many questions, yet no one was saying anything and he felt that he should not break the silence. Asha could feel Pio turning his head this way and that and leaning his body to the side to see objects from a different angle. Honey flicked her ears back and forth every time he wriggled and inadvertently dug his short legs into her sides. Asha was losing patience too; Pio was hanging onto her sore ribs tightly and each time he moved his pointy little chin dug into her.

Honey gave a small pigroot, causing Pio to cling onto Asha more tightly. She blew out an exasperated breath, stopped Honey and whispered something to the warrior nearest her. Suddenly Pio was plucked from the back of the horse and dumped in front of Asha. With one hand on the reins and the other around his middle, she gave him a firm squeeze and shake.

'Be still!' she hissed. Pio needed no translation. They continued in silence for a while, his head still craning to see all he could. However, when the moonlight disappeared, he would clutch Asha's hand and lean back against her, seeking protection from the dark.

Nicanor marvelled at how these men and horses could move unerringly, even without the moonlight. He tried to direct his horse, but soon gave up, as that was the only time it stumbled. It was far more able to negotiate the meandering track than he. The path wove around the boles of enormous ancient trees, down small fern-lined gullies, through small creeks, and up the other side. Logs often crisscrossed the path; the horses calmly picked their way over them, content to follow each other. They seemed to sense obstacles and holes and would step over or around them. When the moonlight reached them, the forest was bathed in a beautiful blue-grey light. As they rode, the natural noises of the forest returned and he relaxed. Now and then he felt Lucia's indrawn breath, as something scuttled off through the undergrowth, and patted her hand reassuringly. This was normal. Yet, he would still occasionally stiffen, unable to shake the feeling of eyes upon him.

Baldev's scouts had found a rocky goat track that descended through a maze of trees and shrubs down to the river's edge. Here it opened out onto a long sandy stretch interspersed with large, half-buried flat rocks, backed by a near vertical bank that towered above them. The striations in the layers of soil transitioned from heavy clay to top soil embedded with roots that tenaciously held it together. Part of the bank was rock which, eroded by water, formed a long half cave. It was roomy enough to fit many of the men and horses. Content with the skill of his sentries, he allowed the horses a short rest.

Ratilal's scouts had headed off at what the younger of the two, Jabr, thought was a sedate pace.

'Mas'ud, should we not be pursuing the enemy with more vigour?' he whispered hesitantly.

Mas'ud replied in disgust, 'That, boy, will just get you killed quick. We're not a two-man assault team. We are scouts … and we're scouting.' Jabr looked as if he was about to speak again when Mas'ud hawked up a great gob of mucus and spat. 'Enough, boy. Do you want to run headlong into the next trap? Wind up like those poor bastards back there?' Jabr shook his head vigorously. 'Right, just watch and learn.'

'They'll be long gone.'

'The only way home for them is The Four Ways. Their horses will need to rest somewhere. We'll scout them out—if we're lucky we'll get ahead of them. If that happens, you go to the crossing to warn the guard as fast as you can and I'll head to Faros for more men. Got it?' The boy nodded eagerly. 'Stay behind me now, I don't want you fouling up any tracks. It's bloody well hard enough to see as it is. And tie down your loose gear. You make enough noise for ten.'

Quickly Jabr realised that the irascible Mas'ud did, in fact, know what he was doing. The passing riders had sprayed water from the rain-filled potholes across the surrounding road and left clear hoof imprints, even in the moonlight. At times, the road grew rocky and Mas'ud had to dismount to look for signs of their passing. Jabr suddenly realised that Mas'ud had increased their pace. He urged his gelding along to keep up; it trotted along obediently.

Mas'ud glared at him. 'Quietly, boy. You should be able to get that nag to stretch out in a walk; to stride so fast it's like another's trot. Don't they teach you anything?' he derided.

Jabr felt like a child—a dimwitted one at that, yet he persevered and soon had his horse keeping the ground-eating pace Mas'ud had set. A myriad of questions entered Jabr's mind, yet he was reluctant to voice them, not wanting to receive the sharp end of Mas'ud's tongue. He noticed that the older man's attitude was changing. Mas'ud was becoming more intent, like a hound with a scent.

Abruptly he turned his horse off the road, away from the river and into the undulating fields beyond. Mas'ud paused, holding his finger to his lips. 'Follow,' he mouthed. The boy, wide-eyed and suddenly nervous, nodded. They moved cautiously amongst the low hills, slowly doubling back in the direction of Parlan. Mas'ud dismounted and left Jabr holding the horses while he scouted on foot. Sitting alone in the darkness, the boy felt his courage slipping. All he could think of were childhood tales of terror and murder. He nearly screamed when Mas'ud, unbeknown to him, returned and touched his leg.

Mas'ud remounted, looked at the boy's terrified face, and took pity on him long enough to explain in a thin whisper, 'We lost their trail on the road a short while ago. I kept going for a while to make it look as if we thought they had continued.' Jabr appeared mystified. 'Do you understand? They did not travel further on the road—they are hiding somewhere about. Now we find them. There are not many places to hide so many riders. These low hills were the most obvious choice, but I think too obvious.'

They continued cautiously scouting the hills before veering in the direction of the road again. Mas'ud left Jabr minding the horses behind a copse of trees between several hillocks and he wove his way cautiously back to the road.

Mas'ud crouched down in long grass, surveying the road dissecting the terrain before him. By his reckoning, he was very close to where the tracks of the fleeing horsemen stopped. He had seen no sign that they were among the small hills behind him and noticed no tracks through the vegetation or soft soil showing they had departed this side of the road at all. That only left the river side of the road. *Somewhere rocky, maybe.* He slunk through the undergrowth, peering intently at the other side of the road as he went. Trees lined the far roadside, too dense for the passage of horses.

He was about to give up his inspection and backtrack, but the thought of facing Ratilal without success made him persevere. He moved slowly, patiently, waiting. Then he saw it. He was peering at what looked like a solid wall of trees when viewed from the front, except that there was a gap. A wild cherry, with its cypress-like weeping fronds, stood to the rear of the other trees, creating a gap between them. There was a narrow, rocky track between the trees, which they had overlooked in the dark. Mas'ud knew the gods were smiling on him, for moonlight shone on the spot now. He saw a branch move, yet there was no wind. *Sentry. Thanks be. If we had noticed and investigated earlier we'd be dead. As it is they must think we passed them by.*

Mas'ud retreated and travelled away from the entrance toward Faros, hopeful that he could cross the road undetected to spy on the enemy. *First I'd better check on the boy—make sure he stays put.*

Jabr was proud of himself—this time he realised Mas'ud was approaching. Although, he thought despondently, that was probably because Mas'ud wanted him to know and not scream like a girl in fright.

'I think I've found them. Stay here, boy.'

Boy! Jabr knew he was inexperienced, but how was he to learn anything stuck here holding the horses like a child. *I should tie the horses up and follow*, he thought rebelliously. He debated the idea for a while, then, frustrated by his own weakness, he tied the horses to the trees and followed Mas'ud.

CHAPTER TWENTY-FIVE

MAS'UD pressed against a tree trunk and peered down on an angle at the riverside. The enemy were below him on the riverbank, partially hidden by an overhang in the embankment. Although they were cautious, he could still hear the tell-tale movements of men and horses. He moved to a better vantage point. Careful now, old man. It looked to be the full force, but as yet he had not seen lords Baldev or Karan. High Lord Ratilal had said to scout and report back, but he had his bow with him—one well placed shot could end this war. He just had to be certain of his target. Surely he would be rewarded for initiative?

Mas'ud lay flat, carefully easing himself under the dense undergrowth and peering down the steep bank to his left. He could see Baldev's mountainous form standing next to Karan's cloaked one. They were partially under the overhang. *No room to shoot.* They did not speak as the horses rested and drank. Ready to leave, Mas'ud paused as he watched Karan lead Mirza forward. He frowned, noting the easy body language between horse and rider was absent. As Karan stepped fully from cover, a gnarly tree root protruding from the roof of the cavern caught on his hood and pulled it from his head. *It's not Karan!* Mas'ud watched as he quickly pulled the hood back up. *Where the blazes is he?*

Despite the sense of urgency flooding his mind, he inched his way backward slowly and quietly, coming to a crouch at the edge of cover. A hand shot over his mouth and yanked him back. He felt the cold steel of a knife pressed against his neck. It pierced his skin. Blood welled and ran down his neck, then—nothing. The hand across his mouth became lax. The knife at his throat fell quietly into the grass. Mas'ud turned his head quickly to see young Jabr, eyes wide, with his knife firmly planted in the neck of the enemy sentry and his hand clamped tightly over his mouth.

Jabr looked as if he might throw up or pass out at any point. Mas'ud held his finger up against his lips, then gestured that he should lower the body slowly to the ground. Jabr nodded, collecting himself. They rolled the body quietly under the bushes. Jabr made to rise. Mas'ud's hand on his shoulder stopped him, while he looked for signs of another sentry. Nothing. Mas'ud nodded and they cautiously made their way back to the horses.

'Well done, lad!' Jabr was silent. 'First time, eh?' Jabr nodded. 'You did the right thing.'

'I disobeyed orders.'

'Thank the gods for that—this time.' The boy seemed in a slight daze. 'No harm done lad, you saved my life.' Mas'ud patted him on the back. 'Come on, mount up. Good lad. Now you are going to ride through these fields and avoid the road until you're well past the enemy and get back to High Lord Ratilal. Look at me now, boy. Listen well. Tell him Karan is not with Baldev.'

Jabr straightened, alarmed at this news. 'Where is he?' he squeaked.

'Buggered if I know, and that's the problem. Just tell Ratilal. I'm off to warn the crossing and get more men from Faros.'

The terrain grew increasingly steep. The path they followed was, at times, only a narrow track—barely wide enough for one person to walk on, yet at others it vanished completely. Elena had remained silent the entire journey. She clung to Curro, terrified, now that the track continued along the side of a precipice. She turned her head away from the sheer drop and closed her eyes tightly. Curro had one hand on the reins, while the other was entwined with one of her hands around his middle, his thumb gently caressing the back of her hand.

Lucia had given up feeling scared after the first few steep descents and climbs out of slippery gullies with burbling little creeks running down them. Her stomach had been in knots and she had begun to feel ill. She thought of Umniga giving her the knife in the wagon. Of the three of them, this old wise woman had trusted her to be courageous enough to use it. Umniga had seen something in her that she had not thought existed.

Recalling this woman's faith in her made her feel that perhaps she could live up to that—perhaps she should. It was clear that these people had taken a huge risk to extract them from Ratilal's control. To *save* them. The thought of his heartless eyes staring at her still made her shudder. Her spine had straightened. *Look at what you have survived so far.* She had found herself grinning. Since then her fear had slipped away and she now sat loosely behind Nicanor, trying to pay attention in the fleeting moonlight to their surroundings.

Lucia thought that in daylight this terrain would probably be picturesque; in the blue gloom it was beautiful and mysterious. When they set out through the forest, it had been very quiet, even the horse's hoof beats were deadened by the pine needles. It was as if the world were holding its breath. As they moved deeper into the forest, the noises had returned; the horse's hoof beats were louder. The variety of terrain had surprised her. At times it was boggy in the gullies; though she could not see in detail, she could hear the horse's feet squelch in the mud. Then they would climb a ridge and it would be rocky with little undergrowth between the trees. When the moonlight shone through the trees here, she gasped, for amongst the darker trunks were tall straight white ones that seemed to reflect the moonlight, almost glowing.

They were departing from one such ridge as the narrow track followed the contours of the hillside and wove its way downward. The sound of a river had been flitting in and out of their hearing for some time. It became louder as they began to reach the base of the hillside; a veil of mist had begun to creep amongst the trees. The towering sentinels were thinning, smaller trees and bushes were taking their place, and the moonlight flooded in. Lucia noticed the leaves on these trees appeared, in the moonlight, to be varying shades of grey. *They must be turning. What will this look like with the dawn?* The noise of the river grew to a dull roar. Then over the tops of some low lying shrubs she spied a massive set of rapids. Water rushed amongst and over huge boulders as the river dropped. Their trail veered away from it, twisting and turning, around its own set of boulders for some way before opening to a wide clear expanse beside the now quiet river. Before them lay Hunters' Ford.

'The water has risen again, my lord,' said the warrior next to Karan.

'It matters not; I never intended for the horses to cross. Get the boats ready.'

Men disappeared into the undergrowth and carried out canoes that they had used to cross the river earlier in order to rendezvous with Karan. Those remaining urged the strangers to get off their horses.

Asha dismounted and helped Pio down. She had been trying not to think about this moment. Quickly, she removed her shield and quivers from Honey's saddle, tempted as she did so to run her hand affectionately over her neck and murmur to her, but she did not— she could not. Asha unsaddled her and removed her bridle, placing them next to her gear. She turned her back upon her horse, then walked over to Karan.

'My Lord Karan,' Asha said. She had resorted to formality to give her fortitude.

'Mistress Asha,' Karan responded. He could hear the strain in her voice.

'My saddle, my weapons … may I bring them?' The words rushed forth. 'They were gifts.' She stumbled over her next words. 'I know I must … Honey … but can I take them … is there room?' Karan wished he could comfort her, but he could sense her hold over her emotions was tenuous and believed if he did they would overwhelm her. He knew Asha—she would feel weak if she succumbed to them before the men.

'There is room. Come, I'll help you.' Honey was waiting patiently beside Asha's tack. Asha could not look at her. She could not think. She picked up her saddle and followed Karan in a daze. She passed it to be stowed in the boat, turned and immediately walked straight into a soft muzzle—Honey had followed her. Karan gripped the mare's mane and led her and Asha away from the shore to the tree line, where he left them without a word.

Next he approached Umniga, who was swearing as she stretched her legs one by one.

'I am too old for this!' She leaned on Nasir's back and peered in Asha's direction. Asha was standing with Honey's forehead resting against her chest as she stroked down the sides of her face. 'How is she?'

'How do you think?' Karan was abrupt. 'How are you, old one?'

'Stiff and sore. I can't remember the last time I spent this long on a horse, let alone bareback. I ache in places I'd forgotten about and my legs feel like jelly. Damn you and Baldev, and your wagon. You've made me soft.' Here she paused. 'And you gave me Nasir. You know his name means "Helper", don't you?' With this she rubbed his neck affectionately. 'Bah! I'm soft in the head too now, thanks to you!' She lowered her forehead down against Nasir's side. 'Take his bridle off for me.'

Karan removed the bridle, and gave her shoulder a gentle squeeze. His men had loaded everyone into the boats. The first few had begun to head across the river. The last two waited only for Asha, Umniga and himself.

'Asha, Umniga!' He felt cruel as they obeyed him and headed to the canoes. *Five more minutes won't make it any easier.* The horses were all unbridled and had wandered off to pick at greenery along the shore line. He snapped a thin branch off a nearby sapling and walked up to the one nearest the trail entrance. He gave it a good firm switch, driving it back through the trail. The others took off after it in their efforts to escape him. He had hoped that Honey and Nasir would follow. Honey, ears forward, watched the others disappear, but did not move. She snorted warily as Karan approached her; he gave her a good switch and she bolted to stand trembling beside Nasir. *Gods, damn it!* He walked briskly up to Nasir, but before he could use the switch Nasir kicked it from his hand and spun to face him. 'Some helper you are!' he muttered. Nasir flattened his ears at him. 'Fine.' Karan turned and stomped to the canoes, feeling like a complete bastard. Reaching the canoes, he muttered, 'Let's go.'

Asha sat unmoving, staring ahead at the opposite bank. It did not matter that in the mist and moonlight she could not see that far, she was unable to look elsewhere.

'It's so wide!' Pio whispered awestruck.

On the bank, Honey paced the shore. Nasir stood between her and the water, matching her movements, blocking her. She tried to dash past him and plunge into the water, but he cut her off. Honey emitted a panicked neigh as the boats disappeared across the water.

Asha gripped the side of the canoe in a bid to stop trembling. The last canoe travelled gracefully and swiftly, yet as it approached the middle of the river the men paddled more strongly, fighting the current to get to the other side, and spurred on to escape Honey's desperate calls. Their brows were beaded with sweat, despite the chill night air. They knew they were slowly being forced sideways away from their landing point. As the current eased, they angled upstream and prayed that they had not drifted further in the mist than they had planned. The mist parted to reveal the other canoes beached on the shore before them. Jaime was on the bank waving at them, before helping lift and carry a canoe away. Curro and Nicanor grinned, pulling their paddles with renewed vigour. It felt good to be doing something helpful.

Honey neighed piteously, and darted toward the water. Nasir blocked her yet again, tossing his head and attempting to bite her.

She pivoted on her hind legs, spraying pebbles in his direction as she escaped him, then stood quivering on the shore. He had driven her further away from the water. Nasir closed on her, his eyes never leaving her. She snorted, pawing the ground and shaking her head at him. Her sides were becoming slick with sweat. She sprang sideways, trying to gallop past him. She almost made it, but he cut her off just before the water's edge. Nasir snaked his neck out and bit her. She squealed and backed up. He advanced on her again, eyeballing her as he did.

Honey returned his gaze, her head held high. Nasir snorted and reared toward her, pawing the air and striking out in her direction, forcing her back. When he landed, he spun and kicked just beyond her nose. He had now herded Honey further along the shore, upstream from where the canoes had disembarked. Honey found herself trapped in a natural cul-de-sac formed by the narrowing of the beach, an overhang and a fallen tree. Nasir stopped, his long ears forward, and continued to stare at her. Slowly, Honey began to lower her head.

Karan's canoe pulled into shore and they quickly disembarked. The beach was pebbly, as on the other side of the river, but shorter, meeting the root-encrusted riverbank that towered some six feet higher. Along this bank were more of Karan's warriors, men and women.

Asha began to unload her gear. Karan quietly took some of it up the riverbank. She stoically carried what was left up the short pebbly beach, then staggered as she tried to heft it up the steep and, thanks to the others, now slippery path to the top. Tree roots formed some natural footholds and at some point some large square rocks had been strategically placed behind roots to form more lasting steps, but the crossing was little used and damage from previous rains and floods had taken its toll. She paused, frustrated, miserable and angry. A hand reached down and took her load from her. Asha looked gratefully into Āsim's face. He gave her a sad smile and a wink, and hauled her up.

The canoes were carted to the steep bank, sat on their ends and then pushed up, as those above grasped them and pulled. They were then whisked off to their hiding place.

Asha sat on the bank, dangling her legs over the edge. There were no longer any despairing neighs from across the river. She should have been relieved, but instead she was depressed.

'They'll be fine. They'll give up and follow the others,' Umniga said as she joined her and passed her a water bag. 'They'll go home, or back to Parlan and Deo.'

Fihr landed beside Asha and sidled up to her in concern. Devi landed beside Umniga.

'Can you send Devi to see, please?'

Umniga pursed her lips, thinking that it may be best to assume they were safe, rather than know the truth.

'I know that look, Umniga. I'm no longer a child. Don't treat me as one. I need to know.'

The old woman sighed. *I am getting old and soft.* 'Fine, but if he drops dead from exhaustion I'm blaming you.' Devi eyeballed her, gave a short abrupt bark and took off. Asha threw her arms around Umniga in gratitude.

Karan was impatient to leave, but he and Āsim had seen and heard Umniga and Asha's exchange. 'We'll rest here a short while— tell the others,' Karan instructed the older man.

Umniga moved away from the edge of the riverbank and sat cross-legged, waiting for Devi, with Asha beside her.

Asha grinned, suddenly lighter in spirits. Thinking of Devi's indignant departure, she said with an uncharacteristically nervous giggle, 'Devi's a funny old one.'

'Umph!' Umniga grunted. 'You try living with him for sixty years.' She took Asha's hand. 'It shouldn't take long. They have probably left.'

Honey stood cowed, her head lowered and licking her lips before Nasir. He snorted softly at her. Devi landed on a branch of the dead tree just over the water.

Umniga's eyes grew wide and she swayed slightly as Devi merged with her, sending her a brief glimpse of Nasir and Honey. 'What are they doing?' Then, unusually, Devi blocked her out. She tried to re-merge with him, but there was nothing. 'What is going on?'

Interested yet wary, Karan and Āsim moved closer.

Nasir approached Honey, lowered his nose to hers and breathed softly beside it. Devi sat watching, fending off Umniga's demands. Honey was calm. Nasir walked to the water's edge and she followed to stand downstream beside him. He flicked his head at her, ears back, and she moved upstream to his other side. Nasir was diagonally facing the opposite landing point, even though through the mist he could not see it. Devi gave two successive short barks and took off, flying in a straight line across the water. Nasir and Honey waded into the water. It was not long before they were swimming and vanishing into the mist.

Devi flew over Umniga, banked and returned over the river, finally allowing her to merge with him again. As he flew low over the water she saw Nasir and Honey, swimming valiantly across the river.

Umniga broke from Devi, murmuring, 'Great Mother, Great Father, givers of light and life, help them. Great Father, Jalal, let your river support them, lend them strength, guide them home.'

'What's happened? Umniga? Umniga!' Asha asked her anxiously.

'They're crossing the river. Karan, they're coming from upstream.'

Asha shot to her feet and tried to peer through the mist.

Nasir saw Devi fly across the river slightly upstream and pushed Honey in that direction. The current was at its strongest halfway across and their struggle intensified. Honey drifted downstream into Nasir, who used his shoulder to guide her back on course. Nasir concentrated on Devi and forced himself to keep moving. Out of the mist, he could see Umniga standing on the high bank. Honey's head dipped below the water; he nipped her, urging her to fight. They were still too far away.

Karan had nimbly climbed down the haphazard steps with several of his men and Asha. They had retrieved a canoe and on seeing Nasir and Honey emerge from the mist, they set out across the water. 'Pull! *Pull!*' he urged. Honey's head was barely above water, her nostrils were flared wide with exertion. Drifting up beside her, Karan placed a rope behind her ears and crossed it under her jaw and over her nose, using it as a makeshift halter. He threw the end to Asha. 'Talk to her. And keep pressure on the rope.' He leaned out and placed his hands under Honey's head to help keep it above the water. The canoe listed precariously. The men pulled furiously on the paddles.

Nasir, relieved of assisting Honey, swam for shore with renewed vigour. Soon he felt the bottom of the river brush against his feet and he waded ponderously ashore. Seeing Umniga waiting for him, he let out a joyful racket that started as a whinny and ended as a bray.

'Damn fool mule!' Umniga chided as she gave him an affectionate pat and looked over him for injuries.

'You do realise how clever he is, don't you?' Karan asked, as Asha led Honey from the water.

'What?' Asha and Umniga said simultaneously.

'They came from upstream.' The two women remained uncomprehending. 'They swam with and only partially against the current. I heard Honey scream when she was left behind. I bet she would have plunged, heedless, straight into that river and been lost.' Umniga and Asha were speechless. 'Your damn fool mule just saved that little mare.'

The warriors who met them on the other side of the ford had brought enough spare horses for everyone, and were riding strung out behind Karan, who held Isaura tightly before him on his horse. She looked paler and felt colder. Whatever the Kenati had planned, he knew it must happen soon. A grin crossed his face as he looked at Umniga riding Nasir. Despite his ordeal, Nasir had become thoroughly cantankerous when she prepared to ride one of the new horses in order to rest him. Honey was beside Nasir, looking decidedly weary, although less bedraggled than when she left the river. Asha was riding another, with Pio asleep before her.

They were now in the Forest of the Asena, heading to their camp. This section of forest, in daylight, was a myriad of colours with the many deciduous trees readying for leaf-fall. Yet as the forest climbed the Bear Tooth Mountain range, conifers, dark firs, pines and cypresses predominated.

Karan beckoned Umniga to him. 'What are you planning to do for this one?'

'The Ritual of Samara.'

'You will do it tonight,' he ordered.

'But I will need all of the Kenati and the sacred site at the lake.'

'The Kenati are here at this camp, not at the lake. You should know by now, I always plan ahead.'

'Without the site, I cannot guarantee success.'

Karan stared at her gravely. 'Look at her. She is fading. You are not guaranteed success even at the site. She will be dead by the time you reach the lake.'

Umniga's face took on a fatalistic cast and her lips turned down bitterly. She had been holding onto one last remnant of hope and it was beginning to crumble.

Karan took pity on her. 'There is another site near where we have made camp. Never forget, Umniga, I plan.'

'I know of no such site.' Umniga was indignant.

'No, you don't. My mother planted the site when she was betrothed to my father.'

'She never said. I would have tended it.'

He shrugged. 'She was to leave her clan and wanted to honour the gods. When she saw the place, the whim struck her. She told me of it when she died. I think she thought that if no one knew and it flourished on its own, then it truly was meant to be. I sought it out when these lands became ours.'

'And, has it flourished?'

'You will see.'

When they reached the camp, Karan carried Isaura near the fire and left her with Umniga. He watched his people efficiently settle in to camp and was pleased to see the newcomers trying to help attend to the horses or anything else they thought ought to be done. They would have to earn their place here to be accepted by the clan, but this was a good start. He thought of Hunters' Ford. If the river kept rising, Ratilal would be able to do little other than hurl insults at them. Nevertheless he had left a squad there to keep watch. He returned to the fireside and accepted a bowl of hot stew.

'Karan, we …'

'Food first, Umniga—for everyone. A few minutes for food and a brief rest I'm sure will benefit you. Correct?' Despite having said this, he walked to Isaura and placed his hand on her brow.

'What do you see, Karan?'

He frowned, puzzled at her question, for the answer was obvious to him. 'She is a little warmer here, but she is fading—she is less bright.'

Umniga nodded, but in truth she saw no such change. She looked questioningly at Asha, who shook her head and shrugged.

'Make sure the newcomers get enough food. See if there are some cloaks for them. It will get colder before dawn,' Karan instructed. Soon Āsim joined him. 'How are your men?'

'They'll settle in quickly,' Āsim replied. 'They'd rather serve under you than Ratilal.'

'I meant it when I said they would not have to fight Ratilal. Their task remains the same: protect Asha and Umniga. I sent for Pravin before we set out. He will join you at the lake. Together you will continue their training, and the training of these strangers.'

'Pravin? He is still alive? He must be ancient.'

Karan snorted in amusement. 'I believe he is not much older than you.'

'You know that they will fight Ratilal?' Āsim asked so only Karan could hear.

Karan nodded as he stared into the fire. 'It may come to pass, but only in defence of those under their protection or their clan members here. Make no mistake—we will protect the citizens here. They may have been the Boar Clan's once, but now they are ours and …'

'It can only be helpful for them to see Boar warriors who have defected to you, working here with you to safeguard them.'

Karan winced at his insight. 'My father chose you well.'

CHAPTER TWENTY-SIX

IT was still night when the two men sent by Ratilal entered the outskirts of Parlan. The night had been unnaturally quiet but, after the chaos, they had found that a boon and were glad to be away from the wrath of their high lord. They had been forced to slow their pace because their horses were nearing exhaustion, and had spent their time hypothesising over the future course of events and whether they would be better off with a new lord.

'He's a hot head—has always been.'

'But new blood could be a good thing. Gods rest his soul in Susurrah, Lord Shahjahan was a good clan lord in his day, but that day has passed.'

They rode a short distance into the village before one reined in his horse and stopped the other. 'Where are the guards? Surely we would have seen some by now.'

They looked about warily, seeing no one. Suddenly the silence that they had found peaceful felt ominous. 'Keep going. We're too far gone now.'

Their horses, sensing their tension, pricked their ears forward and walked skittishly through the village, expecting trouble. They reached the tree in the square without incident and noticed that the door to the lodge had been jammed shut.

Having dismounted to investigate, they warily approached the lodge. It was then that they noticed the dead dumped in the shadows beside the building. They kicked the timbers jammed against the door free and tossed them aside. By the lamp light inside, they discovered their fellow warriors wounded and trussed up.

They unbound Vikram, who was nearest to the door. 'Karan came back and took the strangers Shahjahan had promised him,' he mumbled through his bruised mouth. 'We tried to stop them.' He rubbed his wrists gingerly as they unbound his hands. 'Our Kenati were in on it,' he finished bitterly.

'Both?'

'Yes.'

'Traitors! We could have used their skills.' Vikram looked curiously at him. 'We were ambushed. Caltrops—half the men and horses injured.'

'Damn!'

'Bloody disaster, that's what it is! Young hot head should have known better than to hare off in the dark.'

'I'd keep such thoughts to yourself if I were you,' Vikram chided. 'The high lord is young, but he was justly enraged and no doubt thinking only of vengeance for the death of his father.'

'No doubt,' was the acerbic reply. The soldier helped Vikram to his feet and they untied the other warriors. 'Why did they leave you all tied up?' he asked as he eyed the strangers with disgust.

'They're scared. Stuck in the middle of something they don't understand. They have helped the wounded as best they could ... At least Umniga and Asha left their kits,' Vikram replied.

'Asha I can understand, but Umniga?'

'Nothing we can do about it now. What were your orders?'

'To return with the wagons and supplies for our wounded.'

Vikram laughed bitterly. 'You'd better go and see if they are still here.'

It was not long before they returned to Vikram. 'The horses are gone, all of them!' one spat. 'The high lord will damn us to Karak if we don't come through for him.'

'Calm down. Wake the head man—Deo.' Vikram indicated the direction of his house. 'See who about has horses we can use ... Curse it! I'll come with you, make sure he cooperates.' Vikram straightened, his face greying as pain burst forth from his ribs. He put a hand against the wall to steady himself. 'Gods, damn it!'

'Captain?'

'Give me a minute.' He nodded, attempting to collect himself, then they headed slowly to Deo's house.

They pounded on the front door. 'Deo!' Vikram bellowed. 'Wake! Rouse yourself, in the name of High Lord Ratilal.' He nodded at the door and the man with him pounded on it again. 'Get your old arse out of bed!'

Deo fumbled at the door, opening it slowly. 'What do you want? Why wake the whole household in the middle of the night?'

'Sleeping, were you?' Vikram replied sarcastically.

Deo narrowed his eyes. 'Aye, that I was. Why?'

'You didn't hear fighting earlier? Wonder what was going on?'

'Haven't heard nothing since I hit the pillow. Had too much ale earlier at the celebrations. Most of us had.' He felt Vikram's cold appraisal.

To anyone else's eye, he had the appearance of a man who had been roused from deep slumber; his hair was tousled, he was wearing only a crumpled, drink and food-stained, long shirt. But he could not hide the alertness in his eyes from Vikram. *Yes, you heard nothing. Well, old man, you can keep your secrets.*

Deo knew that Vikram was not fooled. He tried to hide his surprise and relief when Vikram did not pursue the issue. 'Do you have horses?'

'Yes, one,' Deo replied.

'We're taking it.' Before Deo could protest Vikram continued, 'You'll get it back when we are finished. I'm sure the high lord will appreciate your cooperation in this hour of need.'

'Fine, take it.'

'Who else has horses?' Deo gave them a list of local farms nearby. 'Anyone else in the village with a horse or mule? It will take two for each of the wagons we've got.' Deo reluctantly gave him another name. 'Thank you. I'll make sure that the high lord knows how helpful you were.' The guard next to him sniggered. 'Go on, get the others, get the horses. Hitch up those wagons.'

When the guard left, Deo looked at Vikram and spat. As he tried to shut the door Vikram put his foot against it. 'Oh, I'm not finished, old man. You will be coming with us, you and your wife. Your presence will help convince the others to come and lend a hand. We need all the help and wagons we can get for the wounded and dead.'

'Ratilal can go to Karak!'

Vikram's face drew taut. 'I would be very careful what you say, old man. Those words could get you killed, should the wrong ears hear them.' He lowered his voice. 'Do you know what Ratilal would do to this village if he thought you sat idly by while his men were slaughtered? Do you want that?' A slight look of guilt crossed Deo's eyes. 'We both know you heard the fighting, don't we? If you want to come out of this unscathed you should lend all the help you possibly can right now.'

'He's right, Deo,' came Nada's voice from the dark interior. 'Do you think two people from each household with a wagon would suffice?'

'It should do. We'll need as many first aid supplies as you can find for men and animals. If we arrive with a convoy of wagons, it should hopefully impress Ratilal of your loyalty. Get ready to leave right away. We'll pick up more wagons from nearby farms as we travel.' Vikram spun and left.

'What in Karak is going on with him?'

'Don't curse. I'm sure your judgement already hangs in the balance; the gods may yet send you there when you pass,' Nada scolded as she rummaged through the cottage gathering supplies. 'And your grand-babies are starting to copy you.'

'I don't damn well think now is the time to be chiding me about my language,' he grumbled back at her. 'I'll let the gods worry about where to send me later. Right now I'll bloody well swear if I like.' He stormed to the front door, pausing with his hand on the latch. 'I'm going to get more supplies from the others. I'll be damned if I let that sneaky little shit Ratilal say I'm disloyal!'

'You might want to put some pants on first.'

Ratilal had sent several riders off at first light to locate a farm nearby to accommodate the wounded or at least the horses. Most of the farms in this backwater were small. The caltrops had been cleared and collected. The uninjured horses, too few in his opinion, were used to drag the carcasses of the dead horses from the road and the small valley. They now formed an ugly mound in the adjacent grassland before the valley entrance.

The high lord was hot, sweaty and disgruntled. Between the still healing lash marks on his back and the injuries from his fall he was in agony. He was using the shadebell tea sparingly—he did not want to run out and he did not want his men to see him taking it.

Niaz sat down beside him, offering him a water skin as he did so. 'We should burn the horses.'

'We've not enough fuel to do so. We'd need oil and timber. All we'll do is stink up the place quicker.'

Niaz nodded, saying nothing but staring at the bodies of men lined beside the road. *Besides, we'll have our fill of cremations before we're done—thanks to you.*

'My lord, one of the sentries is dead,' one of Baldev's captains said breathlessly as he approached the clan lord.

'Damn! Who?'

'Ramesh.' Baldev's face curled bitterly. 'My lord … my lord, I am sorry.'

'How?'

'It looks as if it was a couple of enemy scouts. We found the body under some shrubs … I can't believe they got him.' Quickly the man collected himself. 'Judging from the tracks I would say Ramesh found them spying. There was no sign of the scouts.'

'Ramesh was a brave warrior. Tie his body upon his horse—we

will take him home.'

Baldev ran over the possible scenarios before them. Two enemy scouts; had they gone back to Ratilal, or onward to The Four Ways? If they were smart they would have split up and done both. He looked across at his captain. 'We have to assume that they were clever enough to send word back to Ratilal and on to the crossing.' Baldev summoned all his captains to him. 'We're going to have to fight at The Four Ways.'

The sun hung low in the sky as Mas'ud had flogged his poor horse mercilessly in his efforts to reach the crossing guard. The Four Ways was now almost in sight; just another bend in the road and it would come into view. His horse slowed; he drove his heels into its sides and flogged it yet again with a switch. It gave a rattling squeal and struggled valiantly on. Come on, just a bit further! Mas'ud rounded the bend in the road; the crossing was in sight. He spun in the saddle, thinking he could hear a distant drumming of hooves. Nothing. Several times on his journey he thought he had heard the sounds of pursuit, but each time there was nothing behind him.

His horse stumbled, regained its stride, then stumbled again. It slowed, sides heaving, finally staggering to a halt. Mas'ud kicked it savagely, but it remained immobile, bar its now trembling legs. 'Damn!' The horse dropped, its legs simply collapsing under it. Mas'ud leapt off as it did so. 'Ah, you poor bastard!' he cursed. It breathed raggedly, blood-flecked foam coated its nostrils, clods of foam covered its body and the welts from his whipping crisscrossed its hide. He retrieved his weapons and ran as fast as he could across the remaining distance to the crossing guard.

Mas'ud's feet pounded out a desperate rhythm. The guards stood alert, weapons ready, as he raced toward them. They began pointing in the distance beyond him. He looked over his shoulder. Beyond the body of his prone horse, a large group of riders approached. *Oh gods, no!* With a final burst of speed Mas'ud made the guard post at the bridge.

'Quick, defend the bridge. We are at war. They have murdered Shahjahan. Do not let them cross,' he yelled.

'Move it, the lot of you. Shift those wagons there,' bellowed the garrison commander. He looked at Mas'ud's sweat streaked, grey face. 'What in Karak happened? Report.'

'Horse and Bear betrayed us. Murdered Shahjahan ... after he made peace,' Mas'ud said breathlessly. 'High Lord Ratilal pursued them ... was ambushed. He sent me and another to scout ahead. I found them ... came here to warn you ... sent the other back to the high lord. Karan is not with them. He's bloody well lurking about up to gods know what, sir.'

'*After* he made peace? Makes no sense,' the commander muttered. He roused his men, rapidly yelling commands. The garrison was constructing defences near the bridge, none of which were yet complete. They had erected three sides of a timber fort that bordered the road and river. Watchtowers stood on the roadside corners; one overlooked the bridge and the other overlooked the junction of the road to Parlan and Faros. The other watchtowers and wall farthest from the bridge had not been completed.

'Get those bloody wagons moving!' One was positioned across the bridge road at its junction with the road to Faros and level with the watchtower. The other wagon was placed at the bridge edge to shore up the existing barricades and make access for their enemies from across the river more difficult. Foot soldiers wielding spears poured out of the fort to fill the gap between the wagons. Archers manned the towers and the walls.

The commander grabbed one of his officers. 'Defend the fort. I'll command here on the road. Keep us covered. Pick off as many of those bastards as you can.' As the other man ran toward the fort entrance, the commander bellowed out, 'Watch the bridge too!'

Mas'ud watched as the horses were hastily loosed from the wagon shafts, and the troops speedily took up their positions. He saw the flurry of enemy activity across the river. *Damn it!* He paled as he realised that they would have to defend the bridge from both sides. Naturally, the enemy troops stationed over the river would fight to cross the bridge in aid of their fellows. *Two sides, they can't do it. They'll be spread too thin.*

'How long can you hold out?' Mas'ud asked hurriedly. The commander shrugged as he watched his troops finally position themselves. 'I'll go to Faros to get more troops.'

The commander glared at him. 'You'll run, you mean,' he said in derision. 'They'll never get here in time and you know it.' He appraised the enemy's rapid approach and Mas'ud's exhausted appearance. 'Damn it! Someone has to go, if only to warn them and get some help for the high lord. It may as well be you. You'll be bugger all use to me in the state you're in. Go!'

Mas'ud needed no further urging. He fled to the nearest horse and leapt upon its back. A soldier nearby grabbed him. 'Bloody coward. Get back here!'

'Leave him,' bellowed the commander. 'He goes to Faros to warn them.' Mas'ud wrenched the horse's head around and spurred it on, never once looking back.

The commander watched as Baldev's force thundered toward him. 'Hold!' he bellowed at his troops, as the enemy loomed ever nearer. The horsemen rode directly at the bridge, appearing as if they would careen into the wagon. At the last minute, their force split, with one group swerving around the wagon, galloping parallel to the road, toward the river. 'Hold fast,' roared the commander. The soldiers braced their shield wall, spears bristling from within it.

The group heading toward the river lobbed arrows overhead, into the foot soldiers behind the shield wall and at the archers in the watchtower and on the wall walk nearest them. Screams could be heard from the wall as archers fell. The archers spread out further to take the place of their fallen comrades. The defenders' attention focused on this assault; they must hold the bridge at all costs. The sound of bowstrings and loosened arrows created a rhythmic twang through the air. They trained their arrows on the horses; several were hit and fell, their riders now easy targets. The commander stepped back as several spear men near him fell to the ground with a dull thud. The enemy circled out of range and moved around for another assault.

Baldev led the second group of riders. After they veered off before the wagon, they rode parallel to the wall of the fort along the road to Faros, all the while targeting the archers along the wall. The archers in the nearest tower were fixated on the bridge assault force, leaving only those on the partially completed wall to shoot at Baldev's group. Baldev knew the far wall and watchtowers were not complete, and it was to this gap in the fort's defences that he led his men. They rounded the wall and were faced with a shield wall of soldiers defending the gap. Baldev hurled one of his axes at the line, embedding it in the brow of the man before him, who toppled backward.

Baldev swung his other axe at the head of the man nearest him as he crashed through the shield wall, nearly decapitating him. His men poured through behind him, dispersing the shield wall and engaging the enemy at close quarters. Swords flashed, booted feet lashed out from horseback at the faces of their assailants who tried to drag them from their mounts. The defenders thrust spears at the bellies of the horses and their screams rent the air. Baldev's charge had placed him well within the fort.

Armed now with his kilij, he dismounted, and he and his personal guard deftly cut a swathe through their enemies. The archers on the wall walk facing Faros Road were now engaged hand to hand with a squad of his men. The corral within the fort was filled with jittery horses. Their hay was stored nearby. Spying a cooking fire, Baldev fought toward it.

'Let those horses out!' he commanded as he picked a brand from the fire and ran toward the hay. His path was blocked by the smith, a mountain of a man, still in his leather apron. 'Shit!' Baldev hurled the brand with all his strength toward the hay, hoping it would hit it and the hay would ignite. It fell short. The smith swung his kilij at

Baldev. Baldev parried with his shield, forcing the smith's sword away while slashing viciously toward the man's torso. The smith was quick, but barely dodged the slash. One of Baldev's guards attacked the smith, forcing him to alter his stance. The smith's side was now vulnerable. Baldev savagely swung his kilij diagonally down, connecting with the back of the smith's leg and severing it above the knee.

'Finish him,' he spat, before racing to the burning brand and tossing it into the hay. The fire spread rapidly. The jittery horses had cowered in a corner of the corral, but once the fire started they bolted through the open gate and ran pell-mell through the fighting, creating even greater chaos before racing through the open wall.

Outside, the first group had made another pass along the road to the bridge, firing arrows into the enemy. They saw the smoke rising from within the fort and realised that the archers' attention was now held by a greater threat from the rear. The horses were close to exhausted. They approached for what must be their final charge. The wagon that blocked the road had been placed so hastily that its shafts lay on the ground, toward the tower base. With this charge, the group split again. Two riders veered off and aimed for the gap between the wall and wagon. Simultaneously, the other riders, armed with javelins and throwing axes, charged directly at the shield wall. The smell of smoke and the sight of the oncoming horsemen caused some of the troops to break.

'Get back in line. Hold!' hollered the commander, just as the two horsemen jumped the wagon shafts, swinging their kilijs ferociously. The head of the commander toppled from his body. At the same time, javelins, axes and horses hit the shield wall, destroying it.

Seeing the battle unfolding before them, the Horse and Bear warriors across the river were desperate to join the fray. Their archers had been targeting the nearest tower as their troops attempted to move across the bridge. They were exposed to the tower archers and the few archers stationed on the road; their progress was slow—many were wounded. However, with this assault on the shield wall and the burgeoning fire, they were able to surge across the bridge. Thrusting the barricades aside they joined the bloody brawl. The battle at the bridge did not last long. Minus their commander, the fort now prodigiously aflame, overwhelmed and with no archery support, the foot soldiers quickly surrendered.

Baldev surveyed the sullen, dejected and frightened men sitting before him. 'Take all their weapons across the river,' he commanded in a quiet voice.

'What will you do with us?'

Baldev ignored the question, but eyed the fellow with such dispassion that he did not speak again. Instead he chose to stare at the ground, desperate for Lord Baldev's attention to be anywhere else but upon him. The shrill cries of the severely wounded horses dissipated as his men dispatched them. Luckily, they had not lost as many soldiers as he would have expected, but many had injuries from which they would not recover. They would regroup at the river, tend the wounded and then head to Bear Tooth Lake to meet with Karan.

The original bridge at The Four Ways had been laid on ancient, pre-existing stone foundations, with huge solid timbers that had been lovingly carved with the symbols of the gods and the Boar Clan. These timbers were now being doused with oil.

'Understand this,' Baldev addressed the defeated men, 'we have never wanted the land south of The Divide. We do not want it now. We were content with the peace agreement signed with Lord Shahjahan—a man to respect, a man of honour. We did not break this treaty. *Ratilal*,' Baldev spat his name, 'a man of no honour, deserving of no respect, killed his father to fulfil his own lust for power.'

'Liar!'

'No! I and others witnessed it. Karak take his soul. You have heard the rumours. You will see the truth of him soon enough.'

Baldev, flanked by his guard, began to cross the bridge. The oil was ignited in their wake and rapidly a wall of flame devoured the old bridge. Baldev looked at the burning images of the gods and begged forgiveness.

CHAPTER TWENTY-SEVEN

THIS part of the Forest of the Asena was little travelled, with the few inhabitants of this eastern part of Altaica preferring not to dwell too near it. Karan carried Isaura deeper into the forest. Everyone from the camp followed him in a solemn torch-lit procession. This was a momentous occasion. They were witnessing history; the performance of a ritual that was the stuff of legends.

The torches bobbed their way through the rising fog, like will-o-the-wisps. They wound their way along a gentle slope between two maples, their large leaves a brilliant red. They walked through an avenue of birch trees, whose pendulous branches were decorated with fine yellow leaves. The slope and trail, such as it was, ended as they passed beneath a large oak tree into a natural clearing. Directly opposite this, at the other side of the clearing, was a young, yet sizeable, willow tree on the edge of natural spring. The clearing was surrounded by more birch and dotted by silversguard plants.

'Your mother did this?' Umniga was in awe.

Karan nodded, proud. 'Aye. The oak and maple were here, but not the willow, nor birch. They are younger. She planted them. The silversguard has come on its own. A sign perhaps.'

'Indeed. I wish I had known earlier.'

'Until these lands were ours, I would not have told you. Even then, I would have preferred this remain mine alone.'

'I'm sorry, Karan.' Umniga put a hand on his arm, suddenly aware of the intrusion into his memories.

Too casually he replied, 'It was not to be. Come, you must begin. Where do you want her?'

'In the centre of the clearing.' Umniga seated herself next to the prone form of Isaura, arranging her hands so that the henna tattoos on her wrists would align with those on her body. The other Kenati began to form a wide circle around her. Anil and Suniti for the Bear; Hadi and Munira for the Horse. They sat cross-legged, planting their staves diagonally into the ground before them, then resting them on their shoulders.

Asha took Pio's hand, smiling reassuringly at him and his parents as she led him to the circle and they took their place. She had no staff, instead planting her bow in a similar fashion. Finally, all their guardians landed and took positions beside them.

Umniga spoke a prayer, which the Kenati echoed. 'Great Mother, Great Father, givers of light and life, help us. Grant us the strength and the wisdom to guide this young one, this *Isaura*, home.'

Pio listened, then copied them, his slightly nervous, breathless young voice carrying their prayer into the mist. Asha beamed at him, and bade him play his flute.

Elena stood with Curro and the others. As Pio began to play, she said, 'What is going on?'

'Ssh!' was universally hissed at her. Umniga's eyes bore into her, commanding silence.

Curro, seeing her chagrin, stood behind her and wrapped his arms about her, planting a kiss on her head. 'I think they are trying to help Isa,' he whispered. His natural joy at this was like a knife twisting in her gut.

The Kenati were all merged with their guardians, their bodies slumped forward, their staves keeping them upright. Asha was shocked when Fihr used his sight to show her Pio. His aura was like nothing she had seen—vibrant shades of red, with flashes of violet and orange and brown. Pio's haunting melody pulsed with the colours of his aura and wove its way like an intricate web between the Kenati, the guardians and Isaura. Although playing just for Isaura, Pio entranced all his listeners as the tendrils of his web meandered through the crowd and travelled into the misty forest.

Umniga and Devi watched Isaura. Her aura was dull and grey, the streaks of violet and red were nearly non-existent. Umniga felt despair claw at her, yet as Pio's music touched Isaura, the violet and red in her aura became a little stronger. Umniga's heart leapt; Isaura was still reachable.

Asha could feel Fihr's concentration shift; once again she had a brief feeling of immense space that was speedily shut off from her. Then she felt a tug on her energy, as it fed and pulsed through the music to Umniga. *Fihr must be doing this. All the guardians must be doing this*, Asha thought.

Umniga felt the influx of energy along the musical web and braced herself for a blast of power, but instead she felt it hit a barrier and coil around her. The power that reached her was a steady flow that could supplement and sustain her. She was surprised to realise that while Devi was connected with her, it was not their usual deep bond, but far shallower–a bond he had restricted. The experience felt similar; she was still connected to his mind, but experienced none of the physical sensations that their bond usually brought. He was protecting her. *Come, old friend, we must find her.*

In Devi's care, Umniga travelled at an astonishing speed to where they had found the ship. The faint aura trail she had noticed during the rescue was gone. *Devi, do you remember the way?* Devi led on in the direction in which they had last seen the aura trail. His sharp eyes scanned the air before them, looking for any sign of the girl's passage. The enormity of their task was beginning to have an impact upon Umniga. They had no idea if the girl had travelled in a straight line or not, or whether she had succumbed to the lure of the wild energy around her and simply wandered aimlessly, until it subsumed her energy into its own.

Even with Devi to anchor her, Umniga could feel its seductive pull. She was beginning to tire. She had no idea how far they had come. *Just a bit further.* She could feel Devi's reluctance, but he complied. *By the gods, how far did the girl go?* Finally a faint trail appeared before her, a mere mauve haze that was dissipating in the ether. *We have her. Come.* Devi baulked. *Devi, no!* He was returning homeward. Umniga knew she could not make him continue. She could no longer feel that reserve of energy coiled about her—they could go no further. She suspected they now had only enough power to make it home on their own. Umniga knew Devi would sense her regret, but she sent him her thanks, pride and love at what he had managed to achieve. To go further would risk them both.

As they returned to the circle, Umniga was pleased to see that the auras of the Kenati were still strong. They would be tired, as she was, but they had not been damaged by the experience. There would be no further attempts to find the girl. *At least we have the boy.*

Putting on a brave face she sat up. She looked at Karan and shook her head—his visage soured. 'How are you all?' she asked the Kenati surrounding her. One by one they nodded at her, but all remained seated.

Asha took Pio's hand and looked at Umniga. 'No luck at all?'

'Oh, I found her trail, but even combined we will not reach her. The distance the girl travelled is remarkable,' Umniga replied sadly. Pio squeezed Asha's hand tightly, then let go and began to play again. Asha gently stopped him; his face crumpled.

Karan felt the hairs on the back of his neck rise. 'Be alert!' The pre-dawn light was filtering through the trees, and with it came something else. Each of the guardians took flight, leaving their Kenati alone. Out of the mist, between the trees, materialised large shapes. They prowled between the onlookers.

'Wolves!' Gabriela gasped, clinging to Jaime. Curro and Nicanor placed Elena and Lucia behind them. Karan's warriors surrounded them, blocking them from any possible move against the creatures.

Asha's guard moved their hands to their swords.

Karan barked, 'No!' The warriors of the Horse quickly ensured their restraint.

One young Boar warrior whispered, 'So it's true.'

Āsim answered, in a hushed and reverent voice, 'Aye lad, it's true. I never thought to see the like. The Asena have come.'

The Kenati were equally stunned. The Asena were rarely seen in the lowlands. It had once been their home, but now they were almost exclusively to be seen in remote parts of The Plateau—the Fields of Naji—the home of the Horse Clan, and even there rarely.

Umniga had no idea what was going on. 'Stay seated. Stay still. They are not our enemies.'

Pio was terrified. His face was ashen. Frantically he looked for his parents. 'Pa!'

'Pio!' Asha's hand shot out and hauled him back down to the ground before he had even got halfway up. 'No, Pio. Be still.'

'Asha, wolves. *Wolves*, Asha!' The last was a high pitched, panicked squeak.

'Wolves?' Asha frowned. 'No, *Asena*. Good.'

'Good?' She nodded but kept her hand firmly on his. Pio's eyes became enormous, a combination of wonder and terror, they seemed to fill his face. He trusted Asha, but he did not want to sit here, yet he could not take his eyes from the huge creatures that were approaching the circle. One was heading directly to him. *Not a wolf*, he told himself. *Not a wolf.* It certainly wasn't a dog—he'd never seen a dog, or a wolf, this big. The head, out of which stared vivid blue eyes, was the size of a bear's. Its long coat was a silvery-grey colour, the tips of which were almost blue. A magnificent ruff covered its neck and forequarters, tapering to a graceful feathering down the back of its front legs. A large silvery-grey, blue-tipped, bushy tail completed it. Pio held his breath as it stopped beside him and dropped to the ground.

Asha was awestruck and nervous. She had never beheld an Asena. She gave Pio her most reassuring smile, hoping that it would work. Each Kenati now had an Asena sitting beside them. The Asena were focused on the centre of the circle—on Umniga and Isaura. Finally, there entered into the circle two Asena who were larger again. They were clearly older than the others and one appeared older than all the rest. They walked directly to Umniga.

In all her long years Umniga had only glimpsed an Asena once and considered herself blessed for having done so. She was overwhelmed with joy. Tears filled her eyes, and she could not help smiling broadly. Instinctively, she knew that the oldest of the Asena, who now stood before her, was their ancient matriarch.

'Old mother, welcome,' Umniga said reverently as she bowed her head, exposing her neck to her. The matriarch lowered her muzzle and nudged Umniga's face. When Umniga hesitantly raised it, she rubbed her ruff along her face, before lying down beside her. The second Asena lay down beside Isaura.

Umniga felt a nudge at her consciousness as the matriarch stared at her. She took a deep breath. 'I think we can … should try again.'

The Kenati looked confused. 'But they are not our guardians.'

'No, but … just relax. I think …' She stared into the blue eyes of the matriarch. 'It will be fine. Put your hands on them.' She lay down with her hand buried in the Asena's coat.

'Asha,' Pio said worriedly. The Asena beside him was nudging his hand, which he lifted away. 'Asha …?' The moment he lifted his hand up, the Asena had placed its huge head in his lap. Pio's expression grew distant, then he smiled beautifully.

'Pio? *Good?*' Asha asked.

'Good. *Very* good!' he said happily. Pio felt warmth spreading throughout his body, along with a surge of joy and a sense of safety. He grinned at his frightened parents, waving excitedly with his other hand.

Asha placed her hand on the Asena beside her. She could sense the power thrumming around her, but it was firmly locked away from her. The Asena were tightly in control of this exchange. It was not like joining with Fihr. There was no emotional connection; she was still able to control her body. She wondered if she was even necessary and was startled to see the Asena next to her snort and curl its lip when this thought crossed her mind.

Pio began the melody he had previously played, only this time there was a wildness underpinning his tune. It was as if two songs had been combined, one that beckoned you home, and another that promised vitality, strength and freedom, and revelled in the joy and power of all life. It seeped into Asha's soul and she forgot all else.

Nicanor and Lucia watched their son with wonder. Pio's fingers moved skilfully along the flute, at times his melody grew haunting and at others it rippled along like a vibrant river.

Karan watched the ritual with interest. *It seems Umniga was correct. The gods did favour us.* He could hear and feel the power around him, but he was not swept away by it. Dwelling on The Plateau, he had encountered the Asena before in the wilderness, albeit not like this; merely as glimpses in the distance, or with the mere prickling of his skin and certainty that he was being watched— judged. The faces of the strangers and of Asha's guard reflected a mesmerised, terrified wonder; thank the gods Karan's men remained cool-headed and had restrained the others from acting out of their fear. The appearance of the Asena proposed other potentialities. *If the Asena return to the forest again, then the Boar Clan need to lose their old hatreds and fears. Too much is at stake.*

Umniga stood, blue and opaque, beside the ghostly blue silhouette of the matriarch and the other Asena. She looked at the circle of Kenati and Asena. Each pair made a pillar of blue light that stretched skyward like a beacon. The web of Pio's music pulsed around them and flowed directly to the circle's centre. Umniga could feel none of its power. She tried to reach for it and found herself unable to do so. A low growl sounded in her mind. She felt a slow probing of her mind, which she was unable to resist, and her earlier search replayed itself.

What followed was a massive jump to the location of the sea rescue. Where previously Umniga had not been able to see Isaura's trail, she could now see a faint haze. She was stunned as she met what she could swear were the slightly amused eyes of the matriarch. Next, they travelled to where Umniga and Devi had regained the trail, but had been unable to continue. This was unlike any travelling Umniga had experienced before. There was no passing of scenery, even at a blur. It was simply as if the world folded and unfolded between one destination and the next. Umniga had never felt so helpless, but with each jump the trail grew stronger.

They reached land and here the matriarch slowed their journey. The trail followed a river, which narrowed at the coast, moved through expansive marshlands and then widened as it dissected the countryside. Nothing seemed untoward. The farms and villages nearby looked intact and productive. However, as they travelled further inland, they witnessed more parties of soldiers camped across the countryside. They passed a large city on the edge of the river, showing evidence of substantial repairs underway, and which was clearly a base for these soldiers. Here they found a mass grave. The matriarch did not linger.

They followed Isaura's journey to a small, looted village, where her trail made it obvious she had explored.

This must have been their home. These bodies once her friends. The trail was much clearer now. *How has she remained, even with Pio's help? Her very life's energy is dissipating, merging with the wild.* Umniga, despairing, looked back at the way they had come and was shocked. Isaura's aura trail was gone. If she had a guardian and training this would not have happened. *How long can she last?* The matriarch flashed agreement through her mind and picked up their pace.

CHAPTER TWENTY-EIGHT

THE trail ended at a small cabin in the woods. Umniga and the Asena stopped before an old hollow tree that should have been long dead, yet was sprouting new growth. There was no sign of Isaura. The Asena walked around the tree investigating it and the ground closely. Umniga had no idea what they were looking for. Isaura should be here. The fact that she was not filled Umniga with despair. They were too late. The matriarch sat before the hollow. Curious, Umniga moved beside her and peered in. Nothing.

Pio's music, hitherto unheard on their journey, cascaded loudly and vibrantly around them. Pulsing with the colours of his aura merged with that of the Asena, the music gambolled about the clearing. Umniga could feel its power reined in, like an unruly pup, and directed solely at the tree. Umniga was sure the matriarch was calling to Isaura—trying to reach whatever kernel of her was left. Umniga wanted to call to her, to use her name, but her abilities had been curbed; she was not sure the matriarch would allow her to. The matriarch simply stared at her. *You know everything I think, don't you?*

'Isaura, come forth. Isaura, friend to Pio, come forth. Isaura, return!' Nothing. Umniga finished with an unmistakable quiet plea. 'Child, please, return to your friends.' *What am I doing? She won't understand me.* Amusement emanated from the matriarch, but was quickly cut off, as she gazed intently into the hollow.

Pulling, tugging, pulling. First to The Wild. Now back. Here was warm, safe, but also free and vibrant. The robin and the stag showed the way. The call was always there, following it had been natural—

easy. There was no regret, no pain, no weariness. Now another pull. The energy that was Isaura was being dragged back together from the comfort of oblivion. This pull—this call, was inescapable. The Wild was seductive and tenacious, it fought back. With each fragment of Isaura's energy that it lost, it beckoned with renewed promises and reached with greedy tendrils attempting to ensnare her power for itself. But the way back was blocked. With each little piece that was recovered from The Wild, more of Isaura was resurrected and the new call became harder to resist. The call coalesced into sound— music coupled with an inexorable will.

Umniga watched, amazed and fascinated, as the power of the music invaded the ancient tree. She was poignantly aware that she was being allowed to see this. A pulse of music broke off, and like a hound with a scent it tracked Isaura's trail around the clearing. It spooled her aura back into itself, finally arrowing joyously into the hollow.

Slowly a violet light began to glow dully within the prison of the hollow tree. The light coalesced into the outline of a tree—a willow tree. Two trees. *Gods, it's the pattern!* Umniga thought. The glow began simultaneously at the trunks and then flowed out along the branches and roots—everywhere that Umniga and Asha had painted. There was no image or projection of Isaura's body, just the ghostly violet trees. *Something of her must still be here.*

The matriarch watched the trees intently as she drew Isaura's spirit forth. The image moved toward them, but stopped as if anchored. Umniga saw a thin tendril that still connected Isaura's energy to the ancient tree. Umniga could have sworn she heard the matriarch huff with impatience. However, the cold, determined cast never wavered from her features. A blast of energy the colour of Isaura's aura left her and plunged into the willow image. By the gods! Now Umniga knew why Isaura's trail had vanished after they travelled along it. The matriarch—she spooled it. With that blast, the last greedy tendril of The Wild, clinging to what was Isaura, had broken. The new growth on the old tree withered.

Pio's playing has improved. Gods! Does he have to play so loudly? Isaura thought as she was dragged awake. Her thoughts came to a jarring halt, when she realised she was still in the tree. Isaura had no recollection of what she had been doing after she entered the tree to rest, other than that she had felt warm and safe and had forgotten the pain that had brought her here. Now, she remembered. Pio's playing continued. *What is bloody well going on?* She noticed three shapes watching her. *Three spirits.* Two scarily huge wolves and an old woman. Wary, she sought the safety of the tree, but a vice-like grip trapped her.

She looked closely. *I've seen the old woman before … on the boat.* Isaura felt vulnerable, exposed and weary. *Why are they looking at me like that?* Self-consciously, Isaura looked down at herself. *Shit! Where have I gone? … I'm a tree?* She was panicking. She knew she was panicking, but really … *a tree?*

A deep, droll, female voice sounded in her mind. 'You are not a tree, young one. You have only to fully remember who you are, what you looked like.' There was a pause. 'Strengthen your image as you did before.'

'As I did before …' Isaura concentrated, watching carefully as her image returned and the willow and oak faded but did not disappear. Suspicious, Isaura remained within the safety of the tree. 'How did you know what I did before? Where were you?' Isaura assumed it was the old woman who had spoken, yet when she looked up, she saw only a beautiful younger woman in a grey robe, with vibrant blue eyes and waist length silvery hair that ended in blue tips. *First trees, now this!*

Laughter rained down around her and through her. She felt a tremulous spark of joy take root in her and explode forth in answer. She quashed it. 'Who are you? How did you find me?'

'Prayers, Isaura—your friends' and yours.'

'I never …' Isaura paused, struck dumb.

The lady smiled. 'Yes, you did. On the mountain you prayed for strength to help your friends survive. How do you think you lasted this long? On the boat, you prayed for "someone to get you out of this shit." I believe that was your phrase.'

Isaura's mind raced. *She looks so different, yet she speaks the common tongue. A god … goddess?* The lady waited with a supremely serene look upon her face. 'The old woman?'

'She is a priestess,' she paused. 'She is … mine. I made sure that she found you.'

'You are a goddess then?'

'I am many things, but goddess will do.'

'Where are the others? The old woman? The wolves?'

'Not wolves—Asena. You need not fear them. They are … useful to me. They are still here, but unaware of our conversation. I do not speak your common tongue. In this realm there is no language, merely thoughts.'

'What! You're in my head? Get out,' Isaura demanded.

The woman's face grew stern. 'Be grateful, child. Without my power you would be lost.'

'I was right where I wanted to be.' Isaura's eyes narrowed in challenge as she goaded her. 'So, you're a goddess then? Why should I believe that? Everything you've told me you could just pluck out of my head. For all I know you're just another spirit, and so are they.'

The lady's face retained a slight serene smile, yet it did not reach her eyes. 'If I were like you, then how can I read your thoughts, when you cannot read mine? How did I know where to find you? You'll have to show some faith, Isaura.'

'You can see into my mind. How much faith do you see there?' Isaura replied sarcastically.

'You have faith enough. Faith in your friends. I would be your friend if you would let me.'

'Gods don't have friends, they have playthings.'

'I thought you didn't believe in gods?'

'I don't have faith in them. I don't even have faith in myself.'

'You had faith in yourself.'

'*Had.* I couldn't even protect my friends. I killed a child. My own father tried to kill me and if I'd left him where he wanted to be, I would have saved him and Gabi's parents. I *failed*. You turn up out of nowhere and drag me back to face this and you want me to have faith, to believe you want to be my friend. A friend would have left me alone. Where were you earlier, before everything went to shit?'

The smile vanished. 'Where was I? Watching. You needed this, without it you …' Abruptly she changed tack. 'Stop trying to goad me, Isa. It will not work. You want me to end you. I will not. That is your decision alone.' Her visage softened. 'Child—Isaura, you are blaming yourself for things over which you had no control. You were honouring your mother's memory when you chose to bring your father. You had no way of knowing …'

'I knew he'd be difficult …'

'Difficult is not insane. Isaura, in the end he chose his path.'

'And Gabi's parents?'

'They made their choice too. We all make choices every day. We can't know all the ramifications.'

'The girl …' Isaura said quietly.

'Yes, the girl. You flail yourself with that one small life, who would have died anyway. What about that bothers you? The reaction of the others? Why should *you* care for the opinion of others? You are not a murderer, and you know it. What really bothers you? That you did it, or that you'd do it again?'

Isaura winced as she broke eye contact with the lady.

'You had the strength to make tough decisions. Do not deride yourself for it. Without you they would most certainly be dead. Stop feeling sorry for yourself. You wanted change, you wanted freedom to be yourself. You ran from the Zaragaria. Now you run from who you are. You can't run from what you did. None of us can. Nor can you change it.'

Would I? I would certainly have left Hugo behind. I should have trusted my gut on that one. The girl …

'The sum of all your experience, all your decisions have brought you to this one moment. They have made you. Now your fate hangs upon your choice. What will you choose?' The lady waited.

'So, this is my moment of judgement? What I choose will decide if you send me to the paradise or the underworld? Somehow I didn't think I'd get a say in it.'

'You get a say, because you are not dead. You slipped into the spirit realm and in your misery and self-loathing you returned here. You have a new home waiting with your friends.'

'I am home.'

'Do you really feel at home here? Pio misses you. He bombards me with prayers for you.'

Isaura smiled wistfully, briefly, but suspicion still nagged at her. 'Why did you really come for me? If it was just about prayers, then I'm sure the others on the boat prayed harder than I did.'

'Because you asked for help. Because I heard you … You and Pio are rare. Your presence can be felt in both realms. That is something I have not encountered for a very long time.' She shrugged. It was a remarkably human thing to do and allayed some of Isaura's natural distrust. 'And because your courage moved me. You can be reunited with your friends, but you must want it. I can drag you back, but unless you want to go, it will not work. Part of you will always stay here in … The Wild.' She canted her head. 'That is an apt name. You think of it as an entity?'

'You already know the answer, but yes.'

'Will you stop running? You must choose. If your spirit remains here any longer you will die.'

Pio's music surged forth, calling her home. Isaura smiled wryly. *He's as persistent as always.* 'How do I get back?'

'Let go of what brought you here. We will take you back.'

Let go? Isaura's gaze left the lady as she looked at her home and thought of the village—all filled with the dead. Was it worth it? *Yes, if they still live. The guilt and misery? No, but it changes nothing for me or them. If I stay … nothing. No pain, but nothing else.*

When she looked back, the lady was gone. Before her stood only the old woman and the Asena. The matriarch eyed her knowingly.

Umniga was bewildered. Between one moment and the next, the image before her had transfigured from that of the trees into Isaura, yet somehow she had missed the transformation.

'Isaura?'

Before she could reply, the lady's voice whispered, *Do not tell them what transpired.*

'Yes, who are you?'

'Umniga.' *She understands me?*

'Who are they?'

'The Asena.'

Isaura nodded, as if she knew that already.

Umniga's brows shot up. 'The elder is the Asena matriarch,' she said reverently.

Isaura stared at them both, thoughtfully and expectantly. Finally she said, 'I thank you for finding me. I want to go home.'

It was past dawn, yet still very early morning. The fog seemed to surround the sacred grove but had not entered it. Karan was the only one to notice, the others were engrossed with watching the ritual. Pio's playing, which had been vibrant and wild, was now more restrained. It still spoke of joyfulness but also of peace, like resting at home after an arduous day or journey. Slowly it became more subdued.

Karan noticed a build up of pressure in the air, just as before a storm. He watched the centre of the circle intently. 'Do you feel that?'

Āsim, reluctantly roused from his reverie, shook his head.

Pio's playing stopped. He dropped the flute and collapsed.

'Pio!' came his mother's frantic cry, but the guards prevented her from interfering.

Then Karan felt a warm wave break over him, travelling through his limbs and settling near his heart.

Isaura moaned, stirred and curled into a foetal position, covering her head with her hands as she began to shake uncontrollably.

Karan strode through the circle, heedless of the Asena and Kenati. 'Āsim, check the boy and see to the Kenati.' Quickly he threw his cloak over Isaura, wrapping it about her and covering her face with it. 'Ssh. All will be well.' He could still feel her shaking, so he lifted her into his lap and held her against his chest, all the while rubbing her back and arms. 'I have you. Ssh,' he murmured. She was clinging weakly to his coat.

Isaura was cold. She felt as if her very marrow was frozen. She could not stop shaking. Her teeth were chattering loudly. Everything around her seemed deafening and even the dull, grey, early morning light was too bright. She curled up, weak, frightened and overwhelmed. A quiet voice spoke to her. Strong arms held her. After so long of being unable to touch anything, of thinking she would never be able to touch, feel, or hear anyone else, she was overwhelmed with emotion, with gratitude. This voice was so calm, so soothing. She felt absolutely safe.

Karan held a water skin to Isaura's lips. His heart went out to her as, still shaking, she tried to hold it but fumbled. He tipped it slowly and she sipped at the water, too weak to do little else.

'That's it, but not too much now,' he said softly as he withdrew the flask. She tried to open her eyes, but was blinking furiously even in the dull light. He pulled the hood of the cloak about to shelter her face.

'Thank you,' Isaura murmured. Very slowly she opened her eyes and looked at the man who held her with a grateful smile. Karan drew a sharp intake of breath. Her eyes were a deep green, but flecked with a glowing vibrant blue that also rimmed her iris. The same blue as the eyes of the Asena.

ASENA
BLESSED

THE CHRONICLES OF ALTAICA BOOK TWO

At the whims of Gods and Men…

Isaura has emerged from the spirit realm forever altered. No longer a pariah, she embraces the future offered in Altaica, but learns that her survival has come at a price. Her transformation is the perfect weapon for Elena to use against her.

The mysterious Asena and The Lady vie for Isaura. Caught between two ancient powers, Isaura must try to make her own path.

Master spy Vikram launches a counterinsurgency against Ratilal and Faros, weaving innocents into the plot to bring him down. Ratilal prepares to wage war against Karan and Baldev. Desperately, he seeks clandestine means to wreak revenge on them in the very heart of their territory, with devastating results.

With enemies nearing, Isaura must learn to master her powers. Aid arrives from the most unlikely source—one who knows no rules and respects no one.

Having run from one war she will not run from another…

The battle is joined.

Available now
www.books2read.com/asenablessed

LET'S KEEP IN TOUCH

Hearing from readers is awesome! Feel free to email me with feedback or even better leave me a review somewhere–the good, the bad and the ugly they all count.

Want more from Altaica? Sign up to the newsletter and get:

- Free short stories
- Deleted and alternate scenes
- News on upcoming books
- A chance to join the ARC team

Sign up here

www.tracymjoyce.com/subscribe.html

ABOUT THE AUTHOR

Tracy M Joyce is an Australian author of speculative fiction. Her novel, *Altaica: Book I in The Chronicles of Altaica*, is published by Cassilis and Co.

Her stories are gritty, a little dark and morality is like quicksand. You won't find any unicorns or fairies here. Tracy particularly likes novels that deal with deep characterisations and that don't flinch from the grim realities of life. This and her fascination with the notions of "moral greyness", that "good people can do bad things" and that we cannot escape our past provide the inspiration for her writing. Combine that with her love of history, horses and archery and you have Altaica.

She grew up on a farm in rural Victoria, in a picturesque dot on the map known as Glenburn and spent half of her childhood riding horses and the other half trying to stay out of–the only way she did that was by reading books and writing stories. Tracy lives in Melbourne with her husband, two crazy dogs and a brother and sister duo of young cats (aka Satan's kitties). Because she'd go completely bonkers if she lived in the city all the time, she travels to the "cabin in the woods" in the Victorian high country as often as possible where she and Miss Lucy the quarter horse have their own adventures exploring the forest together.

Tracy holds a BA (Hons) from Monash University, spent many years in a variety of administrative roles and fortunately never gave up on her childhood dream to become a writer. In her spare time she tutors a select and unlucky group of students in English.

www.tracymjoyce.com

AUTHOR'S NOTE

I love history and I have cherry picked from various periods of history in creating *Altaica*. The pile of books in my research comprises everything from castle and fortification construction, mythology, Roman cavalry training tactics, field surgery, weaponry, armour, poisons, mules, archery (but that is also a hobby of mine), herbology, sword fighting techniques, staff fighting etc (Osprey publications probably deserve a special thank you for their military books.) I have combined them all in creating this world.

In the course of my research I kept returning to the weapons of the Mughals and, particularly, the Ottomans because I loved their combination of beauty and lethality.

Researching wolves, I also stumbled across the Turkic myth of the Asena, which I immediately felt would work with my story extraordinarily well. It seemed fitting that I use it since I was featuring Turkish weapons, and when I saw the term *Altaic* used to describe the language family including Turkish, Mongolian and Tungus, I knew therein lay the title for my novel.

I hope by adapting a much-loved Turkish myth I have caused no cultural offense. I would like you think these things have been an inspiration for a creative mind and hopefully the result will provide much reader enjoyment.

Thank you.